Glide in Slowtime

Barry Rosenberg

Published by Barry Rosenberg, 2024.

This is a work of fiction. Similarities to real people, places, or events are entirely coincidental.

GLIDE IN SLOWTIME

First edition. March 31, 2024.

ISBN: 979-8223990772

Written by Barry Rosenberg.

With much love to my beautiful wife, Judith.

Chapter 1

"Whoops, it's coming!" Mary clapped her hands over the swell of her belly.

"Yes, dear." John lowered *The Namba National* a fraction and gazed at his wife through his pinz-nez glasses. "What is?"

"My waters have burst."

"The tap again?" When the going got tough, John got going.

"My waters, John! My wa...ters! The baby is coming!"

"Oh!" Suddenly aroused, John leapt to his feet. His knee went up and hit the table. The table went down. "My keys, my keys! My kingdom for my keys!" Putting the table back on its feet, he searched along its surface.

"Have you tried your pockets, John?" Though they were happily married, sometimes Mary had to fight to keep the impatience out of her voice.

"My pockets? My pockets?" He clapped his hands over his waistcoat as if he were beating on a tambourine. He next slid his fingers into his brown canvas trousers. He felt a bulge and the panic washed out of him. "Oh good, here they are. Let's go. I'm waiting, waiting..."

John put a hand under Mary's elbow and guided her as if she might break at any moment. Since she had indeed broken, she thought him a little late for that. But she was grateful when he helped her into the car. Though modern steam cars with pipes had replaced the old-fashioned boilers, the door was still an awkward height off the ground.

John was about to start the car when a Ne'verman held out his blue hand. "Got a dollar, mister?"

Ne'vermen were not common in coastal towns. They usually kept to their own desert settlements. Tall and long-limbed, the original inhabitants of Ausphalia were not very popular either. One cause of difference was their colour. Having broken away from *Homo Saps* at some distant point in time, their blood carried less oxygen than the non-indigenous and gave their skin a blue tinge. Naturally, rednecks called them Blueys.

Another difference lay in their development. While the rest of the world had followed the ancient G'eeks and promoted technology, the Ne'vermen had focussed more on living with the land. They had also promoted mental development. What some, with a sneer, called magic. Not that any of it survived technological testing, of course. The reason? Well, they gave the same worn out excuses as western mediums. They had to be in the right mood for the magic to work. Well, who didn't have to be in the right mood to work, magic or otherwise? But their lay-back lifestyle put them at odds with mainstream society.

Rarely meeting a Ne'verman, Mary was intrigued. "Why do you want money?"

"I wanna get a beer."

"I thought alcohol didn't mix with your blood."

"One beer! An' I was gonna drink it not mix it with me blood." The man thrust his hand out. "That's all, just the one."

Mary's stomach sent her a painful message. "Here you are, then." She leant forward and handed the Ne'verman a coin. Oddly, as their fingers touched a curious tingle ran up her arm. A moment later and she realised that her body pains had receded.

"Thanks, missus. That boy you're gonna have, great potential in that boy, real great."

John glanced anxiously from his wife to the stranger. "We'd better get going. We don't want you giving birth in the car."

At that moment, Mary realised that a shadow had lifted and that there was more light. She glanced up. Oh, a balloon. It had only been a freight-carrying air balloon. All the same, it felt like a portent, a good one. With a smile, Mary nodded to her husband then leant back against the worn leather. John turned the key in the ignition. The electrical circuit started the air compressor and the car immediately fired. Thirty seconds later, the steam pressure built up and they chugged away. Mary sniffed. She knew she wouldn't be able to smell steam since the water system was sealed. Still, in her heightened state, she imagined that she could smell the odd escaping molecule.

As the car pulled away, the young Ne'verman turned the new dollar in his hand. Intuition told him never ever to spend it. Its metal was charged with Mary. With it, he could always find her or her child. He slipped the coin into a pocket. He didn't drink beer, anyway. Nor did he normally beg. He'd just responded to the moment.

With the pain in her belly reduced, Mary quite enjoyed the short ride to the hospital. Gliders, air ships and solar-powered flitters dotted the sky as people made their way to work or were simply at play. Maybe one day, they'd go up in a glider. John always spoke about it but they'd never had the nerve. Well, one day, but it wouldn't be today.

John ushered Mary into the hospital, a long low building used only for births. Deaths and accidents were in a completely different building. He slowly hurried her to the receptionist who in turn summoned the medics. Still distanced from any discomfort, Mary was hoisted up, locked down and generally made ready for take-off. John hovered on the periphery as the medics took over. But on the Richter Scale of Births, this delivery was rated just a breath above zero.

"Too easy," the medics said and hurried on to more urgent matters.

Even the local newspaper that published the new births every week forgot to include their photo. For a boy expected to show great potential, he certainly didn't start with a bang. In fact, only John and Mary really took any notice. They, of course, were delighted.

John counted, "Ten perfect little fingers, ten little toes, two big eyes, two funny noses... Oops." Mary had punched him. "One perfect little nose, one mouth."

They had decided to call their son, John. John, the father, had been named after his father, John. And the current John, an accountant by profession, was not one to flout tradition. Even so... Even so... They were at home and he took a moment to stand by the window. Namba was a small town, about two hours north of Brissie if travelling by fast steam car on a clear road. Half an hour to the east were pricey resort towns. Half an hour in the other direction were the snooty hill towns of the hinterland. Namba itself was a tradies town, dominated by the sugar mill.

There was a sugar mill because they lived in sugar cane country and a well-loved dinky-toy train brought the cane into town. Few, however, loved the dirt rain that came from the processing of the sugar. Nor did people like the burn-off of the crops. When the sugar fires raged, fresh laundry was turned black. Namba was not the smartest place in which to live.

John, though, had never voiced any complaint about the sugar processing. Well, why would he? He never voiced complaints about anything. *Don't argue* was his motto. *Live and let live* was another. Yet on the birth of his son, he was for once moved to make an amendment. Maybe he'd half heard the Ne'verman's prediction. Maybe it was his own sense that the boy had a rare and useful Talent. Whatever it was, he decided that now was the time for a change.

"I've been thinking." He screwed up his face to signal thought. "John is okay but I also want another name."

"Another name?" Mary was quite taken aback.

"Yes, another name," John sang, sounding like a character in a Gildert and Sulliban chorus.

Mary, slightly puzzled, held the baby to her breast. John wasn't given to surprise announcements.

"Yes," John repeated and put out a finger. He was amazed as a tiny hand clutched at it.

"What name, John?"

"Glide."

"Glide?" Mary looked askance at her husband. "Well, that's an unusual name for a baby."

"His second name can be John. Or Jack."

"But why Glide?"

John, son of John, pursed his lips. He was a man of medium height and slightly less than medium build. His face was regular though easily lost in a crowd and his brown hair was thinning.

"Well, you know how I always wanted to fly?"

"Yes?" Mary was cautious. She had the vague idea that her husband might start flapping his arms and go *cluck, cluck, cluck*.

"But all my life I've worked in a bank."

Mary raised her eyebrows. "You could always have had a try on the weekends."

"I know. I could've. But I didn't. But well, there you are." And John pulled back his shoulders as if he'd actually braved the air.

"Right," Mary said. She didn't like to argue, especially when John had made such a rare and definite statement. But she did think that you couldn't call a person Glide and expect him to be normal. She, too, gazed out of the window.

John, used to his wife's silences, said, "Still waters run deep. What're you thinking?"

"Oh, nothing." Mary rocked the baby.

John peered over his glasses. "Ah-ha, you're not Tolkien about it, eh? You'll develop bad hobbits."

Mary smiled. Except for their son's name, she knew where she was with her husband - safe, secure and terribly punny.

Despite his name, Glide passed easily through toddlerhood, showing no tendencies to glide off the roof, flap his wings, or to attach solar panels to his arms. A sturdy boy, at age five, he was enrolled in Namba Primary. On his first day, both parents took him to school. They watched with moist eyes as Glide turned at the door and waved. He disappeared, eager to make new contacts.

John sighed. "A good boy." He gazed at the empty door with pride. "Takes more from your side of the family, though."

"Probably," Mary agreed.

Glide's emerald eyes and the odd tint of skin colour = blue, could it be blue = had to have come from somewhere and Mary's grannie had always claimed to have a touch of Ne'verman. Mixing did happen and the offspring were always unpredictable in appearance. Still, whatever his forebears, with other sad-eyed parents, his parents left the school. John dropped Mary at the clinic where she worked part-time as a nurse then he steamed on for the Council offices. He'd moved there two years ago after he'd had qualms about his bank. That institution had followed Amerika into sub-dime loans and his conscience had considered that a little too dodgy.

On his first day in school, Glide met Jonathon.

"My friendsh call me Johnno." The little boy had a marked lisp. "What'sh your name?"

"Glide."

"Glide? That'sh a funny name. We'll call you Glido."

"Glido?"

"You've gotta have a nickname."

Johnno was correct. In true Aussie fashion most names were shortened. Yet neither Glido nor Gli nor Glio seemed to work. So, though it was most uncommon, Glide remained as Glide.

There was another uncommon aspect to Glide. It came out because his father kept chickens. On their quarter acre block, one area was enclosed by chicken wire. Inside it were the chooks – another sign, even perhaps a symbol that John always wanted to fly, but never did. After work, John normally threw handfuls of seeds to them.

Glide usually stood at his side, big-eyed and clutching at his father's canvas trousers. At age seven, though, he put a hand on the bucket. "Dad, can I feed them?" he said.

Though John was risk-averse, even he didn't regard chooks as dangerous. "Of course," he replied and handed Glide the bucket.

Soon after that, the boy ventured into the enclosed area and began to collect the eggs as well.

Mary watched him enter the chook house. "He really likes animals," she remarked.

"Too right." John put down his paper and thought. "Funny thing, though, the pythons have stopped trying to get into the chicken coop."

"Because of Glide?" Mary frowned. John shrugged. He was quite happy to let it go. But Mary couldn't. "John, just go out after he's started feeding the chooks and see what else he's doing. I've got a funny feeling about this."

John went. What he saw made his boots shake with fear. Glide was feeding meat scraps to a python. "Don't do that!" he cried. "You'll encourage the snakes to go after the chooks."

"But, dad," Glide protested, "if I feed them then they won't need to go after the chooks."

"Hmm, yes." John saw the logic but added, "But that means that your mum is doing the shopping for the snakes."

Mary came out. "Glide," There was a sharp edge to her voice, "I don't mind for whom I shop. But I do worry about who eats whom. Feel free to feed the possums or the magpies. But please, please, please don't feed the snakes."

"Okay, mum." Glide made a face. "I won't."

But he did, secretly stuffing his school bag with scraps.

Namba, between the coast and the hinterland, abounded with small hills. One afternoon, Glide and Johnno scrambled up one. Their reason? Lack of rain had brought the kangaroos close to town in their search for water. The two boys were crouched down, gazing with fascination at a mob when a noise made them look up. A big roo had bounded right over them!

"Wow!" Glide exclaimed. He was thrilled.

"Mate!" Johnno cried. He was scared.

It was an experience that reinforced Glide's passion, a passion for animals.

"He belongs in a zoo," his mother remarked.

"He's not that wild." John chuckled.

"I mean as a keeper."

"Well, I hope he gets over it" John opened the paper to the financial pages. "There's no money in it. No jobs. Accountancy, now there's a profession. You can always get a job." Unbidden, he imagined a lite-plane flying over the deep blue sea. "Or you can work for yourself." The plane crashed into the hard brown earth. "Hmm, I'll just go over these." And he read the latest news about Council spending.

At seventeen, John said to Johnno, "What're you planning to do after school, son?"

"Business Studies" Johnno didn't even have to think about it. "I'm no academic but I'm pretty good with an abacus. Anyway, I reckon anyone can be a business executive."

"That's good." John turned to Glide. He didn't really want to ask. His son hadn't got over his passion for animals. If anything, it had got worse. "What about you, son?"

"Ecology."

"Economics?" His father hopefully cupped his ear.

"No, dad, ecology."

"Oh." John sank deep in thought. Eventually lifting his head out of the previous century, he said, "And that is?"

"Oh, dad! You know: animals, plants and the environment. How they all fit together."

"Animals and plants? But what for? There's no money in it. Plants and animals don't pay. Why don't you do Business Studies with Johnno?"

"Oh, well, you know," Glide replied and he made the sort of soothing sounds that he used on injured sugar gliders or koalas.

Mary came in from the garden. "Landscape Gardening would be nice. People always need their gardens doing."

"Oh, mum, that's physical. Moving rocks around and things. You know steam cars use coal, and coal mining affects the environment. So does chopping down trees. They affect all the natural systems. I want to know about pollution, the water shortage, using solar power. It's all about systems."

"Cisterns?" Mary was tempted to copy John and cup her ears as if she, too, hadn't heard correctly.

"Mum! Systems."

John snorted. "What do they teach these days?" But it wasn't clear whether he meant his wife or his son.

Not that John had much chance of swaying Glide. After twenty years of lower to middle management, he was used to conceding. Glide wasn't. Plus Glide was receiving subversive support from his mother. Maybe she believed in the Ne'verman's premonition. Maybe she just wanted her son to have a more colourful life than his father's. It has been known for mothers to nurse such ambitions for their off-springs.

Fortunately, both Glide and Johnno did well enough in their exams to go onto the Sunny Coast University. Johnno stuck with his choice of Business Studies. Glide opted for Environmental Studies.

"Gotta get a car," Johnno said. "By the time a bus arrives, it's time to go home again."

"How? Anyway, what about a covered trike?"

"You see that blonde?" Johnno pointed across the campus. "You think you'd even have a chance if she had to peddle?"

Glide felt torn. A steam car wasn't exactly good for the environment but nor was the build-up of testosterone exactly good for him. "How are you going to buy a car?"

"Get a job, of course."

Though not yet convinced about the need for a car, Glide joined Johnno in trolling the resort coffee shops for work. It didn't take long and on the second day, Glide rushed home.

"Mum, mum," he cried, "I've got a job at *The Coffee Bean*."

"Head chef?" Mary was drying cups and saucers.

"Come on, mum, just waiting at tables."

Mary eyed their dining room table. "You could practise here."

"I can't do that," Glide said sincerely. "Not now I'm a professional."

After a few days of work, Glide put in a good word for Johnno. As a result, the two of them ended up sharing shifts and waltzing between the crowded tables. Between study and partying, they also managed to save. It wasn't long before Mary heard the words that she'd been expecting, but had dreaded.

"Mum, me and Johnno are thinking of sharing a townhouse."

Surreptitiously wiping an eye, Mary murmured, "That'll be good."

John, however, wasn't so sure. "You're what eighteen, nineteen? Bit young to be moving out, aren't you?"

"Oh, dad, a lot of uni guys share." Glide pulled out his trump card. "And we'd be so much nearer to the library, we can study more."

"Chase more girls, you mean," John grunted. He liked to look back and think that he, too, had had a life. But that was only in thinking.

"Oh, dad! But only studious girls, all right?"

It was a fearsome world but what could John say. He liked to use an abacus. His fellow workers preferred the computer. Certainly that was faster when its vacuum tubes didn't burn out. He wore canvas breeches. The modern man wore tight trousers with flares. He also thought the Ne'vermen should live their own lives, out of sight, out of mind. Modern youths were into magic.

So almost with their parents' blessing, Glide and Johnno both moved out of home. Yes, there were girls and there were drinks and there were parties. Yet they didn't completely distract Glide from his studies. Nor were they his only diversion. In his first year, as a change from surfing, Glide had a go at archery. To make sure that there was another beginner, he dragged Johnno along as well. On the first day, Glide surprised the instructor by hitting the target. Johnno fired short.

"How the bloody hell did you do that?" Johnno demanded. His best shot hit the stand in the knees.

Glide twanged the bowstring. "I just see an arc from the arrow to the bullseye. It's easy. You must see it, too."

But Johnno didn't. He didn't even know what Glide really meant. After a month of frustration, he was moved to complain, "I just don't see the point"

"It's on the arrow." Glide waved the tip in the air, providing possible evidence of a gene for terrible puns.

In the second year, Glide decided to take up fencing, mostly with foils. Johnno was given no choice. Glide quickly learnt to parry, riposte and to disengage when strategy required. His reactions were fast and he was soon beating more experienced players.

"You're fast." Johnno was panting. "You on steam or something?"

"I'm not that fast." Glide thought for a moment. "I just anticipate earlier."

"Obviously. The question is how?"

Glide removed his helmet and used it as a fan. "I dunno. I just seem to see... Oh, I don't know, I just seem to see a sort of connection from my foil to your chest."

Johnno still didn't grasp what Glide meant. Nor did Glide. He had a Talent but didn't recognise it for what it was. Understanding only began when, one day, Johnno took a good look at Glide's study book.

"What's a Krebs Cycle?" he asked.

"Oh, that's about electron movement in the mitochondria."

"The mito-what?"

"Mitochondria," Glide repeated, studying the picture. "For both males and females, the mitochondria in every cell comes only from the mother. The sperm gets to the egg and the eggs say, 'No male mitochondria in, thank you. We've got all the mito we need.' Strange, eh?"

John tilted his head. "But what's it mean?"

"Dunno. There's DNA in the mito. Maybe our common sense comes from our maternal DNA?"

"From our mums? No way!" Johnno traced the interactions with a finger. "Good thing, you don't have to memorise that stuff."

"What's the problem?" Glide handed Johnno the book. "Ask me some questions."

"You're kidding." Johnno held the book so that Glide couldn't see the contents. "What's the formula for citric acid?" He looked quizzically at Glide. The young man gave it. "Right. What about... isocitric acid? Right. Malic acid?" Johnno was stupefied. Though he had the bleached hair and wide shoulders of a surfie, he was no idiot. Even so, his memory cells blanked out in the face of these complex formulae. He randomly picked another page. "What does a haemoglobin molecule look like?"

"Let's see." Glide, using his Talent, turned pages in his mind. "It's blue. Like a thick blue sausage that's been folded up. They're the polypeptide chains. There's also the little flying saucers. They're the iron heme."

"Jeez!" Johnno whistled. "How do you remember that?"

"I don't." Glide frowned. "I don't remember it. I just see it."

"You see it? That's bloody magic."

"Nah, everyone does it."

"Well, I don't."

"That's 'cos you're funny."

"Who you calling funny?"

Glide pushed John. Johnno pushed Glide and in a moment, they were in a friendly tussle. Their conversation forgotten, Glide wasn't given the time to realise that he had a gift, a very rare gift indeed. It was the ability to visualise. The screen of his mind was more than a metaphor. On it, he could project images in complete detail. It was a pity that neither Glide nor Johnno knew the word *eidetic*. It would've been so helpful. It was as foreign to them as any Ne'verman word. Yet this ability was going to mean so much.

Chapter 2

Between study, work and play plus the other activities that flesh was heir to, three years of uni passed in a flash. In December, after exams, Glide and Johnno went down to Maloolaba Beach. It was packed. Kids played in the shallows. Adults with boogie boards went up to their waists. Bigger kids on surfboards bobbed up and down on the waves. Young women in tiny bikinis sauntered past on their way to *Loo with a Vue*. Those who had already surfed sat at the many cafés, duty done and ready to fill up on calories. With their boards tucked underneath their arms, Glide and Johnno headed for the beach. They sat on the sand, watching the waves.

"What're you gonna do now?" Glide brushed along his surfboard.

"Surf," his friend said laconically.

"No, you drongo. I mean after uni, Johnno."

"Jonathon to you." Johnno threw a handful of sand at his mate.

"Jonathon. Jeez! Sir. Mate." Glide tried again. "Well, Jonathon, what're you gonna do now, later, next year?"

"I'm joining *OceanCool*." Jonathon pointed over his shoulder. They both turned to look at the building complex behind them.

"*OceanCool*? That bloody hotel chain?"

"Yup. Junior Assistant Executive Manager. Bottle washer in other words. Still, it's a start. What about you?"

"Well, *Jonathon*, I just don't know. It's crunch time. To go fourth or to go forth?"

"Is that a riddle?"

"A fourth year of study or go forth and get a j-o-b."

Jonathon pretended shock. "You? A j-o-b? No way. Wash your mouth."

"Yeah, well I did stick my nose out and it didn't smell too good." Glide indicated the scaffolding around a new building. "It's okay if you're in admin or you're a tradie. There's a shortage." He sighed. "Knock down a tree? Yep. Protect a tree? No. Make a possum homeless? Fine. Shelter a possum? Nop."

A Ne'verman was walking along the sand. He had a tray and was selling sugar-coated macadamia nuts. "Home-groan," he called. "Nuts and sugar, all home-groan."

"Home-grownnn." Glide twisted his mouth. "Home-growwnnn. How does he do that, make it sound like groan?"

"Why does he do it?" Johnno cast a beady eye at the Ne'verman. "Is it meant to be a joke?"

"Don't know." Glide watched the blue Ne'verman with a friendly interest. "When I was born, one of the Blueys told my mum that I was gonna be a star."

"Huh!" Johnno began then he paused. "Well, you do have that memory ability. It's useful for exams." He shook his head. "Can't see that it would have any other use, though." He stood up with his board. "You've got a degree now. What about working in the Civilian Service?"

"Go down to Canberry? Bloody cold down there. And no waves."

"What about the regional council? You know, checking out habitats before they put up houses."

"Yeah, to make sure they disrupt the most animals. No way!" Glide fell back onto the sand as if he'd been king hit. The sky was a dazzling blue, full of the temptation of a radiant life. "No, I still want my freedom. I guess I'm gonna have to do honours."

"Honours for you and money for me. Come on, mate." Jonathon ran towards the sea. "Forget the bloody honours and make like a dolphin."

Glide followed his friend into the waves and decisions were put aside. But the holiday passed and, as they were still sharing an apartment, Glide was able to witness Jonathon prepare for his first day of work. It was a bit of a fairy tale, like seeing a toad being turned into a prince. Jonathon wore black three-quarter length breeches, a waistcoats and a cravat. It was enough for Glide to drop his toast.

"Hell's bells, a gentl'man! A right gentl'men. Breeches and a cravat. Bloody hell, John... Jonathon are you actually selling real estate?"

"You may laugh." Jonathon pivoted. "But wait till you see my pay cheque."

"Your pay cheque! But you're selling your soul."

"And I'd do it for half the price. You bet."

In reaction, Glide put on his most gaudy board shorts and brightest tee shirt. That was the way to dress for honours, the only way. Yet despite his casual gear, Glide put in long hours. Perhaps even more than Jonathon did. He was testing water quality in rivers to determine the effects of new building developments.

"None," the developers said. "It's just cement, mate. Clean enough to eat."

His results said otherwise and, mid-year, his supervisor brought him news of a small success. One that he immediately wanted to pass on. He picked up the speaker on his candlestick phone and turned the rotary dial. It beeped and hissed until the speaker was lifted at the other end.

"Hey, Johnno." Glide was so excited that he was shouting.

"Jonathon, please."

"Yeah, yeah, whatever. You know I'm doing this research on water quality?"

"Yes."

"The Council is giving me a grant."

"Good, great. How much?"

"Two thou!"

"Two thou." Jonathon was not impressed. "It's cheap labour, mate. If they put out a tender, they'd have to pay ten times that amount."

"Come on, Johnno... Jonathon. I'm not into the business side like you are."

There was a small silence. Finally Jonathon said, "Maybe you should be."

Glide's heart sank. This, he sensed, was the beginning of the end. At the very least, it marked a change in their friendship. Two thou might not have been much for Jonathon but for Glide, the money granted him his first few seconds of his expected fifteen minutes of fame. He felt recognised. He felt... paid. The symbolic value of a few extra dollars was amazing. Of course, it meant that he worked even harder. Not that he became a monk. He still went to parties, boozed too much and did his sports. He even managed to pop down the road once a month to visit his parents. Well, that was compulsory if he ever wanted a decent feed. But the study paid off. Glide made it and made it well. He finished honours with a first class degree.

A first? Terrific! Champagne all round. But what next, what after the champagne? The choice of the previous year was reincarnated but at a higher level. Who could he talk to about it? The Prof? No, he'd be too biased. His parents? Maybe. Johnno - now Jonathon? Well, sure, he saw his friend everyday in their townhouse. He could certainly talk to him. Indeed, he would. But after some thought, Glide decided to wait. On weekdays, his friend was in business mode. He'd wait till the weekend. Sunday was probably best.

At seven in the morning, relatively early for a Sunday, Glide knocked on Jonathon's door. "Mate," he called. "You decent?"

"Sadly, yes."

Glide opened the bedroom door. "How about *The Coffee Bean* for breakfast?" he asked.

Jonathon sat up so that he was resting on his elbows. "What, you working there again?"

Glide threw a mock punch at Jonathon's feet. "Come on, mate, you know I haven't worked there this year."

"I thought you might've regressed." Jonathon rubbed his eyes and looked at the grandfather clock that ticked silently in the corner. "All... right. But we gotta go in my car."

That was fine with Glide. *My car* was a curvy roadster with an electrically controlled twenty-pound multi-parallel-circuit steam generator with one millimetre bore tubing. If they were going to cruise into breakfast that was a much better deal than his old double boiler bomb. With the sea as an invitation, Jonathon leapt out of bed for a quick shower and put on his new leisure suit. White with extra wide lapels, it looked good enough for a yacht.

Under the summer sun, they drove to Maloolaba. It was already hot, with fleecy white clouds cruising against the blue sky, and Jonathon stopped to roll the hood down. Driving alongside the beach, passers-by admired the roadster while Glide gazed at the sails gleaming on the water. Jonathon, looking like a rising executive in his casual gear, even managed to filch a parking space. They strode from the car park and across the road and into the coffee house.

Glide sat. "So," He spread his hands. "I've finished uni." A waiter came. Glide smiled at him. "How's study?" he asked.

"Fine. I've made it to second year."

They ordered croissants and coffee.

"Jeez, don't the new students look young?" Jonathon remarked.

"They do?" Glide gazed at the young student. "I've stopped noticing."

Jonathon poked him. "Time to grow up, mate. Time to grow up."

"Yeah, that's what I'm thinking." Glide gazed across the road to the rolling waves. "But I'm thinking what next?" He sighed. "To PhD or not to PhD? That is the question."

Jonathon spread butter and jam onto his croissant. He bit, chewed leisurely then swallowed. "Back to the grindstone, Glide? Look, take a look at yourself." Jonathon indicated the thick glass windows of *The Coffee Bean*. Glide saw his reflection - lean build, dark skin with just the faintest hint of blue, and bright green eyes. "You should be feral, mate. You ought to be a ranger or on an oil rig or something. You don't want to be hunched over with one eye in a microscope and the other on your list of publications."

"It's better than Business Studies."

"No way. B-S, and we all know what that stands for, is much more of a challenge." Jonathon grinned. "You certainly get more wildlife."

"You do? Where?"

"In Management. They're as wild as they come." Jonathon looked intently into his coffee-reflection. "Plus you've got that imagery ability. That must be worth something."

Glide grunted. Basically, he agreed with Jonathon. He didn't want to live with one squinty eye peering down a microscope. He didn't want the excitement in his life to be just the result of publishing an academic paper. No way. He wanted a life, a real life, more real than microscopic accuracy. He wanted to study crocodiles or dingos or whales. And weren't the Ne'vermen claiming they still saw Bunyips and Yowies in central Ausphalia? Yeah, he was a touch feral. He agreed with Jonathon. He'd better apply to zoos and wildlife centres and national parks.

Easier said than done. Glide had the John-gene for shyness and it was a big effort for him to just front up to possible work places. He found it easier to write asking for application forms. But there were masses of people with the same hopes as Glide. Not as shy, they went to the Parks and said, "Here I am. Gimme da work." So though Glide dutifully filled out form after form, he didn't even get an interview. After all, who was going to balloon him to Dorwin on the off chance when Dorwin Crocs Inc already had a dozen volunteers waiting for a job?

Somewhat depressed, he visited his parents. At the least, he'd get a decent meal. Though that meant he had to submit himself to the usual interrogation.

"So how's the job hunting going?" John asked.

"Not so good, dad."

His father nodded wisely. After all, what could you expect from a degree in Ecozology... Ecozoogy... He could never remember. He didn't want to remember. He held out some forms. "Why don't you try this?"

Glide read the heading. "The Ausphalian Civilian Service. Why would I do that, dad? Why would I want to be a pen pusher?"

"They've got an Eco... whatsit Department. You could work on environmental issues."

"Yeah, policy issues. I'd still be a pen pusher."

"Well, think about it anyway."

Glide was desperate enough to take the forms home. Watching Jonathon set off for work made him even more desperate. He lay the forms out on the table and in a desultory fashion filled them in. Meanwhile the Parks sent him more rejections. Glide had to face it - he was never going to be a ranger, never be a feral. With nothing to occupy him, he became more and more despondent. But one reply hit him like a barrel of bricks. Jonathon came home that evening to find his friend brooding over a heap of papers.

"Oh, jumping jeepers!" he exclaimed. "Have I missed your birthday?"

Glide flicked an envelope. "I wish."

"Another miss?"

"If only." Glide picked up the thick brown envelope and waved it at Jonathon. "An acceptance."

"Bloody great, mate!" Jonathon considered his friend's gloomy expression. "Well, it is, isn't it?"

"Is it?" Glide tore the envelope to bits. "In Brissie? With the Ausphalian Civilian Service? It doesn't exactly require a slouch hat or Wellington boots." He picked up a butter knife. "Call that a knife?"

"Mate, it's not a hunting knife but it's still a knife." Jonathon read the letter of acceptance. "You've got to start somewhere, mate. Take it and keep looking."

"Yeah, right. Take it. Where else is there to look? C'mon on, let's go out. I think I'm due for a bender."

That night, Glide soaked himself in beer. And he did it once more on the following night. And the one after that as well. A week of headaches later, he again visited home.

His father, of course, was delighted. "It's better than my start in the bank. In fact, it's a very good start. Security. Promotion. Pension. Superannuation!" His eyes sparkled. "You've got a place for life."

Glide rolled his eyes. "You have, dad. Times have changed. I've just got a three year contract."

"Yes," John waved his hands, "but they keep renewing. Unless you do something really terrible, they never throw you out."

"What's terrible, dad? Killing the Civilian Head of Department?"

"That's certainly bad, Glide. And, yes, they might fire you for that." John rested his chin on his fingers. "I was thinking more along the lines of leaking classified policy papers. They'd certainly fire you for that."

"Leaking is worse than murder?" Glide held out his plate for second helpings. "Thanks, mum. Look, maybe I'll just do a year.

Save some money then go up north, work on the barrier reef or something. Maybe go overseas."

"Yes, dear," Mary said. "You could always teach Auslish in Nippon."

"I don't think so." Glide paused, holding his hand over his mouth until he could speak. "Actually, you may be right. That could be fun. Maybe next year?"

Next year, however, never came. Something went wrong, terribly wrong. It began when Glide moved to Brissie and rented a trendy townhouse in trendy Paddlington. He did that on the basis of having a real salary. The reality of his real salary, however, didn't hit him until his first pay cheque landed on his desk. He studied it and his jaw dropped. Even after tax, the amount was enormous. He just had to ring Jonathon.

"I can't believe it," Glide shrilled. "It's huge! What do I do with it?"

"Spend it. Get used to it" His friend chuckled. "You'll soon be wondering how you ever managed to exist without it."

"No way. Impossible."

"No way? All the way! Mate, a salary is subtly seductive. You'll see. Anyway, what're you doing to earn it?"

Glide's tone lost some of its enthusiasm. "Gathering data on crisis housing."

"You like it?"

"Yeah, it's all right," Glide said slowly. "I don't dislike it."

"Is it important?"

"Yeah, I think so."

"Don't sound like there's any animals in it."

"No, just stats and computers. I try and use the abacus when I can but we're not really set up for that."

"Well, there you are, mate. Gotta go. See you."

Glide put down the phone and stared out of the window. He was in a hi-rise and this building went up six storeys. People and steam cars hurried along the street. The work was okay he had to admit. But it wasn't animals. And it wasn't outside. It was okay but it wasn't him. Was it too late? He again started to search the papers for jobs. Then, like everyone else in his office, he regularly perused the *Civilian*. But Glide just didn't have the heart to send out any more applications. It was easier to stay where he was and wait till he was pushed.

When the push came, it was upwards and Glide was promoted. With one salary increase, he bought a new car. With the next, he took out a loan for his own trendy townhouse. By risking nothing, Glide let strands of money engulf him and he became as trapped as a fly in a jar of honey. It was all too easy. And being easy made it hard.

After yet another promotion, his father rang. "Only one more year," he pronounced, "and you'll be into middle management."

"Yes, dad." Glide's tone was flat.

John noticed. "Is something wrong? I thought you liked the work."

"I do like it, dad." Glide tugged at his long black hair. "But it's not me." He was hit by a realisation. "Even when I like it, I hate it."

John rolled his eyes at the phone. How could he get through? "Security," he said firmly. "Your super."

"I'm super?"

"You know, superannuation."

"Oh yeah, super."

But super was not super for Glide. A grey pall had settled over him. Feeling blue, he replayed what he'd just said to his father: "Even when I like it, I hate it."

What a terrible thing to have to admit. Glide dropped his head. He had to change his life.

Chapter 3

Glide wasn't making friends. At work, his only contact was Matt, a roundish fellow in his mid-twenties. One water break, thinking exercise might be the change that he needed, Glide approached his workmate.

"You interested in foils?" he asked.

Matt's round face broke into a grin. "Foils? I'm often foiled."

"I'm mean as in sword-fighting."

"Wow, a samurai!" Matt patted his round stomach. "I could lose some. But sword fencing, that Error Flynn stuff, I don't know."

"Go on. I want to try a class."

Matt started to move away from the water cooler. "You could go by yourself."

"I could but... I can't."

Glide had a sudden vivid image of years ago and tootling along in his old car with a surfboard sticking out the window. He'd try anything then. Now that he had a new car, he hardly ever went out. Matt, however, well understood. He'd gone through the same process.

"Okay," he said slowly. "When?"

"Straight after work? At six."

Matt threw his plastic cup into the bin. "Okay, see you then."

Glide looked forward to the foils. He'd been so good at it while at uni. But it turned out that his heart wasn't in it. After a few sessions, he began to whine, "It's not working."

"What's wrong?" Matt asked.

"It's too elegant," Glide complained.

"But you're so good!"

"No, I want more bash for my buck." Glide went over some of the other activities that he'd tried. "What about kendo?"

Matt whipped his foil so it made a satisfying whoosh, whoosh, whoosh. "Just when I'm getting to grips with this!"

"Kendo is better. We get to whack each other with sticks."

"But I don't want to be whacked."

"Well, of course, whack the other person first."

Matt made a face. He couldn't see himself whacking anyone. And he didn't. Paired with Glide, he was whacked, whacked, whacked. Paired with Marie, he was whacked. Paired with Otto the octogenarian, he was whacked. On the other hand, Glide managed to whack nearly everyone. He really enjoyed that part of Kendo. But he didn't enjoy the bowing, the sensei-ing and all the other zen-type formalities.

"It's too pseudo-spirituo," he said. "Let's go back to foils."

"But you said that foils were too poofy."

"I could take my kendo stick there."

In that, Matt only saw trouble. "And whack people? How about the gym? No swords, no nothing. Just you and the weights."

Glide thought for a moment. "Oh, yeah. May as well give that a go."

They went to the gym and started to pump iron. Between pumps, Glide sniffed around. Behind a curtain, he discovered a punch bag.

"Oh, yeah!" Glide cried and whacked it with his fists.

That suited Matt. Glide could beat up on anything as long as it wasn't Matt. Only the curtain billowed in and out with his fury. For it was a fury. His frustration was growing and his moods were getting darker. One day, Glide was so dark that he rammed the bag with his head. K.O! With a groan, Glide fell to the ground.

Hearing the noise, Matt rushed in. "What the hell!"

Glide's eyes were open. "Do you see stars?"

"No."

"Oh!" Glide held up his hand. Coloured lights flickered around it. Gingerly, he climbed onto all fours. "Bloody damn and strawberries! That hurt. Bloody inanimate object!" His speech slurred, Glide tottered around, rubbing his head. "It's better when I take it out on others."

"Oh, no! Not foils again? Not Kendo?"

"Nah." Glide rubbed the bright red patch on his forehead. "Punching and kicking? How's about that Korian martial art, Taikwon-dont."

"Taikwon-dont?" Matt squeaked. "I thought it was Taikwon-do?"

"Nah, that's got too many rules. Taikwon-dont is better."

"Mate, where do you get these ideas?" Matt threw out his arms in protest.

"I dunno, Matt, my mate. But have you looked in a mirror lately? You're looking really svelte."

"Svelte, eh?"

That stopped his protests. Matt breathed in to svelte himself even more. Consequently, when Glide went to *KickButt*, his co-worker followed. As Glide had said, Matt was losing weight. It was the fear, of course. Fear was causing him to sweat buckets.

KickButt was somewhat therapeutic. Matt held a kick pad and Glide kicked it. Glide held a kick pad and Matt kicked it. In a strange Can-Can, pairs travelled the width of the dojang, one leg flashing out after the other. It certainly provided some release. Yet less than Glide had expected. He found, to his surprise, that he was holding back. He could kick harder but he didn't. He could punch wilder but didn't. He might even and unexpectedly produce his kendo stick, but didn't. The reason, he didn't dislike anyone enough to really risk hurting them.

"It's no good." Glide was standing by his car after the workout. "It's the office itself. I've got to get away from the office."

"What's wrong with the office?" Matt was fanning himself with his Taikwon-dont jacket, showing off his newly developed muscles. Now that he was loosing fat, now that he was svelte, the girls at work were starting to notice him.

Irritated, Glide slapped the car's bonnet. "Oh, just the air-fans, the bloody computer, the four walls, the same four damn walls. The writing! The reports! The paper! The endless bloody sameness." Glide flung his exercise bag into the car. "I'm working on crisis housing but if I switched to heritage or wildlife, the work doesn't change. It's still shoving bloody paper around and around and going to bloody committees and doing the same old yak, yak, yak!"

Matt was horrified. "You don't like the Civilian Service?"

"No, I goddam hate it!"

"You do?" Matt was astounded. "Well, I like it."

Glide fought to control himself. After all, there was no reason why Matt shouldn't like it. Matt was one person. He, Glide, was another. "Look, mate, I'm sorry. It's me. I just don't think I'm cut out for it."

Glide slid into his car, self-pity sitting with him. He had problems, bad problems, and the walls were closing in on him. He turned the ignition to start the electric air compressor and, with a bad-tempered wave, drove away. He thought he had a leak and something was smelling bad. But on the slow drive through Brissie's busy streets, he had a realisation, a realisation of the worst possible kind. It was true that he hated the office. But the whole thing went deeper than that. He was not at the office now. So he shouldn't be feeling full of hate. No. He understood that it wasn't really the office that he hated. It was himself. That was the bad smell. It wasn't coming from his car. It was him. That was why he couldn't shake off those feelings. He was living totally against his grain. He had wanted a real life but instead he had settled for an easy life. Yet making it easy was making it hard. He had wanted magic but had stopped at security. Like father, like son. Bloody father, bloody son.

Comfort was gnawing away at him. He was feeling blue, depressed and blue. His mood was so blue, it verged on black. The next day, Glide had to force himself to go to work. The day after that was even more difficult. Each day was worse. He had been a clerk, a pen pusher, for four years! How had the time slipped away? On the penultimate night of his fourth year of pen pushership, Glide opened a bottle of vodka. It wasn't to celebrate. It was to commiserate. On the last morning of his fourth year of pen pushership, Glide crawled out of bed. Jackhammers pounded at his skull. His head was going to be pounded off. If only it would. If only!

Another Monday with the blues after another Sunday with the blues after... The jackhammers continued to pound. The shower threw daggers. His olive face was lined with blue-black patches. The pollution of his mind was infecting his skin. He tried to massage the patches upwards and out. It didn't work. Glide resorted to his stagnant eidetic ability and tried to visualise the blemishes as being drawn upwards. In his imagination that, at least, began to work. Cranking the motor of his mind, the blemishes gathered into a blue cloud above his head. That was his life, a blue-bruised mushroom cloud. He groaned. Where was his destiny? Where was his fate? The cloud settled above his head, a misshapen doughnut pretending to be a halo.

Glide left his trendy townhouse and walked slowly towards the bus stop. Every so often, he lifted his hand. Something was pressing down upon his head. The doughnut couldn't still be there, surely? Was it a storm? He looked up. A stormy sky? No, radiant blue. Still feeling the pressure, he stopped. But twist and turn as he might, he couldn't see through the top of his own skull. With a grunt, he gave up. What did it matter anyway? Was living under a cloud of bruised-blue any worse than being embalmed in a grey pall?

A few steps away, a black magpie cocked red eyes at him. It strutted away, wings folded like an old headmaster. Glide scowled, what did the maggie have to complain about? The bird didn't have to go into an open-plan office. He cranked the rusty projector of his mind. A detailed picture appeared. "Was that a magpie?" he thought. "Shouldn't it have yellow eyes?" He gave a silent and bitter laugh. "Maybe the maggie also has a hangover."

He felt so miserable, Glide suffered an inner lurch. How far he'd strayed! "What's happened to me?" he mentally cried. "What's gone wrong, so bloody wrong?"

As if to externalise his words, a white cockatoo screeched. Three kookaburras laughed hysterically. The noise rippled out, collided with tree trunks and died. Waves of a silent scream continued onwards. A bus halted at the stop.

Glide entered along with a burly Islander, a slim Asian and a knobbly Aussie. "G'day," they all said to the driver.

Glide felt alien. "Is it just me?" he thought. "Why aren't they unhappy?"

Entering his open-plan office, Glide sat in front of his workstation. Between the computer icons, he saw his reflection, no more than a vague ghost of a being. He began to tap the side of the keyboard, muttering, "It's wrong, so wrong. It's all so bloody wrong." Unconsciously, his voice rose.

"What's that?" Matt peered over his partition. "Who's Wong? Did you go out with a girl called Wong?"

"Wong, Wong? What's Wong?" Glide hadn't realised that he'd spoken aloud. "Nothing, nothing." He waved his hands in denial.

At six, he went with Matt to *KickButt*. At the end of a tough session, the punch bag was free. Glide kicked and punched it until he fell down. Matt helped him up and he immediately launched into it again. The instructor came over. Gently putting his arm around Glide, he led him away. Glide saw himself in the wall length mirror.

Steam issued from his nostrils and his eyes were scarlet whirlpools. Now he knew. He'd gone over the edge.

With aching limbs and with aching heart, he went home. He should've been exhausted and gone to bed. But he was beyond exhaustion and instead, he stayed up late. The later to bed, the slower came the morning. When his eyes were gritty, he tucked himself away. Yet as soon as he gave up on his thoughts and tried to sleep, a cloud of blueness sat above his head. For a moment, he considered it. Oddly enough, the dark cloud seemed not to be threatening but soothing. Still, blue was blue and he wished it away. He didn't want to be blue anymore. The next morning, he was drained. Good, he'd be too numb to notice that he was in the office. Glide stumbled into the shower. He didn't take too long in case it snapped him awake. Besides, he believed in saving water.

With a towel around his waist, he began to shave. He held the blade to his neck. Quickly he struck down. A tiny cut appeared. What more could one do with a safety razor? He leant against the sink and peered at his reflection. The blue-black cloud had reappeared.

"G'day," Glide said. "How ya doing?" He imagined zigzags of lightning shooting out of the cloud. "There will be local thunderstorms," he muttered. "The Head Land will be dark and there will be gusty squalls in Stomach Land." He gave a dry laugh.

He set off for the bus stop, taking the bruised cloud with him. As before, though, this blueness seemed to be more positive than negative. As before, if anything, it was vaguely comforting. Huh, he must be accepting his craziness.

The next morning, his mini-mushroom cloud returned and his head was again enshrouded in mist. Glide shrugged. So what? Blue, he decided, was more fun than tepid grey.

"It's Fleudian," he told himself on his morning walk to the bus. "A dissociation of what I think of work." He sighed. "Is that what

I really think of work? Damn and strawberries!" He reached a high hedge. On the other side was a small park. He looked longingly at the green as he entered the bus. Inside, though, he thought, "Why me? Everyone has hassles. Why should I get a blue thunder cloud lumbering above my head?" He gazed out of the window at the passing houses and daydreamed. In his daydream, the cloud settled inside him. Unexpectedly, he saw himself in the desert.

A word popped into his mind, and the word was, "Stroll-about!"

Glide dragged himself through work, went to the gym, and went home. After another sleepless night, the blue seemed more profound. His halo/mini-mushroom was almost a second head. As he dragged his feet to the bus stop, the sensation was virtually tangible. The cloud was a reality that dwelt above his head, around his head and inside his head. Suddenly, though, there was a stretching tension and he had the strange sensation that the cloud was pulling away from him. The cloud was a blur of blue elastic.

Slowly, like a genie out of a bottle but where the bottle was his head, the cloud began to take shape. A human shape! The blue cloud took shape at his side! Excitement, like a dash of premature arthritis, briefly stirred in Glide. Fear came, too. Fear wrapped in a cloak of scientific scepticism pushed aside the excitement.

"I don't believe this," Glide snorted. "I just don't." He plodded on, not daring to look to the side. The nearly solid cloud wavered, became less substantial, and eventually was almost translucent. Glide ploughed on until only a misty candyfloss of shape remained. "And that's where it belongs," he thought grimly, "in the dark cobwebs of my mind."

Yet just moments later, it occurred to him that the darkness was the nearest to lightness that he'd felt for months, for ages. The darkness was a challenge and Glide knew that he needed a challenge. Lethargy was okay, he thought, as long as he didn't get sluggish about it.

He arrived at work. The vacuum tubes were fine today. His cards and paper tapes spewed out data. It was a typical day that he quite liked but deeply hated. At the end of work, he consulted his diary. Not a punch bag day, today he went to archery. Usually, however bad he felt, he hit the bullseye. This time, unusually, his first arrow didn't ever reach the target.

"Visualise the trajectory," the instructor said.

"Yeah, right." Usually, Glide didn't need to be reminded.

As he had so often done before, Glide thought to imagine his boss on the bullseye. To his surprise, he again missed. Next, he thought to imagine Matt. Yet for a third time, he missed. On the fourth time, he imagined himself. Bullseye! Bullseye? Bullshit! A deep well of self-pity surged up. Yet it was so dense, so dark, that it was almost a parody. It was as if he was so blue that he was falling out the other side. The cloud, he told himself, must've been an omen. Its breaking away was a touch of magic. Or more likely, it was the touch of magic that he denied himself.

Having no idea what he meant, Glide made his way home. As usual, he delayed going to bed until he was too exhausted to think. At first, sleep embraced him, a deep dreamless sleep. Then it gave way to a dream, a curiously vivid dream.

Oh, Glide thought in his dream, *I've had this dream before.*

The blue cloud took shape. It took shape and spoke. In a reverberating voice, it praised Glide and his Ability. The voice called him a hero.

"A hero!"

In the dark of the night, Glide awoke, his body taut with excitement. He believed the dream. He wanted to believe. He was a hero. But gradually, as dawn fingered its way into his room, scepticism took over. It was a dream, after all, just a dream... a fantasy.

Glide, wondering what could bring excitement to his dismal life, slept again. The darkness in him grew. In the morning, the blue cloud was even more solid. He thought he might be able to lift it like a hat and say, "G'day."

But he did not dismiss it. Better, he mused, to have a dark fantasy than to have a grey life. Accepted, the shape became more definite. It became less a part of him and more independent. Glide shrugged humorously. Him, humorous? Since when? He set off for work and had just reached the park when the cloud totally separated. It took a clear shape and kept pace on the opposite side of the hedge. Then to Glide's utter amazement, the blue-black cloud called out to him.

Chapter 4

"Hey, mate."

"Go away."

"It's a lucky thing," the cloud said.

"Go away. I never speak to clouds."

"It's a lucky thing," the voice repeated, "that you don't believe in me."

"Yeah, right."

"Else you'd be speaking to nothing."

"I am speaking to nothing," Glide snapped. Two schoolkids gave him a wide berth. "See?"

"Nah, they saw me." The voice was dark and gravely. "It's your tone of voice they were avoiding."

The two boys hurried on without a backward glance. They must be confused, Glide thought. They were imagining that he was speaking to a real person. He turned his head. Was he? What was he speaking to? He slowed his pace and took a good look through the hedge. He blinked. On the other side, the park's side, the darkness had coalesced into a strange figure, a very strange figure. Though it should not have been. Not in Brissie, capital of Quinsland. What, or rather who, stood before him was a Ne'verman.

This was not so odd in itself. After all, the occasional Bluey did come into town. When they did, though, they dressed for it. This one hadn't. He simply wore the traditional golden shorts with the silver fringes. He also stood in the traditional Ne'verman posture with his weight on his left leg. His bent right leg was horizontal so that the heel, at waist level, could be cupped in the left hand. His right hand held a spear. In theory, a Ne'verman could stand for hours with his weight balanced between his left leg and the vertical spear. This one didn't. He fell backwards in rigid slow motion, only a moment later to pop upright again. It happened again and again. A slow fall followed by a sharp upright.

Glide shook his head. He should've been frightened but wasn't. The sight was just too strange. It might've been scary at midnight but now it was daylight. He actually wanted to laugh. To laugh? That was so unlike him, he tried instead to be depressed. After all, it was Friday. Just two more days and he had to be back at work. Then another Friday, followed by another two days of bleak anticipation, then once again back at work. The endless cycle. But depression wouldn't come. Instead, he giggled.

"Buzz off." He flicked his hand at the apparition. "I don't believe in you."

"Right, mate. A lucky thing, too, otherwise I might've appeared in your office."

"You what?"

"That's right. I might've appeared on the bus, sitting right next to you."

"As if." Glide shrugged, still walking slowly.

The figure wobbled, fell back yet somehow stayed the same distance away. "Glide," the Ne'verman murmured.

"Go! Away!" Glide said. "What part of *go away* don't you understand?"

He glanced around. It was bad enough being depressed. Was he going mad as well? Luckily, he was on the uncrowded side of the park. It was only around the corner that he'd join the busy part of Paddlington. Well, that was a relief. It was one thing him for him to know he was potty. It was another for other people to believe it. Not that he knew any of the other people. Nor did they know him.

Peering through the hedge, Glide mumbled, "So now it's really happened. Gone loco. I've gone loopy. Misery and frustration have done for me."

Yet try as he might, right now Glide did not feel miserable. Nor did he feel that he was cracking up. This strange apparition excited and enlivened him.

"Glide." The Ne'verman spoke again. "I am Ne'wang the Ne'vermaker."

"A Ne'vermaker? A magician? They don't exist."

"We don't usually show ourselves to pinkfellas. But we are real and we do have magical skills."

"Real? You're simply a real figment of my imagination. Magical? So now, why don't you just magic yourself away?"

"Because... because I need your help." The man was now as solid as a blue thundercloud.

"Sorry, can't help." Glide shook his head. "I'm really busy right now." Which sounded pretty silly even to him. He started again. "I'm sorry but I've had a scientific education. I just don't believe in you. You're an illusion. I'm demented. Go away, vamoose and leave me alone."

"But, Glide, that's why we need you. Because of your scientific education."

"Oh?"

"We need a sceptic."

"Yeah, I'm a sceptic, a sceptic tank. Well, no t'ank you. See? I'm rambling. I'm demented."

"You're not demented."

"No? Well, you're wrong, see. Why else would I be talking to you? So just leave me alone and let me be miserable in peace."

"In peace?"

"In pieces, then. I'm falling apart."

Glide walked faster. The vision, however, kept pace, toppling and righting, toppling and righting. As it appeared and disappeared, Glide passed a hand over his eyes.

"Damn and strawberries!" he cried. "Can you stop doing that?"

"Glide," Ne'wang said, "you said your life was miserable and frustrating. But do you really worry about it?"

"Worry about it?" Glide stopped in his tracks. "Worry? I don't have to worry about it, I live it."

Having stopped, Glide took another good squizzy at the figure. It was much more solid now and the falls were less frequent. "Damn." He hugged his briefcase to his chest. "I've really made you now."

"You have." The Ne'verman put his weight on his spear, "But then again, you didn't."

Glide frowned. "Yes, I did!"

"No, you didn't!"

"Did!" Glide dropped his voice to a hiss. "I can't believe this. A shouting match with my own hallucination."

The Ne'verman wasn't falling at all now. "Well, you did evoke me," the blue man conceded. "Though not me as such. It's just that you're so desperate to be outside, to go stroll-about, it was that what called me. Your desperation along with your vivid imagination."

Glide pouted. "I don't imagine."

"Yes, you do."

Glide sighed. A woman hurried past. She looked at him and then peered through the hedge. Apparently satisfied, she nodded briefly and continued on.

Glide looked at his watch. "Damn, I've missed my bus." With another sigh, he set down his briefcase. It was made of stiff black leather and bristled with combination locks. Civilian Servants used them to carry their sandwiches, jigsaw puzzles and impressive looking computer printouts. "Ah, well," he said. "Now I'm late, I may as well go crazy without all the hassle." As he idly twirled a combination lock, he recalled a discussion at Taikwon-dont. The instructor was talking about the hidden causes of tension. Somehow, he'd gone on to discuss Karl Yung and his theory of archetypes. Suddenly Glide understood what was happening.

"I know," he exclaimed, "you're my shadow, my dark side, the me I try to repress."

With grim hauteur, The Ne'vermaker drew himself up to his full height. "No, mate! I'm dark but I ain't your dark side. Don't you try and therapise me away!" The figure made a wide sweep with his arm, narrowly missing Glide with the spear. "Oops, sorry." Regaining his composure, he intoned, "I am a gateway, a portal, the way. I am, Glide, even though you think I am not."

"Like hell you are." Glide pointed at the bushes between them. "You're like that tree in the forest. It doesn't exist if nobody sees it. I bet... I bet... I bet that if I looked away, you just wouldn't be there." He quickly turned. "Oh!" A dark blue shape had appeared in front of him. "There must be two of you." He turned again. "No, three! Four! Bloody hell, five!" He whirled dizzily.

"It's no good, Glide," Ne'wang said. "The philosophical tree remains."

"Huh?"

"The philosophical tree..."

"Yeah, yeah, I heard all that. But what do you know of philosophy?"

"That was Bishop Berknee, Glide, a famous philosopher." Ne'wang stroked a pretend wispy beard. "Or was that Kant? I kant quite remember. Ha-ha."

Glide kicked his case with annoyance. "Hey, you're my hallucination. How come my hallucination knows more than me? No, hold it, hold it. I know. As Yung said, you're a projection from my unconsciousness and my unconsciousness knows things that my consciousness doesn't. And if I were not conscious, I wouldn't know these things and you would cease to exist!"

"Good thinking, Glide. Just the kind of thinking that we need. Why not knock yourself out and prove it?"

Glide's face brightened. Then darkened. "But if I knock myself out...?"

"Precisely. How would you know anything?" It was the Ne'verman's turn to sigh. "So much for a scientific education." His tone was ironic. "So much for your fantastic faculty of critical analysis."

Ne'wang began to waver, to become a smoky outline. Glide threw up his hands in despair. "All right, all right, from my point of view you're just a projection, but from your point of view you're more than a tree in a forest. I mean for you, you're real. Okay, let's just cut the metaphysics. The point is: Who are you? Where on earth do you come from?"

"Where on earth? Mate, that's a difficult one. Let's leave that for the moment. As for who." The dark face split into a huge impish grin. "As I said, I am Ne'wang the Ne'vermaker."

"N the N." Glide scuffed at the briefcase at his feet. "Look," he said. "I know and you know that you just come from inside my head. So in simple terms, where do you think I think that you come from?"

"Ah well, that's the rub."

"It is?"

"You think life is evil."

"Ye...es?"

"But you ask yourself what is evil?"

"Right. What is it?"

"It is what you are living."

"Oh!"

Glide passed a hand over his eyes. The two of them, or the two of him, were going round and round in circles. Worlds of words span around his head, making him dizzy. But it was true. If he reviewed the past weeks, months, years, he'd lived the very opposite of the life that he'd intended. He never went bush. He had almost no contact with animals. The very sense of adventure in him had been stifled, perhaps killed. In every way, he had become curtailed.

"My life is pretty bleak, I suppose. I have been feeling pretty blue." Glide rubbed his face. His eyes were on the verge of tears. "And so, do I as you, have an answer?"

"No." Ne'wang was becoming misty. "I as I don't. But I, as we, think that you do."

Glide refused to be confused. "Right, you mean in my subconscious." He paused. His subconscious had stumbled over a word. "We, you said we. What do you mean, we?"

Like the Cheshire cat, nearly all that now remained of the dark face was a luminous smile. "If I told you," the Ne'vermaker began.

"Then you'd have to kill me. I know. I know."

"I was going to say that that would just be words. If you want to escape, let me take you there."

"Take me there?" Glide tapped his head. "What, to disappear up my own subconsciousness?"

In disbelief, Glide looked around him. The sky was a bright blue. The grass was a lush green. Across the park, shiny tops of cars with their steam outputs chugged along the road. The shouts of schoolkids reached him. The world couldn't have been more concrete. Yet just in front of him was the smoky version of a man, a genie of the bush, a romanticised image that could be found on a celebratory postage stamp. But such an icon was totally unlikely here in inner city Brissie.

With hope, Glide blinked. But to no avail, the figure remained. Well, if the outside wouldn't change, what could? He dipped into himself. What were the options? Work and depression? Or not work and going crazy? Of the two, crazy without work seemed to be more fun. Even just to think of work normally filled him with a blackness. Not the blue-blackness of the figure in front of him. No, that was a luminous sort of darkness. What haunted him was the empty blackness, a draining blackness, an awful sucking void of blackness. In contrast, crazy was a beacon of glorious lightness.

"All righty," he declared, "you've convinced me. Take me to your leader. You've got a problem? Well, I'm your man with the solution. I'll make it straight, straight as a roo's hind leg."

"That's beaut, mate!" Ne'wang cried, "You definitely won't be sorry."

"You kidding? I'm sorry already. Still, go on." At Glide's words, the Ne'vermaker raised both arms in a dramatic gesture. Without the support of the spear, though, he slowly toppled. "Oh, jeez," Glide groaned, "some illusions do have 'em."

With an embarrassed cough, and a purpling of the skin that might've been a blush, the blue man sprang up. "Sorry, mate, lost me concentration. Too busy working on me spell."

"Try using a dictionary."

"Me magic spell."

"Yeah, sure." Glide pretended to undo his combination locks. "You want to borrow my frog's eyes and newt's tongue? Not a problem. Don't you worry about me. I've got all day to hang around. It isn't as if I've got to go to work or anything." At the mention of work, he expected the usual pall of grey to descend. It didn't. "Work?" he repeated. "Go to work?" It still didn't come. "Jeez, I must be believing this more than I thought! Go on," he exclaimed with Mary Pooppins enthusiasm, "sing me a song, spell me a spell!"

The Ne'vermaker looked at him curiously. "Olright," he said, "if that's what you want. W-a-h-r-o-n-g-a, W-o-l-l-o-n-g-o-n-g, W-a-g-g-a, W-a-g-g-a."

He stopped. Glide looked at the Ne'vermaker, looked around the Ne'vermaker, then looked back at the Ne'vermaker. "So," he said, "nothing's happened."

"Why should it? I just spelt out the spell. Like you asked."

"Oh." Glide did some more looking around. Some grey did enter his heart. Perhaps life wasn't meant to be easy? Perhaps he wasn't going to get out of work, after all? "Look," he said, "I don't think we're communicating here. Like, weren't you supposed to magic me, to take me somewhere?"

"Oh, yeah, sure. The fact is, mate, I've not really acted as a whitefella portal before. So while I was trying to spell, I lost me spell."

Glide reached for his case. "I might just as well go to work," he sighed. "I can't even be disturbed properly."

The cloud remnants darted in front of him. "No! Hold on, mate! I'm just getting into me swing."

The Ne'vermaker suddenly stretched to his full height. His arms reached up and up. He was reaching to the heavens, bringing the heavens down to him. Blue met blue. His voice was a strong incantation. Suddenly, Glide shivered, not only on the outside but inside as well. The incantation was a vibration deep inside of him. He had to admit, he was impressed. For a moment, he fully believed that the proud figure in front of him was no figment of his deluded imagination.

"Hey," he called out, in sudden alarm. "What did you say your name was?"

The majestic sound paused. "I am Ne'wang the Ne'vermaker."

"And a Ne'vermaker is really a magician?"

"Really."

"Oh, hell! Oh, damn and strawberries!"

The majestic sound continued. Glide felt hazy. Did the blue sky wobble? The landscape? Reality? Everything was slowly wavering as if in the grip of a tremulous heat haze. Glide tried to hold on to something: the flickering air molecules, the wavy blue cloud, or the sight of the waving branch of a tree. But there was no substance to hold on to. He tried to shout. Perhaps a passing schoolchild would save him. Or a sceptical scientist. He closed his eyes but it was too late. His mind exploded. The landscape shattered. Shards of blue light shot through him. His ears popped and his legs extended. A powerful electric current swept him away. He was a wave pulsating through waves. He was the music of the spheres – a concerto written in heavy metal. He was a black hole that sucked in light. Once more, he tried to shout. Then, out of nothingness, his feet hit the ground.

"Ouch!" He crumpled backwards.

Lying on his back, Glide opened his eyes. That was a mistake. A huge grey wall was rushing at him! With no way to escape, Glide closed his eyes and opened his mouth.

"Let me out of here!" he screamed. "Let me out! Ouch...!"

Chapter 5

There was a confusion of sounds. A roar. Squeals. Glide's squeals. The rough hiss of something huge skidding to a halt. Dirt flying. Voices shouting. Pandemonium, chaos. Then there was a sudden hush, the hush of suspended activity. Glide remained curled up. His eyes squeezed tightly shut. He had the distinct impression that the hush was centred on him. After all that frantic hubbub, the hush was now worse than the noise.

He held his breath for a week, for a month, for a year. In that fraction of a second when his eyes had been open, he'd glimpsed a great grey wall hurtling towards him. He waited for the crash to come. When it didn't, he risked a slow breath. When the sky didn't fall, he began to uncurl. When uncurling did not result in calamity, he dared to open his eyes. Big mistake. Calamity loomed! The great grey wall was falling! Falling down on him! Eyes shut! Curl up! Glide rolled into a ball.

The sense of action suspended continued. Glide remained in a tight ball for so long that he became aware of the ground pressing its grainy particles against his side. There was a dry smell and a pleasant breeze. Uncrushed, he had time to think. Could he really have seen what he'd seen? No, it was impossible. It was even more impossible than having seen the Ne'vermaker. Surely. Surely? It was quiet now, except for heavy breathing. Whose breathing? His? No. An industrial vacuum cleaner's? Could be. Could he believe his eyes? Could he believe anything? Start at the beginning, he told himself. Deny everything, as Draycart the French philosopher had once said, begin at the beginning and see what he could see. Though, on second thoughts, maybe that was Mary Pooppins?

Okay, to begin with, he wasn't crushed. Well, that was pretty hard to believe. After all, he had seen that incredible grey wall rushing towards him. Except it wasn't a wall. It was something else altogether. Hard to believe but there it was. Its image was imprinted on his mind's eye. Plus its afterimage. In fact, Glide shuddered beneath the apparition of a whole infinity of after-afterimages. That was the problem with eidetic imagery. It captured everything.

Glide shifted through each image and each one shouted one thing, one incredible thing: *elephant!* Elephant? Ridiculous! Well, one moment he'd been on his feet and talking with a blue-black cloud. Now he was on his back and cowering before an elephant. Wasn't that ridiculous? It was. Damn! Well and damn! Damn and strawberries! Glide didn't like to swear but, for once, he could get little further than those *damns*.

He rewound the projector of his mind. He didn't have eidetic hearing. But he was pretty sure that it was the elephant that had roared. It certainly hadn't been a mouse. Nor Glide. Okay, he might've squealed. Yes, he had to admit, he might've done. He might even have wet his pants. But definitely, it was the elephant, the pachyderm that had given a deafening bellow. The elephant had roared, "Oh, no! Oh, no! Oooooo... nooooooo!"

Glide was still curled up and persisting in being a Draycartian Philosopher when a warm wet thing slobbered over his face.

"Oh, no!" He curled up even tighter. "I survived the crash but now I'm going to be eaten."

"Hey," said a voice. "Knock, knock. Open up. Open up."

"No," Glide mumbled. "Go 'way."

"No. G'wan." The wet thing slobbered over him. "At least, open your eyes."

"Nop."

"G'wan. Do I have to keep licking you?"

"You've got me licked. Please do not continue."

"I'd rather you opened your eyes."

"No. I might see what I think you are."

"Ahem." The elephant made a disturbing noise. "I am definitely not what you think I am. I am what I am – despite whatever you think I am."

"Jeez, a philosophical eleph..."

"Careful, careful! Don't say it! Watch your language."

There was a pause, and a silence. Glide, unfolded a little. Cautiously, very cautiously, he cracked open his eyes. A grey and hairy tube floated in front of him. His incredulous gaze travelled up. The tube broadened and joined to a massive bony grey head. An elephant! It was an elephant! Glide quickly closed his eyes again. But the trunk slobbered all over his face for yet a third time. He had to look. A panting pachyderm peered back.

"No!" Glide scrambled backwards. "You are an elephant!"

"No, no I'm not!" The creature reared upwards. "I... I just happen to be big and... and grey and... and with a long sloppy nose." A huge foot stamped down and the ground trembled.

Glide edged further away. He didn't think it a good idea to argue with an ele... Um? It was bad enough to be looney. He didn't want to be a squashed looney as well. "Er." Another realisation hit him. "Excuse me. But did you speak? Words? Actual words?"

"Did I speak? Does the wind blow? Do birds sing? Does moss collect on rolling stones? Eh, eh?"

"Moss doesn't collect on rolling stones."

"Exactly!"

"But you're an elephant."

"No, *snort*, I am not, *snort*, an elephant. Who ever heard of a talking elephant?"

"Um, that's what I mean."

"So I can't be an elephant. Right? Right. So don't even mention it. Right? Right."

"Right."

Glide suddenly realised that he had formed a policy, an instant: don't argue with elephants, especially angry talking elephants, especially big angry talking elephants with a big problem of denial. He sat up and looked around, vaguely hoping for a solution. Or even a well specified problem. Should he believe his ears? Or his eyes? Or neither. Just go with his impending insanity. That seemed to be the most reliable solution, to go with the flow and simply accept his insanity.

But he didn't feel insane. He assumed there must be a certain sort of feel to it. So being of a logical turn, Glide searched for another explanation. For instance, a ventriloquist. That would explain it. The blue Ne'verman man, for example. He might be like an Injun in Injia, they used elephants. So maybe he was throwing his voice. Glide stood to look this way and that. But there was no sign of the Ne'verman, no sign at all. Not within throwing voice distance. Nor was there any sign of the park. Nor of the hedges. There was not even the distant rumble of traffic. Some delusion. This was too much. Glide's legs turned to jelly and he plopped heavily onto the sand. Sand! Sand? It couldn't be, shouldn't be. But then, there couldn't, shouldn't, be a talking elephant either.

"Where?" he gasped. "Who? What?" He flopped onto his back. "And if not now, when?"

The elephant stamped a second time. "Stand up, man. Give yourself some pride."

Staring into the blue sky, the stern voice reminded Glide of all the *sensei* that he'd ever met. In a false calm, he asked, "And who am I anyway?"

"Ah, my very question. Though," the elephant rubbed his trunk over his huge bony brow, "if I were to ask myself that very same question, I'd want a more meaningful answer than Longnose or Narrow Tail or... or... or Strongarm even."

Clutching at straws, the trunk being nothing more than an oversized straw, Glide said, “Are you Longnose, then?”

“No!”

“Narrow Tail?”

“Don’t even think of it!”

“Strongarm?”

“Strongarm, yes.” The creature squinted at his trunk. “Hence this.”

Not familiar with squinty-eyed elephants, Glide said, “Hence what?”

“The trunk, stupid!”

“So,” Glide cried triumphantly, a fool rushing in, “You do admit to having a trunk?”

“Of course.”

“And what has a trunk?”

The elephant furrowed its brow. “Clothing?”

“What animal?”

“An elephant, of course.”

“So you do admit to being an elephant!”

“No, no, no, not at all!” A heavy foot crashed down. A sandquake threatened and Glide hastily backpeddled to avoid disappearing into a newly made pit. “Bronze shields!” the creature shrilled, “It’s all that woman’s fault, that mad, mad woman. Look,” the pachyderm proceeded, “I can see that from your point of view, I might be... mistaken for an elephant. Yes, a great grey beast with a hairy trunk. You name it, that’s me. Inside though, and be very clear about this.” The great grey head lowered. “I’m a man. I’m just a man.”

Glide goggled. He’d heard of cross-dressing. But that was only in terms of clothes. It was never in terms of skins. Except perhaps for werewolves. But they didn’t exist. Or did they? Perhaps they did wherever he was now? His mind tried to adjust and his brain tried to balloon out of his skull.

Carefully, very carefully, Glide said, "Okay, fine, I get it. You're a man in elephant's clothing. But you're not a beast. Definitely not a beast. In fact, except for appearing to be an elephant, you're very nice. Very nice indeed."

"Well, I was," Strongarm admitted grudgingly. "Very nice. And not at all conceited. Even though I was the best archer. And the best wrestler. Even the best poet, I dare say. And dashingly good-looking. The best in the whole country, I dare say."

"In the whole country?"

"The whole country."

"So you were the best in the country." Glide rose to his feet again. There was sand to one side and forest to the other. This certainly wasn't Brissie. "But what country is it?"

"What? Really! Great tusks of fire! This one, of course." And the elephant rolled its eyes as if talking to an idiot.

"Yes, yes! But what is its name?"

"Name, eh? Interesting. You need names. Something metaphysical, is it? A bit like the Witch, eh? You think name is essence? Or name is power? Or is it merely habit, the way you usually talk?"

"Bloody hell!" It was Glide's turn to thump the sand. A talking elephant was bad enough but an ongoing philosophical talking elephant was just too much. He turned away. In the distance, he spotted waving palms. "I know," he said, "I'm in Injia or Barley. I must be in Barley. Is that right? I'm in Barley? You know, that place just to the north of Ausphalia."

He'd no sooner said that, however, than a familiar but definitely non-Injian, non-Barleynese animal hopped into view. It was a big red roo and on its head was an akubra with corks dangling from the rim.

"Oh!" Glide sat heavily on the sand again.

"Oh," Strongarm echoed. "Hernandes."

"Hernandes?" Glide addressed the roo. "And I suppose you're not a kangaroo?"

"Of course he is," Strongarm trumpeted.

"But what do you say?" Glide pointed at the roo.

"Oh, he won't say anything," Strongarm said airily. "He's just a kanga."

"But you're just an jumbo." Those words balanced on the edge of Glide's tongue. Fortunately, discretion got the better part of valour. "This is all very puzzling," he murmured. "Very puzzling indeed."

"That's just the half of it." Strongarm sadly shook his head. Then at a commotion behind a small sand dune, he added, "Oh, oh, comes Hernandes."

A slim tiny figure appeared. Half Glide's height, it slithered and slid over the slippery sand. "Heyo, Horsey." He waved his arms. "You come back heres, straightaway!"

Glide scratched his head. "Are you Hernandes or Horsey?" he said to the roo.

The animal didn't reply but hopped a few steps back to the caller. The tiny man grabbed at the roo's akubra, which now served as reins, and leapt astride. "Heyo, Cisco!" the rider cried, "Heyo, Pancho!" Roo and rider approached rapidly, at the last moment slewing to a halt with a cry of, "Whoa, whoa! Heyo, Horsey, but wots have we here?"

"Who?" Glide said. "Not what."

"Hugh Knotwhat?" the rider echoed. "Never heards of you."

Strongarm snorted. "Very metaphysical he is. Keeps asking who he is. Even tried to speak to Horsey."

The elephant lifted his trunk and bellowed with laughter, creating a local cyclone. It blew off the roo's akubra and the corks whipped around the rider's head.

"Quiets!" the little man snapped. "I wants to think!"

Glide was impressed at how this small person spoke to the huge pachyderm. He thought it must be a magical creature such as an elf or imp. There were Ne'verman stories about them. He'd just never believed them before. Still, they made for a good hallucination.

"Lets me think," the imp said. "Lets me think." He dismounted and stood in the shade of the big elephant. "Ole!" He pointed around them. "Strongarm, did you sees him with anyones?"

"No."

"No ones?"

Strongarm furrowed his brow. "No ones. No twos or threes, either."

"So, no ones? Nobody?"

Strongarm sighed. "No one else was around, Hernandes. If that's what you mean?"

"Si, si, that's what I means."

As imp and elephant established a tenuous link of communication, Glide realised that the imp was Hernandes and Horsey was the roo. The imp now turned to Glide.

"You, did yous see anyones?"

"Me?" Glide said cautiously.

"Si, yous."

"I only saw it... that... him." He pointed at the elephant.

"Him!" Strongarm trumpeted.

"Oh." Hernandes' face fell. "And that's all?"

Glide's mind, once nimble, was now dulled with weeks and months and years of gloom. "Well," he said hesitantly, "there was a someone."

"Exactly, a someones. Who is?"

"Yes, who?" Strongarm shrilled.

"It was..."

"Yez?"

"Yes!"

"Someone Ne'wa... Ne'day... Ne'ba... Jeez, I just can't remember now. But he said he was a Ne'vermaker."

"The Ne'vermaker! See he says the Ne'vermaker!" Hernandes jumped gleefully, his head bumping on Strongarms' underbelly.

"Listen, you," the elephant roared, "if you don't stop that, I'll squirt you."

Still bouncing, Hernandes stepped away from the pachyderm's penumbra. "Et's the promise, the promise!" he cried. "Ne'wang the Ne'vermaker brought yous. Just as he says he would. For us, you will fights the great evil that surround us."

"But, I, er, don't want to fight anyone."

"But you will! You will!"

"No, I don't want to."

"You don'ts?"

Strongarm glowered at Glide, then at Hernandes and then at Horsey. "Just what we need, a pacifist."

"He only thinks he's a pacifists," Hernandes thumped excitedly against his saddle. "When I tells him what happens here, he will wants to help. He will wants to. Listen closely, thees is our problem." He glanced around him and motioned for the others to lower their heads.

"This bending is such a pain in the neck," Strongarm protested. "I'm gonna need a chiropractor."

But Hernandes pulled at a huge ear so that the head followed. "You must have mades a promise," he whispered. "A beeg promise."

Chapter 6

Maggot Thwacka twitched. It began with her nose, a jerky in-out, in-out of the nostrils. With a sniff, she moved her head around. Detecting something, tremors ran the length of her green-tinged skin. Her bony elbows and knees flicked. Led by a nose-driven spasm, her body jerked out of her throne. Her murky green eyes glittered.

"So," she screeched, "he has arrived. Someone has arrived." She paused - and glass on the verge of shattering just about held together. "No," she corrected herself, in a tone of cracking ice, "someone has been brought."

Greenvort, an imp the size of Hernandes, but with the warty skin of an olive-brown cane toad, scampered around her. "Shall I ssee?" he chattered. "Should I sspell him?"

At the noise, a shaggy heap in a dark and webby corner stirred. It looked like a creature would emerge from the heap. But the heap itself was the creature, a great slab of fur-covered muscle. This was Haggort, the Giant Dwarf.

"Witch," rumbled Haggort, "you want I go crush dis creature? Or would dat I bring to you his very best feature?"

Maggot Thwacka the Witch flung out her arms. Instantly, Greenvort the Imp was frozen, his weight balanced precariously on one foot. Haggort the Hulk halted at an impossible angle. They seemed as immobile as two carved statues. Yet a closer look would have shown the frustration of effort on both their faces. Given a day or two and Greenvort would've placed his other foot down. Haggort would've straightened.

"Mindless grubs!" Maggot Thwacka cackled, snapping off a strand of her stiff blue hair. "Listen to me. Hulk, you must skulk. Greenvort, you must court. This person must have powers. If we know them, we use them. If of no use, we crush him. Go!"

The Witch cackled wildly. She was good at cackling. She often practised when no one else was around. She wanted more crackle from her cackle. For a second time, she shot out her arms. Unexpectedly released, Greenvort's second foot jerked forward and stepped on his first. Haggort straightened so quickly his bones cracked. The Witch smiled while the other two shook themselves back to life. Haggort rumbled some curse deep in his throat. But it stopped as soon as a pair of icy green eyes turned on him. He lumbered out of the room and after the imp, their footsteps echoing along the dusty corridors of faded grandeur. Posted along the corridor were suits of armour. They appeared empty yet when Haggort's delayed anger attempted the old one-two against a helmet, the suit neatly stepped aside.

"I'll get you. Just you wait and see." Though other dwarves were known for their fine craftwork and gold jewellery making, Giant Dwarves were known for wrecking destruction and revenge.

After they had gone, Maggot Thwacka stood very still. Her eyes were open but unseeing as her mental vision tracked her henchmen. At Haggort's attempted strike, it was partly her power and partly that of the daemon inside that allowed the metal to move. Haggort was lucky, however, that her real focus was elsewhere or the blow would've been repaid - with interest. She rubbed her hands together but then grimaced. Damn arthritis! But that was the price of her power. Till now. Soon, though, and she'd have that wretched Ne'vermaker at her mercy. Then he could have her pains, all of them.

The Witch moved to the window. From there, she watched as Haggort directed his men. They moved with the reluctance of unwilling conscripts.

"I'll teach you, " Haggort growled.

With a gruff laugh, he picked up one of the men and tossed him through the air. The spinning body didn't crash to the ground but came to a dead halt in midair. It had entered the moat, the moat of Slowtime that surrounded the Witch's castle. Greenvort chittered gleefully as the others huddled away. The imp reached into the field of Slowtime and pulled the man out. The wretch staggered to his feet, only to be buffeted with diminutive cuffs.

"On your way," Greenvort chortled. "On your way or I hitss you again."

The dazed man tried to catch up with his fellows. But that only made them go faster. So the faster that he ran, the faster they did. What a pantomime! Haggort roared and roared and roared.

Maggot Thwacka was pleased. Fear served her well. If only she could spread it further. The domain of her grey-green country was small, too small. She snarled. Her domain was hemmed in by mountain ranges. Above her, yet unattainable, were the bright and dry areas. She rubbed at her aching joints. Up there, the pain would be so much less. Up there, the power would be so much the greater. Up there was Auslan. Down here was Inklan.

The Witch snarled again and with jerky movements strode to the centre of her room. From there, she glared into the corner at a young woman, Cascade. Encased in Slowtime, she was a frozen statue of beauty. Trapped when turning, her silver hair rippled out. Her sky-blue eyes were open wide in surprise - or horror. Her lips were just parted. Like her hair, her dress also showed signs of sudden turning. It pressed against her motionless body and outlined the long slender lines of her limbs.

Yet though the young woman was trapped in Slowtime, Maggot Thwacka the Witch was still jealous of her. She stopped in front of the motionless figure and stamped her foot. Darts of pain shot along her leg and she hopped about with pain.

"Oh, I'll wake you," she screeched. "Wake you and bake you. I'll scratch your fair cheeks till your hot blood creaks. I'll pull out your hair till your scalp is quite bare."

But though she hopped around cursing, she did no further harm. Magic took all of her energy, leaving her weak and allowing the damp mists of grey-green Inklan to seep into her bones. Best to reserve her energies. She muttered to herself. Cascade was her chief bargaining force. If the girl was harmed, the Witch might lose her leverage. So far, peaceful Auslan had not shown a capacity to organise itself to fight. Barbequed nut cutlets on the beach and sandsurfing were its main industries. Growing herbs and looking for god were its main hobbies.

The Devil take them! In a fit of fury, the Witch took a cup of cold water and hurled it over the frozen figure. The stream hit Slowtime, splattered and fragmented into the glistening drops of a halo. Maggot Thwacka snarled.

Chapter 7

"A promise?" Glide demanded. "I made no promise. Who to? Go on, who to? And when? I've only been here for a minute. When could I have made a promise?"

"To the Ne'vermaker, of course." Hernandes bounced around with excitement. "To the Ne'vermaker."

"Oh." Glide had only been *here*, wherever here was, for a minute but *there* seemed a million years away. "To the Ne'vermaker?" His mind went back both a minute and a million years. "Oh, to him." He recalled the blue Ne'verman. *Yes*, Glide had said, *You gotta problem. Well, I'll make it straight, straight as a roo's hind leg.*

Glide simply hadn't anticipated just how crooked the roo's hind leg would turn out to be. It was beginning to dawn on him that he really was some place else. Not just out of the Sunny State, not just out of his mind, but really in some other place. He had been transported to somewhere else. He shivered. How could he get back? This was terrible. Awful. Then he noticed his briefcase on the ground by his feet: a black rectangle with a combination lock. No, that box was truly terrible and awful. In comparison, this was merely a puzzle.

"Oh," Glide repeated but in a totally different tone of voice.

He thought for a moment. Did he want to go back? Really? Sitting on the sand, he sank into contemplation.

The others moved away to give him some breathing space. Beyond them, he saw a thin line of blue. He looked at it in a vacant sort of way. Suddenly, though, Glide straightened. He squinted. The line of blue was moving. Slightly. Up and down. Up and down. Blue! Blue and gold. Waves! Waves and sand! Waves and surf! Surf! Surf plus sun plus sand!

"Far out! For a fantasy, this isn't half bad. I could've done much worse. A helluva lot worse. Where is my bucket? Where is my surfboard?" He turned back to the others. Strongarm was watching him quizzically, his trunk in the air. "Ah," Glide was moving from depressive to manic, "a trunk call."

"Beg pardon?"

"Nothing, nothing." Glide squinted again at the sea, not really thinking, just absorbing. Suddenly, he saw a small dot in the sky. It didn't flap wings and it didn't wander off a straight course. "That... that's an airship, isn't it?" An ounce of hope arose in Glide's breast.

Strongarm and Hernandes both gazed into the far horizon. The imp twisted a long strand of his black hair. "The Ne'verman tells us they's are floating machines. They don't lands here."

Strongarm was also squinting. "They can't land here."

"They can't?" Glide's ounce of hope evaporated. "Why not?"

Strongarm made a circling movement with his trunk. "Ne'wang says that this is or was an area of powerful magic. When Ausphalia was invaded, the old Ne'vermen made this island invisible to the pinkfella."

"Great! That's just great!" Glide kicked the sand. Clearly, waving his Civilian Service I-D card was not going to bring him rescue. He took a few steps, leaving prints in the sand. His, he noted, were tiny compared to those left by an ele... He dared not even think the word. He looked up at Strongarm. "I'm on the beach." He quickly made a little sandcastle. "I can see that. I belong on the beach. But you, an er ele... whatever... what are you doing here?"

"Me?" Strongarm said. "I live here."

"Yes, but right now, what were you doing?" Glide had stark memories of that great grey wall advancing on him.

"I was jogging, of course. What else would I be doing?"

"Jogging?" Glide forgot not to say that word. "Whoever heard of an elephant jogging?"

"What elephant?" Strongarm stamped a huge foot.

"Er, yes, quite," Glide said quickly. "But, still, why were you jogging?"

"To keep fit, of course. All warriors must keep fit."

"All warriors, eh?" Glide was beginning to think that maybe this lovely beach wasn't such a good place for making sandcastles. After all, didn't warriors implied war? "You, too, Hernandes?"

"Oh, si." The imp set Horsey the kangaroo bouncing, lowered an imaginary lance and shouted, "Olè, charge!"

"I see." Glide scuffed sand. "You're in trouble. You're in some kind of war."

"Right."

"With?"

"Not with, Witch."

"Which?" Glide frowned. "You mean with which?"

Strongarm shook his large head. "No, I mean with a Witch. To be precise, Maggot Thwacka the Witch."

"A Witch?" Glide's stomach heaved. "The Ne'verman's bad enough. If you don't mind, I think I'll be going now."

"You whats?" Hernandes slapped his akubra against his thigh.

"I think I'll be going now." Glide walked aimlessly in a circle.

"Well as long as you just thinks it." Hernandes the Imp had a heart-shaped face made for smiling. It wasn't smiling now.

"No, I mean nice knowing you and all that, but I think..." Glide looked around him in a new way, a sort of door-in-the-air sort of way. Yet except for the shimmer of a heat haze, the air held nothing, certainly not a door. There was no sign that said *Exit*. "Um," Glide said, "do you think you might help me here? Sort of show me the way to go home?"

"Whiches way is that?"

"No, no! No Witches. I want home." Glide put on his vacuum-tube computer voice. "Me phone home."

"Home?" Hernandes echoed. Exchanging a quizzical look with Strongarm, he pointed towards the jungle. "Over there. El palazzo awaits you."

"Palazzo? A palace?"

"Home."

"The palace is home?"

"That's right, the palace es home." Hernandes sighed and hopped nearer to Strongarm. Remembering that he wasn't on Horsey, he reverted again to walking. He pulled down a big ear. "Not too bright, eh? You thinks maybe Ne'wang makes a mistake?"

As Strongarm gave a stiff-shouldered shrug, Glide gazed towards the forest. Over there was not home, over there was a palace. So, he was stuck, hopelessly dismally stuck. And all because of that Ne'wang, Ne'wang the Ne'vermaker. Blast him! He was the one. He was the cause. He was. The cause. Glide became abruptly alert. What had the Ne'verman said? In his deep chocolate voice, he'd declaimed that he was the door! He was the portal! The gateway! Without a further thought, Glide opened his mouth.

"Ne'wang," he bellowed, "Ne'wang the Ne'vermaker!"

After a moment's delay, Strongarm lifted his trunk. "Ne'wang," he trumpeted, "Ne'wang the Ne'vermaker!"

Hernandes the Imp stood high in his saddle and also called. Even Horsey the roo made a sort of noise. A terrible cacophony rolled across the dunes. Fuelled by anger, Glide's eidetic ability projected a clear image of the Ne'verman. A shimmer in the air curled around it. A shape formed. It grew dark and solidified. All of a sudden, the Ne'vermaker was there. Or was probably there. Perhaps.

Certainly, someone was there. And that someone was blue. What could be seen of him. That wasn't very much as most of him was packed away in a dark blue suit. Slowly, however, he raised his right foot and cupped the sole of an elegant shoe into his left hand. His right arm went out to use his spear for balance. Unfortunately, he no longer held a spear but merely a short umbrella. It provided no support and, like a falling tree, the Ne'vermaker toppled rigidly into the sand.

"Damn and strawberries! You a comedian or something?" Glide helped him up. "You should be on steam TV."

"I might be," came a strangled voice.

"Is that why you're in this getup?"

Ne'wang sprang to his feet. "I was in a meeting." He brushed sand off of his suit. "We've gotta protect a sacred site."

"You're in a suit!" Glide snarled. "Is your sacred site an office?"

"When in Rome..." the Ne'vermaker began but broke off. "G'day, Strongarm." He grabbed the elephant's trunk and shook it briskly. "G'day, Hernandes."

The imp sniffed. "Don't you g'days me. You were supposed to gets help."

"I've got him."

"Him? He doesn't know what days et es. And he wants go home."

"Wants? Anyone can want."

"And I do want. I mean, I'm not a prisoner here, or something, am I?"

"Nah, mate. I rescued you, didn't I?"

"Rescued! Rescued! I was on my way to work. I said I'd help but there was no mention of wars, or Witches, or dragons."

"Dragons?" The starch went out of the suit's jacket. "Oh, mate, we got dragons now?"

"In a manner of speaking. I mean, talking elephants..."

"What talking elephants?" Strongarm went trunk to nose with Glide.

Glide back-pedalled. "Er, none, none, my mistake. But I still say, it wasn't exactly a rescue."

The Ne'vermaker opened his mouth. He seemed to be wondering what to say when, instead, he pressed his brolly into the ground. Snapping his fingers, dull blue sparks leapt out of them. Reminded of arc welding, Glide jumped back. More snaps followed until a bruised blue cloud formed. It settled above Glide, sank down into him and then permeated into his very bones. Automatically, his shoulders sagged and the blue sky lost its brightness. Everything was seen through blue-grey shades. Everything lost its meaning.

Glide blinked. "Oh yes," he muttered. "I forgot. Yes, I... Maybe you did rescue me." He brushed wearily at his forehead. "That's enough, thanks. If you don't mind." Immediately, the Ne'vermaker jerked a bony finger. Lightning struck the cloud and the dull blue changed. A magnificent rainbow arched over Glide. The colours slid into him and his mouth curved upwards into a brilliant smile. A film star twinkle danced along his teeth. "Jeez, mate," he cried, "don't overdo it! Just tell me. What the hell this is all about."

The Ne'vermaker sighed. "It's about hell all right. How to avoid it? How you can help us to avoid it."

Strongarm trumpeted. "Him? But he's such a whinger!"

"Heem?" Hernandes shrugged eloquently.

"Ah," said the Ne'vermaker, "but you just saw."

"Saw?" Strongarm said.

"Saws what?"

The Ne'vermaker took hold of his brolly. "He images."

"Images? Ah yes, images!" Hernandes struck his brow. "The blue cloud! Now I sees."

"Blue cloud," Strongarm murmured. He nodded, making non-committal but possibly positive noises.

Glide shook his head, wanting to forget how the blue cloud had entered him and become the black dog of depression. But in a comradely way, Hernandes rested a hand on him while Strongarm drooped his trunk across his shoulder. A little nervously, the young man looked around for the Ne'vermaker. He, however, had already disappeared.

"Unstable person, that," Glide murmured.

"Never minds," Hernandes said, "you'll fixes him."

"Fix?" Glide said. "Maybe. I'm not sure. How?"

"Like you make the blue cloud." Hernandes tapped the young man's head as if that were an explanation.

Glide turned and gazed with longing at the rolling surf beyond the golden sand. "Fix the Ne'vermaker," he murmured. "To fix him here. I'll do my best. But what, then, happens to me?"

And for no apparent reason, a premonition ran up and down his spine.

Chapter 8

"Come," Hernandes crooked a finger, "and we will takes you to the Palace."

Glide didn't believe that there would be a palace. A hut, maybe. An ornamental hut, even. But a palace? No. No way. Still, when the others began to walk, he followed. They soon crossed the strip of sand, passed through the dunes and stood on the edge of the jungle. Glide looked back. The distance was just perfect for the classic surfie run, board under arm and zinc on the nose. He glanced sideways at Strongarm. But no, the elephant did not have cream on his trunk.

Still bemused, Glide entered the forest. That, he soon decided, was too strong a word for it. The trees formed more a plantation than a forest. But even that was not really correct. The plantation was also a village. Houses rested on trees. Trees grew in, out and around the houses. Life, work and play all took place in the one area. No need for a black briefcase containing sandwiches. Lunch was straight from the vine.

Of course, Glide had been north of Ausphalia to Barley, too. What Aussie hadn't visited that island? Courtesy of Kookaburra Airships, he had taken his surfboard to Koota. He had even hired a steam car and gone in search of the perfect wave, said to hang out in the environs of Tan-A-Lot.

Glide had passed numerous tiny villages during his Barley trip. He'd seen the villagers, in multi-hued sarongs, busily climbing up and down the coconut trees. He'd seen the carpenters lop the trees for their dwellings. The overall impression was that the huts and trees were intrinsicly interwoven. The village in which he now found himself had the same quality. It had grown out of the forest, and the people with it. They lived with their land, not against it.

A sudden flash lit up Glide's mind. Perhaps he was now on a hidden Barley peninsula? But no, Barley was too small and too densely populated for secret places. He thought it likely that even Ne'wang didn't know the geographic location of this place. He'd managed to transport himself here on magic. Magic did not necessarily have longitude and latitude.

As they walked the forest path, Glide could now also see why Strongarm had been jogging along the beach. He'd have flattened trees and huts if he'd followed the narrow pathways. He might even have squashed the imps. Imps! For the first time, it struck Glide what a weird world he really was in. Hernandes wasn't just a little man. He was a different sort of creature altogether. Mostly human in form, but not quite. His ears were pointier, his lips were wider and his face was more heart-shaped.

Glide was reminded of a play they'd done at school, *A Midsummer Night's Scream*. It had been written by Shakespeer. Had the bard come here? Or was there a magical leakage from here to the bard? He couldn't help looking sideways at Hernandes.

"Puck?" Glide said.

Hernandes shot him a dirty look. "Language! Language! You wants to lose your kneecaps?"

"It's only the name of a character in a play. So you really are an imp?"

"I es an imp? Imps es fine." Hernandes grinned and, surprisingly, managed to look extremely impish.

The forest around them was peopled with imps. No. Glide corrected himself: the forest was imped with imps. And, like the seven dwarves in *Snowd White*, they approached their work in a special kind of way. They didn't just pluck fruit. They also had a fruit-plucking song. They didn't just prune branches. They also had a branch-pruning dance. *Hey-ho, hey-ho,* they turned all work into a cartoon of fun.

"They look really cheeky," Glide said, "and totally untrustworthy. They look like they'd lock your arms inside your trousers."

They seemed so untroubled that the young man was surprised at Hernandes response. "No, they are not happy nows. They used to be. They used to be so carefrees."

"Unhappy! If that's unhappy," Glide retorted, "then I'm a brass monkey!"

"Ah." Hernandes considered him thoughtfully. "So you climbs in trees."

"No, no. I mean, you stick them in front of a computer all day!"

Hernandes looked puzzled. "A comp'ter? What is a comp'ter?"

"It's..." Glide waved his hands, wondering how to explain. "It's when you're stuck in a building all day. The air is artificial and the light is artificial and the windows don't open. You're stuck in front of a screen. Do this. Do that. Then the vacuums blow and you have to do everything again."

Hernandes shuddered. "That is a comp'ter? But et sounds like a prison. Why did you work in a prison?"

Glide shrugged. "It just happened." He gazed at the jungly fields around him and breathed in deeply. It was a long time since he'd felt so liberated. "In your village, you mix the houses and the forest. Where I come from, we all live in houses but the wilderness is outside of the village."

"You dos?" Hernandes looked with disbelief at Glide. "But the trees give us our airs. How do you live without airs?"

"Yeah, right. We cough."

Glide took another deep breath and gazed around contentedly. But some thing, some small thing started to niggle. What was it? While he was staring at the imps, they were staring back at him. Many were female. Both sexes wore striped trousers to mid-calf and multi-coloured shirts. He nodded at them with a puzzling, but increasing, unease. Suddenly, though, it hit him.

"Where are the people?" Glide cried.

"People. They are heres." Hernandes pointed at the imps.

"Sorry, sorry. I mean the humans. Where are the humans? There are other humans, aren't there?"

"Oh, thems." Hernandes sniffed disdainfully. "Over there."

Leading Horsey, he took the young man into a glade where Strongarm already waited. In this area, humans were cutting a tree trunk with long saws. Glide felt an instant relief. He'd begun to fear that there were only two other humans around. Of which, one was an elephant and the other was a transient cloud.

The human males, he noted, did the heavy work. They did the cutting and the hewing, the building and the smithying. Their dress was marginally more sober than the imps, loose white pants and fringed shirts. Many of the women had flowers woven into their hair. To Glide, they also seemed happy. But, this time, Strongarm sighed.

"See how sad they are," he rumbled. "So sad."

"Sad?" Glide snorted. "Huh, they should know what it's like to work on a policy paper."

"Policy paper?" Strongarm's trunk rose to form a question mark.

Glide rubbed his cheek. He was finding it difficult to explain pen pushing. "A policy is that which tells people how to behave."

"To behave?" Strongarm considered this. "In emergencies?"

"Could be."

Strongarm bobbed his head thoughtfully. "Maybe that's why you're here."

Glide halted, nearly bumping into the sinuous trunk. "A policy paper here? I don't think so. I don't think Ne'wang wants just a policy paper on Witches." He snorted at the idea of it.

For an anxious moment, however, he pictured himself with a feather pen, bent over a parchment as he outlined issues and options. Bloody hell! Damn and strawberries! If this was a delusion, surely he could do better than that? The very idea of it was depressing. With an onset of the blues, he sent out a mental signal.

In return, the air spoke. "No, no! Not to write. To do. Only to do!"

"Thank goodness!" Glide relaxed. Write a policy paper here? He'd rather jump out of an airship with a parachute made only of palm leaves.

In response to his mental signal, a blue figure manifested. It balanced on one leg then slowly toppled. It righted again and held for a moment. It reminded Glide of a diver doing for a backward dive from the high board. There was a soundless splash and the apparition disappeared again. Glide looked at Strongarm. Strongarm looked at Glide. The pachyderm did the massive equivalent of an elephant shrug.

They waited but when the Ne'verman didn't reappear, Glide spoke. "Did you hear what Ne'wang said? He said it's not to write, only to do. So, to do what?"

Strongarm looked down his long nose at the slim human. "Well, you might not be doing the doing. That could get a bit rough. You might just be telling us how to do the doing. You know, how to counter magic, how to unspell spells and how to block enchantments. That sort of thing." He tried to covertly glance over his trunk to see Glide's reaction.

"That sort of thing," Glide echoed. He idly kicked at a lump of grass. "Not exactly my field. Witches? Never met one." Kick. "Magic? I've seen a conjurer pull a rabbit out of a hat." Kick. "Enchantments? Rescue Remedy gives me a headache." Kick. "No, I really don't think I can help you there." Glide's idle kicking turned into a manic little dance. "But stabbing in the back? Yes! Yes, I have years of practise. Crawling up the ladder of success? Yes! Phrasing clear thoughts into obfuscatory legalise? Most definitely yes! As a fully-fledged Civilian Servant, I can give you obfuscatory workshops. Yes, I give you Stabbing in the Back, 101."

Entering his manic phase, Glide looked around hopefully. Perhaps Ne'wang had left a door in the air? Perhaps there was a shimmer that he could simply step through.

"But Witches? Spells? Enchantments? No. Sorry, guys. Sorry and goodbye...ee. I've got a Ne... Ne... Ne'vermaker to catch."

But as neither Ne'vermaker nor door reappeared, Glide couldn't catch one. He passed rapidly from elation to puzzlement as the other two patiently waited. Eventually, Strongarm turned and led the way deeper into the jungle, on the way passing beautifully thatched huts. Glide peered inside one and saw that it was small and obviously domestic. Further on, they came to a large barn. Outside it, humans and imps were working together. Glide watched them with interest. Metals were being heated and poured into moulds. The shapes were long and narrow so that he guessed that they were meant to be swords. But the curves and blunt edges suggested large-scale jewellery rather than weapons of messy destruction.

"And they are?" Glide asked.

Strongarm frowned. "They are beating their ploughshares into weapons."

"Into swords?"

"Swords? Instruments to hack with?" Strongarm lifted his trunk. It fell in a hopeless gesture. "Giant brooches meant as shields? Who knows?"

"You don't know?"

"They are not fighters. They don't know about weapons. Hernandes doesn't know. I know but, in this shape, can't teach. They are waiting for your instruction."

"Mine? Damn!"

"You can teach us?" Strongarm didn't sound very hopeful.

In answer, Glide picked up a chest-sized creation. "This is meant to be a shield. But it looks like a Celtic knot. Look at all these holes."

"But es very lights to carry," Hernandes offered.

"Yeah, but can it protect anyone?" Glide held the Celtic Knot shield to his chest. "Strongarm see if you can hit me." The big creature began to prance on all fours, like a boxer seeking an opening. "A medium size hit," Glide suggested. Suddenly, the trunk narrowed and the tip shot out. Passing easily though a gap, it walloped Glide on the chest. He staggered backwards. "Jeez, I should've said touch not hit." He gasped for breath. "Anyway, you see what I mean."

"Rights," Hernandes agreed. "We needs better weapons and better defences. You can policy us on designs."

Meanwhile, Strongarm was turning pink. "Sorry, sorry, sorry," he muttered. "I didn't mean to hit you so hard. Well, I don't think I meant to. I might've done. But you could've moved. You could've ducked. Anyway, we had hoped for more of a warrior. You could've had a bit more grunt. Anyway, the Ne'vermaker... The Ne'vermaker..."

Strongarm's words hung in the air with disappointment. The unsaid finally got to Glide and the worm started to turn. It was time to head butt punchbags, take a crossbow to archery, or a foil to kendo. Smoke burst from his ears.

"So you wanted a fighter, did you? A real fighter? Well, you ain't got one! Ain't got no fighter! But you sure as hell have got a fight!" Glide shadow boxed around Strongarm, which was about as effectively as a mosquito around a rock. "Strongarm, are you? Well, I've gotta strong arm, too. Come on, putt'em up. Bit of arm wrestling. Or trunk wrestling, if you prefer. C'mon, let's see how strong you really are."

So saying, he grasped the tip of the muscular trunk and began to push. But there was no opposition. Strongarm hastily stepped back with a cry of, "Hey, dat's dot my arm, dat's my dose!"

"Oh, damn and strawberries!" Glide dropped the trunk. "Nose wrestling, then."

But the moment had passed. Embarrassed, Glide dropped the appendage. He looked at Strongarm's huge legs. He sure as hell wasn't going to arm wrestle with one of those. One huge foot, however, had already risen. Glide gritted his teeth. What had he let himself in for? He tensed. In sudden relief, though, he realised that he wasn't being challenged. Strongarm was pointing.

Glide turned. He watched. His jaw dropped and his eyes boggled. Now that was funny. Funny? Huh, it was the theatre of the absurd. Yes, it would have been genuinely funny if the intention hadn't been so bloody serious.

Chapter 9

Maggot Thwacka concentrated.

A black raven flew above the jungle. Darkness oozed out of it. Cawing creakily, it circled into Glide's conversation. The bird's sharp ears heard the sounds that were words. His sharp eyes clicked on the shapes the lips made as they uttered those sounds. The bird wheeled and dipped as it transmitted information. When it was above Glide, it released a line of droppings. Yet, without even realising that he was doing it, Glide sidestepped. At the same time, a blue hand burst out of the air and gave him an added shove. With a splat, the droppings made white smears at Glide's feet. He looked up and waved his fist as the large bird winged away.

He turned to Strongarm. "This is getting personal." He scratched his head. "It's a good thing cows don't fly. Ha, ha." He imagined a direct hit leaving a necklace of cow dung.

"They don't?" Strongarm's big ears waggled in surprise. His trunk pointed upwards. A large cow drifted serenely through the air. Amazed, Glide immediately sheltered behind Strongarm's bulk. But since no one else seemed bothered, he quickly relaxed. The cow, it seemed, was not as ill disposed as the raven.

Goresh, the bird in question, was not well disposed at all. Fortunately, although no birdbrain, he was no graduate from Toastmasters either. His transmission of words and pictures to Maggot Thwacka was far from perfect. Oh, she picked up Glide's anger all right and did a bit of fist waving and foot stamping herself. But the words, the actual words that went with the pictures, they verged on gibberish.

One thing was certain, though, a stranger had appeared in Auslan. He had been brought by the Ne'vermaker and seemed to have a penchant for arm wrestling. Or nose wrestling. Well, neither of those frightened her. Yet if the Ne'vermaker had brought him then there must be more to it than that. But the creature was so clueless! How could there be more to him? There must be some potential. But if it were merely potential then that meant that he must yet be trained. And training required time. Good, the more time the better. For now, she'd send out Haggort and Greenvort, the most trusted of her almost trusted minions and they could gather information about this stranger.

She rephrased that thought. For now, she'd send out Haggort and Greenvort, the most least distrusted of her completely untrustworthy minions and they could gather information about this stranger.

But the Ne'vermaker. Ah, the Ne'vermaker. He was a boil in her mouth. She'd have to lance him, do something about him. She went to the window. Mists swirled around her narrow strip of land and her bones ached to be under a clear dry sky. In a sudden rage, she whirled. The full force of her glare fell on Cascade, frozen in the magic of Slowtime. Under that glare, the Slowtime fell from her like hot water running down a sheet of ice. Off balance, Cascade stumbled and her silver hair streamed about her face.

Maggot Thwacka cackled. That was what she liked to see, abasement. But she was not satisfied. Cascade rose with a grave serenity. Though her eyes were as grey as troubled seas, her voice was controlled.

"Let me go," she said, "Let there be peace between our countries."

"Peace! A pox on your peace!" Maggot Thwacka shrieked. "Our countries? You call this poxy strip of swamp a country?"

"This is where you were banished to," Cascade replied, pain in her eyes.

"Banished!" The Witch paced, cracking her knuckles so that Cascade winced almost as much as she. "If I'd known then what I know now, we'd've seen who'd've been banished. Banished? A pox on it! I've been put in a cage!"

"The Ne'vermaker saw only too clearly what you intended. He just never knew how powerful you'd become."

"Powerful!"

"All the same, it pained him."

"Pained me more!"

"Him, too."

"Pain! I'll show you pain."

Maggot Thwacka flung herself around the room in an effort to think. But she was not a thinking person. Mostly, she acted on impulse. But finally, she had an idea. With a cackle, she waved her hand. The room changed. One corner became vaguely spidery, vaguely cobwebby, and vaguely ghostly. It was a space to fear. Cascade saw it and gave little shudder. The Witch, however, decided that the young woman's fear was not yet big enough. She wanted a full-blown shudder. She concentrated again. Her blue brush of hair stood up straight. Horrible images formed in her mind and vile sounds poured from her mouth. The corner became darker, the webs more alive, the spiders more deadly. Now Cascade really shuddered.

"Oh, my lovely," Maggot Thwacka croaked, "it's all so worth it." She rubbed her head. "Despite the migraine." She glared. "This little present is not just for you to admire. This little present is for you to clean."

"To clean?" Cascade gasped. "But why?"

"Why?" Maggot Thwacka cackled. "So your fingers will learn what my fingers have suffered."

"But you've never cleaned."

"Still a good way to suffer."

Cascade sniffed. Though no superwoman, she was no pushover either. Since a toddler, she'd ridden on horses, on roos and even on the occasional unicorn. She could also shoot an arrow straight into a bullseye – as long as the bullseye wasn't a real eye. She'd even had a go with a spear. But as she'd refused to aim at anything vaguely warm and fuzzy, more people had been hit by her drawback than by her actual throw. So though she wouldn't fight, she did have a black belt in arguing.

"A good way to suffer, yes. But why should I go in?"

"Because..." Maggot Thwacka began, "because..." She was almost drawn into an argument. "Oh, drat it!" Her mind clouded with fury. "I don't have to give you a reason!" she shrilled, shaking with fury. "I could just freeze you and drag you in by your pretty silver hair. But, girl, I'll tell you. If you don't do as I say, that thing, that Ne'vermaker, will suffer and suffer most horribly."

At mention of the Ne'vermaker, Cascade paled and her hands clenched. She and the Witch glared ferociously. If she thought she could've made it, Cascade would've leapt at her. But she knew from past experience that Slowtime would hit her first and the next time she came to that her body would be covered in painful bruises. Slowly, she unclenched her fists and forced herself to take a different tack.

"He is more powerful than you," she said. "How could you hurt him?"

"Through you." The Witch cackled, "With you in my control, he wouldn't dare anything. And anyway, he showed his weakness long ago." She frowned in thought. Her head ached as she dug up the memory. "When he let in morality, he also let in weakness."

"No." Cascade shook her head. "He was always honourable. He was honourable and you took advantage of him."

Maggot Thwacka threw back her head and chortled, "I did it once and I'll do it again. And again and again. Till all his kingdom is mine. As it should be. And he is in my power as you are now. Till I have made him crawl from Auslan to Inklan and back. If you think you suffer, girl, see how much more your... your... my... my... the... the Ne'vermaker will."

The Witch's voice rose to a sharp shrill, penetrating Cascade's skull with the whine of a giant hornet. Echoes within echoes added to the cacophony. Her head shook with pain, weakening her resolve.

"Now into the room," the Witch screeched. "Clean it, brush it, scrub it. Spiders' webs entwine you. Tentacles will hold you. Snakes bodies will enfold you. Ha-ha, he-he. Do it, do it for the Ne'vermaker. Ha-ha, he-he, a pox on the Ne'vermaker."

With a sad shake of her head, Cascade moved towards the corner. She tried to tell herself that it was only magic, only an illusion. At its very edge, she stared in. It was a ship's cabin, a hundred years rotten in the murky deep. Dank and musty, a rank smell came out of it. Spiders hung from webs and stared back at her. A dark shape slithered across the floor. She stood as if frozen, unable to make the last step. But a sudden shove from behind sent her staggering across the threshold. There was a hideous cackle as a broom was thrown in after her. Cascade clutched at it, but more for defence than for cleaning. With a heavy heart, she thought once more of the Ne'vermaker. Then as the deepest and darkest fears gripped her, she was immersed once more into the pit of Slowtime.

Chapter 10

"Far out!" Glide exclaimed. "This is the circus, right? They're training for the circus?"

"For battle." Strongarm's voice was a reluctant trickle.

"Battle?" Glide blinked. His ears couldn't square with what his eyes were seeing.

"It's very..." Glide began. He caught himself. "It's somewhat chaotic."

"Yeah." Strongarm waggled his head. "Tell me about it."

"We are not fighting peoples," Hernandes said.

"No." Strongarm waggled his head again. "These folk should not have to fight."

The two shook their heads. Strongarm's swung ponderously from left to right while Hernandes' little head bobbed vigorously up and down. Glide found his own head going both up and down then left and right in sympathy. He caught himself and went back to watching the training. It really was an amazing sight. It was a comedy of terrors.

The target was a pair of fringed white trousers, stuffed with sand, tied to a thick branch of a large tree. An imp on a roo was charging it using a broomstick as a lance. That was fair enough. While at uni, Glide had tried Aiki-dont. For practise, he'd used a broom handle as a sword. But he'd started off with slow swings of his weapon. The imp, however, was pushing his roo to hop as fast as he could. His broomstick hit the target and knocked it backwards. Fine, that was fine. But... not knowing how to absorb the impact, the imp was also knocked backwards. He was sliding down the roo when the target swung forward again. The roo ducked, leaving the imp in mid-air. Hernandes groaned aloud. Strongarm shook his head in dismay. Thud! The imp was knocked into the bushes.

While the watching imps cheered, a second rider charged. He missed completely but his broomstick hit a tree. He, too, slid backwards and fell into the grass. The other imps cheered again.

"That's how they do battle," Strongarm said gloomily.

Glide loosened his collar. "Why don't they try on foot?"

Hernandes turned to him in astonishment. "But they must get used to how the animal moves. How do they do thats if they not rides on the roos?"

"Yeah, how the animal moves is important. But that's a more advanced stage."

After watching two more attempts, Glide put out a hand to stop the imps. As they watched him, he hefted the trousers. Finding they were weighted down with sand. Glide smiled wryly as he remembered how more than once he'd taken to head butting punch bags. From a pile, he selected a broomstick. The centre of attention, he tucked it under his arm and ran at the trousers. He hit hard. His feet skidded and his body recoiled. He just managed to limbo under the target when it swung forward again.

"A good demo," Strongarm said dryly. "Excellent. We should teach limbo dancing?"

"No." Glide brushed himself down. Sarcasm from a talking elephant? That was novel. Not to say unwanted. "Watch again."

This time, he approached the target slowly. The weighted trousers swung back a little and Glide easily absorbed the recoil. He had ample time to avoid them as they swung back again. The imps cheered. Even Strongarm was leaning forward with interest. Hernandes was chewing at the brim of his akubra. Glide attacked a second time. As he gradually acquired a feeling for what he was doing, he increased his speed. Eventually, he was back to his original charge. But now, he was able to absorb the recoil and swing around the bag.

The cheering imps triumphantly threw their broomsticks into the air. Unfortunately, they weren't very good at catching them. As the broomsticks came down, groans went up.

Hernandes clapped. "Excellentes. Very goods."

Strongarm stood with one huge foot lifted in the air. "So that is how you teach folk who are not natural warriors. Well done. It could work. It could."

"Well, I'm only a day-tripper," Glide said, wishing and hoping.

"More'n a day." The air spoke in a gravely voice and a blue shadow momentarily stood on one leg. Then it fell back.

Glide shrugged. Well, if this were Barley, he'd give it two weeks. So he'd give this strange excursion two weeks. That made him wonder how things were going in his office. But he didn't wonder for long. He didn't care. This might be no more than his demented illusion but it was becoming a very nice one, thank you.

Strongarm led him further on. A dozen men, of the human variety, were at swordplay - the emphasis on play. One pair went at it with the speed of snails doing tai chi. They obviously didn't want to hurt each other. One pair went at it full tilt - jumping on tables, leaping over fallen trunks, and swinging their swords in huge swipes. At first Glide was impressed. He soon realised, however, that these two were the Errol Flynn and Zorro of the village. Their moves were well rehearsed.

"Can you stop them?" Glide asked.

"While they're having so much fun?" Strongarm said sarcastically. He lifted his trunk. "Stop!" he trumpeted. "STOP!"

The two men slowed as if their clockwork was winding down. They looked expectantly at Strongarm. "Good, eh?" Errol Flynn did a flashy jump from a table.

"Star quality." Zorro leapt in slow motion.

Strongarm gave the elephant equivalent of a cough. "This is Glide," he said. "Glide would like a few words with you."

"Not words." Glide took one of the swords and used it to trim a couple of stout branches. "Zorro." He pointed at the darker of the two.

"Zorro? Okay." The man accepted the name.

"And Errol." Glide pointed at the other man.

"That's good." The man carefully brushed a lock of hair over his forehead.

"Now you, Zorro, slowly, really slowly, jab at me with your sword." Glide handed the man one of the branches.

"But you've got my sword," Zorro protested.

"The stick is now your sword."

"Oh, a pretend sword." Zorro stuck his nose in the air.

Once he'd made his point, Zorro lunged forward. Glide, expecting this, stepped to the side and rapped the other on the arm with his stick. "What if this were the real sword?" he asked. Zorro went white. "Again but slowly." This time, Zorro complied.

"One attack followed by one defence." Glide demonstrated. "One attack followed by one defence."

Adapting Taikwon-dont training, Glide gradually managed to give the two men the basic equivalent of one-step sparring.

Strongarm was fascinated. "And this will transfer to real swords?" he asked.

"With practise."

The two men turned the branches over in their hands. After choreographed hacking with real swords, real hacking with wood had turned out to be quite painful. Glide rubbed his hands in anticipation. Going crazy was turning out to be fun. Particularly if you could share it. Plus, he was teaching fighting. That was exciting – well, just as long as there wasn't going to be a real fight.

In the pause, he yawned. They were supposed to be going to a palace. Instead, he'd been demonstrating. It must be hours since his breakfast. What about his mid-morning coffee? His chat around the water-cooler? Where was his cappuccino? He could do with a cappuccino. He squinted at Hernandes.

"D'you have coffee here?"

Hernandes squinted back. "Ne'wang has brought coffee here. But normally we use ground roasted yams."

"Oh yeah, ground roasted yams, the taste sensation of the year." Glide wiped his brow. "Anything else?"

Hernandes nodded eagerly. "Waits here." He hopped onto Horsey. Horsey hopped out of the clearing. A few moments later, both still hopping, they returned. "There you ares," the imp said. "Lemonade."

"Real lemonade? Real lemonade as mother never used to make it?"

Glide took a cautious sip. The taste was delicious. As he'd said, just like mother used to make. Not his mother, perhaps, but some ideal mother, somewhere. Hernandes gave another bottle to Strongarm. It looked tiny in the long trunk and its contents rapidly disappeared. Glide also finished his drink.

As the empties went into a collection box, Strongarm asked, "D'you want to see more?"

"Do I?" Glide had been tired. Now, though, he felt a slight buzz. It was the lemonade, he guessed, full of Nature's stimulants. A hint of coca, perhaps? He flexed his biceps. "Onward and outward, mate, I'm ready for anything."

Strongarm gave him a funny look. "Are you sure?"

"I'm still here, aren't I?"

"Yes, but this... this..." Strongarm sighed. "Even I want to run away sometimes."

And with that, they came upon a mixed group of humans and imps. With much jangling of beads and bangling of bracelets, they held hands and progressed in a slow circle. Strongarm looked at Glide and made the pachyderm equivalent of rolling his eyes.

Chapter 11

Glide watched with increasing amusement as with each step, the circle of humans and imps chanted sonorously. The sound created was similar to the strange glottal sounds produced by Tie-beaten monks. It was an extremely electrifying noise, ideal for psyching warriors up before a battle. Unfortunately, it was spoilt when the heel of a large human trod on the toes of a small imp.

"Ow! Big Foot watch where you're going!" The imp hopped about, breaking both the circle and the rhythm.

"Sorry, sorry." The man tried to brush the imp's pain away, but his big awkward movements knocked the small imp down.

"Once more," called a weary voice, tapping a broomstick. "I've seen toads learn quicker."

"Our, er, magic oval," Strongarm mumbled.

"Magic oval?" Glide was bemused.

"It was meant to be a magic circle. They just don't seem to get the concept of roundness."

Beyond the ragged moving line, a group sat cross-legged on the grass. Soaking wet sheets hung between them and the glaring sun. Humans and imps shifted and sweated as sun rays beat down on their necks and water dripped on their heads. Several sneezed and their noses glowed.

"What's this?" Glide asked. "Colour therapy? Or are they trying to make themselves sun-resistant?"

"No." Strongarm sadly shook his sizeable skull.

"Then what? Are they ill?"

"Not ills. Well, some are now." Hernandes fidgeted in the saddle. "They are practisings to focus their minds."

Glide again pulled at his collar. His usual work clothes were designed for air-conditioning. "I don't think I've seen anything like this before."

"Yes, you have, mate," a warm voice said. A dark shadow came and went.

"I have?"

"Yes, mate."

Glide pulled off his work cravat. Earlier, the strange incantation of the circling group had reminded him of... of what? Oh yeah, Tie-beaten monks. Tie-beaten monks...? Tie-beaten... monks? He cranked up his eidetic imagery. Yep, there it was! Monks who sat in the snow with sheets around their shoulders. The idea was to dry the sheets with their psychic powers. He turned a page in his mind. But those sheets were no bigger than handkerchiefs! These sheets were bed size.

"And they're doing this for a reason?" he asked.

"Well, they think so, yes." Strongarm replied. "It's possible." His tone wasn't very convincing.

One of the sitters sneezed. That set off the one next to him. Soon the whole line was sneezing and the wet sheets were bucking up and down like sails in the wind.

Glide sighed. "Perhaps it would be best if you started at the beginning." He paused. "There is a beginning, isn't there?"

"Oh, yes." Strongarm said. "There is. Well, there was - probably."

Before he could go on, Hernandes hopped his roo forward. "Let's not begins now," he said. "Let's begins at Plonkers."

"Plonkers?"

"Over a beer," Strongarm rumbled.

Glide turned in surprise. It wasn't the beer that surprised him – beer he supposed was universal - so much as the rumble. He'd been looking at Hernandes not Strongarm and so he'd heard the voice without seeing the bulk. The pitch was incredibly deep for a man. Though it was rather high for an elephant. Glide scratched his head. Amazing! Size shaped the sound. Now there was an interesting illusion. His eidetic ability threw up an image of a yellow ring. Its left side had a background of bright red. Its right side had a background of dull red. The right side appeared much brighter. Throw in a sound and...?

As he followed Hernandes, a sound was thrown in. And the name of the sound was bedlam.

Glide immediately recognised this chaos. From his life as a student, he knew that excess noise was directly proportional to excess alcohol. His entry to Plonkers was a direct confirmation. The bar was an open-air garden, where all the air was bursting with sound. In this jungly setting, human and imp, male and female, were at their most busy. Their aim? The downing of tankards. With glasses at their mouths, to speak they had to shout. To sing, they had to shout. To dance, they had to shout. This was an undergrad uni bar after midnight, a uni bar after exams.

Hernandes looked up at Glide. "Es a bit happier here," he said.

Glide nodded. Despite the sea of sound, he expected everyone to stare and to quieten when Strongarm the Elephant entered. And so everyone did. The sound stopped as quickly as a switch being thrown. Heads turned. Eyes goggled. Mouths hung open. But why? Was this to stare at Strongarm? No. At Hernandes the Imp? No, again. At Glide? Yes! They were all staring at him.

Similar circumstances caused him to quickly glance down. No problem there, he was all buttoned and correct. Then what?

The silence was as profound as the noise had been deafening. A significant lull was followed by a gradually increasing buzz. And it was all about him, Glide knew, all about him. Blushing like a beetroot, he was extremely relieved when Hernandes ushered them towards a corner. He sat, trying to make himself as small as possible. Strongarm, however, trumpeted loudly to draw attention. At that, a burly man in a leather apron dashed out of the tavern.

"'Oo's that?" he shouted. He glared around until he spotted the looming grey hulk. "Ar, it's only yous, Strongarm."

"And who else would've trumpeted?"

"Ar, you knows, Gabriel the Arkangles or sum'one."

"An archangel?" Glide didn't think he was in heaven.

"Ar, you'd be surprised at the types wot comes in here."

"No one es surprised who comes here, Plonkers," Hernandes said tartly. "The only surprises es who manages to gets out."

"Getting out, ar? So you'd be 'aving Green Mist, is it?"

"Yes, rotguts for three."

"But first," Strongarm said, "can you please find me a chair?"

"'Ang on a mo. I've only got three arms."

"I'll squirt you."

"Olright, olright. One chair, comin' up. An' I 'ope that's the only thing comin' up tonight."

Plonkers trotted into the inn and reappeared a few moments later with a large wooden drum, strengthened with iron hoops. He placed it at the table and Strongarm gingerly lowered his bulk. He settled with a sigh. Plonkers ran off again, bringing three foaming tankards. Glide started to salivate. This was how all hallucinations should be. But then he made a mistake. Instead of just drinking, he peered inside. The contents peered back. Thick green coils, serpentine coils, were crawling up the sides.

Glide became aware that the hubbub had once more died down. He glanced up. As quickly as he did so, a hundred eyes looked down. Even Strongarm and Hernandes were watching him - while pretending not to. Glide sniffed his drink. It had a pleasant enough odour, mild somewhat minty. He sipped. A rich flavour, something like beer, something like mint tea, something like...

Fire. His sip was a tiny flame, a flame adjacent to gunpowder. His belly was a powder keg, waiting to be ignited by a hundred watching eyes. Glide was not a hardened drinker. But he had been a student. As volcanic eruptions gurgled on the brink of existence in his lower regions, he knew that this was one of those times when one had to fight fire with fire. With much the same spirit as taking a foil into kendo, he raised his tankard. He opened his lips and he gulped. He swallowed a third. The pinpoint of fire spread. He gulped another third. Miraculously, in further spreading, the fire diffused. Face aglow, he finished the tankard. The most delicious taste of crème de menthe permeated his body. He radiated mint. Lift him by the collar and dunk him, and he'd make a strong pot of herbal tea. A collective sigh burst out and noise rushed in to refill the vacuum.

Hernandes jiggled with delight. Strongarm thoughtfully dipped his trunk into his tankard and delicately squirted into his open mouth. In a few large gulps, all the drinks were finished.

"Hm," said Strongarm, "so you've been told about rotgut?"

"No."

"You've had it before?"

"No."

"Hm?" Strongarm scratched himself with his long and hairy proboscis. "How'd you know to drink Green Mist like that, then?"

It was Glide's turn to scratch himself, though not with a long and hairy proboscis. "I don't know," he said. "I just did. Having been a student, I guess."

"A stewed dent," Strongarm said carefully. "What sort of dent is that?"

"Very stewed."

Strongarm blinked his eyes slowly in thought. Hernandes, however, happily called out, "More rotguts, please, Plonkers." A little later, he called, "Shame again, please."

With his second glass, Glide began to feel synapses click in his brain as they passed messages from neuron to neuron. The fire burnt through old connections, the mint soothed the new. On the third glass, even stranger things happened. A blue-black cloud condensed. Or nearly did. It toppled before taking form. Glide struggled to recall when he'd seen this cloud before. With each gulp, his brain yielded more and more while the shape stayed longer and longer. On a final mouthful, the Ne'wang the Ne'vermaker was fully formed.

"Keep drinking," he ordered.

"Wha'?"

"Keep drinking."

"Fanks. Fink I will. Hic. Why?"

"For less sanity," the Ne'vermaker replied, "and more reality."

"Less shanitry?" Glide echoed. "Washed my hands thish morning, didn't I? Didn't I?" He squinted. "Shtill here? You here to shtay?"

"As long as you don't not think me."

"Don't not. I don't want to don't not. That makesh... that makesh..." Glide counted on his fingers. "Double negative, double negative. That'sh a poshitive. Sho I do do think you. But that'sh a double poshitive. Sho.. sho..."

"No, you don't think me. Just don't not think me."

Glide shook his head. Briefly seeing an elephant with two trunks, he mumbled, "At leasht, you're not pink."

Strongarm belched. "But you are." He chortled. "Hic! I'm seeing pink peoples."

Hernandes shook Glide's arm. "Don't's not shink him," he said.

"Not shink," Glide repeated. "I'm not shinking as hard as I can." He burped. "My head hurtsh. Ne'wang the... the-somefin. Was' happening? Explain. Pleash explain."

"Sure, mate. But it's a long story."

"Got... got... got all the timesh in the world."

"Just keep drinking."

"Shure, man. Your shout."

"No, my shout." Strongarm hiccupped. "My trumpet."

"Your strumpet," Hernandes said.

The Ne'vermaker poured drinks into their glasses. "It all began..." he began. He sighed. "It's all so difficult, so sad, so unnecessary... You won't believe it. I don't myself. What Oedipal webs we weave. What sad Oedipal webs."

"Sho?" Glide leant forward. "I'm all ears."

"Not as much ears as me!" Strongarm snorted.

Glide ignored him. "Tell me about the Ed Dipple websh we weave."

Chapter 12

"First," Ne'wang stood, sombre as a moral tutor, "what is a Ne'vermaker?"

"You don' know?" Glide hiccupped. Ne'wang's fierce frown pierced his mental fog. "Ah, you do know. Right, sho tell me."

"It was rhetoric." The Ne'verman rubbed at his brilliant emerald eyes. Travelling from there to here was tiring. Talking with Glide was exhausting. "Yes, it was rhetoric."

"Ah." Glide nodded wisely. "You shpeak many languagesh?"

The Ne'vermaker sighed and toppled. Glide blinked and the blue figure returned. "Glide, just listen. Please don't ask questions."

"A'right, a'right. No questionsh. What questionsh? Who asksh questionsh, anyway?"

"A Ne'vermaker is special. He is a magic man, a healer, and a repository of myths."

"A suppository of missh? Missh who?"

"Myths! Legends! The Ne'vertime!"

"Ah, myphs. Sho you admit, thish ish a myph."

The Ne'vermaker's dark hue became transparent. It was a mist that Glide could see through, a fog that hid the whirling thoughts in his mind. He was a cyclone of chaos struggling for coherence. "Drink, drink," Ne'wang urged. "Drink. You're more sane when less sober."

"You're right. I'm too clever-arse when shober." In that moment of insight, Glide downed another slug of Green Mist. Icy fire gripped his mind.

"This is not a myth," the Ne'vermaker said. "This is reality. Years ago, Ne'vermen forged magic paths across the oceans. The mind, or the Ne'vertime if you will, acts as a gateway."

"Oh, I shee, like a science fiction shtory. I just opened the gate and shtepped across the waters."

"Simply put, yes."

"Good, in tha' case," Glide rose, "I'll just open the gate and shtep back through again." He lifted his leg and banged it on the bench. "Damn and strawberriesh, that hurt!"

"Sorry, Glide, it's not that simple."

"Sho, go on." Glide rested his chin on his fist. His elbow slipped and he banged his chin on the table.

"When I was young," the Ne'vermaker said, "I intuitively knew how to find healing herbs. I also had remarkable dreams."

"Too many of those healing herbsh."

"Our Tribal Ne'vermaker saw this and made me his apprentice. He was able to enter my dreams and guide me. After a year of Ne'vertime Dreaming, I gained some control, able to chose a gate, open it and enter."

"Sho this," Glide gasped, teetering on sobriety, "is just something that you've dreamt up?"

Ignoring him, the Ne'vermaker went on, "One gateway suited me more than others."

"Thish!"

"Yes, this one." The Ne'vermaker's face saddened. "I loved this region and spent more and more time here and less and less at home."

"Home," Glide echoed mordantly. Green mist sizzled in his scalp. "Ho-oome," he howled. "Glide phone home!"

"Home," Strongarm repeated and draped his trunk sympathetically across Glide's shoulders.

A trunk with empathy, Glide thought. He wriggled a finger in his ear as a heavy-breathing, sinuous nose curled around him. Lifting the end, he spoke into it as if it were a voice receiver. "Sho you're not from here either?"

"Me? No, I'm from a dishtant country. Hic!" Strongarm released an elephantine burp. It threatened to blow Glide away but he leant into it as his hands gripped the edge of the table. "I wash ashked to train them, the troopsh."

"I shaw."

Strongarm shrugged. A movement that didn't raise his shoulders up but sent his head down. His chin hit the table, causing it to lift. The others quickly threw themselves across it. Plonkers voice drifted out.

"No more Green Mist fer you, yer great heap. Only fer the new one."

"Bronzed shields!" Strongarm sniffed, "I was the new one once. Now I'm just a white elephant."

"Pink," Glide said. He threw out his arms to indicate the inn. "So what ish thish place, anyway?"

"Plonker'z Inn," Hernandes said with a slur. "Though Plonker'z Down would be betters... bitters." He giggled.

"Plonkers Down... and Out," Strongarm added.

The Ne'verman stamped his spear down on the earth.

Glide tried to focus on him. "Shorry, I asked." Glide waved vaguely at the Ne'vermaker. "Pleashe continue."

"This became my home," Ne'wang said. "I mean I did study law in Brissie but mate, when I could, I used to go on stroll-about and this is where I'd be." He leant forward and peered deeply into Glide's eyes. The irises slithered around like greasy omelettes in a pan. "You can stop drinking now. You've fixed me."

Glide rolled his head. "As good a reashon as any to continue drinking."

"Why stay here you may ask?"

"I may? Right, why shtay here I may arshk? Er, you or me?"

"Me."

"Right. Why me shtay here I may ashk?"

"There is the beauty, of course." The Ne'vermaker motioned to the bamboo cottages, the tropical gardens and the colourful birds. "There were no wars, no prejudice, no droughts, no pollution..."

"No problemsh," Glide said. "No problemsh at all." At that, however, the Ne'vermaker became curiously silent. In the pause, Glide had a sudden understanding, a curious tingling in his scalp that verged on the unfortunate state of sobriety. "I know. You met a woman."

The Ne'vermaker sighed. "Right on. And what a woman."

"Watterwoman? I knew a Watterwoman wonce. Wendy Watterwoman. Bit of a washout, weally."

"What-a-woman."

"Right, yesh. She'd have to be."

"A Witch."

"Aren't they all?"

"No. I mean a woman who did magic, earth magic."

"Magic? What with thoshe big wet shits?" Glide cocked his head, testing his last words. "Sheets?" He put down his glass. "Drying those sheets?" As he listened to his words, Glide became aware of new and urgent messages, internal messages. They were coming from his innards. Looking uneasily at the jungle, he mumbled, "I gotta go to the dunny. Where'sh the dunny? In the jungly?"

"A dunny?" The Ne'vermaker frowned, for a moment irritated at being interrupted yet once more. Then the frown lifted and he laughed. "No worries, mate. Follow me."

They went a short way along a path, coming to a row of small thatched cabins. Incense burnt around them, creating a pleasant acrid odour.

"Goes to the sea, does it?" Glide asked.

The blue man laughed again. "Think this is Maroochi, mate? No way. We don't pollute the sea like that. Anyway this stuff, it's bloody good compost. Just add sawdust and grass when you've finished." He opened a cabin door. The only smell was the incense. "We shift 'em around when they get too full." He turned. "See you back at Plonkers."

Glide entered the cabin, muttering when he saw that he'd have to squat. Fortunately, there were handrails. Holding on, he gingerly lowered his body. His knees clicked like castanets while, outside, the birds sang. All in all, Glide decided, it wasn't a bad dunny experience, especially after the cacophony of Plonkers. When finished, he looked around for paper. Of course, there was none, merely a bucket of water.

His bottom clean, if damp, Glide left the cabin. Immediately an imp appeared. He pointed at a pump. "Ne'vermaker says to wash hands," he called. "Wash hands."

"Olright, I was gonna," Glide said. Despite his bigger size, he vaguely felt like a child being chided by its mother.

On the way back to Plonkers, Glide's path was blocked by Strongarm. The latter blushed, becoming a genuine pink elephant.

"It's all right for you," the pachyderm grumbled, "I have to go into the jungle. As for wiping my bottom, I have to use a tree. Of which, its bark is worse than its bite." He laughed moodily. "The Ne'vermaker did once bring newspaper from your region. But who knew what political views I was absorbing?"

"Yeah, still that's putting politics in its right place."

"Politics." Strongarm moved aside so Glide could pass. "The art of verbal warfare."

"I thought war was what happened when verbals failed?"

"Yes. A lot rests on you."

"It does?" Glide wiped his brow. He didn't want a lot to rest on him. That was too much responsibility. And anger was a responsibility that brewed inside him and dragged him back towards sobriety. "Well, we'll soon see about that." The young man strode back to Plonkers and dropped into his seat. "Nice place, Ne'ver," he growled. "I came. I saw. I wasn't conquered. Now, how do I get back?"

The Ne'vermaker sighed. "That's what I've been leading up to, Glide. I can't get you back."

"You won't."

"No, I mean it. I can't.

"You what!"

"Only you can."

"But you got me here!"

"I only supplied the direction. You supplied the energy."

"Me?"

"Yes, that terrible darkness that was building up inside you. The blue cloud that became me. It could've become something else. Exploded and become something murderous, perhaps."

Glide tried to think back. There had been that blue cloud, of course, and it had contained an enormous amount of emotional energy. But murderous...?

"So if you supplied the direction," he said slowly. "Why can't you direct me back?"

"As I said, you have to supply the energy."

Glide groaned. Why were they always going round in circles? That blue cloud, he remembered, had been a symbol of his depression. Yet now he was no longer depressed, what had previously been turned in, now wanted to explode out. Instead of depressed, he was angry. He was furious. In a manic fit, he knocked back his stool and banged down his glass. Jumping onto the table, Glide lashed out at tankards and kicked out at plates. Legs apart, he lifted his head and howled.

Road Rage, in the form of Magic Gateway Rage, boiled up and out of Glide.

Chapter 13

It had been a long day for Glide. Though he assumed that days in this protected region were the same as days back home, it felt that he'd already been here for a century. Having howled himself into silence, he had then kicked the table clear. Stumbling finally to the ground, he upturned the fallen vessels and gulped the remains of rotgut. Plonkers watched. He knew it wasn't safe to intervene. Safe would be was when Glide was comatose.

When the stranger was snoring, Plonkers came out, wiping his hands. "Right, then, yer've 'ad yer fun and a right bloomin' mess you've made ov it. One new blinkin' 'ero an' there goes me best crockery. Olright then, wot I'd like t'know is 'oo's goin' t'pay fer it. That's all. 'Oo's goin' to pay?"

There was a silence broken only by evasive stares. Eventually, Hernandes spoke to the air, "Hows abouts it goes as a donations to the national cause?"

"Yers. That's wot yer said abaht the last 'ero."

"The principal remains the sames."

"Yers. But me crockery don't."

"Chip off a bit of my tusk." Strongarm lowered his head. "Real ivory."

"Nah, nah, couldn't." Plonkers refused reluctantly. "One chip and I'll 'ave old Ne'wang dahn me throat."

"Old?" The Ne'verman glared at the barman.

"Oi didn't say that," Plonkers said.

"Right, nothing heard." With Glide's doubts marinating in rotgut, the Ne'vermaker was more solid than ever. He waved a hand at the broken shards, his long blue fingers seeming to have an elegant life of their own. "Don't you worry about those, Plonkers. I'll fix 'em for you."

"Well do a betta job than yer did last time. 'Arf the cups 'ad two 'andles while the other 'arf 'ad none." Plonkers returned inside, repeatedly wiping his hands on his apron like a hairy Lady Macdeth,

With some sympathy, the Ne'vermaker studied Glide. "Feeling better?"

Glide shrugged. "I've been better." He rested his head on the table and closed his eyes. After a few moments of non-thought, he opened them again. "I'm stuck here. What can I do?" He waved his hand. "Go on, then, tell me the rest."

The Ne'vermaker was making a jigsaw of broken crockery and turned to look at Glide. "Of?"

"Your story, of course."

"Oh, yes, my story."

Above them, a big black bird rustled in the leaves. Half-grasped words formed in its ears and quarter-grasped meaning in its brain. Goresh passed these on to Maggot Thwacka. The distant Witch squeezed her forehead in concentration. Later she'd deal with the migraine. She could already feel it building up, steel bands around her skull that grew tighter and tighter. When they were at their worse, she would free Cascade. Let her suffer, too. Make her. Maybe one day, she could pass all her pains on to the girl.

For a moment, for one single solitary moment, her pain left her unguarded and her thoughts leaked across the connection to the bird. Suddenly, the Ne'vermaker rose. His spear seemed to lengthen as it shot out blue sparks. They rocketed up into the tree. Some hit and so, with a squawk, Goresh the Raven shot into the sky. The blue sparks followed, so that screeching with pain and rage, he flew into the distance clouds.

"What was that?" Glide gasped. "What did you do? Why?"

The Ne'vermaker gave a tight smile. "If anyone tells you, Glide, that here the walls have ears take them literally."

"That was an ear?"

"Of sorts."

Glide glanced at Strongarm. "That size?"

Strongarm gave him a quizzical look but the Ne'vermaker waved to him for silence. "Back home, Glide, you were ready to explode. That was because you had a Talent. Still have. It's almost magical. It is magical. It was that Talent that called me." He paused. "Summoned me. It calls me still. If you want to return, you'll have to develop it."

"Yeah, right, develop it." Glide handed Ne'wang a piece of pot that completed one jigsaw. "Almost magical, as in?"

"I can't say exactly, you'll just have to develop it."

Glide stomped in frustration. "Right, right. Okay then, so how d'you know if it'll help me? How d'you know if it'll help you?"

"You just did help me."

"I did. How?"

"The piece you just gave me." Ne'wang touched the pottery fragment. "You saw how it fitted."

"I'm here to fit pottery? Or is that some sort of sÿmbol?"

"I don't know, Glide!" The Ne'verman banged the butt of his spear into the hard earth. "My intuition knows but my mind doesn't."

"Bloody hell! Magic, intuition, talent!"

Glide glared at the others: Strongarm the talking elephant, Hernandes an imp who rode a roo, and Ne'wang who continuously fell through a magic gateway. The reality of being elsewhere was starting to sink in and he threw out his arms in resignation.

"So let's start at the middle again," Glide growled. "You'd just met a woman."

"A woman, what a woman. Or rather, a girl. We were both young then. Boy meets girl, girl meets boy. They fall in love. That sort of story. At least, I thought it was." The dark face showed pain. "Maybe it was only boy meets girl. She was quick, even in those days. Learnt far more from me than I ever did from her."

"Maybe you had less to learn," Glide said.

"She had nothing to teach," Strongarm growled.

"Oh, but she did, she did." Ne'wang stared into the distance for a moment. "I knew Ne'vertime but she knew Witchery."

"What's the difference?"

"Ne'vertime is more of the mind, Witchery more of the earth."

"The yink and yank of magic," Glide said. "Tell me more. Oops, scrub that. Makes me sounds like a therapist."

"Ne'vertime can create worlds of the mind." The Ne'vermaker stamped his spear against the ground. "Witchery can control them. I showed her how to create. She began to control the creations." He sighed. "At first, they were funny. Then they were satirical. Then..." He shrugged wearily. "By then, we had a daughter. She was gorgeous, young and fresh, our prize creation. Of course, my wife wanted to control her. She became jealous. We began to draw apart. First just a little, as in satire. Then further, into taunts. She sowed seeds, half-truths that split the community. Human was set against human, imp against imp. Before actual war, however, the elders met, both males and females. My wife was banished. Yet she refused to go." A deep sigh escaped the Ne'vermaker. "That was a terrible time. We fought with magic. And I managed to banish her. But magic, as in mechanics, also has equal and opposite reactions."

"So you were banished, as well?"

"Yes, though not completely. You, for instance, can hold me here."

"Why can't Strongarm?"

"He is more physical. You are more mental."

"Yeah, I'm right mental." Glide looked around. The inn was now almost empty. Only a dozen or so people remained beneath a velvet sky studded with stars. Glide gazed at constellations, but didn't recognise any. But, then, he never recognised constellations anyway. Especially when rotgut had hold of his neurons. "So," He rubbed his aching head, "Strongarm is physical and got turned into an elephant. I'm more mental. What will she do to me, turn me into a thought?"

"A thought?" The Ne'vermaker rested his chin on his hand and the blue of his face became darker. After a while, though, it lit up with a silvery smile. "Mate, that could be it! A thought or, maybe, some sort of ghost."

"Aw, hell! I'd die before I became a ghost!"

Ne'wang eyed the young man. "That is the normal sequence."

"Nah, you know what I mean."

"You'd prefer to be an elephant?"

"No, mate. I'd like to stay as sweet as I am."

"You won't get homes, then," Hernandes said. "We are dependings on you. But you are dependings on yourselfs as well. You brought yourselfs here, only you can take yourselfs back." His voice rose. "The Ne'vermaker can shows you how to do it. But only you can actually do the hows."

The imp was bouncing up and down in such an agitated way, it looked as if he were using his seat as a trampoline. Without wanting to commit himself, Glide felt quite touched. In the Civilian Service, his real enthusiasms had been squashed. Here he was being encouraged. And the appeal was direct to him, to him as a person not to him as just a cog in a machine. He was their shining knight in shining armour. Glide again rubbed his head.

"All right, I'll do it. I don't know what I can do, but I'll have a go." He turned to the Ne'vermaker. "You say I've got a Talent. So let's find out what it is." Witch or no Witch, he thought, he'd show them. After all, he was a scientist. No hocus pocus would get to him. No way.

Only one thing bothered him. One tiny... enormous thing.

Glide took a sip of rotgut. Eyeing the great grey bulk of Strongarm, he put his lips close to Ne'wang's ear. "So how did, er, you-know-who become an... an elephant?"

Everyone leant forward. "What? Speak ups." Hernandes cupped his ears.

Glide swallowed. "So how did Strongarm become an elephant?" he repeated.

There was a moment's silence. An enormous foot lifted and, for a moment, Glide thought he'd gone too far. But tiny tears, though they were probably huge for a human, trickled down the trunk. In a human way, the elephant tried to use a huge front foot to wipe them away.

"Out of love, Glide," Strongarm replied, "out of love." His voice broke and he remained too choked up to continue.

Chapter 14

The silence stretched. Eventually, Ne'wang spoke again. "My wife's name was Argot."

"Argot?" Glide echoed. "Argot? That word means slang."

"Not here, Glide, not here. Her hair was spun gold." The Ne'vermaker sighed, creating a disturbing sensation. As the Ne'verman sat facing Glide, another more shadowy version, slowly toppled backwards. Glide, dizzy, shook his head and sipped his drink. The two versions fused and a voice from somewhere inside of him said, "Keep drinking, stop thinking." Obediently he did so. The Ne'vermaker firmed. "Argot," he went on, "was a master, mistress, of herbs and potions. Initially, she used her skills for healing. But as her power grew, she wanted to control people as well. *She* knew what was best for them. But she also used her herbs to loosen their minds so that they did silly things. She said spells over her potions, adding to her power."

"Her power?" Glide startled. Wasn't the Ne'vermaker's voice also a power? It was dark and rich with harmonics. "Your power, too. Is this...? Is all this just some form of hypnosis? A posthypnotic suggestion?"

Strongarm snorted. "You think I'm just some sort of posthypnotic suggestion?"

"Well...?"

"I'll sit on you. See if you can unsuggest me."

"In some sense, Glide," the Ne'vermaker said pacifyingly, "all magic is suggestion, a consensual suggestion. Your reality is a suggestion. To see through it is the difficulty. Here, in this place, there is an enormously strong collective belief that Strongarm is an elephant. So, immediately you were with him that is how you saw him."

"Oh?" Glide rose unsteadily to his feet. "Uh, you mean a sort of mass hypnosis? That if I didn't see him according to what people here believe then I'd see him as he really is?"

"Well," the Ne'vermaker gave his silvery smile, "I wouldn't go that far. Let's just say you'd see him as a man."

"Isn't that what he *really* is?"

"Really is a deep deep word, Glide."

Glide mused. "Hmm, now you're being mystical." The Ne'vermaker inclined his head. Glide shook himself. "You haven't been feeding me any of your herbs?" he demanded.

"Green Mists is enough," Hernandes snorted.

"It's your thinking, Glide." The Ne'vermaker looked at the young man. No, he looked into the young man. "It's beginning to change."

Glide frowned. He'd always been proud of his thinking. He was analytical, but not limited. Not limited, yet not weird! Till now.

"That's why you're here," Ne'wang continued. "That's why I'm explaining. I was saying that Argot combined herbs with spells. There was one mixture in particular which fascinated her, the flower of time."

"Oh," Glide hiccuped, "I cook with thyme."

"Time with an *i*."

"Oh."

"Not o, i."

"Right, i as in time." Glide hiccuped. "Or better still, time and a half."

"As in," Ne'wang agreed, "but opposite. It was more like time minus a half. Or time minus nine tenths, or time minus ninety nine hundredths."

"Not much drinking time."

"Not much time at all. None."

"Jeez!" Glide shivered. This, he knew, was where he came in. "This is some sort of anaesthetic, or neural block, something like that?"

"Exactly. A light dose is great. The world slows down, relaxes. Everyone goes ultraslow. Like doing tai chi in honey. A heavy dose is... heavy. You can do brain surgery in it. Time and the mind freeze. But no one feels good about it. Somewhere there's a little trickle of consciousness and that little trickle knows that time and the world are passing by, but that there's no catching up to it."

"I get you," Glide said, "it's like just before you present your honours thesis, the world freezes. Except for your stomach." He shuddered. "I don't much like this flower of time."

"Argot did. She was a real scientist in her way. Analysing, experimenting, refining."

"All that? On who?"

"The animals, at first. It wasn't totally harmless and we should've stopped it, but we were fascinated. We've paid since, though. By doing nothing, plenty has happened. From nothing, plenty." The Ne'vermaker smiled sadly. "What's that phrase: evil happens when good folk do nothing. Well, we did nothing."

Glide thought of his father. He'd been a great one for doing nothing. Not idle, though. Not lazy enough to be idle. Not committed enough to do nothing. His nothing was: don't stir the waters, keep your head down, they cut down tall poppies, don't they. See where it had got him. Glide was all for sticking his neck out. Except where it had mattered. And where had that gotten him? In an office. Like father, like son.

One person acts. If for good then a paradise is created. For bad, then hell. *Evil happens when good folk do nothing.* In that moment, that heady moment, Glide committed himself. He'd help. He'd act for good. There was just one thing, another one thing, this flower of time. An inner voice said, "Hold on, don't tell them you're committed yet. Find out more. You might yet make a committed withdrawal." Aloud, he said, "Isn't there an antidote for this time business?"

"For the herb, yes."

"But not for?"

"Herbs plus spells. Or just her. The combination is in her. Just as a rabbit will freeze before a snake, she has that power. She learnt to focus the flower of time so that with one look, she could freeze you."

"Oh, come on! Suggestibility. A temporary shock."

"Knowing the flower, a very powerful suggestion."

"Then since I don't know it, I must be immune."

"Glide!" The Ne'vermaker grabbed him. "Don't be such a fool. We are not talking metaphors. Strongarm is not merely a metaphor. It is not merely a temporary aberration that he manifests as an elephant!"

Glide, however, hadn't been listening. When grabbed, he'd reacted by twisting the Ne'vermaker's wrist. The latter was grimacing with pain until a great clout sent Glide flying. He was then peppered with punches.

They ceased only when the Ne'vermaker cried, "Stop! Stop immediately."

Hernandes stepped back. Glide shook his head. He glowered at Strongarm. "That's not fair, hitting me with your... your... your nose."

"I could've kicked you," Strongarm growled, lifting a foot that would've sent Glide a continent away.

But Ne'wang was grinning. "No worries, mate." He patted Glide on the shoulder. "It's just what we want, the fighting spirit. But you don't yet have the skill. You wouldn't be immune. It's like, oh, like electricity. You can't see it or hear it or smell it. But stick your fingers in a socket and you'll certainly feel it. Argot, as she used to be, hits the electricity in your neurones. Your nerves no longer conduct, they're suddenly frozen."

At that, the Ne'vermaker waved his spear. Glide felt the air around him thicken. He moved and it felt as if he were underwater. Another move and it felt as though his arms were glued to his sides. He tried to shout. The words were slow bubbles that reached his mouth but dribbled into nothing. There was a silence, a thick silence, the silence of a hungry lion approaching on soft pads. Then, with heartfelt relief, the world broke through again. Sight and sound tumbled in. Glide gasping, groped for the bench.

"What," he croaked, "was that?"

"Just a suggestions." Hernandes grinned smugly.

"Not for real," Strongarm added.

"That was Slowtime." The Ne'vermaker sat back and watched.

Glide put his hand to his mouth, wanting to retch. As he did so, Plonkers came out. He sniffed the air. "'Ere," he said, "'oos been doin' magic? Come on, own up. Yer know the rules, no magic at the bar."

He glared at them. But Ne'wang slowly raised his spear again. Without waiting for an answer, Plonkers gathered up his apron and rushed back inside the inn.

"Right, mate." Glide removed his hand from his mouth so that he could again hold onto the bench, "so it's not all suggestion. What about Strongarm? I don't want to be turned into no elephant."

"It has some benefits," Strongarm said gloomily.

"Yeah? What are they?"

"Like this. Calling one, two, three. Calling one, two, three."

"What the hell's that?"

"A trunk call. Ha, ha, ha." With a down-turned mouth, Strongarm stomped into the forest.

Glide stared after him. "Was he always like that?" he asked. "Or has being an elephant addled his brains?"

"The idea of a trunk call must've travelled through the gateways." The Ne'vermaker ran a hand through his hair. "Ideas seem to seep both ways."

Glide jutted his chin forward. "So is this gateway on another continent? Do you know that for sure?"

Ne'wang shook his head. "Not a continent. The magic extends over a number of islands and this is one of them. The gateways go to several places in Ausphalia. The old folk also knew about Afrika and Amerika. I think it once went to Atlantis, as well. So we get some odd people here and we don't always know where they came from."

"Crazy." Glide shook his head from side to side then quickly stopped. It hurt too much with the rotgut sloshing from side to side.

"But as for Strongarm?" the Ne'vermaker shook his head. "He's lucky he wasn't changed into a toad. But still, it's not easy for him, Glide. A sacrifice was made for him. A sacrifice to which he would never have agreed. An unexpected sacrifice for which he can never forgive himself."

Chapter 15

"Strongarm comes from a family of heroes," the Ne'vermaker began. "There was Strongleg, Strongbow, Strongneck...."

"Redneck?"

"Strongknee...."

"Strongnose." Glide tried not to smirk. "Okay, okay, I get the picture."

"Two years ago, at the age of eighteen."

"He's only twenty! He's a big boy for his age."

"A few thousand kilo," the Ne'vermaker said vaguely. "But elephants are big, you know. Good thing they don't hop like roos."

"Jeez, no! You'd disappear into their footprints."

"Well, Strongarm could be a heavy walker if he wanted to. But brains, too, and plenty of initiative. He came here in search of adventure."

"Like I came?"

"Not quite. In fact, quite different." Ne'wang stamped his spear into the ground. "He travelled by boat from a distant land. And, after the usual collection of heroic journeyings, he fell through a gateway and arrived here."

Glide felt a dash of envy. He, too, had wanted the usual collection of heroic journeyings. It wasn't his fault that he'd worked in an office. Well... maybe it partly was. But hadn't he... he... Well, he'd head butted punch bags? What had Strongarm done?

"So what," He tried to sound nonchalant, "was the usual collection of heroic journeyings?"

"Oh, you know. Rescuing maidens from dragons, some dragons from ex-maidens, plus he moseyed with minotaurs in a maze."

"Huh!" Glide grunted. "Nothing to what I had to face in the Civilian Service!"

"Just so." Glide's jaw dropped at this quiet agreement. "Your fantasies were pretty horrific. The greyness, the never-ending greyness. Strongarm's adventures were much more concrete and picturesque. He hadn't, however, found his own true quest. Not till he came to Auslan, that is, and here he fell deeply in love with Cascade."

Cascade! At the name, a thrill ran through Glide. He didn't know why but he immediately pictured her as silver and green. Suddenly everything made sense and he knew why he was here. To meet her. To rescue her. Why else would he help Auslan?

Auslan? Glide startled. "Is Auslan the name of this place?"

"No one's told you?" The Ne'vermanker looked doubtfully at Glide.

"Er, I don't think so." The young man scratched his head. So much had happened in so short a time, he couldn't remember.

"Auslan is here." Ne'wang again stamped his spear onto the ground. "Inklan is down there." He pointed at the forest. "As is Cascade."

Once more, Glide tingled at the name. At the same time, he resented her link to Strongarm. Just fancy. How could a beautiful girl like that fall for an elephant.

"Cascade," Ne'wang continued dreamily, "my own daughter. She was, I can honestly say, a beautiful young woman, a beautiful spirit. Every man was in love with her. Every person was. Only Strongarm, though, could match her in luminosity."

Acid was honey compared to the way that Glide said, "So you set him a mighty tusk."

"He set himself one."

"Jokes," Hernandes cut in. "Haves some more Green Mist, it helps the jealousies."

"You jealous?" Glide asked the imp in surprise.

"He did say every mans. I am of the gender mans if not quite of the species Homo Saps."

Just then, Strongarm re-emerged from the forest. "Cascade?" He waggled his huge ears. "Are you talking about her? Ah, Cascade. What wouldn't I do for her?"

"What did you do?" Glide muttered.

"In those days," the Ne'vermaker said smoothly, "Argot had been banished to Inklan. I, well, I only had an intermittent grip here. It gave Argot the opportunity to use her understanding of the flower of time to set up a barrier, the Slowtime. To step into it was to totally freeze."

Glide shuddered, first with fear then with anger. Didn't he know what it was like to freeze? Hadn't he done time in the Civilian Service? "So," he said, "and Strongarm tried to break down this barrier?"

"In a way." The Ne'verman sighed. "So many things to tell. Argot wouldn't let her followers escape. Though many wanted to after a little time with her. Her new persona."

"Persona and a halfs," Hernandes said.

"Three and a half," Strongarm said. "You may as well tell the lot."

"The lot!" Plonkers shouted from the bar. "Includin' stealin' me best swanmead."

"Yes, you see once Argot found the essence of time, in a way, she became it. With eyes and fingers, she could control it. As there was a barrier of Slowtime around Inklan, those that wanted to escape had to confront her. The few who faced her became a lesson to the many that wanted. With that victory, Argot became bolder. She started to kidnap the people of Auslan."

"Far out!" Glide exclaimed. "She must be awesome!"

"Not her alone," The Ne'vermaker sighed, "she had enough willing helpers."

"From here?"

"No, from far lands, other gateways. Giant Dwarves and green imps, for instance. Plus people who had always been in conflict with Auslan."

Glide shook his head. "Did... did you just say Giant Dwarves?"

"Yes."

"Isn't that a sort of contradiction? I mean, aren't dwarves small by definition? Isn't a Giant Dwarf just a sort of knobbly man?

"Ah, well." The Ne'vermaker scratched his head. "Yes, I suppose. In the same way that a gorilla is just a sort of hairy man."

"Oh!"

"You want some differences. Well, for one, and this one is enough, dwarves are magical. Argot's helper is Haggort and he can make himself invisible."

"Haggort his names and Haggort his natures," Hernandes hissed.

Glide snorted. "Invisible, you say? I'm a scientist and I say that's impossible."

"You do, do you, mate?" the Ne'vermaker said. "What about crocs, you ever see crocs?"

"Uh, yeah, in Krockadu." Glide pictured one. He could remember eyes, just eyes. Then they, too, disappeared. But they still watched. He knew that. A thrown fish had been gulped immediately. Otherwise, they were, and a light dawned, invisible. "I see," he murmured. "So that's Haggis, is it?"

"Haggort. Lumpy and dumpy. Short legs and wide arms. Wide across as he is tall. Absolutely still and he merges. Like a rock, probably has some troll in him."

"A Giant Dwarf with a touch of troll?" Glide shook his head in wonder.

"If I could get my hands, er legs, er trunk on him," Strongarm trumpeted.

"A friend of yours?"

"An ignorant stump! That's all he is, an ignorant stump."

Strongarm stamped the earth so hard that grass flew up and hit another group. They began to protest but the Ne'vermaker held up a hand. In the ensuing silence, he said, "Don't forget Greenvort, the green imp. A true mischief maker, an organiser, a carrier of Argot's magic."

"Who is Argot no longer," Strongarm said sadly.

"Who is Argot no longer," the Ne'vermaker echoed. "Argot of the golden skin and the golden hair. More and more, she shunned the sun and more and more, she dwelt in the dark. So that with her alchemy, her skin changed and her hair changed. No longer Argot, by a wicked humour, she called herself Maggot, Maggot Thwacka. She sold her beauty for power."

"And that was your wife?

"And Cascade our daughter."

"Oh, jeez, this is sort of Friedian, isn't it?" Glide felt sick. Families sure knew how to create a hell or two. "It's Oedipal or something? Your wife kidnapping your daughter!"

"No, no," Strongarm groaned. "I was the one they caught! When they first began to take people from here, I started to train them to fight. When I had some trusty men...."

"And imps!"

"And imps. We attacked. I led the way."

"Wasn't there this, er, barrier of Slowtime?"

"Not yet. We approached at dawn, not a good time for the Maggot. But her eyes in the raven, Goresh, saw us and warned her."

"Her ice in the raven, Goresh?" Glide blinked. "Her ice in the raving Goresh?" He turned to the Ne'vermaker. "My parsing's gone. Please explain."

"Goresh is a bird," Strongarm trumpeted, "a raven. Maggot Thwacka the Witch can see and hear through the raven. So she heard of our attack. Though if it hadn't been Goresh, other of her... animations would've warned her."

"Animations?" Glide was being swamped with new ideas. None of which he liked. "Don't tell me Bugs Bunny is on her side?" He drummed the table. Strongarm and Cascade? Cascade and Strongarm. He couldn't come to terms with that.

"Don't mock, Glide," the Ne'vermaker said. "She commands strange forces, forces which live in armour."

This was too much. "Oh," Glide said glibly, "you mean ghosts which go clank-clank in the k-night."

"You're don't believe in ghosts?"

"Never heard of one which could stand in the light of science."

"Hmm." The Ne'vermaker looked down at the ground. Then, without raising his head, he moved his eyes to stare at Glide. The latter took half a step back. "You might have a problem there, son," the blue man said. "You just might."

"Oh!" Glide's mouth formed a small 'o'. Pulling it straight, he managed to squeeze out, "Nothing wrong with scientific analysis."

"Maybe." The Ne'vermaker suddenly beamed. "On the other hand, ghosts may simply be projections from other gateways. Very scientific. Who can say? So Strongarm, what were you saying?"

Matching Glide's drumming of fingers, the elephant had been rhythmically thumping his trunk on the table. Glide put his hands on the top and his arms vibrated.

"We easily made it through her men," Strongarm said.

"Mens in the broad senses," Hernandes put in.

"In the broad sense," Strongarm concurred. Then added, "Oh, shut up, Hernandes. Stop being so defensive, there's good and bad in all. Except maybe in elephants." He shook his massive head. "Still who's to say since I'm the only one around here. Still." There was a heavy silence, the sort of heavy silence that only a sad six-ton elephant could make. Then, with a swish of his trunk, Strongarm swept it all away. "We brushed them aside like flies," he cried, "and entered the Maggot's domain. Only two rows of armour separated us from her. Two rows of armour," he muttered.

"And Haggorts the Giant Dwarves. And Greenvorts the Twisted Imps."

"And Greenvort." Strongarm was silent again, remembering. "He was the one. Through him, the Witch could invoke wicked homunculi, spirits that occupied the armour. They could be seen as green lights behind the visors, green fireworks. I chopped off the head of the first one but its mouth still bit the unwary. I lopped off the arm of the second but the stump still slashed. I hacked off the legs of the third but then they kicked me from behind. In short, the more that I cut down the more that I had attacking me.

"In no time, my men fled. Who could blame them? But I was surrounded and so fought on till my body had become like butter. Then a shadow moved in the shadows. Stealthily, swiftly, it moved. I caught only flickers from the corners of my eyes. But I knew it was Haggort. It had to be Haggort! He'd been motionless for the whole duration of the fight. Now he moved. A net flew through the air. I rolled. But fragments of that cursed armour blocked my way. Another net enveloped me. I cut at it but a metal ball struck my sword away. A third net trussed me."

Strongarm gasped for air, reliving the panic of the moment. "My men had been allowed to escape but only in order to tell of my capture. I was alone. Then Maggot Thwacka the Witch appeared. I hadn't seen her before and seeing her was a shock. The Ne'vermaker had told us how beautiful she had been and, as the mother of Cascade, I couldn't expect her to be otherwise. Yet, now, she was not beautiful. Not ugly either. Worse, something much much worse. Her hair was blue, a crinkly blue, and it crackled as if an electrical storm raged through it. Her skin was tough and mottled as if pinched from an old crocodile."

"She probably ates the poor croc," Hernandes said.

"Swallowed it 'ole," Plonkers shouted. "She'd go the 'ole 'og, that one!"

"Sounds like you had a rough time," Glide murmured.

"Rough? That was nothing. The worse thing was her laugh. Laugh? Her laugh was like hyenas in a graveyard. No, the worse thing was her walk. Walk? Her walk was like the scuttle of a spider with arthritis."

Glide had never seen a hysterical elephant, certainly not a talking hysterical one. But Strongarm was definitely that now. His voice rose shrilly and sweat flew off him like a broken down shower.

"In short," Glide said, trying to make light, "you didn't like her."

"In short," Plonkers bellowed, "she was 'orrible!"

"In shorts. And in longs," Hernandes concluded.

"She fixed me with Slowtime," Strongarm whispered, still shivering. "Manacled and trussed into Slowtime, I didn't stand a chance."

There was a silence. Plonkers came out, wiping his hands on his apron. He shook his head. "The worst is yet t'come."

"But you're here now," Glide said. "You did get out."

"Yes, I did get out." A big tear trickled down the long grey cheek. "I did get out. Love released me."

"Love? Cascade?"

"Cas...cade."

"Strongarm had no idea what was happening back home," Ne'wang said. "And I had only a temporary foothold. So Cascade took it upon herself to trade. Her for him. No one could stop her. I flickered in and out of their world, a ghost unable to help. Strongarm was captive in Slowtime. Frozen in time, he was carried out of their castle by Haggort. The Witch released him and he staggered towards Cascade. They embraced, only for him to see her run towards the castle. The Witch laughed. She reached inside Cascade's mind, searching for what she loved. With the combined powers of Haggort and Greenvort, she linked the two great loves of Cascade's life. And made a mockery."

"An elephant?"

"Brought when Cascade was young. There was a great thunder of feet and a huge trumpeting. Strongarm had been transformed. He rushed in a blind rage towards the Witch but I managed to head him off. I could sense the field of Slowtime. Strongarm went beserk. He crashed down trees, overturned rocks and crashed through walls. I wasn't able to stay here for long, yet when I did, I went directly to him."

"Hell!" Glide shook his head in shock. "That was terrible. And you can't turn him back?"

"No."

"Can anyone?"

The Ne'vermaker looked directly at Glide.

"Me? No. No way. I can't do it. I don't even know how to start."

"You have a special skill, Glide. Your mind called me and it is only your mind that can fix me here. It is no exaggeration to say that the future of Auslan depends on you."

"On me? Oh, no! Oh, bugger!"

The enormity and horror of what was being asked of him finally struck Glide. He looked frantically around, searching for an escape. In desperation, he turned to his only source.

"Plonkers," he shouted. "Plonkers, a rotgut. And make it a big one."

Chapter 16

Green Mist exploded in Glide's overworked brain like steam through paper. In imitation of Ne'wang, he toppled backwards. He hit the ground, his mind a blank. Immediately, the Ne'vermaker also toppled. But he didn't hit the ground, he just vanished out of Auslan. Showing a remarkable fluency in multi-lingual abuse, Hernandes rushed to Glide. He lifted his head and lightly slapped him across the face. Strongarm dipped his trunk in a bucket and squirted cold water. Between slaps and slurps, Glide came to. He was relieved to see a familiar constellation of stars circling above him.

"Just a dream," he muttered, "a crazy dream." He raised a hand and it went right through the stars. "Not stars." He waved his hand about. "Concussion. That's the constellation I got when I used to nut the punch bag."

A face floated in the air above him, as disembodied as the Cheshire cat's smile. He blinked a few times and the face seemed to come and go. Tentatively, Glide poked at blue flesh.

"Hey, mate, keep your fingers to yourself."

Glide growled back, though mentally. It was no good, whatever he did, this delusion had a reality of its own. With reluctance, he sat up. An elephant, an imp and a Ne'verman swam within his field of vision. Making the effort to focus, they resolved into individual figures.

"Damn and strawberries!" Glide looked at each in turn. "It's a nightmare, a horrible nightmare."

"Well, it ain't a dream," Ne'wang said firmly. "You're here whilst I'm between here and there. But we want to swap places. So tomorrow, we start your training."

"Oh, yeah?" Glide struggled to his feet. "What did you say it's for?"

"So you can leave. So I can stay. So Strongarm can return to being a man. To free Cascade. And to save Auslan."

"Is that all?"

"It's a start."

Glide gazed at the people around him, at the tables of the inn, and beyond to the forest. It should all have been so peaceful. It wasn't. Wherever there were people, there was trouble.

He sighed. "What do we do?"

"We work up the same skill that called me."

"Oh?" Glide fumbled for the few thoughts that had accompanied his last moments on familiar territory. They slipped away. "How was that?"

"Your ability to visualise."

"Visualise? Oh, yeah." His head pounded. "I think I'm gonna be sick." He remembered now about visualisation. It was how he'd done so well at anatomy. He could see pictures in his mind. But to do it, he'd just have to concentrate. Concentrate? That was just another word for nausea. He had to lie down again. To close his eyes and to shut out the world. "Bed?" he groaned. "You gotta bed for me? We were going to the palace. What happened to the palace?" Glide pushed up from the bench and staggered a few steps. Strongarm heaved forward just in time to catch him. "A trunk call," Glide mumbled. "A trunk fall. Trunk fool. Drunk fool."

As the young man slid into semi-consciousness, Hernandes, Plonkers and the sometimes-present Ne'vermaker lifted him onto Strongarm's wide back. Hernandes gently rearranged Glide's untidy limbs. They made a solemn procession back to the forest. Glide had the vague impression of being placed on a bed of leaves at the foot of a tree.

"I didn't mean a flower bed." He opened his eyes and saw a strange figure coming and going. He quickly closed his eyes again. "Wottabout my palace?"

"It's safer outside," the Ne'vermaker said, his voice also flickering.

Placed horizontally, Glide sank from nausea into nausea. As his mind swung from one state to another, the Ne'vermaker either blurred or sharpened. After a while, though, Glide gave up. At that, the Ne'vermaker groaned and multiple images of a blue man tumbled through each other. Then he was gone and the air ringed with his absence.

Strongarm shook his vast head in disgust and wheeled off. Hernandes, however, jumped astride his roo and raced after him. "Hey, where you goings?" he shouted.

"To finish my jog!"

"Is it that importants to keep fits?"

"It's not the keeping fit. It's to keep my blood from boiling out of my ears. We need a hero and what do we get? A Glide! A pen pusher. A dreamer. An analyst."

"Well, muscles didn't works."

"What!" Strongarm rose massively on his hind legs. Balanced like an avalanche, he trumpeted, a shrill uncomfortable sound. High above, a raven cackled. Strongarm looked up. He recognised Goresh as the raven's laughter funnelled mockingly into his big ears. "Caw... Caw... Cas... Cas... Cascade, Cascade." Strongarm balanced briefly in the air. Then his weight crashed down and his head sank between his knees.

Hernandes reached upwards and stroked the huge shaggy dome. "It'll be olrights," he murmured. "You'll see, it'll be olrights."

Echoes of that shrill trumpet penetrated Glide's sleep and caused him to dream. In this dream, he triumphed, miraculously conquering the Witch and rescuing Cascade. To a triumphant brass band, he returned home, home to Brissie. Funny, though, but the dream left him sad. Where were the others, his new friends? Where, most importantly, was Cascade, the beautiful Cascade? But when there were no repetition of Strongarm's heavenly trumpets, Glide drifted into the nether world of Green Mist. A few fermenting neurones popped but there weren't enough to conjure either ghosts or nightmares.

Glide awoke at dawn. A pinkish blue light came in from a window. He looked around, wondering where he was. He'd been transported. He remembered that. Then he'd... He wasn't sure but it had ended with drink. That he remembered as well. Now, he appeared to be inside a thatched cottage. Nice, he thought, very rural.

He drifted off again to be woken a second time by the cheerful sounds of people going off to work. Did he hear steam buses and steam cars? No. Oh-ho! The light was brighter now and the window let in a brighter patch of blue. There was also a dark figure, ever falling into itself. *That's a dream I've had before*, Glide thought, and his eyes shuttered closed again.

The third time that he awoke, Glide saw a grey flying snake. "Hmm, it's a dream within a dream." And he waited for sleep within sleep to claim him again. When it didn't and a blue face appeared beneath the flying snake, he grunted. When a ruddy round face appeared beneath the others, he really began to worry.

"You readys?" said a ruddy voice.

"Readys? Readys for what?" Glide came up on an elbow.

At the sight of the three faces, though, the events of the previous night came flooding in. He'd been placed on a bed of leaves and that bed was in a thatched hut. And the three faces that were staring at him were familiar faces. And instead of his clothes, cool linen pressed against his skin. Linen against his body! His bare flesh!

"Where're me clothes?" Glide wildly looked around him.

"Those smelly things!" said the top voice with the long grey snake of a trunk.

"For offices only," said the bottom voice.

"They're being washed, Glide," said the dark middle voice.

"Look, mate," Glide hissed, "You want me to fight your battles. Right? Right! Then olright. But damn me if I'm going to do it in the nuddie. Starkers. Blow me if I'm gonna face a Witch without a stitch!"

"Oh, the Witch has a stitch," the Ne'vermaker said. "Like a bloke has a spoke."

"What's that got to do with the price of cheese." Glide rested his chin on his bent knees. "Get me some clobber."

"On the chair, Glide." The Ne'vermaker pointed with his spear. "We'll wait outside."

The three heads withdrew. To Glide's right was a cane chair with a bundle on it. He picked up the first item. It was a pair of white linen trousers, with a cord through the top and flairs at the bottom. Rather pleased, he pulled them on. The shirt was a pebbly white with a deep vee at the neck and fringes all around. Now he was getting somewhere. These were hero's clothes. Not bad. The outfit was completed with soft but sturdy moccasins. Glide dressed and stepped outside.

"Well," he said grudgingly, "here I am."

"Here you ares," Hernandes agreed. "Not bads. Not bads at all."

"You look fit enough." Strongarm walked around the young man. "A few muscles here and there. You must've used a heavy pen."

"Some of his muscles are in his head," the Ne'vermaker said.

Glide winced. "You're not wanting me to think now, are you?"

"No, not now. Not in the way you mean."

"There's another way? How does one.... oomph"

Strongarm had closed Glide's mouth with his trunk. "Not now. No more questions. Breakfast first."

"Good idea," Glide said inside the trunk.

Strongarm quickly pulled it away. "Hey, that tickles." He sneezed, sending Hernandes flying.

Glide burst out laughing. Immediately, the Ne'vermaker also flipped endlessly backwards. "Stop laughing, Glide." His voice came in fading waves. "This is serious."

But that only set Glide off more. Hernandes rose, cross-eyed, and staggered forwards. Glide held his sides. "And you're at war, too," he roared. "You must be a gas when you're at peace." His mirth, delayed hysteria, only came to a stop when Hernandes stamped on his foot. Glide hopped on one leg, spluttering. When he finally came to a halt, he weakly said, "Oh, well, what next?"

A dark voice took shape by his ear. "Breakfast for you, Glide. I've got a sit-in to attend to."

"A sit-in? As in a protest?"

"Yup. There's a coal mine scheduled at a sacred site. They've gotta keep the steam cars going."

"Oh? What'll you do?"

"The usual, I guess. Bang my head against police batons. Put myself in jail for a few days. May even manage a holiday in hospital. But don't you worry about that, I'll be okay. You go ahead and eat. I'll catch up with you later. Ouch!" The voice came from far away. "That hurt!"

Glide gazed into the air with guilt. Ausphalia could be tough for the Ne'vermen. The cup that was half-full promised that when he got back, he'd do something to help them. The cup that was half-empty wondered if he'd ever get back. Being between cups, Strongarm nudged him forward until they arrived at an open-air kitchen. Glide gazed around puzzled. The spread of tables and the skyline of trees were vaguely familiar.

"This is, er, Plonkers, isn't it?" He lifted the corner of a white linen tablecloth. Underneath were the scarred tables of the previous night. "It is." He held his head at the memory.

"That was Plonkers' Tavern," Strongarm said. "This is Plonkers' Breakfast Bar."

Glide extended his arms. "In the spirit of capitalism, I name thee Plonkers."

"Better the fruit of the vine than digging up coal, Glide," a distant voice observed.

Then, as they sat at a table, Ne'wang the Ne'vermaker offered progress reports on his sit-in. It meant that Glide's fruit salad was deliciously speckled with insult and his toast was smoothly spread with injury. Glide squinted into the hazy air.

"You clever bugger!" he swore. "You sure know how to use guilt! You certainly know how to pull my strings! Okay, I'll now help you! Now, and not when – correction, if - I ever get back to Ausphalia!"

Chapter 17

"He's awake, you say! Thank you, Haggort, thank you. Your powers of perception are amazing! You are Captain of the Guard, the Chief High Fighter and the Keeper of the Fist. But that's all you can tell me? That he is awake!"

"Bud your..."

"And that he likes toast!"

"Bud..."

"With milk in his coffee!"

"B..."

"Do you know what Slowtime is? Do you know what it feels like when the whole of your present hangs before you in excruciating detail, knowing that your future goes on without you, passing you by? Do you know? Do you?"

Maggot Thwacka's voice reached a peak of shrillness. Haggort, desperately not showing it, shivered. His guts turned to warm jelly and threatened to run down the inside of his legs. Behind him, Greenvort was trying to hide. His skin had turned to the green of a sick frog, a very sick frog.

"I want to know why he's here," the Witch hissed, her blue hair crackling. "And I want you to tell me more than I can get through the dumb head of an arthritic raven more than an hour's flight away."

"Yeah, yeah, your Witch...."

"Your Maggot...ss, your Honour...."

"I'll crawl to my pitch,"

"And ss...soon we'll discover,"

"Wot makes him tick."

"Go!" Maggot Thwacka screamed. "Go before I act!" The two turned and scuttled out. The Witch paced the room, her bones cracking with every step. "Fools for henchmen," she cried. "And they think they're poets." Her gaze turned to Cascade, frozen in her webby corner. "I'll get you to join me yet. See if I don't." In a grand gesture, she threw her head back to laugh but three vertebrae in her neck painfully popped. Being a Witch wasn't meant to be easy.

Haggort and Greenvort slunk past the suits of armour. The Giant Dwarf made a threatening gesture at one but the homunculus within hit out with a fist of iron. Haggort cursed and leapt aside. Greenvort, though, whipped out a piece of chalk and scrawled graffitti on the metallic back.

That little act of defiance was enough to cheer them. Chuckling, they crossed the Slowmoat to where a man was working. He tried to scurry away but, in a bout of good humour, Haggort picked him up and held half of him upside down in the moat of Slowtime. The man looked sick as signals sped from one part of his body to crash into the traffic jam on the other. They giggled when Haggort dropped him, leaving one arm free, and the man scrabbled frantically to pull himself out with it. When the two henchmen were further on, another man fearfully came to help the first.

"Look at that," Haggort growled, "while we work, dey shirk."

"It's an unfair thing," Greenvort agreed. "Sstill, one day, you'll be the king."

"Yeah, king, den I'll definitely have my fling." A smiled smeared itself across Haggort's face, a smile that would've made a crocodile jealous.

On their way to spy on Glide, they took secret paths between huge rocks, pushed through narrow tunnels and stood immobile among clumps of thin trees. In this way, they managed to evade imps on roos and men on horseback. With sly winks and nudges, they congratulated themselves on their cleverness. That is, Haggort congratulated Haggort and Greenvort congratulated Greenvort.

Nearing Evertall, the village in the jungle, they spilt up. Not into their constituents parts, unfortunately, but just in the sense that they went their separate and evil ways. The Imp merged into the greenery above Glide's hut. The Giant Dwarf climbed into a high tree overlooking the training area.

With no training happening, Haggort looked for ways to occupy himself. A butterfly fluttered by, enjoying the breeze, it touched lightly on the leaves. Haggort waited, breathing internally only, not letting a particle of self to escape. The rainbow creature drifted too close. A huge hand shot out. Wings battered heedlessly against the enclosing palm. With a broad grin, Haggort popped the butterfly into his mouth. A few grubs served as dessert.

At a change in the air, Haggort froze. Glide came out of Plonkers Breakfast Bar with Strongarm and Hernandes at his side. The Giant Dwarf was pleased to see that they were headed in his direction. The hairs in his big ears vibrated like antennae as they picked words out of the air.

"Where's Ne'wang?" Glide asked.

"Are you ready to work?" Strongarm replied.

"What sort of work?"

"What do you think?"

"To teach fighting?"

"You don't think I can do that?" Strongarm's tone rose defensively.

"Er, yeah, sure. You just need to break it down a bit more. You know, like do one-step sparring before you do free sparring." They were walking from the shade provided by Plonkers' trees towards the open area used for training. Glide looked across the space. His scalp tingled with a curious unease. Yet he saw nothing disturbing. "So what is the work that I should be doing?"

Strongarm wriggled his trunk as if making pictures in the air. For some moments, it pointed straight at Haggort and the Giant Dwarf froze. "Think," Strongarm said. "Think hard. What is the Ne'vermaker asking you?"

"To fix him here."

"That's right." Strongarm drew the outline of a man with his trunk. "It's to do with your ability to visualise, Glide. You have to learn to visualise the Ne'vermaker. To concentrate so intensely that you fix him here."

Glide wondered what could make him visualise so intently. He couldn't just furrow his brow and make it happen. No, he had to approach the task indirectly. He needed the emotions that underlie the intensity and that meant those dark emotions of yesterday. Yesterday? Yesterday, he had awoken drowning in self-hate, awoken to his constant baggage of self-pity. He felt again for the darkness that had accompanied it. Depression had enveloped him so completely it had numbed him to the rest of the world. He had been so blue that it had seeped out of him and congealed into the surrounding air. The darkness had, in fact, become Ne'wang the Ne'vermaker.

Even as Glide imagined it, the air shimmered. The ground seemed to rise up out of itself. Again and again, it rose but only to fall back. From above, Haggort watched. So this was it, he saw. Glide could summon the Ne'vermaker. But what an effort. The blue man was no more than a shimmer of light on the surface of a flat pool. Huh! No problem. One tap from Haggort's horny hand would bring an end to that illusory effort. He chuckled. They had nothing to fear from here.

Or did they? For despite his failures, Glide continued. The shimmer came and went and came again but with more substance. Eventually, though exhausted, or perhaps because of it, Glide managed to solidify the Ne'vermaker. But what a difference to his previous appearance. This time, the Ne'verman was wearing jeans and his shirt was torn.

Glide was shocked. "What happened?"

"A civic protest."

"The police?" Glide's eyes opened wide.

"Nah, it ain't always the white fellas. Our people're the same as yours. This time it was blue - white and brindle against blue, white and brindle."

He stuck his spear into the ground, raised his left leg and cupped it into his right hand. He opened his mouth to speak. But then, in his usual fashion, he first stopped to listen. The Ne'vermaker listened with all his senses, having what Strongarm the elephant lacked: animal smarts. Strongarm still thought of himself as just a man and so, except for his awkward bulk, he denied the reality of also being an elephant. So he never used his new senses to their full, never used his newly given intuitions and instincts. The Ne'vermaker, however, had worked hard to extend himself. All the time, he was like an animal that had just gone down to the water's edge. Senses that had no name were always alert. Before he spoke, they rippled out. As they did so, a tiny disturbance tweaked the edge of his mind. Ne'wang closed his eyes. He began to sniff. His nostrils widened. With a slow in and out breath, he tasted the streams of flowing air. Unnamed senses became sharper and more focussed.

In his bower, Haggort tried to become stiller than still. He tried not to breath, to contain every last particle, to prevent the least molecule from escaping. But in a body as dense as his, even his thought molecules were as pungent as most people's armpits. And particles, delighted to escape from Haggort, tumbled and rolled happily on flowing streams of air. Streams of air that continued to enter the Ne'vermaker's questing nostrils. Into nostrils that were remarkable instruments for the testing of molecules.

"Somewhere near," the Ne'vermaker said, "is a Giant Dwarf."

"Haggort!" Strongarm roared. Rising on his hind legs, he trumpeted, "It's Haggort! Haggort is here!"

In a contrasting mildness, Ne'wang said, "Yes. Probably."

"Shall I find him? Trample him to dust?"

"No, no. He will slink away before we can find him. No." The Ne'verman gazed thoughtfully at Glide. "But if he can come this close, it means that we need to hide you while you train."

"Hide?" Glide said.

"In a big hut?" Strongarm looked back towards Plonkers' Breakfast Bar.

"Undergrounds?" Hernandes hopped on Horsey, listening out for below ground echoes.

"No. Glide must develop two skills. One for him, one for us." The Ne'vermaker turned on the spot like a slowed down top. His spear pointed. "He has to adjust to the outdoors. So we must hide him in the open."

"Can't I just wear a false moustache and a wig?"

But it was too late for Glide to make a suggestion. Ne'wang the Ne'vermaker had stopped turning. He wore a dreamy look. He was about to use more magic.

Chapter 18

"Hides him in the open?" Hernandes said. "How? Turn him into a puff of winds?"

"My wind?" Strongarm suggested.

"Hey, guys." Glide threw out his arms in protest.

"Now, now," Ne'wang tapped his spear on the earth, "stop squabbling. Strongarm fetch logs. Hernandes find thatching. Glide, bring your bedding."

With mutterings from all three, they trotted away in different directions. The Ne'vermaker walked thoughtfully to the centre of the empty training area. At one spot, he dug his spear into the ground. Holding it with one hand, he turned the other palm to the sky. After a few moments of absolute stillness, he shook his head. He tried again and again until at one spot, he gave a satisfied nod and drew a circle in the earth with his spear.

In his nook, Haggort frowned. "A power site," he muttered. "Dat might be okay for you. What about fer him?"

His frown turned into a sneer when Glide stumbled into the clearing, a mattress bouncing on his head. "Put it down." The Ne'vermaker motioned him over. "I want to try an experiment."

"Experiment?" Glide tapped at his pockets. "Test tubes? Bunsen burners?"

"Hmm." The Ne'vermaker scratched the back of his head with his spear. It made a scraping sound. "That's me thinking," he said, "the cogs whirring. Nah, we might do that later. For now, I just want you to imagine me."

"Imagine you? What's the point? I can see you."

"What? Oh yeah, that's right." There was a blur as the Ne'vermaker fell through a gateway. "Right, now imagine me."

"Where are you?" Glide peered into thin air. Seeing no one, however, he shrugged. "Never mind." He closed his eyes and told himself to visualise. At first, nothing happened. Yet as he continued, he forgot to tell himself anything and actually concentrated instead. A blue outline formed in his mind.

"Not bad, not bad," said the voice in his ear. "Walk a few steps and try again." Glide opened his eyes. "Keep them closed! Keep them closed!" the voice commanded.

Eyes screwed up, Glide carefully moved forward. As he did so, the image sharpened. He edged to one side and it blurred. He went to the other and it became sharper still. "Good, good," murmured the Ne'vermaker. "Now fine tune it."

"I'm tired," Glide complained.

"Puff of wind," Strongarm rumbled.

"Wind maker!"

Glide began to shuffle around the field, his awareness focussed on the inner image. It was an effort, though, and he yawned. Wouldn't it be nice just to go back to sleep. But one more step and he was jolted awake. His spine buzzed. The inner image sparkled and the hair on his head tried to climb out of his scalp. He opened his eyes, expecting to be reclining on a cloud. The outside, though tinged with blue, was otherwise normal. The Ne'vermaker was again at his side, smiling broadly.

Glide had found his special spot. Yet it did have unexpected ramifications.

"Booger!" Haggort muttered.

"Caw!" Goresh screamed.

"Ai...ii!" Maggot Thwacka keened, picking up the vibes. "Bloody raven!" She unfroze Cascade in her cobwebby corner. "Work!" she shrieked. "Work!"

Though Glide was not consciously aware of those ramifications, his unconsciousness was. "What the heck was that?" he exclaimed as spikes shot up in the depths of his mind.

Ne'wang, knowing only that Glide had projected him, said, "You drew me."

"Drew you? Looks like I bloody painted you in as well."

"Drew me *to* you."

Glide thought for a moment. He wasn't sure that he liked the implications. "What, I think of you and you appear? Hell, you mean I've got a instant bloody chaperone?"

"It's for your safety, Glide." The Ne'verman pointed to the spot left by his spear. "You're doing good, mate. That was my centre." He pointed again. "Yours was a toe away. We're in harmony." He scratched his spiky hair. "Well, occasionally. You'll see." He clapped Glide on the shoulder. "No worries, mate, we'll win yet."

"With us." Strongarm grinned. A grin so wide, it was scary. "Right, Hernandes?"

"Sure, sure," the imp agreed vigorously. "We are togethers, together. We might teases you, we might prods you, but we'll always spurs you on. In short, you can relies on us, man and imp."

"Elephant and imp."

"Elephants!" Hernandes whipped off his hat on threw it on the ground. "Calls him a man and he say he's an elephants! Calls him an elephants and he say he's a man!"

"I only said...!"

"And I saids...!"

"Quiet!" Ne'wang swung his spear in great arcs. Sparks shot out of it, tumbling over their bodies. The three jumped. Their mouths closed as four arms and one trunk brushed away the sparks. The spear came to a stop. "With friends like these..." the Ne'vermaker muttered.

There was a silence followed by a ragged and insincere chorus of sorries.

"Okay mates, we've got work to do. So let's do it."

They began the task of building a hut, finding that two men, one elephant and one imp can do an amazing amount of work when they acted together. Which they sometimes did. In just a couple of hours, they had a small thatched hut established in the centre of the training area.

"We'll post a guard at all times," the Ne'vermaker said with satisfaction. "No one will be able to get at you. Nor will they see what you're doing."

"Good. Great." Glide clapped his hands. "And what will I be doing?"

The Ne'vermaker carefully looked around. "Not out here," he said. "The trees have ears."

"I thought it was the walls?"

"The trees have walls?" Ne'wang turned to observe the trees.

"No, the walls have ears!"

"Corn has ears," the Ne'vermaker remarked absent-mindedly.

"Er." Glide shook his head. "You're right, not out here. Tell me inside. It might make sense."

"Wait, I feel a pull."

The Ne'vermaker silently entered the hut. He moved to the far side, his dark shape merging with the shadows. Glide waited a few moments then went to find him. But now there were only the shadows.

"Fine," he said to the air, "so don't tell me." He turned to the others. "Gone again. Amazing, isn't it?" Since no one else spoke, he felt compelled to answer himself. "Yes, very." Strongarm gazed at him from outside the hut. Glide shrugged. "Sometimes I'm in two minds."

"Forget your minds. Think about bodies." Hernandes bit at a cork dangling from his hat. "We need some foods."

"Good idea." Glide headed towards the door but a shadow passed over him. He paused and the next moment, he was nose to nose with a blue face. He jumped.

"Sorry, mate, got pulled away," the Ne'vermaker said, "Also I forgot to give you this."

Glide looked down. "What this?" He took another two steps and stood in the doorway. "A tin whistle. Is this a tin whistle from the Two-Dollar Shop?"

"No, mate! It's a very small trombone from the Opera House. Mate! Of course, it's a tin whistle."

Glide began to lift it to his lips. "No, don't!" The Ne'vermaker caught his wrist. "It'll blow my head off. This whistle will aid your visualisation. But, mate, only use it when you need me. And then, only in extreme circumstances." With that, he vanished.

Once more, Glide put the whistle to his lips. These were extreme circumstances. Just being here was extreme. He couldn't think of anything more extreme. He breathed out and then he prepared for one long and very deep breath in.

Chapter 19

Despite appearances to the contrary, Glide sometimes did actually listen. He stood for a moment in the doorway of the thatched hut as, holding his breath, his face went redder and redder. But before he exploded, he took the whistle from his lips and breathed out. He turned the short cylinder in his hands. He licked it and felt the coldness of the metal. He tried to play his fingers along its length. But it wasn't very long and only had one hole. He stepped into the light to take a good look at it. He hefted it and felt its weight. The whistle was just a school whistle. Pretty ordinary. No, wait! His old whistle did have one magical quality. One toot and all the stray dogs would come running.

Glide did do quite a few things with the new whistle - tasting it, hefting it and sniffing it. He even put it to his ear. Perhaps he'd hear the surf or, better still, echoes of Ausphalia. But one thing that he didn't do was to blow it.

He turned to the others. "D'yous have one, too?"

"Does this count?" Strongarm waved his trunk. "I don't think I could play a thing that small, anyway."

"I don't haves one," Hernandes said.

"Ever?"

"Never."

"Must've thought of et after Strongarm, er, you knows..."

"Converted."

"That's rights. Converted."

"Turned into a bloody great elephant," Strongarm said moodily. "Still, could've been worse. Cascade could've liked goldfish."

"The Witch would've turned you into a goldfish!" Glide was truly shocked. An elephant seemed comparatively human.

"Certainly," Strongarm replied, "with a leaky bowl."

In a thoughtful silence, Glide looked up at the sky. The sun dazzled him as if seen through a cracked goldfish bowl. "Right" He licked his lips, suddenly thirsty. "Plonkers."

"Haggort's still around," Strongarm said. "We'd better post a couple of guards."

Glide looked puzzled. "Where would we post them to?" His face cleared. "Sorry. Understood. Yes, we must get into the habit of posting guards. Any idea who?"

Hernandes opened a saddlebag and pulled out a paper that Horsey immediately tried to chew. "No, no, Horsey." Hernandes twisted aside. "Ne'wang gave me a lists. Naturally, he suggests imps. Two imps, in particular."

"Two imps?" Strongarm dropped his big head between his big legs. "Two imps! No, no, not those two! Not them!"

"Yes, those two." Even Hernandes didn't sound too keen. "Guildencrantz and Rosenstern."

Glide mouthed the names, Guildencrantz and Rosenstern. They were familiar. Weren't they from a story? No, a play. That was it, a piece of theatre. It was *Omlet, Omlet* by Shakespeer. Omlet, he remembered was the more than slightly cracked Prince of the Ausphalian Tennis Open. Glide had once played him. Reminded of the piece, his eidetic memory took over. As if reading from a script, he said, "To Pee Or Not To Pee." Glide coughed lightly and adopted a heroic pose.

"To pee or not to pee? That is the question:
Whether it is nobler in mind to relieve
The burns and strains of a bursting bladder
Or to cross my legs and hold my sea of troubles,
And by waiting, play on. To score, to serve;
Yet more; for by a serve to say we ace
The receiver and the thousand practice shots
That his strokes are heir to; it is a winning hit

Devoutly to be wished. To score; to serve;
To serve; perhaps to fault. Ay, there's the rub;
For in that serve of nerves what faults may come,
When we have sliced the ball off this finite court,
Gives bladder pause – there's the respect
That makes calamity of holding on too long.
For who would bear the deuces and the double faults,
The too high ball, the low bend of knee,
The impact of a volley, the fast return,
The doubt of a line call, and the shouts
When a foot fault is unworthily cried,
When he might just flush his stream
Through a bare bodkin? Who would litres pour
To grunt and sweat within a little loo,
But that the dread of concentration lost,
The loosened focus from whose choke
No player returns, puzzles the will,
And makes us rather face the net than piddle
Where others would have us go with the flow?
Thus conscience does make continence of us all,
And thus the native desire to pee
Is prevented by the pale cast of thought,
And tournaments of great pitch and fervour
With this regard turn my currents away.
Oh, piss! Oh, damn! To make my waters work
I needs must run the tap."

Hernandes clapped. "Olé! Terrifics. But what does et mean?"

Glide bowed. "Mean? I'm not sure. I'm just trying to find my place here." He turned the pages of his rusty eidetic ability. That was not informative and so he selected another book from the library of his mind. "Ah ha, here it is! Someone else wrote a follow up play, also about Omlet, but taken from the point of view of two minor characters. Yes, that's it. That's where Guildencrantz and Rosenstern come in. There definitely must be leakage through the gateways."

"Those two are a leakage, all right," Strongarm said gloomily.

"To rights." With a resigned shrug, Hernandes folded the paper and mounted Horsey. "Ne'wang says to fetch them so I'd better finds them."

They watched Hernandes leave, Strongarm humming on one note. "Pity a trunk doesn't have holes then I could play a proper tune."

"That's not a pity." Glide stretched out on the grass to enjoy the morning sun. "If you used your front legs to play your trunk, you'd constantly be falling on people."

Glide was thinking it was time to move into the shade when he felt ground vibrations. It was Horsey. Hernandes was walking behind the roo and towing two identical imps. Their trousers and shirts were made up of brightly coloured triangular patches. Their flat hats were like Danish pastries. Their shoes had bells. Everything about them clashed with the surrounding bush.

"These twos." Hernandes dropped his leash.

Strongarm stood tall, a great looming grey shape. "Attention!" he boomed.

Startled, Guildencrantz and Rosenstern saluted. Their hats fell off. "Hat-tension?" Guildencrantz said.

"At! At! At!" Strongarm bellowed. Haggort almost fell out of his tree with laughter. "Never mind." Strongarm pointed to the hut's doorway. "You're to stay on guard here. If anyone tries to get in..." He thought for a moment. "...or out, call us immediately. Don't you tackle them. It might be dangerous."

"Fie!" Guildencrantz sneered. "We sneer at danger."

"Faith!" Rosenstern sneezed. "We sneeze at danger."

"Fine." Glide tried not to giggle. "As long as you sneer or sneeze loud enough to warn us."

"Good works, boys," Hernandes said encouragingly.

The two imps puffed out their chests with pride. But that didn't last long. As soon as Glide & Co had left, their pecs slid down to their tummies.

Guildencrantz, at one side of the door, yawned. "Hot day for it."

Rosenstern blinked slowly. "My word, it is." They both adjusted their weight until they could balance with their eyes comfortably closed.

Glide looked back at them from a distance. "Are they safe?"

"Possibly." Strongarm waved his trunk uncertainly. "Though it might be to our advantage if they were actually imp-napped."

"They're that bad?"

Even Hernandes nodded.

Entering what had been Plonkers' Breakfast Bar, they now found themselves in Plonkers' Midday Munchies. That was achieved by replacing the linen tablecloths with bright tapestries.

Plonkers, on seeing Strongarm, called out, "G'day folks. T'day's special is fish. Yer like fish? Three lots ov fish?" Three heads shook vehemently. "No? Not fish. I've got steak. Huge steaks. Elephant-sized steaks. Oops! No, not elephant size. No steaks, especially not elephant-sized. I've got shrimps. Bi-ig shr-imps. Oops! Nothing wiv imps in it. Silly ov me t'suggest it. Bread? I've got bread. Nice bread. Dried bread. Untouched by human-hand bread. Untouched by anything-type bread."

At three sombre nods, Plonkers returned with slabs of fresh bread. They were accompanied with chunks of cheese and slices of salad. "To the 'eroes of Auslan," he said. "I'll put it on yer credit."

"We've got credit?" Glide asked, building a giant sandwich.

"Mostly discredit," Strongarm groused.

Carefully moving from tree to tree, Haggort observed them with interest. At the same time, he was communicating with Greenvort. This involved a network that would've done steam telephone proud.

For though they were only a short distance apart, all messages had to be relayed from raven to Witch and back through the raven again. Fortunately, they weren't timed calls.

"Dey've built a hut," Haggort whispered into the air.

"Connecting you," a voice crackled.

"I t'ought we were connected," he hissed.

"Have you put in your dollar?"

"Dollar? What's a dollar?"

"Please put in your dollar."

"Dollar! Dollar!" Haggort screeched. "I t'ink you've got the wrong connection."

"Sorry," the voice crackled, "have a nice day."

"What's with the sexy voice, Hag?" Greenvort asked.

"What voice?"

"The one asking for a doll."

"Doll? Nah, dat was fer a dollar. Wrong connection. Hey, Greenvort come over here and get into da hut."

"I've got a hat."

"Hut! Hut!"

"Okay, okay. You don't have to shout."

Haggort scratched bark from his tree and viciously crumbled it into dust. Moments later, a light breeze stirred the grass. Since there was no breeze, Haggort knew that what now moved the grass was the carefully blending-in body of Greenvort.

From the edge of the clearing, the green imp studied the hut. With a few deft smudges of earth on him, he sidled towards it. He saw, however, that the entrance was still being securely guarded. Coming closer, he was challenged by Guildencrantz and Rosenstern. Zzz... zzzz challenged one. Zzz... zzzz... zzz... challenged the other. Greenvort disdainfully pushed past them.

"Forsooth," Guildencrantz cried, "but do not push."

"Fivesooth, but t'were not me," Rosenstern protested. "It were you."

"Not I." They looked around but Greenvort blended in too well. "Perhaps we were touched by the pangs of hunger?" Guildencrantz suggested.

"Aye, the pangs of hunger can do that," Rosenstern agreed. "With just one touch."

"Then let's lay down our arms and get us some food."

"You think? We are supposed to be on guard."

"But there's no one around. Fie, let's lay down our arms."

"Forsooth, let's do it."

As one, the two dropped. They began to drag themselves along the ground. "Four sooth or more." Guildencrantz panted. "Is this what Strongarm meant by lay down your arms?"

"Sooth," Rosenstern replied. "But what would an elephant mean?"

Guildencrantz spat out grass. "Lay down yer trunk?"

"Could be. Could be. Or maybe it was yer tusks? Lay down yer tusks?"

Guildencrantz considered this. "But wouldn't they get stuck in the ground?"

"Too true." Rosenstern rested. "Could it be he said to take up your arms?"

"True, that's true, too. But you've got to put them down before you take them up."

Thus engaged in meaningful meditations on military manoeuvres, the guards of Auslan crept off the field. Greenvort explored the hut. There wasn't much: just a chair, a bed and a table. There wasn't much light either. But that didn't bother Greenvort. He could see quite well from the moonlight reflected off a blade of grass down a deep well. More importantly, he could see that nothing was hidden anywhere. Even more importantly, he saw that there was nowhere for him to hide. Yet if he were going to spy then he definitely needed to hide. Greenvort considered the thatched roof. Tempting. But he was pretty sure that the Ne'vermaker would sense him and jab his spear through the roof. No heart, that man. He'd treat a poor imp like a pincushion. Nor were there any nearby trees to which he could retreat. As a place to spy, Greenvort didn't like it. But if he didn't spy then Maggot Thwacka wouldn't like it. Greenvort felt caught between a rock and a hard place.

Two ideas came to Greenvort. One: he could make tiny cracks in the wall and hope to spy through them. Some hope. The Ne'vermaker would easily detect him. Two: he could read their vibes. That was possible but he'd better be good at it. Otherwise, it was Slowtime for him and the real possibility that he become Maggot Twacka's next handbag.

A hiss broke into his reverie. It was Haggort, giving his warning. Greenvort gathered in the psychic hints of his presence. Holding them close, he crept to the doorway. No one was near and so he slunk away, well away, into the neighbouring forest.

Hernandes, however, was attuned to the presence of other imps. He slid off Horsey and into the hut. His senses flared. "Quicks!" he cried. "Greenvort was here. He's gone in that directions."

Greenvort turned around. "Grut!" he snarled. "He's read me." He headed towards Inklan, telling Haggort to do the same through the medium of Goresh.

Hernandes came out of the hut and searched around. "Too lates. We'll never catches him."

"Does it matter?" Glide asked.

"Of course! We don't want them to learn what you learn."

"I suppose not." Glide looked inside the hut. "Well, I haven't learnt anything yet so I guess it doesn't matter. Anyway, there's not much room in here for learning."

"No?" Strongarm knelt and got half a trunk inside the door. "No," he agreed.

"It is whats Ne'wang is wantings," Hernandes declared, "so it must be rights. We will just have to devibes it each times Glide goes outs. If there's anythings to devibes."

"Depends on what I've eaten." Glide was feeling put out by being constantly put down. "Still." On a sudden inspiration, he took out the whistle. "Greenvort was here." He waved it around. "This must constitute an emergency."

Putting the whistle to his lips, he blew. There was a hissing sound, followed by a whoosh and culminating in a thud. The ground heaved upwards. The air pushed downwards. From within an air-ground sandwich, the Ne'vermaker emerged.

"Jeez!" he exclaimed. "You've got good wind!"

"Did I do that?"

"I don't usually bury myself ten feet deep."

Glide glowed. "See," he said to Hernandes with a lift of his eyebrows.

"But I hope you've gotta good reason for calling me."

"Greenvort was here."

"Greenvort!"

"Where are Guildencrantz and Rosenstern?"

Glide shrugged. "They're our best guards," the Ne'vermaker said loudly. "The very very best." Goresh, high in the sky, squinted his ears to listen.

The Ne'vermaker winked as he entered the hut and extended his arm to hold the others back. "Those two will actually make an excellent diversion," he said. He turned his palms out to use as detectors. "You're right, mates. I can feel Greenvort's vibes. No matter, we'll just be extra careful. Strongarm and Hernandes, you twos keep guard outside, real guard. Glide, you sit.

"Now, we really begin the Work."

Chapter 20

There was one cane chair in the hut. Glide sat in it. "What about you, mate?" he asked.

"That's up to you?"

"To me? You wanna sit on my lap?"

"No way!" The Ne'vermaker smiled briefly. "I'm going to sit in your mind."

"Sounds fun. How?"

The Ne'vermaker raised his left leg to cup the foot in his right hand. Holding his spear at arm's length, he used it to balance his weight. He now looked as stable as a tree grown out of the earth. His words, however, expressed the opposite. "I'm not fixed here, Glide. Another place has a stronger call. Yet the more I stay here, the more fixed I become. You can make me permanent."

Glide uneasily looked around. The small hut was dim except for chinks of light. Through a small window, he could see a blue patch of sky. He sighed. It felt like he was right back in school.

"Ol-right," he said, "tell me what to do."

"Dream. You have to learn to dream."

"You want me to sleep?"

"And snore? No. I mean Ne'vertime dreaming. It might be what pinkfella call lucid dreaming. But you gotta visualise me. You gotta see me in your mind's eye. You gotta," Ne'wang made a vague gesture, "you gotta mentally experiment with me."

"Yeah, right. I'll put a mental Bunsen burner under your feet."

"Excellent if you could. For now, though, just concentrate and project me onto the wall." The Ne'vermaker faded.

"On the wall? No worries." Glide worried.

He closed his eyes. Oh, he knew exactly what the Ne'vermaker wanted. He also knew that he was resisting it. The problem was that he only knew one way to create the energy to see Ne'wang. And that meant that he had to revive the feelings of hatefulness, emptiness and depression that were associated with his years of pen pushing. Revive them in such a way that he actually fully experienced those feelings. The hate ran so deep that it united the various layers of him. In Yung's terms, he would be uniting his shadow side with the light-of-day side. No, he didn't want that, not at all. Yet he had to do it. He had to but there was a problem. Glide liked the Ne'vermaker. So if he visualised him, Glide became all warm and fuzzy. Those feelings, however, counteracted the ones that generated the required energy.

Glide opened his eyes. There was a faint outline of Ne'wang against the wall. "Not doing too well, mate," a voice whispered. "I don't wanna be a ghost."

"Yeah? Well, it's hard. I can't just switch it on."

"This is only the beginning, Glide."

"Jeez!"

"There is still Maggot Thwacka the Witch."

"Yeah, thanks for reminding me." A quiver of fear ran through Glide.

"Ah ha!" he thought, catching that frisson. "Fear may not be hate. But it's still a bloody good motivator." Plus he had this idea of Cascade, a young woman of innocent beauty. Hmm, he could hate the Witch. He just about could. Glide pulled his shirt over his head and concentrated on the resulting darkness. In it, he put the fearful Witch. Subservient to her was the lovely Cascade. A sense of revulsion grew. A revulsion that generated its own twisted energy. The energy built up. His scalp tingled. A cloud mushroomed out of his head and curled against the wall. He pulled down his shirt. The Ne'vermaker was a smoky storm cloud twisting and turning against the wooden timbers.

"Great, mate." The Ne'verman beamed. "Beaut, toot. How d'ya do it?"

"Em, uh. The Witch. I thought about the Witch."

Glide didn't want to explain. He didn't want it known that he was motivated by a fantasy, by the image of a woman, Cascade, that he'd never even met. Something else also niggled at him: that the concentration was also an invocation. He'd dialled the Witch and, though he'd given her no space in which to answer, he had this uneasy idea that a low-level connection still existed. He'd put down the phone but hadn't yet disconnected. He wiped his forehead.

"Thirsty work," He didn't want to think about not disconnecting. "How about a pint?"

"Water?"

"Nah, Plonkers' beer."

"Faerie juice? Imp Tea? Troll Coffee?"

"Come on, mate! How about a pint of rotgut?"

"Green Mist? No way, Glide! You've got to be sober. You've got to take this seriously."

"Ah right, ya dingo! Make it a juice, then."

Outside, Strongarm was flapping a huge ear. "Juice, d'you say? Coming up, sir. Just put a napkin over me trunk, Hernandes." With a flourish, the imp laid out a towel. Strongarm then raised a beaker and poured liquid into four glasses. "To life after Thwacka." He raised his glass in a toast.

"To life after we thwacks her!" Hernandes said.

"Hey guys," Glide pulled his shirt down. "I haven't done anything yet." He sipped at a juice that combined chocolate with orange and yet he never even tasted it. "I've got a migraine coming on." He'd pulled his shirt up again. "Never had one before. Not till I came here."

"Then how d'you know it's a migraine?" the Ne'vermaker asked.

"I can see stars and spots."

"Stop pulling your shirt over your head."

"What? Oh, yeah." Glide sheepishly adjusted his shirt. "No migraine."

Ne'wang downed his juice. "Back to work. The hard part."

"The Bunsen burner?"

"Could be. We're certainly gonna turn up the heat."

"Metaphors," Glide muttered. "Don't yer just hate them?"

They entered the hut. "Voilà," the Ne'vermaker said, pulling a candle out of his pocketless silver shorts. "Gotta light?"

"Me?" Glide searched in the pockets of his fringed trousers. "I thought you'd be rubbing sticks together."

"Always found cigarette lighters best myself."

"Rubbed together?"

The Ne'vermaker smiled thinly. Clearly his humour hadn't crossed the gateway with him. Flickering briefly, he reappeared in a suit.

"How d'you do that?" Glide cried. "How can you just go from anywhere?"

From one pocket, Ne'wang drew out a cigarette lighter. "I mentally connect to a gateway." He held a flame over the candle. "You're first task, Glide, is to see me in the flame." The candle flared in the dim hut, the yellow flame rising then narrowing to blue.

"See you in the flame? The yellow bit? You're not exactly Nordic, mate. How about in the smoke?"

Again the Ne'vermaker flickered, appearing once more in a loincloth. "Better still, if you can."

Glide sighed, closed his eyes and again pulled the shirt over his head. It was dark. He could concentrate. Was going to concentrate. The Ne'vermaker coughed. "Yeah? What?" Glide spoke through his shirt. "What is it now?"

"You're supposed to see me in the smoke? How can you do that when you can't even see the candle?"

"Huh? Oh, yeah." Glide pulled down his shirt. "You mean see you? Actually see you?"

"Actually, yes."

"Not metaphorically?"

"No."

"Okay." Glide squinted. "The candle's gone all funny."

"Just pull your shirt down a little further."

"Oh, no wonder. Jeez, it's bright."

"Curiously enough, it's just one candlepower. But you could try turning the power down."

"Ha, ha. Very not funny." Glide watched the smoke. It curled and writhed upwards with an independent life of its own. "So, you want me to see you in that?"

The Ne'vermaker, becoming insubstantial, nodded. Glide tried to sink into the hate but it wouldn't come. The Ne'vermaker was too warm a presence. So was the candle, in its own way. They nullified hate. But what other feelings went right down to the depths of his being? The fear? He tried it again but it wouldn't work for a second time. What else? What else could integrate him? What was there, but was positive?

Glide drifted back in thought, to the time before work, to the time before finals. Right back to the time when he'd enjoyed his studies. Yes, there was a something. Had been a something. There'd been a time when he'd been as motionless as a Haggort in a freezer. He'd been so focussed, so concentrated, it was only afterwards that he'd realised that he'd been so completely motionless, so completely integrated.

Glide recalled the image. He'd been at Byrone Bay, south of Brissie. A currawong bird had dive-bombed a goanna. The lizard had probably been after the bird's eggs. The bird was driving it away from its nest. The goanna had waddled onto a thick root. By not moving, it had become virtually invisible against the tree's bark. Fascinated,

Glide had also frozen. For ten, twenty minutes, only the goanna had occupied his attention.

He was supposed to be surfing. But he kept going bush to practise stillness. Motionless, he'd seen snakes basking in the sun, kookaburras dive for mice, possums forage for food. He'd seen an echidna waddle from under a bush, the spiny creature unaware of being watched. He'd loved it all, absolutely loved it. That time before work. That time in the bush. And that feeling was returning.

It began with faint shadows. There was the faintest touch of that intense stillness. It resonated, becoming stronger. A hint of a shadow formed in the smoke. The shadow acquired an outline. Glide went further into the stillness, and the outline was given a rendering. He blinked and the smoke broke away from the candle. Holding onto the stillness, he projected the Ne'vermaker against the wall. In the candle flame as well, there was a tiny image of him.

Flush with success, Glide relaxed. Immediately, the projection fragmented. A leg floated away, the head dissolved and an arm broke off. The candle image faded. Glide sighed and the genuine Ne'vermaker reappeared. He seemed, though, more real than before, his blue skin had a deep lustre, almost iridescent.

"Mate, you pack some energy. You're a natural," the Ne'vermaker said. "An excellent start."

Glide held his head. It was pounding. "I'm buggered." He rubbed his eyes. They felt sandpapered. "That was hard work!" He looked at his watch. "An hour!" he exclaimed. "I've been in here for an hour. I thought it was about ten minutes."

"Time is relative, Glide."

"Yeah, right, it's my Aunt Fanny." Glide lightly massaged his scalp.

"Want to rest?"

"Rest? No, just get me outside of my head."

"Okay, okay, have a break. How about training the troops?"

"And compete with Strongarm?"

"He's more on the, ah, cavalry side, right now. You can teach hand-to-hand combat."

Glide yawned. "Yeah right, let's get physical."

The pounding in his head receded slightly although, on leaving the dim hut, the sun's rays became daggers thrust against his eyeballs. As he blinked and groaned, Hernandes rode up on Horsey.

"Finished so soons?" he asked.

"I'm knackered, mate."

"In such a short times?"

Glide grimaced. "You wanna try it? Be my guest."

He motioned towards the doorway. The Ne'vermaker, however, glided between them.

"Glide's doing very well," he said, "plus right now, I'm needed elsewhere." He disappeared but promptly reappeared. "Forgot, please give Glide the troops." He promptly vanished again. Glide's mouth was still fly-catching when the Ne'vermaker manifested yet again. "And don't forget, give me a call in the morning."

"A call? A telephone call?"

"No, a mental call." The Ne'vermaker shook his head. "Exactly what we've just been doing."

"Oh." Glide's arms fell to his side. For a brief dazzling moment, he'd hoped that *Dr Whom* might be around the corner along with his phone box. But no such luck. Instead, a noise made him turn towards the forest. It was Strongarm. "Hey, mate," Glide entered the open area around his hut, "the old man told me to train the troops. That all right with you?"

"Yes, fine." Now that Glide was pulling his weight (Glide's not Strongarm's), the elephant's manner towards him had completely changed. "I'll just give them the last trumpet." He held up his trunk. Hernandes fumbled in his pockets for a harmonica. It went into the trunk tip and Strongarm began to blow. Sad notes floated over the clearing.

"Isn't that a retreat?" Glide said.

"Yes." Strongarm stopped blowing. "But that's what they need to practise the most."

"Yeah?" Glide threw back his shoulders. "Well, we'll soon see about that." People were beginning to gather in the clearing. Glide thought that it was time for an encouraging speech. "Friends, humans and imps," he shouted. "Lend me your ears."

"Lend him our years?" Rosenstern said.

"Fie, he said to lend him our rears." Guildencrantz scratched his skinny buttocks.

"Ears or rears," Strongarm muttered. "He'd disappear inside of mine."

On the wings of fervour, Glide added, "Take up your arms and fall into line."

"Take up our arms and fall into line?" Rosenstern glanced sideways at Guildencrantz. "Been there, done that." Lifting their arms, they both fell. The milling crowd applauded.

"This is terrible!" Glide cried. "Pull out your swords," he bellowed. "Ready your staves and string your bows." The mob suddenly disappeared. "Hey, come back," he shouted.

"They've gone for their weapons," Strongarm rumbled. "I hope."

"If they come for training, they should already have them!" Glide paced in front of his hut as in ones and two, the crowd returned. Once more, he shouted, "Fall in!" Before there was more chaos, however, he added, "No, no, cancel that. Form lines, just form lines."

A few dozen erratic lines formed. Obviously, these were just family groups. Glide groaned. He thought of the movie where the tough sergeant breaks in the new recruit. He sighed. This wasn't going to be that way. In this movie, the recruit breaks in the sergeant.

"Form two lines," he called. "Two lines only." The family groups split, reformed, joined friends, shouted and left friends. Glide tugged at his hair. "This is worse than entropy," he groaned. "I'll number you," he shouted. "All you lot are ones, all you are twos."

With much tugging and turning, he managed to line up all the ones. By evening, they were able to do it themselves. Though they didn't all face the same way. By night-time, he was exhausted but able to claim that he could turn a milling mob into two lines of armed warriors. Well, almost-armed, almost-warriors.

Finally Glide muttered, "I'm done for." More loudly, he added, "Time to knock it off." After a brief pause, Guildencrantz swung his staff at Rosenstern. "Stop!" Glide screamed. "I didn't mean knock him off. I meant knock it off. *It* as in *finished*."

Guildercrantz moved his lips. "But there isn't a *t* in *finished*."

"Damn! Damn! Damn and strawberries!" Glide groaned. "Where's the Green Mist? Top me up on rotgut."

"So much for training," Strongarm said sympathetically. He sighed.

"I'm sure Haggort, Greenvort and the Witch are wicked. But these...?" Glide pointed at the ragged lines. "My head hurts." He made one last effort. "Dis-miss!" For once, he gave an order that was well understood and the warriors quickly dispersed into their forest home. Glide just had time to point at Guildencrantz and Rosenstern. "Except for Ne'wang's two volunteers, of course. You have guard duty."

Though they both groaned, they obediently headed back to the hut. Dragging their weapons, they made uneven furrows in the earth. Hernandes hurried after them.

"Come along," he said to Glide. "I must devibes in case Greenvort comes back. In fact, with these two as guards we are sures that he will comes back."

"De-what?" Glide asked.

"Devibes. You'll sees."

Glide stood in the doorway when the imp entered the hut. Hernandes stood near the candle, closed his eyes and concentrated. His tawny skin began to glow, not all over but in small patches. Glide thought of radiation in reverse, an implosion. Hernandes was a radiation vacuum cleaner. The imp opened his eyes.

"You've gots some outputs there," he said. "I've devibes the best I could."

"You mean I've left an imprint on the walls?"

"You hads. Now et's gone."

Glide rubbed his eyes. "Thanks, no wonder I'm so knackered. Let's head for Plonkers."

Glide's feet knew the way by now. They arrived to find that all pretence of tablecloths had vanished and the wooden surfaces were now free to show their true, scarred nature. Plonkers Inn was in its usual noisy glory and lantern light gave an almost cosy atmosphere. It was an extremely pleasant night to those that were there.

To those not there, to those left behind to guard a flimsy hut in an open field in a starlit night, to whit Goldencrantz and Rosenstern, it was a dark and stormy night that bore the terrible threat of Greenvort and Haggort.

Chapter 21

"Umm." Guildencrantz coughed and rocked on the balls of his feet.

"Uh hum," Rosenstern responded, too quickly, also rocking on his balls – ouch - the balls of his feet.

"Nice night fer it. Forsooth."

"Ye-ers." Rosenstern studied the sky, which was now the livid green of a well-worn billiard table. "Nice night for what?"

"Um.... Sewing socks? Sitting by the fireside? Reading? I like reading. I once read this play. About a midsummer's night dream. No, no, I'm mistaken, it wasn't. I remember now, it was a midsummer's night scream. That was it, a midsummer's night scream."

Rosenstern again eyed the bilious sky. The trees at the edge of the clearing were waving ominously. He didn't feel like waving back. He felt like doing a bit of midsummer's night screaming. "Who wrote it?" he asked, his voice increasing an octave with each syllable.

"Um... Wobble... No, Shake... Shake... Shake something."

"Milkshake?"

"No, more foreign than that. Shake... Shake... Shak-a-spear. That was it, Sheik El Speir. A real foreigner."

They were now rocking so much on the balls of their feet, they could've been used as pendulums. A noise stopped them. Only the rocking on their balls and the knocking of their knees continued. A dark shadow had separated itself from the trees. Not that they would've felt any better if it had been a light shadow. No shadow would've been their preference.

"Guild?"

"Rose?"

"Did you see what I saw?"

"I saw nothing."

"Yup."

"That sort of nothing?"

"Yup."

"Exactly."

"Right."

There was a moment of silence broken only by the rocking and the knocking. Haggort stood at the edge of the forest and opened his arms wide. He closed them, seeming to embrace the whole field. And them with it.

"Um." Guildencrantz coughed again. "Nice night fer it."

"Yep." Rosenstern lifted one knee to his chest. Then he lifted the other. "First gear." Then he lifted faster. "Second gear."

"What gear are you into?" Guildencrantz asked.

Rosenstern paused and fingered his jacket. "It's a nice little cotton thing. Designed it myself."

"I mean what's with the knee lifting and first gear and second gear?"

Rosenstern raised his legs higher and faster. "Dunno exactly. Glide used it during training."

"Right. Looks useful." Guildencrantz began to copy his companion.

By now, both sets of knees were a blur. "Fourth gear!" Rosenstern cried. "Overdrive!" He shot forward.

"Reverse!" Guildencrantz screamed and shot backwards. He hit the hut, ricocheted off and caught up with Rosenstern, still going backwards.

Greenvort immediately ran to the hut. "Kill the jibes...s," he hissed, "while I read the vibes...s."

Haggort stood solidly in the doorway. "No imp will come near," he rumbled, "while I'm standing here."

In the hut, Greenvort sniffed, his nostrils working like bellows. Climbing onto Glide's chair, he turned with arms outstretched. His skin gleamed like a frog fresh out of water. A green mist radiated out of him. It touched the walls but there it evaporated.

"That Hernandes...s," Greenvort screeched. "He's...s devibed it. He's...s no fun. I can't find out what they've done."

Greenvort's mist condensed into thin shells and formed fragments of fingers that picked at the cracks. But Haggort suddenly bent. His big ears twitched. "Quick, quick," he cried, "and find a clue. An angry elephant will soon come to view."

Greenvort, however, still didn't move. He was trying to extract at least a micro-bit of information from the air. It was only the fast approach of pounding feet that broke his absorption. In a trice, he leapt from the table and onto Haggort's shoulders. The Giant Dwarf gave one flex of his muscles and then he sped off.

Haggort fled into the depths of the forest. In dense growth, he climbed a tree, becoming invisible even to the sharp eyes of Goresh. Once hidden, Greenvort again marshalled his thoughts. Most of which should've been court martialled. He began to transmit. Goresh sensed bits amongst the bytes and endeavoured to pass them on. Maggot Thwacka concentrated, collecting only fragments. She gernashed her teeth in despair.

"Smoking Ne'wang," she mumbled. "Has he taken up smoking? A candle, he smokes in a candle? This is twaddle. I want details. Get me details." Reversing transmission, she hurled a neural stab that zigzagged in psychic waves from Goresh to Greenvort to Haggort.

While his archenemies arched, Glide returned to the hut. He was led by two imps who, somehow, always managed to lag behind.

Rosenstern was still in shock. "2B or not 2B?" He stared at his flat Danish pastry-shaped cap. "Who knows what size? But it was big and there was at least a dozen of it."

"Of what?" Glide forced himself to be patient, wondering if there was any sense in this gibberish.

"Of him," Guildenscrantz said. "Maybe two dozen."

"But we held them off."

"Fought to the last."

"Thought it was our last."

"Fought? Thought?" Strongarm looked down his (very long) nose at them. "Guards? Call yourselves guards?"

Guildenscrantz frowned and looked sideways, wondering how to put it. "Er, no," he said at last. "Not really."

"Actors, maybe," Rosenstern suggested.

"Fruit pickers on the field of being, perhaps."

"Foils on the stage of life, possibly."

"But guards? Frankly, no."

Just then, Hernandes bounced past. A moment later, the roo bounced past him. For a fraction of a second, a puzzled Hernandes looked between his legs. Then with an amazing recovery, he leapt aboard the roo. A cork on his akubra swung out. Then in. It hit him on the nose. He fell off again. Cursing, Hernandes leapt up. With eyes watering, he leapt onto the roo for a second time. He beat the others to the hut.

"Stands back," he cried. "Lets me." He entered and as before radiated out waves of gold. Glide's mouth watered. If only Hernandes was an onion, lightly fried. "Yes," the imp declared, "Greenvorts was here."

"Greenvort?" Rosenstern echoed. "But we saw Haggort."

"The big one."

"Big and ugly."

"As big as an elephant and as ugly as an ele... as an... as...." Guildencrantz faltered as a trunk hovered threateningly in front of him. He took a deep enjoying-the-air breath, and rubbed his hands together. "Ah yes, Rosenstern," Guildencrantz went on, "time for, er, nitpicking. On the, er, pickpockets of life. Foils on the, er, turning into ploughshares. Going, um, just going." He raised one leg and slid straight into fourth gear. In a moment, Guildencrantz was a mere pimple on the horizon. Rosenstern was a wart behind.

Glide threw up his arms. "What does it all mean?" he demanded. "Haggort! Greenvort! All these oughts!"

"Meaning?" Strongarm replied vaguely. "Oh, much as usual."

"Then why all the fuss?"

"What fuss?"

"Well, er, you know." Glide waved a hand equally vaguely. His hand collapsed. "What," he whined, "is happening?"

Strongarm blew a bubble. "Basically," he said, "Greenvort was here and reading your vibes."

"What was lefts," Hernandes said.

"Reading my vibes," Glide echoed. "I see. Well, I don't really but I get the idea." He sat on the grass. "Receivers and transmitters. I'm a doer, a transmitter. Ne'wang is a receiver. And the Witch? What is she, a receiver or a transmitter?"

"She's just interference on the air waves, mate. She's white noise, black white noise."

Glide looked around but the Ne'vermaker was nowhere to be seen. His voice was here but his body was defending a sacred site in Western Ausphalia. He thought the untouched site was sacred. The people pitted against him believed their mine was sacred.

Glide thoughtfully chewed on a piece of grass. He now had some idea of what he could do. But he needed to think about it. The best place for thinking was in his hut. But it needed real protection. With Strongarm's help, he selected twenty imps. Five at a time were posted around the hut. If they did two hours each, he should be safe for the night.

Then Glide rolled out his bed. He felt quite relaxed. More relaxed than he'd felt for a long long time. This, he thought, was good. It might just be the rotgut, he admitted. But he was sure that it was more than that. He felt more alive than he'd felt had for ages.

He didn't admit, though he did sense, that he was also in some sort of danger. Possibly that added to the feeling of aliveness. Yet as he sped towards sleep, his released thoughts and feelings floated up. Goresh reeled them in and though not understanding their content, he passed them on to Maggot Thwacka.

The Witch considered this free-floating data and cackled. So that's what this stranger could do. She cackled again. Knowing what he could do, told her what she would do. And that was quite simple, really, she'd turn this stranger inside out, upside down and into a mental pretzel.

Maggot Thwacka sat on her wooden throne. Her henchmen said that this stranger liked animals. Well she, herself, had a way with animals. So if she couldn't drive him away, she'd switch to Plan B. She'd use a joey, a young roo. Or maybe she'd use a baby possum. Something with big eyes. She cackled with glee. He'd get his animal. The plan was so natural. It must be one of her best. First, though, she'd see how Plans A, C and D went.

Chapter 22

The Ne'vermaker sniffed. "Too much Green Mist," he observed.

"Too right," Glide mumbled. "Anyway, I only drink it for you." There was a smidgen of truth in that. "To fix you here."

"Well, now I'm fixed. So start saving your brain cells, you'll need them for the big stuff."

"It's the big stuff which is driving me to Green Mist." There was more than a smidgen of truth in that.

Glide held his head. It was vibrating. At least, he thought it was *his* head. He also thought the cause of its pounding was the Green Mist. He had yet to realise that the real cause was a bad case of psychic tinkering by Witch & Co.

The Ne'vermaker absent-mindedly scratched his back with his spear. "Yeah," he said, "those two were here last night. Didn't get much, though. Still, we'd better confuse them."

"The devibing didn't help?"

"Sure did. But we also need to give them some red herrings."

"Sorry, all my herrings are still unread."

The Ne'vermaker smiled briefly and lit a candle. "We'd better start with some R and R."

"Rest and recreation?"

"Review and revision."

"Right." Glide sat upright in the cane chair. His head still revolved. Forcing his mind to hold still, he had the vaguest sensation of a mental tug.

"Concentrate on the flame," the Ne'vermaker said. "Just see me in it for now."

Glide set to it and was surprised. Despite the Green Mist, or maybe because of it, his images were strong and long lasting.

"As yesterday," the Ne'vermaker said, "now separate the image from the flame."

"Righto."

Glide bent his mind to the task - it was getting more and more bent with each practise. The effort was in finding the stillness, holding the stillness and using it to move the creation. He tried and tried. And tried. Slowly an image moved out of the flame.

"Yes!" Glide punched the air.

"Almost right," the Ne'vermaker said. "But now, we want it bigger."

"Bigger, okay." The image fragmented. "But in bits? I don't think so."

"Shows what happens if we fail, Glide. So, put your mind to it."

"Put my back into it."

"And your nose to the grindstone."

Glide spent three hours at it, the concentration turning his mind into jelly. "I gotta stop," he said. "Gotta eat. Gotta drink. Gotta do the other end, too."

His mind slithering out of his eyes, Glide staggered from the hut and into the glare of the sun. Under the shade of a tree, he hung onto a branch. His mind drifted, only partially aware of Strongarm's heavy approach. Footsteps were followed by a pungent spray. Glide inhaled it, letting the cool mist settle over him.

"What's that?" he asked dreamily.

"I makes it," Hernandes declared proudly. "Venomade. Frog's breathe, toad's gaze, and dragon's footprints. Stirred but not shaken, fermented in freshly filtered dew. Works every times."

"It's good." Glide blinked. "No, I think I'm going to faint."

"Oh! Works nearly every times."

Glide blinked again. "I still think I'm going to... No." He looked around, surprised to find that he was still standing. "Hell, I felt great, bloody fantastic." Imitating the Ne'vermaker, he rubbed his hands. "Even good enough to get back to bloody work."

"Sees," Hernandes announced. "Every times."

With an amazed shake of his head, Glide returned to the hut. He was going to make it this time, he promised. He was going to crack it. It helped that the Ne'vermaker stayed with him most of the time. Some of the time, though, Ne'wang was with a bunch of people in a lush valley. He was protesting against the building of a billion dollar dam. It was strange but only the Government didn't know that this particular dam was so shallow that the evaporation rate made it useless. Nor did they know that it would force a rare and sacred fish to become extinct. They did know that this area didn't vote for the Government. They also knew that they would have to flood the lush valley, a food bowl for southern Quinsland. Bye, bye food bowl. Bye, bye rare and sacred fish.

But Glide didn't know about those matters. He just kept on keeping on. With aching head and glazed eyes, he stared at the candle. Images formed, pulled out of the smoke and plastered against the wall. From ephemeral, they became more and more substantial. As the day passed, the detail became more and more lifelike. There came a point when Glide could no longer distinguish between the image and the real Ne'vermaker.

Ne'wang clapped his hands. "You're good, mate. Better than I ever expected."

There came another point, though, when Glide could not continue. He stood, but finding that his limbs were as soft as spaghetti, he collapsed. He had to cling to the walls to haul himself upright.

"I'm sugar starved," he groaned. "I want chocolate. Feed me doughnuts. A pizza, a pizza, my kingdom for a pizza."

"What's a pizza?" Hernandes asked. He and Strongarm had been on guard all day.

"It's food. It's carbohydrates. It's big and it's round." He pointed at the afternoon sun. "Big like that." He sat heavily on a tree stump, saliva dribbling from his lips.

"He's a..." Hernandes screwed a finger at his temple.

"Venomade?" Strongarm suggested in an elephantine whisper.

Hernandes inspected their buckets. "Good idea. Venomade on the rocks."

Strongarm dipped his trunk in a bucket. "On the rocks," he repeated.

A gentle spray enveloped Glide. He flopped onto his back, his mouth open. "That's a start. But where's my pizza?"

"Ah ha!" Hernandes looked around. Certain that the Ne'vermaker was not currently in Auslan, he dipped into a saddle and brought out a bottle. "Thees do?"

"Probably." Glide sniffed it. "Yep." He swallowed and, after a bout of healthy gurgling, returned the bottle. Hernandes peered inside then upended it. A few drops dribbled out. The earth smouldered. Glide put his ear down. "Funny, I've never heard grass hiccup before."

With the potent brew fizzing in his stomach, Glide took a deep breath and dipped back into the hut. A few moments later, the potent brews exploded. With a strangled cry, he tottered to the doorway.

"Goodbye shanity... sanity," he cried, eyes swivelling. "Inshanitry... insanitry is just the word for a dirty mind."

Head pounding again, he turned around and blew onto the candle. The flame flared. It cackled. Glide, holding onto his chair, corrected himself. The candle crackled. It was the Witch that cackled. The flames crackled. His brain sizzled. There were two flames now. One cackled. One crackled.

Glide slapped his head. It was time to pull himself together. Start with the eyes. Glide squinted at his nose. Two noses. *Moses supposes his noses were roses. Well, the more noses, the more roses.* But no, no good. He shook his head. Not a good idea, the potent brews shook it back. He squinted harder. The right eye peered into the left eye.

Right, now there was just the one image. One image but it had two sides. Two sides? He tried to think. His nose had two sides, didn't it? A right and a left. Ah, but it also had a middle. Perhaps he should see three sides? Three sides? One, two or three? He couldn't work it out.

What else could he see? Glide's gaze gradually gravitated down to his knees. Two knees. Was two right? No, one was right. The other was left. Was that right? His mind strained. Yes, he could definitely remember two feet and somewhere, back there, they joined to two knees, separate knees. Right, getting somewhere. Glide felt pleased with himself. Could he...? Should he...? Would he...? Yes! With a quick lift of his head, he looked at the candle. One table. Great. And on it, one candle. And on that, one flame. He sweated. Touch and go, touch and go. But he seemed to be in control again. Now to make a Ne'vermaker. But first to unmake the cackle. What cackle? Whose cackle? He stuck his fingers in his ears. But the sound remained, a low sinister noise in his mind's eye – in his mind's ear.

Glide shook his head. Mental fatigue and potent brews shook with it. Once more, he realised that he had to force himself to hold still, to be still. He made himself visualise being back in the bush and watching the unmoving goanna. Gradually, he did become still. In that increasing stillness, though, he became aware of something else, something not right. It was something not quite nice, something like a fish struggling on a hook. In a blinding flash, Glide finally understood. Through his imagery and her intermediaries, the Witch had forged a link! He was the fish!

Unfortunately and unbeknownst, his current endeavours were now being transmitted. While Glide had been trying to order pizza and the Ne'vermaker was protesting a dam, Greenvort had been able to enter the hut and submerge himself in the roof's thatching. Absorbing the vibes, he sent a message directly to Haggort. The Giant Dwarf passed it onto Goresh. The airwaves crackled. Maggot Thwacka cackled. At last, she was getting useful information. She pointed a finger. A thin line of electric blue jaggered out of it and into a cobwebby corner.

Cascade stirred. Slowly, ever so slowly, her right hand floated up. With the exquisite grace of a Barleynese dancer, she brushed a strand away from her face. With a slow twist, she evaded a creepy crawly. With a dignified lift, she withdrew her foot from a scuttling something. In her dim and dusty corner, she performed a dance that made the Queen of Sheba look like a country bumpkin.

The Witch laughed. This was what she wanted. Let the girl perform. She was merely bait. The airwaves crackled once more. Her relay points twinged with her energy. Haggort cracked his big knuckles. If only she'd keep her arthritis out of it. He passed on the vibrations.

Greenvort twitched. That hurt. He almost jumped out of the thatching. He almost jumped out of his skin. Quickly, pass it on. Glide blinked. He had just managed to project an image of the Ne'vermaker against the wall. His eyes watered at the stab of a new neural pain. What the hell was that!

And what the heck was the image doing now?

Chapter 23

Guildencrantz raised his tankard. "Fie, but we did right last night, didn't we, Roshen... Roshenshtern?"

"Brave, we were, brave. Right up to the... the... the... beginning."

"Shoon as we shaw Hag... Hag... Haddock."

"Haggort and Maggort."

"Maggort?"

"Like, hic, Greensnort."

"Greenvort and Haggort. Poetry in loshion."

"Moshion?"

"Locomoshion."

"Ah, yesh, loshion."

There was a profound silence, broken only by the sound of gurgling. Two tankards hit the bench. "Plonkersh," Guildencrantz cried, "anovver shquare."

"Anovver square?" Plonkers queried. "Wot's that?"

"It'sh... it'sh like a round, but two each."

"I dunno that I should give yous any more. Aren't yous supposed t'be on duty."

"Fie, yersh, duty."

"Duty callsh."

Guildencrantz tilted his head. "I don't hear anything. Shush, don't answer."

"No, no." Rosenstern waggled his head vigorously. "I speak meta... meter... meterfrolically."

"Meter frolically?" Guildencrantz echoed wisely. "They can meter it now, can they?"

The two imps nodded at each other. It slowly dawned on them that neither knew what either was talking about. Nothing new there. Plonkers held his breath. At this point, they either became maudlin or murderous. Sometimes both. They chose the former.

"You shink we should've gone back?" Rosenstern asked.

Guildencrantz eyed his empty tankard. "And fought?"

"Yersh."

"We are impsh, after all."

"Impsh. Of the finest blood."

"Or if not blood, of Green Mist."

"Yersh."

"Yersh."

"Right."

"Right."

"Now?"

"Now!"

As one, they rose. As one, they toppled. Some moments later, they pulled themselves up.

"That way!" Guildencrantz cried and pointed left.

"That way!" Rosencrantz pointed right.

Following their fingers, they collided and went down again. Plonkers took pity on them. Hauling them both up, he faced them in the right direction.

"That way," he whispered.

"That way," they whispered, putting their fingers to their lips.

As they clung to a table, their good intentions headed towards the hut. Inside it, Glide was still watching smoke. With great concentration, he had created an image of the Ne'vermaker. He had projected it against the wall. It expanded and now, to his surprise, it was taking on a life of its own. The skin, a dark blue, was acquiring a golden hue. The short hair was being drawn out into layers of silver. The emerald eyes were turning blue. The clarity didn't last very long. But Glide instantly knew who it was, to whom this beauty belonged. It was Cascade, the Ne'vermaker's daughter. He tingled. If ever he'd wanted to fine tune an image, it was now, definitely now.

Glide tried to concentrate. Yet he was torn. His mind said Ne'vermaker. His heart said Cascade. The Witch was bending his intention. An image formed in the candle. It was part blue, part gold. Short hair streamed into long silver strands. Glide visualised a lance of light that reached from his forehead and into the image. The end of the lance, he carried to the wall. By then, the image was three quarters gold and the hair was all silver.

Glide's whole heart went into the image. It began to get bigger but, instead of fragmenting, it simply stretched out. Glide then saw what he hadn't been able to see before. Cascade was dancing. In slow motion, her hand floated, her hip twisted, and her foot lifted. He was enchanted. This was the dance of the seven veils. No, the hundred. No, the thousand. And each veil was a shimmering web. But Glide didn't see the web. He saw only the dazed beseeching look in Cascade's eyes.

He didn't need to make any more images. This one was etched into his brain. Speechless, he stumbled out of the hut. Strongarm took one look and lightly sprayed him with venomade. Hernandes held out his flask.

Glide inhaled. He inhaled. And inhaled. He was fixating on that one image when the good intentions of Rosenstern and Guildencrantz arrived on an incoming breeze. They wobbled in the general direction of Glide's nostrils. Drawn in, they permeated his brain. They reinforced an idea that was already germinating. Glide gazed around him, good intentions to the fore. There was Strongarm, trunk hovering uncertainly. He would help. And there was Hernandes. He would, too. And the Ne'vermaker? Surely for his daughter. He raised his arms. Against the lowering sun, he prepared to exhort his warriors.

"Elephants, imps and humans," he declared. He hoped his speech would go better this time. "Lend me your ears. I... I...." He glared.

Hernandes was shaking his head. "This lendings of ears is not good." Suddenly, he went white. With a groan, he pointed at the hut. "We haven't been guarding properly. By now, the walls haves ears."

Hernandes moved towards the hut but Glide was still in his state of fervour. No matter if the walls did have ears - or noses or mouths, he wanted to rescue Cascade. Going to the other side of the training field, he switched to military-movie speech.

"Right," he said, "we're going in."

He raised his fist. The others stared.

Strongarm waved his trunk. "But you've only just come out."

"No, no," Glide cried. "Going in." Drowning, not waving, he added, "Er, as in rescue."

Hernandes moved his lips. "But there's not evens a 'g' in rescue."

"I mean to rescue Cascade."

"Ah," Strongarm raised his trunk high into the air. "Cascade!" he trumpeted.

Hernandes took off his hat. "Cascade," he sighed.

Strongarm brought his trunk down. "But can we rescue her?"

"I have a plan," Glide stated.

"Then let's go." Strongarm pawed the earth, sending up grass.

"Yes, let's go." Hernandes slapped his hat back on.

Enthusiastically, they strode forward. Hernandes leapt onto Horsey, shouting, "Hurrah!" A cork swung out from his akubra and popped him on the nose. The slight delay allowed a thought to pop into his mind. "Why nows?" he asked.

Glide shrugged but Strongarm was also curious. He paused, one huge foot hovering. "Yes," he echoed. "Why now? Why you? Why Cascade?"

Glide didn't want to explain. He could hardly tell Strongarm that he fancied Cascade, that he'd seen her image. "Well, er," he stuttered and his mind raced down twisted avenues. "I can project the Ne'vermaker now." That seemed right. "Yep. That's what he gave me to do and now I can do it."

"You're sure?" Strongarm asked uncertainly.

"Of course."

"Of course, what? Of course, you can project or of course that's the reason?"

"Of course, yes. So are you coming or not?"

"Me?" Strongarm rubbed his head with his trunk.

"Or are you chicken?"

"Chicken?" The elephant-man laughed. "More sort of pterodactyl."

"Right." Glide turned to Hernandes. "What about you?"

"Magics against magics?"

"Aw, look. I'm going. You can follow me or not."

Glide headed towards Plonkers. By now, Rosenstern's and Guildencrantz's good intentions had batted around in his head for long enough to know that this wasn't their home. Each rushed for a nostril, popped out and returned to their owners.

Plonkers was busy. Drinking was at work. Through the noise, though, Glide discerned an apparently empty table. When he reached it, two sets of hands clawed at the table's edge. With moans and groans, two flushed faces fought their way up.

"Hic," said Rosenstern.

"Haec," said Guildencrantz.

"Hic, haec," they said together.

Glide glared at them. "What're you two doing here?"

Rosenstern waved feebly. "Drinking."

Guildencrantz was equally accurate. "Falling."

"You're supposed to be on duty. Why're you drinking?"

"We're drinking to forget."

"Forget what?"

The two blinked owlishly. "We don't know. We forget."

"We were following our good intentions," Rosenstern said.

"But they came back," Guildencrantz cut in.

Glide sighed. "Well, if it wouldn't be too much, GET BACK ON GUARD. That way, at least, if Haggort comes we'd hear the screams."

"Scre...ams?" Guildencrantz said. He unravelled the knots in his tongue. "We didn't scream, we uttered brave war cries."

"He disappeared from us in a cloud of dust."

"Because you were running so fast. Look, it's all right to be frightened," Glide said. "But be good fellows and just go back on guard, right?"

So encouraged, Guildencrantz puffed out his chest. "Right," he said.

Rosenstern raised his head. "Right."

As one, they faced their destiny. And, as one, they rapidly walked backwards.

Strongarm sighed, causing Glide's hair to stream back. "When I first came here," Strongarm murmured, a loud murmur, "I wanted to fight just to save Cascade. But with these crazy people, now I want to save them, too."

Glide was surprised. He looked at Strongarm, expecting to see irony. Yet as far as he could tell, the elephant was serious. Hernandes gazed at Strongarm and smiled.

Glide rubbed at his eyes. "You're right," he said, "and they're right, too. I was wrong. So two rights do make a wrong. Plonkers," he shouted, "three doubles and make it quick!"

"Yers, yer hero. An' anyfink fer the others?"

"Ha, ha."

"An' wottabout these?" Plonkers held a limp imp in each hand.

"Two more doubles, of course. Now," Glide leant forward, "has anyone got a pet mouse or a pet canary? We need one for my plan."

Chapter 24

Goresh the Raven rode the air currents in despair. There was such a babble in Plonkers, he couldn't make out a single word. He plummeted downwards, skimming the inn's roof. Hernandes, however, noticed the glint on glossy wings.

"Visitors," he murmured. "We needs a decoy."

Glide looked at two recumbent imps. "Zzz." came from one and "Zwzz," from the other. "Them?" he suggested. "They do want to help."

Strongarm nodded. "They're just what we need right now."

"You mean?"

"At the first sign of trouble..."

"They run!"

"Right, then that's decided. Good decoys."

"Decays," Goresh sent. "Two more tankards... and creep up in the night... no more for yous two... I zed...."

"Zed? Said?" Maggot Thwacka spluttered. "Rubbish! This is complete rubbish!" Despite the anguish, she cracked her knuckles. The resulting stab of pain shot Goresh a hundred feet upwards. He tumbled down again with icicles in his wings.

The Witch summoned her not-so trusty henchmen. "This stranger," she screamed, "is planning an attack! Double the guards, hire another Giant Dwarf, get me more homunculi. Stop this man. Get him!"

"Duh," Haggort began, loathe to let another Giant Dwarf knuckle in on his territory, "it's only one man. A mere man."

"With," Greenvort put in, "only one plan." He was tired of supplying homunculi.

"You defy me!" Maggot Thwacka hissed.

"Oh, no, no. We, er, just wondered."

"Er, yeah. Why are you s...so bothered?"

"I have to explain every little detail? What's he doing, this stranger? He's doing what Strongarm did! He's organising them! Alone, the Ne'vermaker can be nibbled away. But organised and he's a totally different power. Stop them," she shrieked. "Make Glide slide."

Her voice frizzled with electricity and sparks crackled across the blue wire of her hair. The hair on Haggort's arms also rose up. Even the hair in his nostrils began to spark. With the acrid smell in his nose, he glared suspiciously at Greenvort. "You make dat pong?" he asked.

"No," the imp replied. "It's your nos...se."

Haggort's nostrils did a frenzied dance up and down the knobbles of his face. Twisted turnips, it was him! He was on fire. His nose! His armpits! Flapping his big biceps against his sides, he slapped at his nostrils. As smoke poured out of him, Maggot Thwacka laughed and laughed and laughed.

The fire out, Haggort stopped leaping. The Witch, however, began to prowl. Trying not to be noticed, the hulk tried to skulk. But that didn't help. The Witch raised her arms and her long bony fingers pointed down at him.

"Stop them," she hissed. "Double the guard. Stop them or else."

Maggot Thwacka pointed. They didn't need to be told twice. Haggort and Greenvort crept to the door. The Giant Dwarf turned the handle in his huge fist and angrily flung it open. There was a curious backwards shuffle of metal.

"Snooping!" Haggort growled, glaring at the armour. From within, an unblinking olive green light glowered. At the last visor, Haggort stepped up the intensity of his glare. But the light inside didn't flicker for a moment.

Greenvort tugged at Haggort's sleeve. "Bide your time," he whispered. "Bide your time, you'll yet be king."

Haggort's fingers closed on the imp's shoulder. "Yes," he echoed. "I'll be da king. I'll be da king."

They shuffled out together and passed unharmed through the moat of Slowtime. In the distance, men stopped at their work. Haggort grunted in their direction, took a big knobbly mallet and with great swings, he beat on the echoing surface of a hanging drum. This was a boom loud enough to shatter eardrums at fifty paces. It was a summons. The men, however, knew trouble when they heard it. As one, they turned a deaf ear. In many cases, a deafened ear, and they resumed their work. Not to be outdone, Haggort beat out a slow tattoo. Reluctantly, the men set down their tools and came forward to form a ragged crowd.

Haggort glared at them. "Make lines!" he bellowed. The men hastened to obey. Haggort moved amongst them, treading on tardy toes and banging heads together. "Right," he roared, "how many lines we got. One, er, two, er, er, ..."

"Three," Greenvort suggested.

"Three. And... and... and many. Now, men, what is your duty?" No one spoke. "WHAT IS YOUR DUTY?" There was a whisper. "I CAN'T HEAR YOU!" Haggort bellowed.

"Mumble, mumble."

"WHAT?"

"To defend our country."

"DID SOMEONE SPEAK?"

"Defend our country!"

"When I'm king," Haggort muttered, "I'll make you sing."

"Or necks...s you'll wring," Greenvort chuckled. "Oh, how you'll s...sting."

"So, get to it. Make groups of..." Haggort held up the thick bunch of bananas that served as fingers. "Dis many. How many many is dat?"

"Five."

"HOW MANY?"

"Five!"

"So get to it."

There was a listless shuffle. No one wanted to be the first to move. Greenvort drew one of Haggort's big ears down. He dipped his head into it, pushed a bush of hair aside and murmured, "Make a s...speech."

"A speech?"

"Yes...s, you know, words."

"Words, right." Haggort glared at the men. "So get to it or I'll personally pull off yer heads. In Slowtime."

"No, no. I mean inspiring."

"Inspiring, eh?" Haggort frowned. Then his face did a horrible thing. He smiled. Earthquakes have happened with less strain. "Once more to da breach, beer hens," he quothed, "or close up the wall with your Inklan's bread."

"'Ere," someone muttered, "'e's takin' the mick."

"Nah," said a second, "'e's takin' the rise."

"Yeah, well, none of us will rise if we close up that wall."

"Quiet!" Haggort roared. "A... ttack!" There was more stunned silence. He looked down at the gaping faces. "Duh...?"

"Defend?" Greenvort suggested.

"Defend!" Haggort bellowed. "Well?" He grabbed the nearest man, Swallow, and with one hand lifted him high into the air. "Why aren't you defending?"

"Gurgle, gurgle, glug, glug."

"What? Speak up!"

"Grr... glu... g...."

"Allow me," Greenvort said. "In groups...s of five you'll patrol the border. Any s...sign of trouble and you'll call us. Got that?" There was a slow nod of heads. "And don't think that you can es...scape. Nor that they'll get in to rescue you. A moat of S...Slowtime stretches all the way along the border. Heh, heh, heh." He laughed impishly which, coming from Greenvort, wasn't impish at all. "Now we'll divide you into groups...s of five."

"Yeah, each one of you." Haggort laughed dwarfishly. Which was even worse than impishly. Swallow, released, crept away, his head still echoing.

Greenvort's first magnificent Five headed north. The next patrol went south. In all, he had twelve patrols take turns in spying out the land. Haggort and Greenvort made up the thirteenth patrol and they went directly to the border.

On the second night, the men of the Tenth patrol pricked up their ears. Swallow turned to his companion, Gulp. "Your ears are pricking," he said.

"Big prick or little prick?"

Swallow raised his lantern. "Big."

Tenth patrol swivelled their eyeballs. Their knees knocked. Their stomachs churned. Life had just become interesting.

"Walk away?" Gulp suggested.

"What if they find out?"

Gulp drew the edge of his hand across his throat.

The men of the Tenth looked to Swallow. He swallowed. "All right, all right," he muttered. "I'll go." He got off his horse. The animal nuzzled him but Swallow rapped him smartly on the bottom. "Oh dear," he said. "My horse has run off." He put a pebble in his shoe. "And I've been injured." With exquisite care, he limped in the general direction of Haggort.

From the distant ridge, Rosenstern looked down. "To see or not to see," he whispered. "I see nothing."

"What sort of nothing?" Guildencrantz whispered back.

Rosenstern squinted. A lone figure bobbed up and down in the distance. "A one-legged roo?" he suggested.

Guildencrantz made a telescope of his hands. "With clothes on?" he asked.

"Maybe it has a dinner appointment."

Guildencrantz adjusted the telescope of his hands. "Nah, it's a man with a limp. Or is that an imp with a l-man?"

A thought hit Rosenstern. He hit it back. "Oh, fie," he moaned, "I think we've been spotted."

"That's just your complexion," Guildencrantz half rose. "Follow me."

By the crescent moon, Guildencrantz crawled back to his men. "We've been seen. We could stay and fight or...."

"We'll take the or."

"Right. Then walk this way."

"That's not walking."

"True, true. Creep this way."

The bold amurai, bold as samurai but missing a bit, crept along the dark ridge. Only their occasional shadow could be discerned as they travelled back north. But that was enough for Haggort. Not waiting for Swallow's report, with Greenvort on his shoulders, he thundered furiously towards his enemy.

Chapter 25

Guildencrantz and Rosenstern led their band north with Haggort tracking them. That was perfect for Glide. He was heading south. At the ridge that marked the border, he stopped.

"I'll go on alone now," Glide said.

"You can't," Strongarm protested. "You don't know the way."

Glide held up a small cage with a sleek chocolate-coloured mouse in it. "Key will help me."

"But he sleeps all the time."

"Is not sleeping," Hernandes put in. "Is thinkings."

"Whatever." Strongarm tried to shrug but only managed to bob his head. "If he doesn't move, how d'you know if he's in Slowtime or not?"

"Strongarm," Glide said firmly, "I can't use you. I think you're sort of noticeable."

"I... I... I can merge into the shadows."

"A pretty big shadow would be needed for that. And elephant shaped." Glide pointed down the rocky slope that led to Inklan. "I'll take Hernandes, then. How's that?"

Strongarm grunted. As the other two began to slip and slid down the dark slope, he lowered his great bulk over the edge. Trunk in and legs folded, he resembled a rather odd rock. Listening intently, his ears stuck out. suggesting a rock with wings or a wall with ears. Ears that twitched erratically at each dislodged pebble and every mumbled curse.

Hernandes, out front, suddenly stuck out his left arm. "Hsst," he hissed.

"What?" Glide exclaimed.

"Hssst!"

Glide inched forward. Hernandes, however, waved his right hand frantically. Glide paused, searching out for trouble. But he saw nothing. Then it clicked. Hernandes' left hand was unmoving while his right was waving. Ah hah! The penny dropped. Slowtime! Glide carefully placed Key on the ground. With both feet firmly planted, he took hold of Hernandes' waving hand. Gently, he pulled. Slowly, ever so slowly, Hernandes was drawn out. An acrid smell came with him. Glide's stomach turned. Slowtime was for real.

"Sacre blurb!" Hernandes muttered. "Lucky you hads me to guide you."

"Lucky you had me to pull you out."

"Well," Hernandes went on, "this es where the Slowtime starts. Now you do your scientific magics."

Glide looked around. Behind him was the dark slope of the escarpment. It was mostly low scrub, except for one lone trunk - elephant not tree. Large rocks prevented a straight path. Any route down would undoubtedly lead into this field of Slowtime. But how high was it and how wide? Glide gazed thoughtfully at Key. Key thoughtfully twitched his nose at Glide.

As this deep communication took place, Greenvort was tugging on Haggort's ears. "Whoa!" he shouted. "Whoa!" The Giant Dwarf gradually became aware of pain and raised a big fist. Anticipating this, Greenvort lent forward, waving his hands. "Whoa!" he repeated. "Whoa!"

Haggort slowed. "Wot's dat?"

Greenvort stood on Haggort's shoulders. "I'm not s...sure," he said.

At the pause in Haggort's pounding feet, Guildencrantz and Rosenstern looked back. "Fie, they've stopped," Guildencrantz said.

"Cowards!" Rosenstern shouted.

"Cowards!" his fellow imps chanted.

Greenvort tilted his head. "Now, why would they be calling us...s cowards...s?" he mused.

"I'll show dem," Haggort rumbled.

Greenvort turned his head, sniffing the air. "S...Something's not right. They want to fight? No. They want us...s to chas...se them? Yes, they want us...s to chas...se them." Greenvort considered this strategy.

Meanwhile, Key, sensing bad motivations coming from Glide, increased his rate of twitch. "Sorry about this," the young man said, "but...." Tying the cage to the end of a pole, he extended it to where Hernandes had been caught. Key froze. Even the ever-present twitch ceased. Then Glide withdrew the cage. The mouse looked around and his nose twitch immediately went into overdrive.

"First, let's find the height," Glide murmured. He lifted the cage high and slowly lowered it. At head height, Key's ever-twitching nose, stopped. A fraction higher and it began again. "Hm," Glide mused, "head height? I could pole vault over that."

"No, no! You still don't knows how wide it is!"

"Yeah, right. I'm getting ahead of myself here. I've been in an office too long."

Glide blushing, extended the cage. Sure enough, one vault and he'd have been stuck plumb in the middle. Upside down in Slowtime. Slowtime? Show time! See the upside-down, frozen not-so-scientific person.

It was time to measure. Very quickly, Glide estimated the height and width at several points. They were pretty constant. Now, he rested uncertainly on the pole. He had this. And he had that. What about...? He tapped his foot. What about...? He'd forgotten his basics. What was he getting at? Oh, yeah, the depth. What about the depth? Glide used a flat rock to scratch at the earth. His hand tingled but, carefully, he began to dig. Very quickly, there was a hint of a glint. Hernandes saw it and joined in. They both scraped away. Slowly, they unearthed a fine network of filaments. In the night sky, they gave off an eerie blue glow.

"Wire?" Glide sat on his haunches. "You make wire here?"

"No," Hernandes replied. "We don't makes it. We don't even knows what it is."

"This... this isn't a plant, is it? A Slowtime plant?"

"Not in Auslans. Not those strands. Not underground like thats. And never blues."

"In other words, no."

"Yes, et es nos."

"Nose? Whose nose?" By now, Glide was shouting – in a whispering sort of way. He realised then just how nervous he was. "Oh," he said, "you mean no." He thumped the earth with the rock. The filaments sparkled. "Damn and strawberries! I'd better dig some more. You keep an eye out." Remembering where he was, he quickly changed that to, "You keep guard."

Hernandes shrugged in agreement and looked around for a suitable lookout. He spied a rock slightly higher than the others. In the dark, he clambered up boulders to reach it. A bad move by moonlight. Meanwhile Glide poked about with his stick. A filament loosened. Excited, he tried to get the stick underneath. He poked and he pried, the filament went this way and that. Hernandes watched intently. Even Strongarm became absorbed, squinting along his trunk as if it were a telescope.

In the midst of this blissful concentration, catastrophe struck. Hernandes' convenient rock moved. It was Haggort. With a cry that sent Hernandes tumbling, the Giant Dwarf leapt forward. His arms encircled Glide and lifted him high.

"Ha, ha, ha," he gloated. "He-he-he." He shook Glide as if he were a rag doll. Shook him at Strongarm.

Hernandes gathered his scattered wits and threw himself at Haggort. Having absolutely no effect, he picked up a rock. With all his strength, he brought it down on Haggort's foot. The Giant Dwarf bellowed and kicked out. Hernandes went flying. But it gave Glide a chance. He lashed out. The iron grip loosened and he managed to pull away. Meanwhile, Strongarm had trumpeted mightily and begun to descend like an avalanche. Haggort bellowed again and dived for Glide. He hoisted him onto one shoulder and jumped into Slowtime.

Strongarm skidded to a halt. Haggort ran through the field of Slowtime as if it didn't exist. At the other side, he halted. Glide tentatively moved an arm, then a leg. Flailed then frozen, he had no idea what was happening. Haggort held him up in the air.

"Follow if you dare," he jeered. "Follow if you care. Or just send da chits fer when we send his bits."

Haggort laughed, a laugh that sent razor blades along Glide's spine. The Giant Dwarf backed away. Meanwhile the Witch, using the powerful surge of emotions between Haggort and Glide, strengthened the links that ran between them.

In tears, Hernandes cried out, "Do somethings! Do somethings! Do ... anythings!"

Frustrated, Strongarm stamped at the edge. Suddenly, he stopped. "How wide is this?" he asked.

"How wides? How wides? We don't need sciences now! We need heroes!"

"I need to know how wide," Strongarm insisted.

"Whats? Whats? Oh, oh, I sees. I sees." From Key's end, Hernandes made three steps along the pole. "This longs."

Strongarm snorted. "No length at all."

He slowly advanced, his trunk extended. At the barrier, he felt the unpleasant tingle of Slowtime. Ever so carefully, he advanced another step. His trunk became numb. With it stuck in the air, Haggort imitated it with crude gestures. Strongarm pulled back and his trunk immediately returned to normal.

"Three paces?" he said.

"Yes, three."

"Will you release Glide?" Strongarm trumpeted.

"When we've emptied his brain."

Laughing, Haggort held up the still struggling figure. On the safe side of Slowtime, the Giant Dwarf waited to see what would happen next. He was amused when Strongarm turned his large bottom to him. It was, however, an insult that he well understood. He turned and retaliated in kind. Strongarm, however, wasn't just in the process of trading insults. He shifted backwards and forwards until his rear feet were just outside Slowtime. He carefully drew his front feet back so that all feet were together. With a great roar, he flung his rear feet as far back as possible. For a long moment, he lost sensation. But with the pressure from the front, his rear feet gradually emerged from the field. Three Hernandes' paces weren't much when compared to the span of an extended elephant.

Haggort had made the mistake of watching. He had thought this was just entertainment. Even Glide had stopped struggling. He felt proud. He'd introduced the scientific method to Auslan and Strongarm was using it. He remembered what Newtone had said, or maybe it was Einstine, "We stand on the shoulders of giants." He just hoped Strongarm wouldn't try to stand on top of his.

In fact, it looked more as if the elephant would land on Glide's head. With front feet on the far side of the field and rear feet on the near side, Strongarm knelt down. With a great push, he then threw himself backwards. His front froze. His rear legs strained. His momentum slowed. Yet slowly, ever so slowly, as if pulling against a vacuum of treacle, he slid out. There was a thump. A roar of pain. A roar of anger. A roar of challenge. Then Strongarm was up and charging.

Haggort bolted. Glide's weight was no problem and his big feet pounded pebbles. But unfortunately for him, Giant Dwarves were two-thirds body and only one-third legs. He hadn't a chance. Strongarm caught up with him. His trunk rose to strike. It was coming down when... Haggort held Glide up like a shield.

"Touch me," he screamed, "an' I'll pull off his legs!"

"Touch him," Strongarm bellowed, "and I'll squash you like a tomato!"

"Touch me an'... an'..." Haggort's limited imagination reached its limit.

"Try," Glide suggested, "I'll stuff your tusks down your throat."

"Touch me an' I'll tuff yer stusks, er, stusk yer stuff, er..." Haggort rumbled to a halt. The effort of thought had loosened his grip. He opened his mouth again and Glide put his foot in it. "Duh!" Haggort grunted. Glide, however, had frozen for the grip on him had tightened.

"Don't," Strongarm hissed. A strange sound to come from an elephant. "Let him go and I promise not to touch you."

"An' if I don't?"

"It's better I risk hurting Glide than let him fall into her clutches."

Haggort frowned. He hadn't realised that thinking could hurt so much. "You promise?"

"You don't have a choice. I'm going to count to ten. If you don't let go then I'm going to charge anyway."

"Ten? Is that bigger than three?"

"A bit."

Strongarm began to paw the ground. His ears flapped out to make him bigger. His trunk lifted a big rock and smashed it down.

"Um," Haggort said, "if I just put him down 'ere. Quite clean." He brushed Glide down with his huge hands. "Unhurt." He shook Glide to show that nothing was broken. "An' 'ealthy." Glide fainted. "Right, all yours then an' I'll just be orf." Dropping the limp figure, he pounded away in a haze of small stones.

Strongarm immediately knelt by Glide. The young man was breathing shallowly. Strongarm wanted to chase after Haggort, but this was more important. With his trunk, he blew cool air and massaged Glide's chest. The eyes of the latter flickered. Gradually, they opened.

"Dumbo?" he muttered.

"Dumbo?" Strongarm echoed. "What's that?"

Reality came flooding back. Reality? No, he'd gone through all that. "Don't ask," he mumbled. "Just help me up."

Gently, the trunk lifted him and with its aid, he began to walk. They returned to where Hernandes was anxiously hopping up and down. From the other side of Slowtime, he called, "Is Glides all right?"

"I'm fine," Glide replied. He stood well away from the field. That brief taste had been bad enough. "Hernandes," he called, "use Key. Find this side of the field." The imp obeyed, passing the cage through Slowtime. The mouse froze. When its nose began to twitch again, Glide marked the spot. He turned to Strongarm. "How did you get through?"

"I somersaulted."

"You what?"

"I, er, leapt. Backwards."

"That's rights. I saw. You jumps."

"Like an overweight roo."

Glide shook his head. He couldn't remember the last few minutes. "That's too wide for me." He sighed. "The only way that I'll get through is if you nudge me."

"Like Key in the cage."

"No cage. Just a poke with a pole."

Hernandes removed Key from the pole and then pushed the wood through until Strongarm could grasp it. Hesitantly, Glide approached his marker stone. With a sickening feeling and a prayer, he took another step. Time froze. Thoughts froze. Feeling froze. He was locked into fear, sickness, and prayer. There was a dim sense of existence, struggle, and helplessness. It went on and on and on.

Seconds later, he was pushed out of the other side. He stumbled into wiry arms and cried and cried and cried.

By the time that Glide came to, Strongarm was also through. The latter patted the former gently with his trunk. "It hits us all like that." He puffed a little air over Glide. "You just have to get used to it."

"That's right," Hernandes agreed. "If you goes in with fears, all you feels is fears."

"You can go in without fear?" Glide asked incredulously.

The other two looked at each other then shrugged. Glide didn't push for an answer. He just wanted to get away from that place. Yet Hernandes stopped him.

"What abouts that?" He pointed at the filaments.

"What about it?" Glide responded listlessly.

"We're not used to analysing likes you do. This is new."

Glide sighed. "All right, let's get it."

With the pole, he dug at the filament. The earth pushed aside to reveal a wire as long as his foot. Glide pulled it with the pole until he felt safe to pick it up. He turned it wonderingly. By the light that remained, it appeared to have a blue sheen.

"Real wire?" He bent it and it stayed bent. "Odd, I've not seen any wire here before."

"What's wire?" Strongarm asked.

"This."

"Oh. Grows underground, does it?"

"No. Doesn't grow at all. It's made."

Hernandes cricked his neck to exchange significant glances with Strongarm. "Sounds like magics to me."

Glide nodded thoughtfully. Sunk in thought, he began the ascent of the escarpment. As he fingered the wire, he thought of valves, capacitors, and inductors. A linking thought also nagged at him but he couldn't quite tease it out. Something to do with the events of the night? He bent the wire. Something to do with

Slowtime? He straightened the wire. Something to do with Haggort? He dropped the wire. That was it! He turned to the others.

"Haggort," he declared, "just did the impossible. He simply walked through Slowtime!"

The others turned and gaped.

"Bronze shields!" Strongarm said. "So he did. He did. But how? That disgusting Dwarf just did the impossible!"

Chapter 26

Plonkers didn't have a closing time. As long as there were customers, paying customers, then he was open. There were customers. Ne'wang the Ne'vermaker was one. And Ne'wang the Ne'vermaker was two - maybe three, or even four. For four tankards surrounded him and he was staring gloomily at them. Till a sound sounded. It was a rather rude sound but, all the same, it made his face light up. It was the sort of sound made by someone making a raspberry through a rubber tube. Or the sort of sound made by an elephant wanting to draw attention but not sure what sort of reception he'd get. In other words, it was Strongarm. With him were Hernandes and Glide. They saw the Ne'vermaker and hesitated. Then they spotted the tankards and rushed forward. Ne'wang rose. At his enigmatic expression, however, they stopped.

"Um," Glide scuffed the earth. "You angry?"

"A little."

"Drunk?"

"No."

"Relieved?"

"Yes!"

In delight, Glide hugged him. "Bloody hell," he cried, "gimme a bloody drink." They dived onto the tankards. Eventually, Glide wiped his mouth. "You're sure you're not really angry?"

"What for?"

"Well, you know, going beyond your orders."

The Ne'vermaker scratched his head. "We're not really big on orders here."

Glide slowly sipped to give himself a chance to think. He'd been asked to practise and that was what he'd done. Right, no problem there. He'd just been a bit extreme and put practise into operation. But he'd been asked to help and that was also what he'd done. So it was only his own conscience that was pricking him. His own conscience? Now why was that? Why, indeed, but because of Cascade? He really wanted to save Cascade. Auslan was only incidental. He recalled his vision. Should he tell them about it? And how it had come about? But... How had it come about, anyway?

As if reading his thoughts, the Ne'vermaker asked, "What made you do it?"

Glide cracked his knuckles. The very question. Should he tell? With Strongarm bending an ear? Strongarm, the one who'd rescued him. Strongarm, the one intended for Cascade? No, he couldn't tell. He waved his hands.

"It just sort of welled up out of me," he mumbled. "After all the sitting-around-mental exercises, I wanted to do something, to actually get cracking."

The Ne'vermaker nodded but his dark gaze bore into Glide. The latter could feel that questioning look bounce around within the cavern of his skull. But no, he told himself, it wasn't time to tell. But the image? That was a different matter. He too wanted to know how Cascade had appeared to him. Absent-mindedly, he stuck his hands in his pockets. His fingers touched something flexible. Flexible, but rigid. It was the wire filament. Something else he had to think about.

His thoughts switched. Leave Cascade till later. The wire was a more concrete issue. Given where he'd found it, he had to assume that it was connected to Slowtime. But how? He couldn't say. No idea. He curled it around his finger. Obviously, it also had to be connected to the Witch. The Witch? Was that why the image of Cascade had come to him? When the Ne'vermaker was away, was he, Glide, more susceptible to her? If that were so... He shivered. Bloody hell! Now he really did have a reason for commitment. Self-preservation.

Anxiety mixed with excitement as Glide pulled out the blue wire. "Is this familiar?" He held it beneath an oil lamp.

The Ne'vermaker frowned. "A broken electrical thing?"

"Or a whole one."

"Ne'vermen only get the broken sort. Where's it come from?"

"We dug it out from the ground, at the base of Slowtime."

"Ah!" The Ne'vermaker's face lit up. "It takes someone like you, Glide. We never even thought of it."

"Well, yeah, I was being real scientific."

The Ne'vermaker turned the filament this way and that. "What does this mean, Glide? Has she invented electrics? Has she combined magic with electricity?"

"I dunno. But electrics imply an electromagnetic field. Is Slowtime electrical?"

The Ne'vermaker handed back the wire. He gripped Glide's shoulder with excitement. "Can we check it? Is there anything I can bring, some gizmo or other?"

"I don't know." Glide gazed into the distance. "We did do electrical models of nerves in biology. Dunno how much that'll help." He tapped at the table. "I bought some electric kits when I was a kid." He looked sad. "Wasn't allowed to solder the parts, though. There were just these springs to hold the parts together." Glide rested his chin on his hands. "Somehow it seems that we're dealing with electricity combined with living people."

"Not all livings," Hernandes said. "Haggort is maybe semi-livings."

"Yes and the armour that you told me about? That could be electrical."

"Could be, Glide." The Ne'verman's face was bright with excitement. "It's a new idea to us."

They all gazed at the wire. It seemed so familiar to Glide and yet so strange. His eidetic imagery was turning pages of a catalogue when a sound disturbed him. Clump-clump-clump, clump-clump-clump. Glide shuddered. He was reminded of the pirate with the thin wooden leg, Long John Sliver. He rose in alarm and Plonkers also ran out, a two by four in his hands. The sound grew closer and louder. Clump-clump-clump, clump-clump-clump.

"Long John!" Glide trembled.

"A trifid!" Ne'wang shouted.

"Dragons!" Hernandes cried.

"Dragons?" Strongarm trumpeted. "Oh, if only I had my real arms and my trusty sword, Cohen."

Glide stopped trembling and gave Strongarm a funny look. "Cohen? Don't you mean Conan?"

"No. Why should I?"

Glide shrugged. "Conan was a barbarian warrior. Cohen was a tailor."

"That's okay. When I had Cohen, I had the enemy in stitches."

By now, the sound was closer and more threatening. They huddled together. Clump-clump-clump, clump-clump-clump. The Ne'vermaker squinted. "Two three-legged creatures, two trifids!"

They bunched even closer together. "Wot's a trifid?" Plonkers growled.

"A three-legged, man-eating plant."

"Not imps eating, then?" Hernandes asked hopefully.

"They are supposed to be fiction," Glide said. "But I don't know what to believe here."

The sound arrived at the edge of the woods. Clump-clump-clump, clump-clump-clump. They all goggled. Yet only a moment later and they all laughed. Clump-clump-clump, clump-clump-clump. It was Rosenstern and Guildercrantz. On crutches. They limped forward. Once in sight, they added their moans and their groans. Plonkers lay down his two by four.

Glide ran towards them. "Cheers to our heroes."

Rosenstern leant on his crutch. "Is this a tankard I see before me?"

"Its rim towards my throat?" Guildercrantz finished.

They reached for the tankards and the beer disabbeared. "Fie, did we decoy okay?" Rosenstern asked.

"You were fantastic," Glide replied. "We were able to do more than we could ever have expected." The two imps glowed with satisfaction even though Strongarm was patting them on the head. "It allowed us to find this." Glide held up the wire.

"Is that important?" Rosenstern asked.

"We're certain it is," Glide replied. "Though we're not sure how."

Ne'wang stood straight with one leg cupped. "I'll see if there's anything like this wire back in Ausphalia." He put his weight on his spear. "You keep practising. I think...." He squinted along the weapon. "I think you've put her on the defensive."

"Jeez, I hope so." Glide twisted the wire. "Any ideas on how Haggort could go through Slowtime?"

"An antidote?" the Ne'vermaker ventured. "Or a talisman? That's the magical way of thinking. You've probably got a scientific solution."

"Got nuttin yet, mate. But if she's on the defensive, we ought to be more offensive."

"How?"

"How?" Glide drowned the last of his drink. Green Mist popped in his head. So did a few ideas. "Name's Glide, isn't it? So that's how."

"Names are powerful," the Ne'vermaker said. "They can do powerful things."

"Nah." Glide had the excitement of a dream. "Not what I mean." It had been a hard day and the Ne'vermaker was beginning to fade. "Not what I mean at all."

For Glide an idea, a Gliding good idea, was forming. He looked up to the night sky. He was so excited that his head began to spin and all the stars became shooting stars. Maybe he was going to live up to his name, after all. He was certainly going to try.

Chapter 27

Wobbly with weariness, Glide weaved his way back to the hut. Rosenstern and Guildencrantz clomp-clomped along with him, nominally sober and as alert as guards. On his bed of leaves, Glide fell into a deep and almost dreamless sleep. Almost but not quite. The vaguest of shapes drifted through, like mantra rays in the ocean. One might've been Cascade and that felt good. One might've been Haggort and that felt bad. Her silver ghost was caught in Slowtime while his ugly bulk sped right through it.

Below the level of dreams, Glide felt that his too too solid flesh was too heavy to move. His body, his thoughts and his feelings were all frozen, caught in the horror of Slowtime. Even the night was caught in Slowtime, moving so slowly, it seemed that daybreak would never come. When there were sufficient sun rays for him to crawl up to escape the pit of sleep, Glide sat hunched over a coffee. He barely looked up when a dark shape fell out of the ground.

"Got a radio for you." The Ne'vermaker held out a box. A logo on the side read, *Edison's Steam Radio: Valves to go*.

"Yeah?"

Glide eyed the box with its loose wires and complex entrails. It was bigger than his head and burnt-out valves filled its insides. He rubbed his cheeks for a moment then stumbled back into the hut. Where had he put that wire filament? He felt a sharp point dig into his thigh. It was still in his pocket. He blushed, hoping Ne'wang wasn't watching, and pulled it out. He held it to the radio and vaguely poked around with it.

"What d'you reckon?" He prodded a blackened valve with the filament. "Something connects to something? Something boosts something? I don't know. You tell me."

"Dunno, mate. I'm a Ne'verman and I've never tangled with technology. Too much like bad magic. Never mind, it'll come. You all right to practise now?"

"Yeah, I suppose." Glide stretched. "Hit me with the venomade first."

His words were still hovering in the air when a trunk sprayed him. "Thanks, mate." Glide spluttered. "Talk about the walls having ears. The ears are the walls!"

"Any Greenvorts here?" Ne'vermaker poked the roof with his spear. "No, no one up there. Right, Glide, back to work. But no candle. Just make the image."

"Without the candle? Jeez, mate that's a hard one!"

"Not at all, a simple hallucination."

"It doesn't feel like one."

"Well, it's not really. It's consensus reality."

"Consensus bloody reality! I think an image onto a wall. We all agree that it's there and then we find that *it* is thinking us."

"Good, good." The Ne'vermaker beamed. "That's practical metaphysics. You'll show us yet."

"Show you? I don't have much of a choice."

But Glide did have a choice. As well as his eidetic imagery, he had his name, the power of his name. As Adam and Eve had known, all names had power. So by naming all the animals, they gained dominion over them. Unfortunately, they didn't name themselves and so they didn't have dominion over their own selves. Elohim named them, Elohim being the plural form of El. In other words, a committee had named them, a committee of gods. Fat chance they had. An Eloher rather than an Elohim might've done better in dealing out the names. An Eloher might've been more consistent, too, starting out with an A-dam and an A-damsel

Glide was fairly lucky. He'd been named by his father. Now John had always wanted to fly. But being a clerk by nature, he was averse to risk. Fear held him back. Yet in the naming process, he had passed on something. Skill? No. Experience? Never! Desire? Some. Inherent in Glide was some desire to fly.

Maybe it was something in the blood, Glide thought. Or maybe it was in the cells or even in the mitochondria? His mind projected pages of text. Every cell in the human body, he recalled, contained mitochondria and every one of the latter contain DNA. What was unusual was that for every person, male or female, the mitochodrial genes always came from the mother. So though his father might've given him his name, it was probably his mother who gave him the desire.

The desire? What desire? Was Glide born to run? No. Was he was born to fly? No, not quite! Was Glide born to, er, glide? Yes. Exactly. He quivered. He was born to glide.

As yet, however, he'd never flown. He loved to watch airships but he'd never travelled in one. The nearest he'd got to it, he supposed, was to ride atop a wave. From Namba, the sea had only been half an hour away. From Brissie, never been more than a couple of hours. An interesting thing about the sea was that it stopped at the land, sometimes at a gentle beach, sometimes at a steep cliff. Some cliffs had evolved handglider enthusiasts. These were strange daredevils who had stitched and glued flimsy materials together so that they could throw themselves off the cliffs. It was thought that they'd evolved from lemmings that had survived an earlier bout of leaping.

It was inevitable that Glide watched the handgliders. When the surf was flat, he'd sit on his board and crane his neck to the skies. One day, he'd thought, one day he'd have to give it a go. One day. Even as he prepared himself for Ne'wang's practise, Glide realised that that day had now arrived. That day was today. The thought drifted, even glided, just below the surface of his mind. In the forefront, though, was his practise.

"Concentrate," Ne'wang said. "See my form. See my arms. See my legs. Concentrate on my face. Make my eyes and my nose. Focus on my hands, project the fingers and project the thumbs."

Because Glide wanted to play with his secondary thoughts, he was surprised to see a figure take form, a vague blur. He worked on the image. He drew one leg up, tucking one foot into the hand. An outstretched hand held a spear. Playfully, he even placed a blue-gold aura around the head.

"Flattering," the Ne'vermaker said. The figure fragmented. "Now try for a bit more reality and try to hold it for longer." The cloudy blur became more substantial. "Now move it around."

Gradually, mind took on substance. With more practise, Glide found it hard to tell which was the real Ne'vermaker and which was the conjured. Eventually, the Ne'verman left but Glide continued. Without Ne'wang, however, the image transformed. The dark hair became light, straight lines became curvaceous, and stillness became dance. Cascade! Who else? Cascade and Glide's heart ached.

An inner voice added to the ache. "Here is life. Here is beauty. Here is intelligence. Here is your heart's desire."

An unvoiced voice tried not to cackle. That inner sound, however, chilled Glide's bones. Now that he knew Slowtime, he really knew fear. Even so, he was determined to go on. He managed to put the fear to one side and he strode outside. Now that Ne'wang had gone, the other thoughts were spilling over. He was going to live up to his name, up to his destiny.

"The best defence," Glide announced, "is offence. We are going to be offensive."

"Offensive is good," Hernandes said.

"Now he's starting to sound like a warrior." Strongarm drummed a weighty foot.

"I want broad leaves." Glide held his arms out wide. "Strong branches and fine twine. No more skulking at the border. We are going to take them by storm."

Hernandes sniffed the air. "Tomorrow, then," he said. "It doen't looks like storms today. Don't even looks like rain."

"That's right," agreed Strongarm. "Though I can provide a light spray."

Glide snorted. "I'll be the storm." And he jutted out his jaw.

Hernandes tilted back his akubra. Two corks rested on his nostrils. "Right," he declared, pushing them aside, "musts be time for his Green Mist."

"Or venomade." Strongarm hovered his trunk over the buckets.

Glide pulled himself to his full height. Not much when compared to an elephant but pretty good when compared to an imp. "I've got an idea." He looked around. Was he paranoid or did the grass have ears? "Come. I'll tell you at Plonkers."

This time, they sat beneath thatching in the midst of a dozen conversations. Goresh the Raven settled unnoticed on the tree above them. But Glide was starting to understand when paranoia was just another word for sanity.

"Are any of *them* here?" he asked.

Hernandes held up his palms and turned them. Sensing Goresh, he whipped off his akubra, stepped out from under and sent it skimming upwards. With a squawk, Goresh flew up as the hat floated down.

As the raven forged through the air, Maggot Thwacka the Witch cracked her knuckles. It hurt. Good, she'd take that out on someone. Someone close, someone that deserved pain. Someone who bore the name of Cascade. In the shadowy corner, the slim figure moved. Trapped in the eternal anguish of Slowtime, in infinite slowness, she brushed at cobwebs.

Glide winced. Even in Plonkers, in his mind's eye, he could see her only too clearly. Yet it only strengthened his resolve. The Green Mist also helped and he stood on the bench.

"We will take them by storm," he said. "We will give them shock and awe."

Hernandes frowned. "Or whats."

"What?" Glide looked down bemused. He'd just got a good stride into his voice, a rich ring into it. But drama wasn't him. "Oh, forget it." He sat down again and in a more normal voice, said, "There's plenty of trees and branches around, mates. No problem getting started."

Strongarm lifted his trunk and trumpeted loudly. He knew how a hero should act and Glide was beginning to show the signs. Chief among them were mad certainties and the air around him becoming hazy with excitement.

Chapter 28

In her dark and webby corner, Cascade moved to the infernal dance of Slowtime. Slitting her eyes, Maggot Thwacka cackled at her. It didn't sound evil enough and so she tried again.

"Drat it." She fanned her throat. "I need more practise. There ought to be mirrors for voices." She pulled out a strand of her blue hair. "Perhaps I shall invent one."

She went to the windows. A grey mist rolled over the narrow and colourless strip of country. She hated it. The people that she brought here, however, hated it even more. Well, good.

Above the trees, Goresh the Raven could be seen wheeling and diving. Haggort and Greenvort were hidden amongst the branches. From their mish-mash of thoughts, the Witch built up a picture. The stranger and his men were in the forest and collecting wood. So, another scheme to rescue Cascade. Good, let him. She'd be ready. She cackled again. This time, she hit the right note. Cascade startled in slow-motion. A startle of fear that would go on and on and on.

The Witch left the window and crossed to the high chair that served as her throne. One day, she knew, and she was certain, she would have a throne of gold. But for now, this rough-hewn wooden construction would do. And made by Haggort, rough-hewn it was. Yet not totally unattractive. Its base was cut from a rough trunk. The arms and legs were formed from knotted branches. Titania, the Queen of faeries, would've been proud of such a throne. But Maggot Thwacka the Witch was not.

Her castle was not a huge affair. When she'd been banished, it had been a humble fisherman's cottage. For what she had been, Ne'wang the Ne'vermaker, had added a large hall and provided decoration. Her henchmen had added the battlements. And she had developed the lab.

Anyone could see that it was a lab, from earliest alchemist to the latest steam engine physicist. The walls were basically just shelves. Each one of them was stacked with jars. Some contained dried plants. Others contained moist growing things. Some contained the dried essence of what once had been moist and alive. Those were best if not looked at too closely. Glass tubes led vapours from one heated glass jar to another. Pots boiled and strange gases rattled their lids. Unpleasant odours coiled from one vessel to another. Most people would prefer not to go into this lab. Most people would fight not to go in - even if dragged to it by wild horses.

Haggort might peer from the door. Greenvort might even tip-toe just inside the door. But only Maggot Thwacka actually felt comfortable inside of this room. This was where she cackled the best. Bent over a pot and stirring, the sound just issued out of her. Hard and jagged. Here, she was all cackle. It was as if she were happy, deliriously happy.

In the pot, thin strands writhed with the currents. Glide would've recognised those threads. They were similar, if not identical, to the filament that he'd found. As they boiled, they absorbed power from the liquid. The power of Slowtime. Maggot Thwacka gave a cackle. An excellent one. They absorbed the acoustic power, too. The Witch put out a sensing hand. Yes, there. There the force was strong.

The Witch took some filaments from the bubbling broth. Before they cooled, she twisted them into strange shapes. As she did so, she chanted weird words over them. The convoluted elements vibrated. Like an electric circuit, they emitted waves. This was the antidote, the force to nullify Slowtime. If this stranger wanted a fight, these filaments would be for her army.

***

The stranger did want a fight. Though not at that very moment. At that very moment, he was stuck with his head in the sand and his feet waving in the air. With a huge effort and a sucking sound, he managed to extricate himself.

"Well," he demanded, "wasn't anyone going to help?"

But anyone - in fact, everyone - was rolling around on the ground and holding their sides. With a snort, Glide rose and spat out sand. Nearby lay the buckled remains of what could be taken for a butterfly, if a butterfly had wood for a skeleton. It was a glider of sorts. Well, it had been a glider of sorts. Currently, it was the bits of a glider. Glide gathered up the pieces. With a bit of bending and tying, plus a lot of swearing, he again attached the wings to the framework. Putting himself back in the harness, he clambered once more to the top of a sand dune.

Strongarm, still hooting through his trunk, padded up. "You want me to pull this time?" he asked.

"Pull," Hernandes chortled. He was still prostrate on the sand.

Glide gave them both a withering look. Shrugging himself into a more comfortable position, he nodded curtly at Strongarm. The latter lifted his trunk and gave a mighty roar. Pawing the ground, he sent great clouds of sand into Glide's face. As Glide tried to protect his eyes, Strongarm exploded forward. His great bulk burst into a pounding lumber then a pounding trot and finally a pounding run. This pulled Glide into a walk, a run, a... a flight. He rose into the air. Not very high, still, it was higher than the sand dune. He released the tow-rope and caught a rising wind. He rose higher. In imagination, he soared on the wings of a bird. In actuality, he lurched like a roasted chook. Yet, as far as his genes were concerned, he was soaring. If only his father could see him now.

In his exhilaration, Glide banked and dived and skimmed. He flashed over the gleaming sand, over the sea where the silver-flecked waves sported, and over a gull that somersaulted in surprise. He wanted to go on and on, to go on forever. He wanted to rejoice in the freedom. But he knew that he couldn't. Not now. Not yet. He couldn't take the risk. If he landed in the water, his fragile craft would fragment. Reluctantly, he headed back.

Glide began to lower. The beach came up to meet him. Too quickly, he began to run. Strongarm and Hernandes stopped cheering and dashed forward. Glide's feet blurred but he couldn't keep up. His shoes cut a long trough in the sand. The hand-glider tipped and once again, he was buried head first.

If only his father could not see him now. Definitely, not now, hauled upright on the end of an elephant's trunk.

Hernandes dug out the glider. "Very good, very good," he said, "excepts for the landings."

Glide spat out sand and stumbled around in a circle. When his head cleared, he thoughtfully paced around the dune. How to land? How to land without bombing out? How?

Strongarm was watching the wheeling gulls. "Many martial arts begin by watching animals," he observed.

Glide turned to the gulls. "You think I should shriek?"

"Watch." Strongarm pointed with his trunk. "When they land, they fold in their wings."

"Yeah?" Glide watched a gull came down. It came low to the ground, turned one eighty degrees, and then landed. After that, it folded its wings. He watched a second gull and then a third. They all did the same. Glide rose excitedly. "Mate, you're right. I'll try that."

He again put on the harness and Strongarm began his run. As the wind whistled past his ears, Glide soared up and into the air.

For the fourth time that day, he felt the exhilaration of flying. On his flimsy structure, he rode high into the air. The wind whipped past his face and his muscles comfortably controlled his flight. With the beach a racing blur beneath him, Glide made the decision to land.

He manoeuvred the craft around in one-eighty degrees. The wind now fought it and slowed him down.

As he descended, Glide focussed on the image of a gull landing. As a result of his mental exercises, however, a shimmering form appeared in the air. He laughed with delight. Then as the ground rushed up, he made another one-eighty turn. His speed decreased immensely. He almost hovered. His feet hit the ground at a comfortable trot. Glide came to an easy halt and so strong was the image of a gull that when he stopped he even tried to close his wings.

"Squawk!" he cried. "Squawk! I mean I've done it! I've done it!"

Hernandes dashed along on his roo. "Makes a glider for me, too," he cried. "Makes one for me."

"And me!" Strongarm trumpeted. "I wanna drop on 'em from a big height."

"Yeah, right." Glide laughed. "Look, maybe we can make one for Hernandes. But for you, Strongarm? No, way. One tricky landing and you'd flatten the village. Anyway, I need you two for a very important tusk. I mean task." He decided to lay it on a bit thick. "Without you, my part can't even begin to work. You have to create a diversion."

Strongarm made a face. "Can't Rosenstern and Guildencrantz do that?"

"Well, that's the beauty." Glide thought he sounded very convincing. "They did so before. So if I now take them with me, Haggort will think that we're the diversion and that means that he'll then concentrate on you."

"Whats if we creates a flying diversion?" Hernandes suggested wistfully.

"No, you don't have the experience," Glide replied, implying that he had. "Now, one more go. Beam me up, Strongarm."

Pushed on by success, Glide did an almost vertical take-off. In a twinkling, the other two were just dark spots on the sand. Enjoying himself, he took little heed of another dot on the horizon. Moving high above him, it passed out of sight and hence out of mind. But when Glide turned above the ocean and prepared to slow for the land, it fell like a stone. Glide had just a moment to protect his face from a fierce attack – a fierce Goresh attack. As Glide shielded his eyes with one arm, the other beat out frantically. The bird backed off but circled for another charge. Though he didn't recognise the creature, Glide was pretty certain that he knew who it was. A hideous cackle confirmed it.

Goresh attacked again. Glide tried to turn his body but the harness slowed him. His flailing fist caught a departing body but not before sharp claws had slashed his face. With squawks of triumph, the raven shot away. But not far. Not far enough for Glide. Desperately, he reached inside his shirt. The whistle hung on a leather cord. This was definitely an emergency. He ought to blow. His fingers trembled. They fumbled on a shirt button. He let it go, sure that he would drop both whistle and cord into the ocean if he tried to pull it out. Yet if he tried to land under attack, he was equally sure to crash.

The raven was closing on him for a third time. Glide half-closed his eyes and concentrated. Nothing happened, except that his attacker drew even closer. Glide tried harder. His mind was bursting. He heard a wing beat. His mind exploded. Air shimmered. He projected fiercely. Suddenly there were two ravens. Goresh released a squawk of alarm. Maggot Thwacka saw it through his eyes and forced him to attack. Though frightened of this strange bird with no smell, Goresh threw himself at it. But he went right through! He turned and attacked again. And again and again. Each time, he went straight through. The raven's heart pounded. This must be the ghost of all his victims. Frightened and frustrated, with a final hysterical squawk, Goresh fled away.

Keeping hold of the raven image, Glide wheeled to land. As he came closer to the shore, Hernandes and Strongarm had stones ready to throw. But Goresh had had enough. Glide banked, slowed, and stumbled to a halt. Now he knew. He was no longer fighting for an abstract, he was no longer fighting just for Cascade. He was now fighting for his life.

Chapter 29

The Witch was furious. "You could've had him and scratched him. You could've pecked him and wrecked him. Now, he's more determined. Useless bird, useless mess. Useless raven, useless Goresh!"

Pecking out the eyeballs was an image that appealed to Goresh. As for the rest of the words, he preferred not to understand. Not that it helped. The sizzling in his neurons told him that the medium was the message. He flew back to Inklan and nestled in a tree. Goresh hung his head over a branch. As an evil raven, he was a failure. So much for Mr Edgar Allan Poo and his tap-tap-tapping on his chamber door. If he were lucky, Maggot Thwacka would forget about him for a while.

Goresh was lucky – at least for the moment. The Witch had decided to go on the offensive. On the offensiver – offensive was her natural state. "Greenvort," she paced her throne room, "Hernandes, that nasty do-gooder of an imp, rides a roo. Are there any young ones in Auslan?"

"A joey?" Greenvort thought quickly. It didn't pay to think slowly in the Witch's presence. "Yes...s. If a joey loses its mother in the other place, the Ne'..." The Witch hissed. "He brings them here for looking after."

"Then bring me one. The bigger the eyes, the better. The more cuddly, the better. I want innocence. The more innocent, the better."

"I've heard the stranger s...speak. He likes animals...s."

"We know!" The Witch threw him a furious look. "So don't think. Just do. Go, go, go! Fetch me a joey!"

Greenvort hurried away. On the other side of the Slowtime moat, Haggort was harrying his helpers.

"Leave them." Greenwort lifted his small arms to indicate that he wanted a pick-a-back. "She wants...s a joey."

"She wants a joey, a baby roo? She gone soft in der head?"

"No. I think she has a plan. A plan to catch our man."

"Uh huh." Haggort put a thick finger to his thick nose. "Dat makes sense."

With Greenvort on his back, Haggort galloped towards Auslan. At the boundary, there was another field of Slowtime. As he plunged through it, he felt the tiniest of drags against his short powerful legs. On the other side, he scrambled up the escarpment. In the distance was the forest and villages of Auslan. He trotted towards the trees, Greenvort clinging tightly to his back to minimise the pain of bouncing against the Giant Dwarf's rock hard muscles.

Guildencrantz and Rosenstern were guarding the perimeter. "It's a warm day." Guildencrantz yawned.

"Too hot for any incursions."

"Or excursions."

"Incursions or excursions."

They leant against a tree trunk and their snores competed with the songs of the birds.

Haggort crept up to the sleeping pair. "Should I biff 'em?"

"No." Greenvort pulled his ears to keep going. "If they wake up, they might know they've been biffed."

"I could biff 'em so they don't wake up."

But Greenvort shook his head. "Then they might use real guards."

"Yeah. Yeah, dat's right. Good thinkin', Greenvort."

"I try to think. I think I think better than her." He immediately put his hand over his mouth. There could be one of her bugs around, a bug in the shape of a raven - or even in the shape of a bug.

When Greenvort remained unblasted, he goaded Haggort into a faster walk. Beyond Glide's hut, there was a field with a small river running through it. This was the best place for finding stray roos. They hid behind a wide trunk at the water's edge. A big roo hopped across the clearing and bent his head to drink. Haggort and Greenvort pulled in their thoughts to remain unnoticed. The roo hopped away. Deciding it was safe, a bunch of smaller roos, females, came to drink.

Behind them was a lone joey. It had a fine red fur and large brown eyes. Its front paws were small but its rear legs were as long as its body. It hopped along with curiosity, stopping every so often to smell the roses. It was so cute... so cute. Haggort was tempted to jump right on top of it, to crush it, and to render it into soup. As his big body tensed, Greenvort pulled desperately on the wide lobe of the Dwarf's ear. He didn't want the Witch to render him into soup.

As the joey drew closer, Greenvort whispered, "Pretty, pretty. Come here, pretty."

The small roo sniffed the air. He was smelling the roses but this rose was unfamiliar. If the smell had just been that of Haggort or Greenvort, the joey might well have hopped away. But Greenvort had borrowed one of the Witch's concoctions. One made and saved from a young Cascade. He sprinkled it outwards from Haggort's feet. The innocent joey hopped towards the tree trunk. His head bent. He sniffed and hands attached to arms of iron caught him.

In fear, the joey cried out. But his cry was no more than a cough-cough growl, cough-cough growl. Haggort pressed the roo's face to his chest and even that coughing sound was smothered.

"We've got the young roo," Greenvort whispered excitedly. "So now let's see what the Witch is going ta do."

They raced through the trees, giving Glide's hut a wide berth. At the escarpment, Haggort's big feet pounded down, throwing up stones and making a noise. Guildencrantz and Rosenstern awoke. They saw the cloud of dust and made out the wide back of the Giant Dwarf.

"Huh!" Guildencrantz snorted. "I think we've frightened him away."

"Yeah. He knew what we'd do to him if we were awake."

Proud in their role as defenders of Auslan, the two imps continued their ever-ready patrol of the border.

Greenvort and Haggort entered the Witch's abode. They proceeded along the line of armour, the gangrenous green leering at them. Haggort thrust the roo's gentle rabbit face at them.

"You just stand here," he growled. "We do the actual work."

"They shirk," Greenvort added, "while we work."

"Yeah. Dem's a jerk."

They paused at the thick timber door that led into the Witch's presence. Haggort raised his fist to beat on the wood. By the time that it struck, though, it was just a feeble tap.

"Come." The door squeaked open. "Oh!" Maggot Thwacka clutched her knobbly knuckles to her knobbly chest. "You found me one. That's very well done." A mad smile lit her face. "You may go and play football with our men. Some of them are quite bouncy."

Her henchmen grinned. There was nothing they liked better than using a chubby man as a ball. Actually, there were lots of things they liked better. Such as pulling off the chubby man's arms and legs. But that would have to wait.

They left, leaving her alone with the joey. It looked at her with its gentle rabbit face. It wasn't very bright and, oh, so innocent. The Witch stroked her pointed chin and gazed thoughtfully at her potions. It would soon be much smarter but not quite so innocent.

Chapter 30

Once more, Haggort was carrying Greenvort and the joey. Glide was in his hut while Strongarm and Hernandes stood outside it.

"We gotta draw 'em up to the roo but they've not gotta know it was we wot did it," Haggort said.

"We can put the joey down. The Witch made sure that he won't run." Greenvort led the way to a line of bushes. "Now we go further away and attract their attention."

"I can do that, ha-ha." Haggort unloosened his belt. "Oi you, ya great grey drum. Getta load ov dis." The Giant Dwarf dropped his pants and pointed a huge pale bum at Strongarm.

"Him!" Strongarm trumpeted. "What's he doing this far into Auslan?"

"I came to pinch... to pinch..." Haggort's voice faded out. "Wot would I wanta pinch?" he whispered to Greenvort.

"Their two funny imps."

"Their wot? Yeah, dat's right. I came to pinch yer two funny imps."

"Our guards? Have you got them?" Strongarm pawed the earth, throwing up big lumps of grass. "Glide, stop your practise. We've got to go after them."

Since Glide hadn't been able to concentrate with the shouting, he came to the entry along with smoky images of Ne'wang.

"They're imp-napping Rosenstern and Guildencrantz!" Hernandes cried. "We musts go after them."

"Then let's go." Grabbing his shoulder bag, Glide set off.

Haggort ran with Greenvort on his shoulders. When he was far enough away, he turned and opened his arms. "Huh, fooled ya! We can stop ya trainin'! We can stop ya trainin'!"

He ran backwards, taunting them. Glide hesitated. "Strongarm, Hernandes, stop. There's something funny going on here."

"They're funny enough," Strongarm growled.

"They must wants us out of the hut." Hernandes turned Horsey, ready to go back.

They were stopped, though, by a strange cough-growling that came from around a line of bushes.

"What's that?" Glide nipped behind Strongarm. "It sounds like a wild animal."

"We don't haves wild animals," Hernandes said. "Only those who comes from Inklan."

Glide approached the line of bushes then paused and broke out in a cold sweat. From around the corner, a shadow had fallen across the pavement, a frightening shadow. It had the long jaws of a crocodile but the round body of a big roo. Stranger still, the shadow wasn't solid. It seemed to be coming through a wire figure and where it touched the ground, there was a very faint blueness. As he hesitated, the growling grew fiercer.

"Wait." Strongarm placed his trunk on Glide's shoulder. "Let me."

Glide, however, didn't want to appear cowardly. So he took off his shoulder bag and shoved his right arm deep inside it for protection. Keeping Strongarm close behind him, in case he needed to jump duck behind a shield, he leaned around the corner. In amazement, his jaw dropped.

Startled at Glide's reaction, Hernandes cried, "Tells me! Tells me! Tells me what it is!"

Glide turned to him. "It's a joey. A young roo."

"A joey? Is thats all?"

Hernandes couldn't believe that the strange growling could have come from a joey. Keeping Strongarm close behind, he also rounded the corner. He saw a young roo pressed against the bushes. It was even smaller than the imp and had such a gentle face. Its small pear-shaped body was balanced on wide feet and a strong tail. The colour of its fur was cream and reddish-brown.

"Hmm." Hernandes glanced back at Horsey. "He's a handsome young 'un." He stretched out a hand. "Kangy, kangy." Tentatively, the joey hopped forward, his nose sniffing Hernandes' palm. When he didn't retract the hand, the joey licked it. "Good kangy, good boy."

Glide bent down and stroked the golden fur. "Who do you belong to, I wonder?"

"There are mobs of roo in the forest," Strongarm said. "He could be one of their joeys or else Ne'wang brought him here from Ausphalia."

"He seems very tame." Glide thought back to home. "Maybe Ne'wang found him on someone's property?"

The roo made a low coughing sound and gazed from one to the other with his big brown eyes. Glide stroked him. "All right, you come with us." He looked around, wondering what had caused the strange shadow he'd seen earlier. The link with the Witch made sure he didn't think too deeply. "We'll see you'll be all right."

Hernandes played his palms over the roo's body. "He seems okays. Come on, boy, you can stays with us."

As the joey looked at them with his melting brown eyes, Glide knelt to cuddle him. "He's so soft." His eyes gleamed. "I used to really care about animals. I wanted to work with them. Somehow, I got sidetracked. Come on, Loopy." He looked at the others. "Is that name okay with you? Loopy?"

Strongarm did an I-don't-mind shrug of his shoulders. Not easy for an elephant but the message was conveyed. "Shouldn't be a problem. At least, unless the Ne'verman says no."

"Might he?"

Hernandes jumped onto Horsey. "He mights. We don't always understands why he does whats he does. He might have his reasons."

Glide once more patted the joey. It looked so harmless that his critical sense was nullified. "Come on, Loopy," he said. "Come with us."

The young roo gave its low cough as if it understood and began to hop with them. After a few steps, though, Glide paused. "So what was the growling? What made that odd shadow?"

"Maybe another animals? An animals such as Haggort?" Hernandes stroked Horsey's tall ears. "Sometimes the sun es low and the shadows of the big ears look like croc jaws."

"They do?" The sun wasn't that low but Glide shrugged. Maybe in Auslan the gateways between places meant that light didn't travel in straight lines as they did back home. He patted Loopy's head. "Come on, boy. We're just down the road." Glide felt a pang when he heard himself say *road*. Roads were what they had back on the Sunny Coast. Auslan had forest paths but it didn't have roads. Glide had never thought that he might sometime miss the smelly fumes.

When they returned to Glide's hut, Goldencrantz and Rosenstern were standing guard.

"Halt! Who goes there?" Goldencrantz cried.

"It's me." Glide went face-to-face with the imp.

"No Mes allowed in." Rosenstern stood straight and stiff.

Glide looked at Strongarm for help. "Can you do something?"

"They can be very obstinate." Strongarm placed the tip on his trunk on the top of Goldencrantz's head. He gently inhaled. A pointy hat lifted off. "Oh, I thought that was the shape of his head." Strongarm tried again. On the second try, the imp rose, his spine still straight. Like a living crane, the elephant swivelled and dropped the imp in the shade of a tree. The other imp followed. Loopy hopped up to them and their whole demeanour changed.

"Is this a joey, I see before me?" Goldencrantz leapt up with joy. "What big eyes you've got."

Rosenstern was equally joyous. "And what big ears."

"All the harder to ignores you two," Hernandes said gloomily as he dismounted from Horsey.

Glide fetched water from his hut. "We'd better see if Loopy's thirsty."

"Good ideas. It's a thirsty sorts of day." Hernades twisted his head around. "Where's Horsey? He doesn't usually leave when the saddle's on."

Glide pursed his lips. "She was looking a bit fidgety. I think she went into that glade." He pointed towards a grassed area surrounded by macadamia trees.

"Sometimes that roo can be a bit nutty," Strongarm observed.

"Maybc she's jealous of Loopy?" Glide suggested.

"Maybes." Hernandes tickled Loopy and, for the moment, Horsey was forgotten.

Glide looked towards the sun. It was a little low but he thought that he should put in a bit more training. "Loopy can come into the hut with me," he said. "He shouldn't be a problem."

After a little more patting of the roo, Glide sat on his three-legged stool and tried to see a concrete image of the Ne'vermaker. He was finding the feeling for it when Loopy cough-growled.

"There, there, boy." Glide searched around his hut. "I've got to do my homework." He found what he'd been searching for, a ball made of twigs and coloured twine. It was good to squeeze if his training wasn't going too well. But when he sat with the ball in his hand, Loopy growled louder. "Hey, stop that noise. It's just an old ball."

Glide knelt on the ground and rolled the ball towards the roo. Loopy's mouth opened. To Glide's surprise, it opened wide... wide... and wider. Loopy's snout stretched forward and at the last moment, Glide snatched the ball away.

"Hey, Loopy," Glide gently patted the roo on the nose, "don't be jealous. I just hold it while I practise."

But it didn't work. When Glide tried to concentrate, the cough-growl went on and on. With a sigh, Glide went outside.

"Hey, Strongarm can you look after Loopy while I train?"

"Is he too much of a handful?"

"Something like that."

"I'll take him for a walk." Strongarm nudged Goldencrantz and Rosenstern. "You two keep alert. Okay?"

Goldencrantz threw a quick salute. Rosenstern caught it. "No probs. We were sent to sentry."

Glide went back inside his hut, feeling a strange unease. Unable to put his finger on it, though, he sat on his chair and concentrated. Later, when they all went to Plonkers, he hoped that Ne'wang would appear. He did manifest, but not for long enough. Not sure what was bothering him, Glide didn't imbibe too much rotgut and even managed a fairly straight-line back to home. Before turning in, he put a rug down in the shelter of a tree while Loopy nibbled grass.

"There you are, boy. Almost a room of your own." He rubbed his nose against Loopy's side, feeling for a moment, as if he had pressed against the teeth of a comb. Puzzled, he yawned and shuffled off to bed. He wondered if his puzzlement was because Loopy was so cute. He was almost too cute, like an ad for a retirement village back on the Sunny Coast.

Chapter 31

In the middle of the night, Glide had a strange dream, a very unpleasant dream. It started with a cough-growl. The sound was low at first but gradually grew to fill every corner of his sleep. Glide put his hands over his ears but the sound wouldn't stop. It also acquired a shape. It began as a flat shadow that edged under the gap in his door. The shadow then took a terrible shape, looking as if croc jaws had been grafted onto a big roo body, a body made from wire. In his sleep - he was sleeping, wasn't he? – the shadow stood upright. Yet the shape remained flat, as flat as a cardboard cut out!

With a low moan, Glide turned in his bed. The roo went to his chair and with jagged teeth worried at something on the surface. Glide feared that it was his shirt, his treasured fringed shirt. He moaned again. The flat shape turned its strange, elongated head towards him then backed away. Once more, it lay flat on the floor and slid out through the crack. Glide gave a grunt of relief and managed to fall back into a decent sleep.

In the morning, he sat on the edge of his bed and rubbed his eyes. What a peculiar dream! About a roo, a roo with power saw for teeth. He couldn't remember the details but it certainly was scary. He stretched and shuffled over to his study table. An unexpected and disturbing sight greeted him. His twig and twine ball had been destroyed! Who had done that? A guard? Had one of his guards crept in and done it? No, Glide immediately dismissed the thought. They had no reason to do that and, anyway, none of them were vicious like that. A chill ran through him. Glide unconsciously wrapped his arms around his chest and shivered.

He dressed and with Loopy skipping at his side, Glide marched into Plonkers Breakfast Tavern. A chalked menu was attached to a pole. "Dodo eggs?" Glide tilted the board to make sure that he'd read it correctly. "I thought the Dodo was extinct."

"That's explains the tastes of their eggs." Hernandes came over to pat Loopy. "He a good boy?"

"I... I'm not sure. I had a really weird dream about a strange shadow or something." Glide held out the remains of the ball. "I don't know what's happened here. It looks like it exploded or something."

Hernandes took it. "You didn't sits on it, did you?"

Strongarm tapped it with his trunk. "It looks more as if I'd sat on it."

Glide took back the ball. "Maybe I sleep-sat."

"But sits on your ball?" Hernandes shook his head. "That ball is your favourites security blanket."

"That's right." Glide felt a soft weight press against his calf. "Oh, it's you, Loopy." He looked around. "Where's Horsey. Maybe he can play with Loopy?"

"I don't knows." Hernandes was cracking an egg as big as his head. "He saw Loopy and went skippy away."

"Okay." Glide touched the weight against his legs. "I'll just take you out for a bit of a play."

When he had gone, Hernandes heard a quiet cough-growl at the ragged fence that surrounded Plonkers. "Horsey." He approached his roo. "Where have you been? You wants to play with Loopy?"

He began to lead his roo across the field towards Glide. But Horsey held back. Hernandes put his small hands on his hips. "Are you jealous, Horsey? Jealous of Loopy? I'll takes you over and introduces you. Then you can be friends."

Hernandes jumped into the saddle and bounded across the clearing. "Here you are." He dismounted and holding onto the reins, he tried to lead Horsey closer. But the roo resisted and he had to pull. "You brings Loopy closer," Hernandes called. "I'll holds Horsey."

Glide took Loopy's right ear and drew his roo towards the other one. Briefly, Hernandes thought he saw a blue wire shadow fall over Horsey. He startled and Horsey, released, bounded away.

"Hey, Horsey! Horsey!" Hernandes looked around. Where had that strange shadow come from? With no answer, he looked in the direction of the departed roo. "Really, Horsey. Where are your manners?"

At that moment, Loopy put his little forepaws on Hernandes knees and tried to lick his face. "Good boy, that's a good boy." Hernandes remembered his Dodo egg. "Have I got eggs on my face?"

"You?" It was Strongarm. "Whatever you do, you'll never have egg on your face."

"Thanks you." The imp took out a hankie as large as himself and wiped his face. "That Loopy has a wets tongue."

Glide stretched, cracking his back. "Better get back to work or Ne'wang'll think we're slacking. I guess Horsey and Loopy can look after themselves for a while."

They were crossing the clearing to the hut when a man-shaped piece of sky landed in front of them. "Ow!" The Ne'verman did a dance of pain, trying to blow on his bare feet. "I forgot to allow for the extra mass." He pointed and a yellow-crested cockatoo jumped from his shoulder onto his extended finger.

"Who's this?" Glide tentatively stroked the gleaming white feathers.

"This is my mate, Merlin."

The big bird opened his strong beak. "Hello, Strongarm. Hello, Hernandes."

"Meet Glide."

"Hello, Glide."

Ne'wang lifted his hand and the cockatoo took to the air. "Merlin is my familiar." The Ne'verman stretched back a long thin arm to scratch between his shoulder blades. "Funny vibes were coming over the gateways. I thought I'd better bring him."

"Funny vibes," Merlin screeched, "are not funny." He flew back onto Ne'wang's shoulder, seemingly chuckling to himself.

"Does he really talk?" Glide asked.

"Yep. Got a PhD, this bird. Yeah, he's pretty bright."

"Why don't you call him Cocky or Whitey?" Glide was getting a bit tired of magic. "Why Merlin?"

"Because he's my familiar," Ne'wang repeated.

"Merlin the Magician." Glide made a face.

The young man found that he was more interested in the bird than its magic. The cockatoo reminded him of all the different birds on the Sunny Coast: the kookaburra with its hysterical laugh, the elegant ibis with its long narrow beak, and the galah with its rolling walk. Glide's favourite, however, was the black cockatoo with its enormous wingspan and distinctive way of flying. Just before rain the black cocky would circle the sky, cawing harshly. Much like Goresh, Glide thought. Hmm, now that was a thought and a half.

Ne'wang waved his hands in front of Glide to get his attention. "Right, Glide's gotta practise. I gotta go." He directed Merlin into the air again. "And he can find out what's happening."

The Ne'verman flipped backwards, falling through a gateway. That, too, was interesting, Glide thought. The gateway didn't seem to be an actual hole in real space. It seemed to be more a hole in the psyche. The only problem with that idea, though, was that he just didn't know what he meant by it. On the other hand, when he practised in his hut, he felt that what he was projecting was the hole itself, or from the hole. What an idea! It gave him a headache. The whole hole was headache. It was a relief when Strongarm trumpeted an interruption.

"Time for venomade, Glide." Strongarm dipped his trunk into a bucket and sprayed.

Glide inhaled the spray and blinked. "I wouldn't mind a decent coffee."

"I go and gets it from Plonkers. Horsey! Horsey!" Hernandes searched the nearby glade. "Where es that silly roo? He gone all morning."

They began a search but found no sign of Horsey. Loopy, however, was grazing behind a bush. He stopped and immediately hopped towards them.

"Have you been a good roo?" Glide rubbed the golden-brown belly. "Yes? Yes?"

As Loopy looked at him with his large brown eyes, Glide, for some reason, had a flash vision of Merlin. "Magic," he thought. That was forgotten, however, when Hernandes gave a little gasp. He bent to the grass and picked up a small object.

"What's wrong?" Glide hurried to the imp.

"This es a bit of Horsey's rein." Hernandes turned it. "Look! And this looks like blood. Loopy?" He faced towards the joey. "Was et Loopy? Did they have a fight?"

"Loopy?" Glide gazed into the young roo's gentle eyes. "It couldn't be."

Hernandes sniffed. He couldn't believe it himself. In a comradely gesture, Glide put an arm around the imp. Loopy, however, tried to push between them.

"Not now, Loopy." Glide pushed the joey away with his knee. "Not now."

Unnoticed, a wire shadow fell on the back of their legs.

Chapter 32

Dabbing at his eyes, Hernandes showed the bit of rein to Strongarm. "Look, Horsey's been hurts."

"Hurt? No wonder we haven't seen him." Strongarm absent-mindedly pulled up a clump of fresh grass and put it in his mouth. "Haggort's got a way of creeping in. Could it have been him?"

Glide watched as Strongarm chomped. "He's big enough. And mean enough." Glide took a closer look at the rein. "Maybe he grabbed it and Horsey ran away."

"We have to looks for him." Out of habit, Hernandes lifted his leg as if about to mount his roo.

Glide was still holding the bit of rein when Loopy lifted his nose to it. He bared his teeth and a steady cough-growling came from him. "Quiet, quiet." Glide snatched his hands away.

Hernandes, though, glared at the joey. "There's somethings about that roo, somethings not quite right."

"He's just a joey." Glide bent to pet Loopy. "He doesn't know right from wrong." He stroked the soft fur, frowning with puzzlement as he seemed to feel sharp edges beneath his fingertips.

"He's not just a joeys." Hernandes said. "He's somethings else altogether." For a second time, a wire shadow fell unnoticed across the back of his legs. "He's weirds." He sighed. "I wished the Ne'verman was heres. He could tells us."

"Yes, he could tell us." Glide looked around for the glossy cockatoo. He saw a white streak in the sky. It seemed to be chasing away a black one.

Since Ne'wang seemed to be on a prolonged absence, probably tied up in business concerned with yet another sacred site, Glide decided to also take time off. Instead of sitting in his hut and learning to create images, he went with Strongarm to see their troops.

Goldencrantz and Rosenstern were demonstrating one-step sparring. Goldencrantz punched. Rosenstern stepped back while blocking. Or rather, Rosenstern tried to step back while blocking. Only he didn't quite manage it. Goldencrantz had stepped on his foot.

"That's not one-step sparring." Rosenstern tried to twist his foot free.

"This is better than one-step." Goldencrantz threw a series of mock-punches. "This is half a step sparring. Copy us!" The imp signalled to the amassed troops.

"I see trouble," Strongarm groaned.

He was correct and trouble followed very quickly. As soon as Trooper One trod on the toe of Trooper Two, Two howled and trod back. It turned into a stamping conquest that reminded Glide of Oirish dancing. At least, it provided exercise.

While Strongarm sorted out the mess, Glide searched among the trees. He found one with a wide strong leaf and contemplated carving out a boomerang. It could provide a useful addition to the armoury. But, and he realised there was always a 'but' in the state of Auslan, a thrower such as Goldencrantz might do more damage to himself than to an enemy.

He was adding up the pros and cons when Hernandes rode up on Horsey. "He was in my huts." The imp leapt off of the roo. "Not outsides but insides. I think he very scareds."

"Of?"

Hernandes didn't want to say. Looking at the ground, he muttered, "Loopy, I thinks."

That was not a happy thought and the rest of the day turned out to be an itch they couldn't scratch. Even Plonkers didn't provide much relief. Hernades worried about Horsey. Glide worried about Loopy. Strongarm worried about the two of them. When the moon started to weave a wobbly way across the sky, Glide headed for bed.

"Sleep on it," Strongarm said. "It'll be clearer in the morning." He didn't say it with much conviction. It was just positive thinking. But, sometimes, even positive thinking could turn out to help.

But it didn't help. Hernandes, in particular, was restless. Every time, branches rustled or an owl hooted, he awoke thinking of Horsey. He was tossing and turning when a wire shadow slipped into his hut. At first, he didn't notice it. Then it sprang upright. At the strange sight of the flat, wire shadow of a roo, Hernandes' heart began to hammer. His breath grew wheezy and he pushed back from the weird sight. The shadow cough-growled and the hairs on the back of his neck stood up. With a muted curse, as the flat shadow came round one side of the bed, Hernandes threw himself off the other. He dashed out of the door and ran towards Glide's hut.

"Et's after me! Et's after me!" Hernandes tried to rush through the door. Two stalwart arms prevented him.

"Halt! Who goes there?" Goldencrantz cried.

"Halt! Whom goes there?" Rosenstern said by way of correction.

Hernandes was scared but not of grammar. He pushed through and rocked Glide's shoulder. "The shadow, et es after me!"

"Wha'? Wha'?" Glide opened bleary eyes.

"Loopy's shadow thing! Et's after me."

Glide sat up. "The shadow thing?" He put his finger to his lips. "Quiet, we don't want to frighten Goldencrantz and Rosenstern."

"We don't? Why not?"

"Because they'll run away and never come back." Glide was more awake now. "Where was it? Show me."

They crept back to Hernandes' hut but there were no longer any strange shadows.

"Et's gone now. But et was here."

"Okay, it's gone." Glide yawned. "So you can go back to bed now."

"No, no way." Hernandes shivered. "I'll take my rolls and sleep in your huts."

"Oh, all right." Glide was too tired to argue. "Just don't snore."

"Me snores?" the imp was indignant. "I'm quiets as a mouse."

Normally? Yes. But tonight? No. In his dreams, he saw that strange wire roo as it creak-creaked towards him, its teeth like saw-blades. He put his arms up and cried out. Glide awoke and shook the imp awake. It was not a good night, but proceeded in stops and starts.

Dawn came and brought a charming chorus of magpies and butcher birds. On top of the chorus was the screech of one bloody big white cocky. Glide startled awake, twisted out of bed and plonked his feet on the floor. They met soft flesh.

"My chests," Hernandes groaned. "You're standings on my chest."

"Oops!" Glide lifted his feet, allowing Hernandes to stand.

"Et's not your faults," the imp said. "Et's because of that roo."

Merlin shouted at them from a branch. "Morning, morning. Watch out for that roo." Loopy was at the base of the tree and looking up. "Watch out for that roo."

"Loopy?" With uncertainty in his voice, Glide said, "Come here, boy. Come here."

As the roo hopped towards him, Glide called up his eidetic imagery and projected his most recent sighting of Haggort and Greenvort. He'd been certain that those two had been after the joey. Now, he wasn't so sure. He played and replayed the image. It was impossible to say. Had they been after Loopy or had they actually deposited him? Had their antics been to draw him to the roo? To make sure that he caught Loopy? It seemed so unlikely. Roos were gentle. Though once, he recalled, he had seen two males battle it out. They balanced on their big tails and used their powerful rear legs to rip into each other. But Loopy wasn't big. He was small. He couldn't even balance on his tail so he certainly couldn't let rip with his hind legs.

They all trooped down to breakfast. Glide hoped that he might still find Plonkers Tavern for Rotgut and Associated Beverages. But no such luck. It was just the Breakfast bar. They ate quietly, knowing that they had a serious problem with the joey.

Before he began his practise, Glide brought Loopy into his hut with Strongarm blocking out the doorway. When he lit a candle, the inside was now dim enough for the flame to show. He held it behind the joey.

"Look."

Hernandes and Strongarm looked. The shadow was completely wrong. It wasn't solid. It had holes as if Loopy were made of wire. He was small. The shadow was big. Loopy was plump and round. The shadow was lean and jagged.

"We have a problem," Glide said. "One big scary problem."

Chapter 33

Glide sat and Loopy rested his chin on his knees. Without even thinking about it, Glide stroked the joey. He gave a sigh that was dredged from the bottom of his moccasins.

"Let's see what we can do." He gave the candle to Hernandes. "You hold this."

Glide had a broom in the corner of his hut. For a moment, he stood with it alongside the wire shadow. Then he lifted the broom and whacked it down on the shadow. Loopy made his low cough-growl, but the shadow never changed.

"Et's cursed." The candle flame wavered in Hernandes' hand. "The shadows is cursed."

"I'll try something else." Glide led Loopy into the sun and used one of Plonkers' tankards to focus the sun's rays onto the shadow. Grass smoked. The shadow still didn't change, but Loopy's growls did. They became fiercer and more threatening.

"It's not physical." Glide was sweating. "Damn and strawberries, but we'll have to tie him in the shade and see what the Ne'verman can do."

Glide thought about blowing the whistle. But if this was an emergency, it was one they could wait out. Instead he put his concerns aside and managed to work at visualising. Eventually, he created an image of a blue man in the candle flame. With concentration, he made it bigger and started to move it around. With further concentration, Glide found that he had two of them.

"Two? Damn, I'm only trying for one."

"Glide?"

"Yeah?"

"Glide?"

"Yeah. Wot? You're not supposed to be a talking image."

"Glide, for Ne'vers sake! It's me, Ne'wang. I'm here."

"Oh! Oh, right. I thought I was seeing, creating, double."

"The vibes that Merlin is sending through the gateway are not good. The Witch has been up to something."

"Her!" Glide rubbed at his eyes. "You think she's behind Loopy."

"What better trap for you than an innocent looking joey?"

"You reckon? I had thought Haggort had been trying to steal Loopy. But it could be he's a plant."

"A plant?" The Ne'verman gave Glide a funny look. "I think you'll find he's an animal."

"Ha-ha. I meant they left him here as a decoy."

"Okay, Glide, so let's find Merlin and see what he's got to say."

They went outside. Loopy was still tied to the thin trunk of a Cooloolabah tree. Though he was under the shade and had water and grass, his big brown eyes were sad.

"I'm sorry, mate." Glide spread his arms in apology. "We're not sure what you are."

Ne'wang pointed to a circling speck in the sky. "That's Merlin up there. He's keeping Goresh away."

"G'day, mate." Strongarm had just arrived.

Hernandes soon followed. The presence of the Ne'verman was a magnet that immediately attracted them.

"I'll just call him." Ne'wang whistled, a sound that was at first audible then went supersonic.

The big cocky descended like an arrow shot from a bow. At head height, he did a loop-the-loop, cawed with triumph and landed on the Ne'verman's head.

"Show off." Ne'wang lifted his hand and Merlin waddled onto it. "So Merlin, what've we got?"

The cockatoo opened its strong beak. "Exo! Exo!" he screamed.

"Exo." The Ne'verman looked apologetic. "He can't say exorcism. The word's a bit hard for him."

"Exorcisms?" Hernandes was disbelieving. "We has to do exorcisms?"

"Didn't you say that Loopy has a blue wire shadow?"

Glide slowly nodded.

"I haven't had time to think about it." Ne'wang stroked the bird. "That's why I left Merlin here. "But doesn't that remind you of anything?" At a prolonged silence, he added, "The wire that you found at the base of Slowtime?"

"Of course!" Glide clicked his fingers. "But that seemed such an anomaly that I didn't put them together."

"Magic and science, Glide. Magic and science."

Glide shook his head. It was so hard to think that the gentle-eyed joey could be a real problem. "So an exorcism? You think he's possessed?"

"Something like that. Let's see."

The Ne'vermaker sang to Merlin in a strange language. At intervals, the cockatoo repeated sounds. They all walked towards where the little roo was tethered. At their approach, Loopy retreated against the tree trunk, growling quietly. Then he did the opposite, pulled against the leash and grunted furiously. Ne'wang threw up his arm. Merlin flew into the air then floated to the ground closer to the tree. The grunting increased to a frenzy, the roo frothing at the mouth.

Keeping to one side, Glide lit a candle. A faint but wide wire shadow appeared. Then he turned the flame towards Merlin. His shadow was solid but small.

"Merlin, here." Ne'wang held the cockatoo and again sang to him, saying to Glide, "Keep the candle flame going."

The young man did so and to his surprise, the bird's shadow grew bigger and bigger. As it did, Loopy went into tantrums. He bashed into the tree and lunged against the leash; then he did it again.

Strongarm's trunk suddenly pointed straight out. "The roo's shadow is pulling free!" The elephant's voice was as high as a mouse's squeak.

The Ne'vermaker took one look. "Go!" He threw Merlin into the air.

The cockatoo dived at Loopy. He attacked, a strange attack. The cockatoo flew over the roo, dived at the roo, and circled the roo. Yet he never bit him nor clawed him. On the other hand, the bird's shadow went straight at the shadow Roo. Powerful shadow claws scratched at shadow wires. They stretched them and weakened them. His strong shadow beak crunched them and crushed them. The solid bird shadow buffeted the thin wire shadow. In retaliation, the wire shadow tried to fight. It tried to evade and it tried to run. But there was no escape. Whatever it was, it was ripped to pieces.

Eventually, Merlin stopped darting from side to side and Loopy stopped struggling. Glide watched in amazement as the bird lowered his head and stroked Loopy's face with his yellow crest. Glide lit the candle again. Both shadows were normal.

The Ne'vermaker slapped his hands together. "There, it's done."

"So Loopy's been exorcised?"

"He's been exorcised."

Glide stroked the joey. He remembered feeling harsh lines within the rotund body. Now they were gone. "So he was meant to hurt us somehow?"

Ne'wang nodded. "Some form of Slowtime entrapment."

Glide shivered. "So if we don't go to it, she will find a way of sending it to us?"

"That's how it seems."

"And Loopy?" Glide rested a hand on the joey's head.

"Best if he goes stroll-about with a roo mob."

"And Merlin?"

"He's got his own ways."

There was a long silence. Hernandes broke it, his voice unsteady. "So that's et. If we don't goes to et. Et will comes to us."

"That's it," Ne'wang agreed, "it will come to us."

"Damn and strawberries," Glide muttered, "Take me down to Plonkers."

Chapter 34

In the age-old tradition of barmen everywhere, Plonkers was calling, "Time, gen'lemen, please."

There was a chorus of groans, suggesting that if the walls had ears then the floor had mouths.

"It's early, yet. Me wife's still awake."

"'Aven't 'eard the crow cock, er, the cow crock, the... zzz..."

"But I kin still unnerstan' meself."

Plonkers reached for his two-be-four. "If yous ain't out by the time I counts t'ten, yous all be for it."

"Ten? You can't even count up ta three."

"I can if I starts at nine. Nine!"

There was a flurry of movement and a scurry of feet from those who were still on them. There was also a donk-donk of elbows and a clonk-clonk of knees from those who were not so fortunate. Even the dimmest shade of consciousness reacted when Plonkers' voice took on a certain sort of tone. Right now, it had that tone. When the inn was empty, Plonkers took an unusual care in his security. From inside, he pulled wooden shutters over his windows. From outside, he locked the doors with heavy bolts. Now, no one could get in from out - nor outt from inn. And, as far as he knew, no one was left inside. Not even in the cracks between the floorboards.

Though early by Plonkers time, it was already well into the night. A night that perfectly suited Glide, cloudy and windy. He was waiting in the forest. With him was Strongarm, two dismantled handgliders stacked neatly on the elephantine back. Hernandes was quietly fussing around them. At a disturbance, however, they all drew their weapons. But it was only Plonkers. Leading him were Rosenstern and Guildencrantz.

Plonkers showed himself to be a true woodsman. "Ai," he hopped stealthily, "oi've stubbed me foot. Ah, a tree just bit me! Fizz, there's zomething in me pants!"

In this manner, they arrived a few minutes after their voices did. Hernandes flapped his arms. "Quiets, we don't wants them to knows we're here."

"Fizz!" Plonkers glared at Rosenstern and Guildencrantz. "But they came wiz me."

Hernandes threw his hat down. "Not them. *Them*."

"Oh, yez, them." Plonkers held his two-be-four aggressively. But he jumped when Glide glided out of the shadows.

"Quick," Glide said, "get undressed." Plonkers gave him a funny look. "I mean you've got to change clothes with me."

"Oi, right yez are, then. Right yez are."

Plonkers stripped down to his bare skin. "Ah," Glide muttered, "I didn't mean to take off your bloomers. Just your shirt and trousers." He held his nose. "Jeez, mate. When did you last wash?"

"I wash, my friend, I wash. I just don't want to put on me clean clobber coz I like to keep 'em clean. If you see what I mean?"

For a moment, Glide had thoughts that were strongly desirous of a hot shower and laundered underwear. He shook them off. "Never mind, you stay here. Rosenstern and Guildencrantz, you follow me."

Hernandes eyed the angle of the moon. "Better synchronises our watches firsts," he said.

"Watches!" Glide glanced at his bare wrist with amazement.

"Sures." Hernandes took a small sundial from his pocket. "Damn!" He shook it. "Night times."

Rosenstern held his sundial to the moon. "Check. Night time."

Guildencrantz took out an hourglass. "Night time plus four grains. A day to go."

Glide looked at Strongarm. "Did any of that make sense to you?"

"About the same as you looking at your wrist and saying five hairs past the freckle."

"But that's just habit!" Glide looked at where his watch used to be. Then he gazed pensively towards the sky. He was now pretty good at knowing the time by the angle of the sun – except at night.

Hoisting one handglider, Glide pointed down a tunnel of trees. "We'll go that way. You go south." Plonkers lifted the second handglider. "And Plonkers," Glide added, "please don't risk actually trying to fly."

"Wot me? Cos not." Plonkers winked. "Never take a risk, that's me."

With the stealth of a rhino on stilts, Plonkers led Strongarm and Hernandes south. In the dark, between his two companions and with the change of clothes, Plonkers could easily be mistaken for Glide. The fog of cloud cover also helped. Glide, meanwhile, with Guildencrantz and Rosenstern had entered the tunnel of trees. To judge by its smell - those few odours bold enough to overcome those of Plonkers' clothes - it was an animal track. For Glide, it provided an excellent cover.

As planned, and despite synchronised sundials and hourglasses, they arrived at the escarpment about twenty minutes later. To the south and below the edge of the escarpment, they could spy a steady convergence of dots. The large one, they guessed was Haggort. The small one at his side must be Greenvort.

"Good." Glide rubbed his hands. "They've fallen for it. They think Plonkers in my clothes is me. Now, while they go after him, you two help me into the air."

As Rosencrantz and Guildenstern were getting ready to pull Glide, Plonkers was also wrestling his way into his harness. Haggort was watching from below. "Wot's he doing in dat t'ing? Wings? He's puttin on wings? He ain't hoping t'fly over da moat, is he?" The

Giant Dwarf roared with laughter. "If he comes dis way, his skin I'll flay. Call me an imp, if you see me wimp."

Greenvort held out his palms, sensing energy. "You know he's...s got a wire," he hissed. "Into its s...secrets, he'll enquire. So it must be time for him to expire."

The Witch, sensing their news, flew into a fury. "He dares to fly over my moat," she screeched. "I'll make it higher, stronger! Their blood will water it and their skulls will decorate it. They dare to infringe upon my land." Her voice became darker and more bloated. "As for those two, my fool assistants, my would-be knight and would-be king, I'll put an end to their self-promises." She hunted feverishly among her jars of potions. "This will do. An alembic for their iambic. I'll curse it for their sonnet. Not an iota for their pentameter."

With curious rhyme, she stirred and cursed. An olive-green fog arose from her glass retort. She rubbed it into her hair, cackling at its acid feel. It seeped into her joints, evoking arthritic stabs of pain. But for now, she was beyond pain. In the vessel, green crystals formed around blue wire filaments. She twisted them into strange shapes and impregnated them with her reverberating incantations. This one would go into the crucible of Slowtime. This one would be its antidote. And this one? What would it be, with its devils horns and strange overlappings of circuitry?

Glide adjusted his harness. "You go over the edge," he said to the two imps, "and pull. Soon as I feel some tension, I'll start to run."

"Forsooth!"

Rosencrantz ran to the left. Guildenstern ran to the right. They came to the end of their rope, their feet flew up, and their bottoms came down.

"Oops!" Rosencrantz groaned.

"Just practising," Guildenstern whimpered.

"Damn!" Glide was furious with fear. "We're right to go. We're ready. Surely, you two can just go down!"

The imps jumped to attention. "Yes, sir!" they cried and leapt over the edge. Glide expected to feel a tug on the string. Instead, there was a muted muttering. Two heads popped back.

"You right?" asked one.

"You ready?" asked the other.

"Yes, yes! I'm right. I'm ready." For a moment, Glide had the fear that these two had been magicked in the same way as Loopy. He had to summon all of his courage to cry, "Pull, damn you, pull!"

There was the sound of scrabbling. This was followed by a gentle tug. At first, Glide pulled against it. When the force built up, he began to run. At the edge, he hurled himself forward. For a sickening moment, his feet scrabbled on dirt and the wings pulled against his arms. But the slight breeze from the cooling cliff caught him. He balanced momentarily on tiptoes. A breathless pause and then he was airborne. Below him, Rosencrantz and Guildenstern danced with delight. In front of him, across the narrow strip of land that was Inklan, shone the strange light of Maggot Thwacka's castle.

Glide glided. He soared soundlessly. It was sheer pleasure to dance with the currents. But when he crossed into Inklan, the clear air became murky. By the time that he wanted to land, he seemed to be dropping into a stagnant pool of green algae. At least, no one was about. His diversion must be working. He turned to slow his speed, skimming over the roof. He turned again. Touchdown! A perfect landing! He was on the roof! Fantastic!

Glide slipped off the harness and in the misty darkness, he listened carefully, very very carefully. There were no sounds, none at all. In the moonlight, he saw just a thin strip of light outlining a trapdoor. Cautiously, he lifted it. No one was in sight. He crept down a ladder and landed in a long corridor. All that he could see were two lines of armour. Great, that looked pretty safe. And the ladder had been very conveniently placed, too. His luck was in.

His critical sense was out.

As Glide hesitated, Plonkers was settling into his harness. "Well," He wriggled his shoulders, "are youz gonna pull me or what?"

"But you can't fly it," Strongarm objected.

"Oi knows that an' you knows that. But that gorilla down there don't. An' if they're to think that I'm that potty young fella then the least youz can do is to pull me into the air."

Strongarm looked at Hernandes. Hernandes looked at Strongarm. They both looked at Plonkers. They both sighed.

"Wells," Hernandes reached for a rope, "maybe a small pulls."

"Very small." Strongarm reached for another.

But a pull is a pull is a pull. Especially when aided and abetted by the bulk of an elephant. Plonkers rose. He soared high into the air. At his apex, he took a nip from something secreted up his sleeve and that lifted him even higher.

"Come down!" Strongarm trumpeted.

"Come downs!" Hernandes squealed.

"Come down," Haggort invited.

Plonkers took another nip. Then from the recesses of his glider, he withdrew his two-be-four. During the afternoon, he had thoughtfully studded it with six-inch nails. With a cry of "Geronimo!" he sailed over the moat of Slowtime. He hovered over enemy territory, a terrible sight to behold. A pug-nosed, club-waving barman.

The gathered enemy, most of who would've preferred to be friends, hastily retreated. Only a puzzled Haggort stood his ground. He now realised that this was not Glide. He knew what it was not but he didn't know what it was. Somewhat hesitantly, he ran towards the falling creature with the intention of crushing it within his strong embrace. They met and the next moment, he was skittering back with rusty spikes pounding at his head and Greenvort slipping and sliding beneath his feet.

What Plonkers lacked in good sense, however, he made up with... in... with... nothing. With the fog of Inklan swirling about him but no wind, there was no hope of getting airborne again. Nor did he know about turning into the wind. He touched down. His feet scraped earth and, with a yell, he lifted them up again. Seconds later, his legs blurred as they tried to keep up with his descending body. The handglider passed him as he tried to dig in his toes. But as he was still wearing the harness, the front could only dip down. In a shower of dirt, branches and feathers, Plonkers somersaulted to a halt.

Haggort ran at him. "Got ya!"

"Wa ... wazzat?"

Plonkers stumbled in a circle. Haggort closed on him. Plonkers stepped back but Greenvort had knelt behind him. Haggort trod on his toes and the barman tilted back at an impossible angle. Haggort thrust his pock-marked face into a boozy vein-broken one.

"Dis ain't da right guy," Haggort growled. He lifted Plonkers in one huge paw. "Dis is jest da barman. Where's dat oder guy? C'mon, I'll shake it outta ya." Plonkers had no objection to that. He frequently shook it out. All of it. Including the last slug that he had swallowed. Haggort jumped back, letting go as he did so. He drew back a large foot. "I'll kick it outta ya. See if I don't."

But Greenvort clutched at his leg. "There's something wrong here," he said. "This is just another decoy."

"He don't look very coy t'me," Haggort growled.

"Forget him," Greenvort insisted. "Let's go. Quick, quick!" Haggort hated to let go when he had a good thing going. But Greenvort also pointed at Strongarm. "He's coming through again!" Once more, the elephant had launched himself through Slowtime and was charging to the rescue. "Quick! Quick!" Greenvort leapt aboard the Giant Dwarf's shoulders.

The latter released a half-hearted boot at Plonkers. That was enough to send the barman's incline into a decline. Plonkers disappeared into a blur of bush. Haggort disappeared into a detonation of dust. Strongarm halted in a cloud of confusion. Everyone had suddenly disappeared. Where had they gone? Alliteration had alarmed them all.

Searching around, Strongarm spotted a feebly waving arm in the bushes. Quickly, he plucked Plonkers out, threw him onto his back and continued to charge. But Haggort had crossed the narrow stretch of Inklan and ran through the castle's inner moat of Slowtime. Strongarm halted. Having no idea of its width, he couldn't risk going through. From the other side, his enemies jeered.

At that moment, Glide stood between the two strange lines of shining armour. He took his first step and shuddered. For no discernible reason, he no longer felt so safe.

Chapter 35

Glide knew that he was being watched. For once he was between the metal suits, his skin had started to crawl. He looked back. Had there been movement? Had the suits moved? There were apertures in the armour. But he saw no indications of arms or legs. There did seem to be a faint blue glow reminiscent of valve computers. But that, he decided, was probably the reflection of the moon on the metal.

He took a few more steps. The hairs on his neck rose. They stuck straight out! They quivered like antennae. Slowly, very slowly, Glide turned. Had the blue light intensified? Was this light the same as Loopy's shadow? From the corner of his eyes, it seemed to flicker over the metal. Hardly visible but it was definitely there. Were the lines of armour as straight as before? He had the distinct impression of being crowded.

Glide went over his choices. On or back? Or the third way: become a whistle blower and summon the Ne'vermaker. Ne'wang would come immediately. If he could. If politics didn't restrain him. Glide sighed. He'd come this far. He focussed on the far door. With a sense of increasing pressure on his shoulder blades, he moved towards it. He reached out. He touched the door. As a last check, meant to be reassuring, he turned. His heart jumped into his mouth. He was surrounded. The empty suits of armour were enclosing him. Even as he stood frozen, the door was flung open. The metal arms grasped him and carried him into the room.

A rotten stench rolled over him.

Glide gasped. He gasped again. The person confronting him exuded a foul pox-laden smell. Even her complexion was sick with small bruised-blue patches shifting around under her skin. Glide had seen those dark pouches under the eyes of people suffering from severe strain. This person's whole body suffered from strain. The blue patches bubbled up in one spot, deflated, only to reappear elsewhere.

They reminded Glide of something. It was... Yes. His eidetic memory conjured up the pages of a children's book, *Arthur's Chicken Pox*. This creature was suffering from a bilious case of colouring in.

It, she, had to be the Witch. He tried to tell himself that he was being silly, that he was reacting to a stereotype. But he couldn't help himself, his whole body shrunk away from her. Even the eerie armour was preferable. She epitomised all the wicked Witches and evil godmothers of every fairy story that he'd ever known. And yet, she could have been beautiful. She was tall and thin with narrow features. Her mouth could have been full but she compressed her lips into a slit of contempt. Her eyes could've been bright but they had transformed into pools of muddied hate. Her hair could've been... Who could say? Now it was a strange blue. A blue with a metallic sheen, it seemed to be alive, a Medusa's head of writhing snakes. But this was no fairy tale witch to be laughed at. This was a real life Medusa.

The Witch exuded power. Her aura of jagged black seemed to swallow up the light. Before this pox-ridden evil, Glide was totally repulsed. Physically unable to move, he reacted by mentally retreating. Yet just as the strong arms gripped his arms, so sharp fingers scraped at his mind.

"Bring him in," the Witch rasped. As if he weighed nothing, the armour held him at the base of her wooden throne. He shuddered at the skulls that decorated it. The Witch grabbed his hair. "Ah," she cackled, "but your head would fit nicely."

Glide gulped. He knew he wasn't brave, that he lacked the heroism of Strongarm, but he wasn't a coward either. Even so, his heart sank in that room of stinking retorts, jars of pickled organs and sharp, dripping instruments. He tried, however. He did try.

"Wood's not my colour," he croaked.

"He-he-he," the Witch chortled, "he-he-he. So it's not, so it's not." She picked up a jar. "But it will be. Oh, but it will be."

She cracked her knuckles, grimacing with the pain. In the silence, with her over-ripe stench, the noise was ominous. Glide tried to break away but his arms screamed agony. The Witch cackled again. Her eyes glowed red. Glide saw a tremendous intelligence shine out of them, a mad non-caring intelligence. For a moment, he also saw the wild beauty that she had once been. The vision touched him, showing fleetingly in his expression.

The Witch noticed. "Don't look at me like that!" she grated. "Don't!"

"I saw what you once were."

"Once! Once were! I was a nothing. A fool. A weak-kneed little girl. Now, now I am a something." She rubbed her hands. "And now, shall I show you what you came for? Yes, I'll show you. But you won't be so lucky, not half so lucky." He prodded him. "A bit thin, aren't you? And a bit smelly?"

Glide flinched from her. "Smelly? You're rancid!"

"A few herbs, though," she cackled, "and you'll come up nicely. He-he-he."

The Witch moved towards a corner. It was intricately cobwebbed and the odour of long-dead fish emanated from it. Glide cringed, thinking that he was going to be hurled into that murk. Then his stomach turned. Within the haze, he made out a figure. Cascade. It was her. She of the silver hair and golden skin. He saw, or felt, that she moved within the nauseating infinitude of Slowtime. The Witch snapped her fingers. At a quarter speed, Cascade turned. Glide dry-retched. Glide was entranced.

He threw himself forward. Or tried. But metal fingers held him immobile. He spat into the nearest visor. If the blue glow meant electricity perhaps he could short-circuit it. But the grip never faltered. Maggot Thwacka snapped her fingers again. Cascade froze. Glide still struggled uselessly. In a parody of thought, the Witch slowly stroked her blue-patch chin. The movement gripped Glide.

He tried to look away, but found that he couldn't. Her chin seemed to grow longer and longer with each stroke. So did her nose. Her skin became more mottled and lumpy. She cackled with a sound that cut right through to the worst of his childhood nightmares. He shivered and felt completely helpless. In despair, his inner voice called out for the Ne'vermaker. All the power of his eidetic ability screeched into it.

The Witch strolled around him. "A little bit of skin," she chanted. "A little bit of hair and a little bit of blood, let's see what we can make from this little piece of mud."

Glide shivered again. Two fits of shivers ran through him, once from guilt and once, amazingly, from hope. The guilt was because, as a student, he'd collected and worked on animal specimens. The hope, because... well, because... He had the smidgen of an idea, the faintest ray of hope. Glide sneezed. His head went back, his mouth opened and whoosh, his breath shot out. With it went a little bit of spray.

"He-he-he," the Witch cackled, "nasty germs."

Glide sneezed again. His head went down and his chin hit his chest. He tried to rub his nose on his shoulder. He couldn't reach. Snot dribbling, he muttered, "Hanky."

"Hanky?" the Witch mocked. "Hanky panky?" She took a lizard's skin from the wall. "Will this do?" Glide eyed the rough skin. "No, not soft enough?" She uncorked a bottle. Green smoke billowed out of it. It wrapped around the skin. Scales stood up like razor blades. "Now, this is what I call a hanky. Blow your nose on this one, ducky."

But while the Witch had been busy, Glide had been even busier. He had kept rubbing his nose on his shirt. On the top button of his shirt. On the string underneath the top button of his shirt. On the whistle. The whistle! While distracting the Witch, his searching lips had found the whistle. His head came up and he prepared to blow. A mighty blast to bring down the walls. Yet just as he began, the Witch whirled on him. She pointed a long bony finger. Green light shot out of it. Flashes zigzagged around Glide. His puff was hardly started when Slowtime enveloped him. The minutest of squeaks fell out and his mind froze on the call of, "Ne'wang the Ne'ver..."

But what Glide didn't know was that the whistle didn't really summon. It only focussed. Glide's incredible power of imagery exerted a constant tug on the Ne'vermaker. So the whistle was just a make-sure. Even now as the Ne'verman held the banner, "No more black-coal mines", he felt the pull. But there was not much wattage in it. Glide's intention, however, was the trigger. To blow the whistle focussed his intent. To put Glide into Slowtime was to turn his mind into a constant siren. So he emitted a sharp and constant signal, the kind of signal that allowed a fire engine to speed through a traffic jam.

As the Ne'vermaker's end of the banner dropped, the other end called out, "You all right?"

"Am I all white?" came a fading voice. "Not bloody likely!" A neighbour caught an apparently fainting pole.

Though called, the Ne'vermaker had no idea where he would appear. Consequently, he always put himself into a state of heightened readiness. Though, perhaps, not quite high enough for a guest performance in the Witch's stronghold. But, then, she didn't expect him either. For a long moment, they stared blankly at each other.

"Oh!" the Ne'vermaker exclaimed weakly.

"Oh!" the Witch echoed.

"Oh, oh!"

"Oh, oh, oh!"

This swift repartee was followed by:

"You!"

"You!"

Staring turned to glaring. The Witch pointed. Jagged light spat out of her finger. It danced around the Ne'vermaker and his tight curls stood up straight. The Witch uttered a sharp command. The suits of armour clanked towards the Ne'vermaker and grasped his arms. He didn't seem to resist. Yet when he casually reached up to scratch his nose, the metal screeched.

So did the Witch. She lifted a bowl of steaming putrescence and hurled it. The Ne'vermaker wrote in the air. The head of a huge goanna appeared, a goannasaraus. Its tongue flicked out and lapped up the liquid. The Witch crouched. A javelin of thin green light sparked in her hand. Sweat beading his forehead, the Ne'vermaker spread his hands apart. Silver threads criss-crossed his blue palms. The witch threw the javelin. The Ne'vermaker blew his silver web into the air. The two met. The web drove the javelin back. Spitting furiously, the Witch grasped the end and slashed at the web. Both green and silver evaporated in a burst of magic.

The Witch rubbed her hands, her elbows and her knees. The pain in them was terrible. She was panting. And so was the Ne'vermaker. They were both exhausted. But, luckily, he had none of the pains. Pushing away the homunculi, he approached Glide. In a tongue that was both ancient and terrifying, he began to chant. Slowtime gradually receded. Yet as it did so, a fearful occurrence began. The Witch's hair started to unwind. It writhed like a nest of snakes. Glide came out of Slowtime to see a Medusa's head in full performance. In shock, he witnessed a dark cloud form above her head. It writhed vilely exuding its rotten stench.

Even the Ne'vermaker paled. Facing Glide, he said in a calm but fierce voice, "Feel me, touch me, make me." Glide stared at him in blank incomprehension. The Ne'vermaker repeated, "Make me, create me. Image me!"

The dark cloud had become thicker. It oozed with evil. The smell was so bad that Glide could scarcely bear to breathe. But it forced his frozen brain into a sudden comprehension. The fear energised him. He dived inwards, searching for a feeling. He projected outwards. A giant candle appeared. The Ne'vermaker sweated. From above the Witch's head, a huge blob of a hand reached for him.

"Create me! Me!" the Ne'vermaker hissed. "Not the bloody candle!"

Glide's mind exploding, the candle transformed. In its place was a replica of the Ne'vermaker. The real person jumped within the image. The two moved apart and it was impossible to tell which was which. Though it were still possible to tell which was Witch. The putrescent hand hesitated. The Witch pointed. "Him! Him!" she screamed.

Her hair sparked as the blob hand drifted towards the Ne'vermaker. Urgently, he hissed, "Make another. And another."

A second image manifested. Then a third and a fourth. The room filled with shifting figures. The Witch bubbled with fury. The hand divided. It spilt into many rough strands. Against it, all the images of the Ne'vermaker emitted a silver light. The rays converged on the Witch's hair. The black blobby hand was hit by many rays of silver light. The hand began to melt. The blob dripped into nothingness and with it the terrible smell went away. The Ne'vermaker's images coruscated briefly with silver light. Then they, too, collapsed.

The Witch fell against her wooden throne. Her face was a mask of hate and pain. The Ne'vermaker looked just as pale. He pulled at Glide. "Come on, mate, let's go before she recovers."

But Glide tore his arm away. "What about Cascade? We can't leave Cascade."

"We can. We have to!" The Ne'vermaker's voice broke. "I made a promise."

"To hell with promises. Free her!"

The Ne'vermaker sagged as if knives were being thrust into his stomach. "When Cascade exchanged herself for Strongarm, the

Witch wanted to kill him. She didn't because I monitored the exchange. So she turned him into an elephant instead. She still has a magical hold on him. If I break my promise, she will kill him."

"Ah!" Glide emitted a long sad breath. "Ah!" It turned into a broken sob.

This time, when the Ne'vermaker pulled at him, Glide didn't resist. The blue man threw open the door. They both recoiled. Hurtling towards them were Haggort and Greenwort. The Ne'vermaker stepped forward. This caused Haggort to skid to a halt. So did Greenwort. But not fast enough. His head hit the iron bottom of the Giant Dwarf. His feet kept going.

"I'll clean the floor with you," the Ne'vermaker muttered. He clicked his fingers. Greenvort pouted his lips and began to suck in. "Not as good as a vacuum cleaner, but still. It's a pity that we can't plug you in." The Ne'vermaker clicked his fingers again and the imp relaxed. "Leave us be and you'll come to no harm." Haggort, however, at a signal from the Witch leapt forward. But his fist took on a life of its own. It rose rapidly and hit him on the nose. Haggort retreated.

The Witch reached the door. "Don't let them go!" she screamed. "Stop them."

She leant forward. The Ne'vermaker leant on Glide. Haggort sat on Greenwort. Around them were disappearing projections of Ne'wang. Haggort looked from one to the other. In obeyance to the Witch, yet keeping enough wit for self-protection, he reached out for the images. As he did so, a glitter against his chest caught Glide's eye. He had noticed this glint before when he was caught in the Giant Dwarf's embrace.

"A necklace," he cried. "It's an amulet. Or... or, it creates an interference pattern."

With a final effort, Glide conjured up more images of the Ne'vermaker. He filled the corridor with them. At the same time, the real one sent out a magic flare. It touched Haggort's woolly shirt. That smouldered briefly then shot into flames. His hairy chest also began to smoulder. Before that could burst into flames, he began to furiously slap himself with his huge hands.

A second flash cut the leather around Haggort's neck. The Ne'vermaker quickly snatched at it. A twisted blue wire lay in his hand. He turned now to Greenwort. A flash set his backside alight. Unable to reach it, the imp sat down and began to beat his bottom on the floor. The Ne'vermaker's hand flashed out once more and a second amulet settled in his hand. With a furious scream, the Witch threw herself upon him. But he inter-weaved with the images of himself and she fell from one shadow into another. With another shrill scream, she threw herself at Glide. This time, a solid blue arm barred her progress.

In the confusion, the Ne'vermaker pulled at Glide. "Run, run," he shouted.

With a final glance at Cascade, Glide let himself be drawn. They ran down the corridor with Haggort hot foot after them. Hot arm and hot chest, as well. Greenwort was no help either. Any time that he stopped to try his magic, the Ne'vermaker turned and set their clothes alight.

They reached the outside. But this presented a problem. Around the house was a moat of Slowtime, dense as a thundercloud. "Glide," the Ne'vermaker urged, "get onto the roof and use your handglider. I'll cover for you."

"Wait." The young man snatched an amulet. "Hold onto my shirt in case you have to pull me out." He plunged forward. It felt sticky but he could move! "It works! It works!" he cried and did a wild dance in the middle of the moat.

The Ne'vermaker cheered. Then Haggort came out, still smouldering. The Ne'vermaker took one look and dived forward. Haggort reacted and followed after him. He hit the field and froze, an expression of intense and pained surprise engraved upon his face. He hadn't realised that his protection had been stolen.

Glide and the Ne'vermaker ran on. The men and women of Inklan pursued them. But they were too frightened to catch them and too cowered not to chase. Glide set into an easy trot. It petered down into a slow jog and then into an amble. With relief, they caught up with a still angry Strongarm and a still dazed Plonkers.

"Good to zee yous," the barman cried. "But oh, me head. Oi hit Haggort wiv it but oi wished oi'd hit the ground instead."

"You flew?" Glide snapped.

"Just a little."

"You said you wouldn't."

"But yous wanted a diversion, didn't you?"

"Yes but..." It was too late to argue. Glide patted Plonkers on the shoulder. "I'll tell you what, the next shout is on me."

"Oh, great. Great that is. If oi just didn't happen to own the bloody pub."

They continued on to the escarpment when a faint cry halted them. "Ooh, argh, ow."

Recognising the quality of dramatic agony, Glide hissed, "Rosenstern?"

"Ooh! Argh! Oow!"

"Guildencrantz?" Two small figures crawled out from under the bushes. "What happened to you?"

"Goresh..."

"...the raven."

"He was jealous."

"Because you flew."

So much for being called Glide," the young man thought. *All I achieved was to make a raven jealous.*

He put his hands in his pockets. Tucked in a corner were the two amulets. He took them out and studied them: wire embedded in clay. They reminded him of something. But right now, he was finding it hard to get his head around normal technology. It was something like an electric circuit. Something like a… a… He just couldn't put his finger on it. But he did know that it was important. Very important.

Chapter 36

The Witch slammed the door. She'd deal with her two henchmen later. When she could. When her strength permitted. If only she could be rid of them and start again. But good help was so hard to find. Bad help was even harder. She could send off for another Giant Dwarf. But what was the point. Two half-wits couldn't help one whit.

She went to her throne. It had splintered. Her jars were cracked and green fumes were leaking out. Where the fumes touched wood, it mildewed. The Witch cracked her knuckles and was jolted with pain.

She went to the window. Outside were the sad fields of her estate. Bent men and women moved among bent corn. Around them was the ever-present mist. Green tinged, surely the result of her experiments. She sighed. Was it worth it? Then her gaze fell on Cascade. Bolts of jealousy ran through her. Yes, it was worth it. Her blue hair crackled like electric eels. Her teeth bared and her strong-boned face fell into the archetypal shape of a lunar crescent.

The moon, however, did not control the Witch. If anything, she was solar, aligned to its flares and its power. Power was her addiction. Power over people, power over nature, and power over the elements. How could she have let herself sigh? How could she have despaired? How could she have been weak? She cracked her knuckles and rejoiced in the pain. She'd have power over herself as well. And that gave total power.

Power over... Her gaze shifted to the corner. Cascade. Power... But why did the dratted girl still shine? Why wasn't she downcast? Did time pass too easily for her? Did Slowtime preserve her luminosity? Well, she'd soon see about that. Why hadn't she thought of it sooner? She snapped her fingers. A thin green fire flared but then sizzled. She shook her hands. She was weaker than she thought.

She walked stiff-legged to a cloudy beaker. Pulling out the cork, she breathed deeply as the murky green fumes swirled around her. Her eyes became red-rimmed and her lips turned blue. She held onto the bench until the moment passed. Then she laughed wildly, whirled and pointed. Jagged lightning shot across the room, ionising the air.

Cascade jerked. Slowtime gave way to the filthy world of cobwebs. Spiders crawled along her body. Rats ran around her feet. Snakes slithered into crumbling hollows. Cascade stumbled out of the murk and into a pungent room full of misty wraiths. The mist emanated from the Witch. She pointed a finger. Cascade tried to resist but her feet were forced to lift and she advanced in the grim parody of a dance.

"We'll have your hair, my pretty one," the Witch rasped. "We'll boil it and stew it and stir it. Add a chant and a potent. You won't stay fair and young for long."

"You've hurt my father. You've hurt my lover. There's nothing more you can do to hurt me."

"No? I can show you how your hair turns grey and your skin grows wrinkled."

"No!" Cascade ran to the window and made to open it.

But the Witch only laughed. "Jump," she cried. "Haggort will catch you. Make his day. Make his year. Make his whole life." Below Cascade, the Giant Dwarf spread his arms. A leer crept across his face. Cascade gasped. She backed away. Coming to a flask, she raised it. "Go on, go on," the Witch urged. "That will age you nicely.

Startled, Cascade dropped the retort. The glass broke and an evil smelling liquid oozed along the floor. In its track, the wood turned to dust. She picked up a chair. But the Witch merely snapped her fingers and in slow motion, the young woman toppled. Maggot Thwacka took a pair of scissors. They clicked menacingly in her hands. Cascade tried to struggle but strands of Slowtime held her.

The Witch darted forward. Snip-snap, snip-snap. She began to cut the silver locks.

In Plonkers Day Lounge, Strongarm startled. He trumpeted mournfully.

"What is it?" Glide asked.

"Cascade!" Strongarm exclaimed.

"What?"

"I don't know!"

"Something bad?"

"Yes, yes. Of course!"

"How do you know?"

"How do I breathe?"

Glide pounded on a table. "Hell, we have to go back."

Without question, his small group jogged through the forest until they came to the escarpment. The narrow strip of Inklan stretched below them. But already, it had been transformed. Sharpened poles had been erected around the castle and also on the castle. There was no way a handglider could get in. Men and women were on guard. Haggort and Greenvort were making sure they kept alert.

Glide took out the amulets. There were two of them. "There must be a way we can use these. But we can't just rush in, we need a plan."

Strongarm pawed the earth. "We can't wait or we'll be too late."

They looked set to argue when the Ne'vermaker's disembodied voice cut between them. "Wait! Time is short, yes. But whatever she does, the Witch will give us warning. That way, she knows that we will suffer more."

Glide nodded. "Yeah. She'll want to make the most out of what she does. Come on back to Plonkers. We can think better there."

Strongarm's huge head sank down. "There must be something we can do!"

Glide patted the huge flank. "Plan, we've gotta plan."

On the return, Strongarms' shuffling feet created broken furrows. Unrested, they returned to Plonkers.

The owner eyed them. "Yers," he asked, "wot'll it be?"

"Coffee. We need to think."

Rosenstern and Guildencrantz hobbled up. "What now?" they asked.

"Sit. Coffee. Think."

They sat and brooded. Gloom descended. Glide fell into a trance. He knew that he had an answer. He just didn't know what it was. He became angry with himself and anger clouded his ability to visualise. Partial images replayed in his mind: flying in the handglider, landing on the roof, and being trapped by the strange homunculi. Then the despair of being frozen in Slowtime followed by the excitement of passing unharmed through the moat. So many images, so many disjointed images.

Glide took out the amulets. The twists and turns formed a circuit, he was convinced. He found the filament that he'd dug up and bent it until it matched the design in the amulet. He studied the curves carefully. Then he passed it to Hernandes.

"Can you do a better copy?" he asked.

The imp delved into a saddle and pulled out a lens and a pair of metal tweezers. "Mades by the dwarves of Gondwarvaland," he remarked. "Fine peoples excepts they beats everything flat. Don't leave them without giving them a presents otherwise they beats your kneecaps flat." Hernandes stuck the lens into his eye and made some fine adjustments to the filament. "All we needs now," he added, "is the clays."

Strongarm lifted his heavy head. "I can help you there," he rumbled.

"Great. Where?"

Strongarm blushed, becoming the first pink elephant that Glide had seen while sober. "I, er, like to, er, take the odd mud bath," the very big creature mumbled in a very small voice.

Glide gripped the table with excitement. "So? Can you get us some clay?"

"Yes. Yes, I think so."

"Plonkers," Glide called, "a bowl!"

"But oi've given you the biggest cups."

"Not for coffee. To get some clay."

"Oh, right, make my clay."

The bartender wiped a bowl clean. Strongarm took it in his trunk and trotted into the forest. When he returned, it was full of a white-red lumpy material. Glide took out a palmful and began to knead it. As the moisture dried out, the clay began to harden. Before it solidified, Glide embedded the filament in it.

"Tweezers?" he said.

"Tweezers." Hernandes handed them to him.

"Lens?"

"Lens."

"Sun?"

"Sun. Huh?"

"You're in my light."

"Sorrys."

Hernandes moved. The sun beamed through the lens onto the newly made amulet. Faint wisps of steam rose from it as the clay moved towards drying.

"Dry! Dry! Bloody damn and strawberries, dry!" Glide exclaimed. At that, a dozen lenses fell out of the air. "Thanks," he muttered. He formed a circle with them and focussed the sun. The last vestiges of moisture gave up and the clay quickly dried.

"Good," Glide said, "now we need a volunteer."

"Him!" With immaculate timing, Rosenstern and Guildencrantz each pointed at the other.

Hernandes yanked the brim of his akubra. "I'll goes."

Glide looked from one to the other. "Right, I think I know how to do this."

They all returned to the escarpment. Carefully, they descended to the area marked out as Slowtime. Glide put a borrowed amulet each on Rosenstern and Guildencrantz. The one that he'd made, he put on Hernandes. Ropes joining them at the waist, they walked to the edge of the field. Rosenstern stopped at the marker and looked back.

"Don't worry," Glide said. "We can quickly pull you out."

"I'd prefer if you pulled before I went in."

Hernandes took half a step forward. "Come, we are heroes." He tugged at the other two imps.

Taking heart and with a little cry, Rosenstern plunged in. For a moment, he slowed. But, regaining his balance, he continued on at a normal pace. Guildencrantz followed. Glide looked at Hernandes. The imp bit his lip. Then he put a cork in it. Better to bite on that. Holding onto his hat, he took the other half of his step. He froze! Then, ever so slowly, he began to move. His face lit up and he urged himself on. No faster than a person walking underwater, but he did move! With a big grin, he turned and waded out. Pop! He burst into normal time. There was a hush followed by cheering. Several hands, and one trunk, clapped him on the back.

"I think," Glide breathed, "that we've cracked it. All we have to do now is to dig."

"We can dig that!"

Rosenstern and Guildencrantz grabbed wooden trowels and dived back into the field of Slowtime. With a few shallow scrapes, they unearthed more filaments.

Glide held up the wires. "Tomorrow and tomorrow and tomorrow," he cried, "and we shall all go in."

Yet even as they rejoiced, a black shape flew out of the castle. It grew quickly until it circled above them. To draw their attention, the raven cawed, "Caw-resh! Caw-resh! Caw-resh!" Then it dropped a small silver load. The bundle turned over and over in the air. As it did so, Glide's stomach also turned over and over. With an awful apprehension, he identified the silver lock. It was cut from Cascade's hair. A terrible sense of urgency gripped him. They didn't have tomorrow and tomorrow and tomorrow.

Chapter 37

Sunk in blackness, they retreated to Plonkers. There, Glide immediately downed a Green Mist. That was followed by a Dragon's Claw. Which in turn was followed by a Serpent's Tooth. He went through the cycle again. He was trying to get drunk. He wanted to get drunk. And he should've been drunk, very drunk. He should've been a slobbering mess under the table. But all he could manage was stone sober. Worse, stoned sober. He had all the symptoms of drunk: rocks in the head, old socks for a tongue, and corkscrews for eyes. Yet he didn't feel woozy. If anything, he felt sharp, sharper than sharp. A sort of tighten-the-screws, hone-the-razors type of sharpness. Glide ached. He had never before thought that he might like to kill someone. Now, he did. Glide was ready for war.

The problem, though, was that he was not getting anywhere. He had no plan and nor did anyone else. Plonkers Afternoon Tea Bar had become a black hole of dialogue. Folk arrived and speech was snatched from their mouths. The spring was stolen from their steps. Thoughts were sucked from their minds. A graveyard was merry by comparison.

"Charge them?" Strongarm muttered. He was like a broken record.

"Nop."

"Magics them?"

"No."

"Gettem drunk?"

"No, no, no!" Glider slapped the bench. "I know what to do. I just don't know how to do it."

"Deep," Rosenstern said.

"Profound," Guildencrantz agreed. "Ah ha!" He lifted a finger. "There's only one thing for it."

"True."

"Two true."

They nodded wisely at each other. They were so know-all, Glide glared at them. There was a pregnant pause, long enough even for a pregnant elephant. He felt as if there was a vice across his head.

"So," Glide eventually grated, "what is the one thing?"

"You want to know?" Rosenstern asked.

"You really want to know?" Guildencrantz added.

"Yes!" Glide snapped. "I want to know. I really want to know."

"Call the Ne'vermaker."

"Or whistle for the Ne'vermaker."

"The Ne'vermaker!" Hernandes slapped at his forehead. A cork rebounded and hit him on the nose.

"The Ne'vermaker!" Strongarm trumpeted. He stamped a foot. The earth trembled on a Richter scale of twenty and everyone clutched at the bench.

"The Ne'vermaker!" Plonkers cried and smote one fist into the other, forgetting that they held tankards. Briefly, it rained Green Mist.

"The Ne'vermaker," Glide said to himself. "Of course, the Ne'vermaker."

His reaction was to dive inwards. Forgetting the whistle, his first thought was that he needed to visualise Ne'wang. Going inwards started to lessen the vice across his head. Yet the visualisation was not succeeding. What now should have been easy was proving to be difficult. Why? Why? Of course! The vice across his head. It was the Witch. The Witch was in his head. Beneath the vice, he could sense her cackle. She was preventing thought.

"We're too open here," Glide said. "We need protection. We need..." What did they need? "We need to go into the hut."

"Roight!" Plonkers plonked down the mugs and slipped his apron onto a passing neck. "Oi know eggsactly how many pints there are so don't you be short-changing me."

As the others turned to leave, Plonkers stomped off with them. Their fight was his fright... was his flight... was his fight. He'd fight alongside them. They filled the small hut. Strongarm sat outside, his ears closing off the doorway. In the centre of a quiet circle, Hernandes slowly turned. Glide could sense, rather than see, a fine aura spin out from the imp and touch the walls.

"Now," Hernandes concluded, "nothings can get out."

On walking back, Glide had felt the whistle scratch against his chest. He put it to his lips and squinted down his nose at it, unconsciously creating the required intent. He took a deep breath, pursed his lips and prepared a great blast. A dark figure suddenly appeared.

"Olright, olright," it cried. "I'm here already. Oops!"

The Ne'vermaker left a dark hole as he fell back through a gateway. Glide readied himself to blow again. This time, however, he remembered the Witch. She was there, somewhere, deep inside his mind. Having met, she had forged a link that he couldn't break. No wonder the Ne'vermaker was afraid for Strongarm. But perhaps the link worked both ways. Glide dived even further within. In that depth, he touched an outside tension. He sensed it as a line, as a taut fishing line. He focussed on that line and like a fisherman his imagery pulled it. Like a fish, the Witch resisted.

But Glide's ability to visualise was powerful. He took the image of the fish caught on the line and visualised it as being outside of him. His projection was so strong that even the others could sense the ugly creature wriggling to be free. With a feeling of revulsion, Glide carried the line outside the hut and flipped the fish away. Relief! He felt immediate relief.

Yet the Witch did not give up so easily. She turned the fish into a rat and it sought to burrow back into the hut. But Glide was learning. Magic had to be fought with magic. He imagined a force field around the hut, including the floor and Strongarm. So every time the rat tried to bite through the wall, it burnt its lips. With a sour taste in her mouth, the Witch howled with frustration. Satisfied that they were protected, Glide blew on the whistle.

The Ne'vermaker appeared. "You just pulled me from a party." He pulled off a cravat.

"A good one?"

"Nah, a political one."

"Well, we're stuck. We need help."

The Ne'vermaker's annoyance disappeared to be replaced by a look of deep sadness. He flickered for a moment and his sadness deepened. "By this time tomorrow," he muttered, "Cascade will be gone."

"Gone!" Strongarm heaved to his feet. "I have to help her!"

"Wait!" Glide leapt to his feet. "First see what the Ne'vermaker has to say."

"Me?" The blue man breathed heavily. "What's to say? I don't understand. This should've been a paradise. Instead, it's a war." He sighed. "I thought it was an escape but I carried war within my heart."

"No!" Hernandes protested. "That is guilt from the other place speakings. You have been good for us. Helps us to unite."

There was a profound silence, broken only by the sound of Plonkers nodding. The Ne'vermaker turned to Hernandes. "Thank you," he said. "Thank you." He paused. "Even so, I don't know what to do."

The imp pointed dramatically. "Glide knows."

The Ne'vermaker's face brightened. "He does?"

"Yes. But he don't knows what he knows."

"Oh!"

The Ne'vermaker seemed to shrink. He put his hands on his spear and rested his head on his arms. The group froze. They could've been made of stone. In that heavy silence, Glide felt a tiny tug in the depths of his mind. He put his attention to it and felt the jagged edge of a cackle. Angrily, he snatched for the spear. The Ne'vermaker didn't resist but, momentarily, the weapon did. Once more, he skated on the verge of knowing. Yet insight refused to come. Whatever he knew, the Witch prevented him from knowing.

"Strongarm." Glide shook his head in despair. "You said to charge them. You're right and I'm coming with you."

Without hesitation, the elephant's trunk rose and Strongarm blasted out a challenge. It spilt over the fields and the villages. Moments later, it had echoes. But these echoes were not merely reflected sounds. This was their army preparing to go to battle. Rosenstern stretched to his full height. Guildencrantz stuck out his chest. Plonkers pulled in his pot. War had been declared.

Still clutching the spear, Glide marched outside. The sun glinted on the metal. The Ne'vermaker, however, remained inside. He raised his face. One part remained in shadow. The other gleamed as it reflected the light of the moon.

"Glide." Though Ne'wang's voice was less than the breeze among the branches, the young man instantly halted.

"Yes?"

The Ne'vermaker shook his head. But Glide frowned and walked on. For a second time, a sound less than the wind brought his name. Yet still, Glide pressed on. On the third time, the call was more urgent. Glide turned, anger warping his features.

"What? What? Now is the time for action!"

Ne'wang turned to Glide and there was such a sadness on the blue face that the young man's fierceness dropped away like butter put to a flame. With heavy legs, Glide returned to the hut. He offered back the spear and Ne'wang reached for it. At the instant that they both touched it, Glide's arms tingled and his legs felt weak. Carefully, he had to lower himself into the chair.

"Glide," the Ne'vermaker began, "you said that you know but that you don't know what you know." The young man nodded. "There is a way to find out," Glide's head jerked up, "but it does mean that you must make a journey."

"I made a journey here."

"Another one."

"I'm ready. You know that."

"I know. I do know. But this isn't the kind of journey that you think. It is not a journey of a thousand miles that starts with the first step."

"I guessed that. I'm still ready."

"People suffer, Glide, because they do not journey." The Ne'vermaker's voice was so low that Glide thought that it must be vibrating inside of his head. The spear, like the dark face, now seemed luminous. "Men and women confine themselves. They live in little boxes yet their essence is the hunter-gatherer. To go stroll-about. That is your essence, too, the wanderer-gatherer. Your coming here was part of that. You made a choice and set out on the journey. That is your primeval essence."

"I know. That is the deep me. So let's start before the shallow me gets in the way."

The Ne'vermaker began to chant, his words tunnelling below hearing. Light faded as it funnelled into a sea of sound. Glide rode upon the murmur of that trusted voice. Yet as the sound became more and more indistinct, the meaning became more and more apparent.

In some mental sphere, Glide soared.

In that imagery, as he soared, a white speck flew to greet him. It was a dove, the dove of knowledge. Yet as they drew closer together another shape, dark as a bullet, hurtled towards them. The dove fluttered this way and that to escape. Yet, with a metallic click, great talons closed around it. Around nothing. Before the metal talons could close, the dove had vanished. The dark shape cackled with frustration.

Glide no longer drifted on the murmur of sound. As he went further and further into the journey, he became more and more focussed. He became a tiny bundle of energy, an electron carried in a current of electromagnetism.

"I'm so tiny," he thought, "I can jump light. I can run with light. In no time, I can hop from here to there."

Vast nuclei pulled at Glide. Drawn in different directions, he tried to determine where he was. In an instantaneous flip-flop of thought, he knew. He was charging down one of the blue wire filaments. But going nowhere. Ever moving, going nowhere. Then, suddenly, a rogue nucleus, heavy with protons bore down on him. Its huge force sucked at him. Seven electrons were already in orbital. He would be the eighth. If pulled in, he'd never get out. The atom would be too stable.

"Ne'wang," he screamed, "Ne'wang the Ne'vermaker, I need help. I need a quantum flip. Do something."

Nothing. Blackness. Or maybe that was a something. A whirling vortex. A total flip. He was a sheep.

No, not the sheep! Another flip and he was the shearer. Large metal shears were in his hands. He snipped the air with them, snick-snack, snick-snack. Glide bent to his task. The sheep turned. Its eyes said, "Don't you dare!" Glide recoiled. The look was full of hate. The fleece took on a blue tinge. It felt thin and wiry. A smell of evil wafted around them. Glide wanted to run. He backed away. The shears stretched forward. Balanced between fight and flight, Glide knew where the answer lay and threw himself forward.

He fell into nothingness. Heart-beating, pulse-racing, sweat-dripping nothingness. He tensed, waited, senses alert. Still nothingness. He relaxed a fraction. There was a current. No, the shadow of a current. The vibration of a shadow of a current. The

Ne'vermaker. Glide rested. Into his mind, into the vibration of a shadow of his mind, came words. In the words, between the words, between the cup and the lip, wrapped in the shadow of the words came meaning. A spiral of meaning.

The metal bird, the charged electron, the blue sheep. Bird... electron... sheep.... Charge... blue... metal.... In each situation, the Witch had blocked him. Metal? Charge? Blue? But he had also blocked her. Hadn't he? Metal? Charge? Blue? Yet he'd thrown an image around the hut. So... so it wasn't the Witch who had blocked him. It was... it was... it was himself. The metal... was... charge... himself... blue.... Himself! It was himself. He blocked himself, but he didn't need to.

Click! Glide sat bolt upright. Click! His eyes opened. Click! He jumped to his feet. He laughed, he danced, he shouted. "I know!" he cried. "I know what I know. Now I truly know!"

Chapter 38

"He knows!"

"And he knows that he knows!"

"His nose?"

"And he knows it's his nose?"

"Not nose, knows!"

"Not knows knows what?"

"Quiet!" The Ne'vermaker shouted. In the pause, he shouted again. "QUIET!" His shout was so strong that it blew their breath right out of their mouths. He glared. Then he turned to Glide.

"So," he said, "you know."

"Yep, I know." Yet as all eyes fell on him, he paled and said, "Perhaps I should rephrase that. I think that I probably have an idea of what might, under the right circumstances, perhaps... be... could..."

"You probably might..."

"Under the right circumstances..."

"If..."

"Arrgh!" Strongarm rose to his feet and beat his trunk against the sky. His huge front feet punched at the air. "Do you know or don't you? Do I charge or don't I?"

"I know, I do know," Glide said quietly. "The only thing is if we can do it."

All ears now turned to him, which he found less threatening than having all eyes upon him. Glide began to speak. Even Plonkers listened. At the end, they all turned to the Ne'vermaker.

"Sounds about right to me." He drew a circle in the air with his spear. "But it's definitely a risk."

"Doing nothings is more of a risks," Hernandes pointed out.

"Wotz a risk?" Plonkers shrugged.

"We'll certainly do it." Rosenstern stiffened Guildencrantz's spine.

"You're sure?" The Ne'vermaker looked at each person in turn. Everyone nodded. "Right." He held out his spear. "One for all and all for one."

Hernandes frowned. "I've gots an uncle Juan. Why are we alls for him?"

Without replying, the Ne'vermaker continued to offer his spear. One by one, they reached out to touch it. The metal glowed. A blue light flowed out, illuminating their hands.

"Right," the Ne'vermaker said, "let's be seen to be doing something." And with that, he disappeared.

Knowing now what he knew, Glide set his plan in motion. The first task was to rework Plonkers' handglider. When it was ready, he led the barman to an Umbrella tree. Under its wide canopy, he put his head close to Plonkers'.

"Look as if you're hiding." He gave Plonkers the new glider. "I want you to set off now but make sure that Goresh can see you."

"You want me ta be subtle, roight? Well oi can be roight subtle." Plonkers touched a thick finger to the tip of his nose. He set off, moving slowly through the forest, his team and a handglider with him.

Goresh flew above them, transmitting information. "It's another flying machine."

"Ah ha, another aerial attack. Goody." The Witch rubbed her hands together. They wouldn't catch her twice that way.

In his hut, protected by Strongarm and Hernandes, Glide worked on a project that could easily be yet another handglider. It could easily be something else as well. Though his skills were rusty, he weaved on a leaf here, stuck on some resin there and threaded a branch all the way through. It would be a glider if Goresh saw it. It would be something quite different when Glide needed it.

Meanwhile Plonkers, with Rosenstern and Guildencrantz, had led their team down the escarpment and up to the barrier of

Slowtime. Those that wore amulets began to dig for more filaments. They put them into clay bases and lit fires to dry them. Across the barrier, the Witch's sullen army watched in silence. They would have run away, but Haggort and Greenvort prevented them. Further away, more of their sad army was sinking more of the pointed stakes into the ground.

The Witch was stirring a yellow-green brew. "Another flying device," she chortled. "This time we are well ready for it." She looked at Cascade's corner. "When this is done, you'll be old, my lovely. First you then the others, all of them. He-he-he! He-he-he!" She took a deep breath of the brew. Her skin creaked and her hair writhed.

Cascade, held at half speed, willed her body to move faster. She tottered one step, two steps, almost in attacking distance. But to no use. The Witch laughed loudly, lifted the slim figure and dumped her in a corner. The Witch returned to her brew. In despair, Cascade forced herself yet again to move faster. If only she could grab the Witch or upset the brew. She fought and fought and fought. The Witch cackled quietly. The more fatigued, the better.

When Glide was finished, he headed into the forest. With him was what Goresh saw from above as a handglider. Reaching a dense canopy and guarded by Hernandes and Strongarm, he separated the well-crafted base from the slapdash wings of his device. He hid the base under a mound of leaves. Quickly, he attached branches to the wings to give the impression that the handglider was still in one piece. He headed back the way he had come. Once at his hut, he drifted in and out with bits in his hands as if still fiddling with the device. He also searched the ground as if in search of more material.

"Another flying bird," Goresh reported. "But he keeps changing it. He wants it to look like me."

"Another flying machine," the Witch cackled. "He-he-he."

For the last time, Glide wandered into the woods. The sky now had the emerald luminescence that comes just before sunset. Goresh spied the young man as a dark speck, between a bigger elephantine speck and a smaller impish one The three disappeared beneath the umbrella of the trees. The raven flew in a wide circle. He couldn't penetrate the canopy of branches here but would suffer if he lowered and Hernandes' magic caught him. Still, that didn't matter. When the stranger came out, his eagle, er, raven, eye would spot him.

Glide remained hidden in the thick copse of trees. Though quite still, his forehead was beaded with effort. Facing him was another Glide. It had taken him long minutes to create this image. This was what he'd known but hadn't known. That he needed to make an image of himself. When it was solid, he visualised the figure as carrying branches. With further effort, he sent the image back to the hut with Strongarm and Hernandes. Goresh spied them and sent up a triumphant caw-caw-caw. He hadn't lost the stranger. The Witch wouldn't cause him pain.

When the image reached the hut, it sat. The real Glide then got to work. He didn't have much time. Without his focus on it, his projection would begin to fade. Moving carefully to where he'd buried the modified support, he scraped away the leaves. His fingers touched something hard. Good, his structure of branches and wood and resin was still there.

Glide had been born on a surfboard. Well, almost. He'd actually been born on a bed. But despite having flying in his genes, he was a typical Ausphalian youth. Before he could walk, he could float. Before he'd started school, he'd had a boogie board. Before uni, a surfboard. There was always some mate who was driving to the coast. Ten surfers would pile into a steamer wagon with ten boards strapped on the top. They'd race to the sand, struggle into wet suits and spend the whole weekend doing wingy-wangies, curly-clangies, and dingly-danglies. At night, they'd sleep in, on, or around the wagon.

So what Glide now had under his arm was a surfboard. At least, he hoped that he had. It had the right shape and he'd coated it with enough resin from the trees to feel like one. He only hoped that it would hold together like one. For with the land and the air now blocked, approach by sea was his only chance. If he didn't save Cascade now, she was done for. And so, he believed, was Auslan.

He trekked north in the forest. At the point where he'd glided over the escarpment, he hurried on. Further still and he came to a point where Inklan was so narrow that he could hear the waves beat against the shore. A little more and he could see where the sea threw itself upon the rocks. There, when the waves realised that they were in Inklan, they threw themselves back off again. He descended carefully, his feet scraping along the surface. He picked up what should've been sand but found only particles of flint in his hand.

The sea was a dark green mass edged with white foam. Glide put his foot in and shivered. Only one thing to do, he backed off and prepared to run. At the last moment, a small tube appeared in the air. Puzzled, he took it. Zinc! Another tube appeared. Wax! Following an age-old ritual, perhaps as old as twenty years, Glide rubbed zinc on his nose and wax on his board. The zinc was to prevent sunburn. The wax was... Well, what surfer would go into the water without first waxing his board.

The ritual complete, Glide tucked the board under his arm. With a little run, accompanied by a big groan, he threw himself on top of his construction. The water engulfed him and he flailed out wildly. Soon his body adjusted and he began to paddle at a comfortable rhythm. The current was with him, which was why he'd gone north, and he was soon making good time.

The Witch, however, was no fool. Well, actually, she was. Like a politician, power had turned her brain to confetti. But she still had a strong working instinct and that said keep an eye out ready to sniff any trouble. But, whose eye to use? Which eye could sniff out the best? And who, she groaned, could help her with her mixed metaphors?

Aloud, she addressed her psychic network. "Is he still just sitting there?"

Goresh ducked and weaved to avoid the air turbulence that so often came with the Witch's messages. "Yes," he cawed. "Cor!"

"You're sure?"

"Caws I'm sure."

"There's trouble if you're wrong!"

"Caw! Cor! Caw blimey!"

Then the raven startled. Glide's head had lifted from his body. His right arm fragmented. Some people are easy to see through. This person became totally transparent. The Witch saw the transformation through the eyes of Goresh.

"Fool, fool!" she cried. "You've been fooled. You've been watching an image."

"Ca... aw!" Goresh squawked as static singed his wings and he had to beat faster to cool them. But his body still smoked and from a distance, he looked like a flying cigar.

The Witch cracked her knuckles. The pain it gave her was as much mental as physical. But that was the price. Her thoughts tumbled over each other. Why had this fool created a decoy? To mislead her. So where was she being misled? She'd covered the land and she'd covered the air. Where else? Land. Air. And sea. Sea? Could it be? Was it possible? No one had dared to try that way before. But this one was resourceful. Wasn't he? Was he? Well, she'd soon see about that.

The Witch extended her mind. It spread out like a fan towards the sea. Near her, it was strong and focused. Further out, it was weak and fuzzy. She sensed the sea, the mists that arose from it, and the minds of the huge creatures that swum in it. But there was no stranger. She tried again, forcing out a stronger surge. It penetrated

Cascade's corner, and the young woman stirred a little faster. In another direction, it penetrated Strongarm's bulk. It shimmered and, for a moment, Hernandes could almost see the man within.

Her mental radar spread. Ah, there, got him! A blip appeared on the scope of the Witch's awareness. There on the sea. She couldn't get a clear focus but that didn't matter. She had her ways. She had her hook in the depths of his mind. And what a depth!

Glide startled. He paused in his easy paddle and looked around. A nameless terror gripped him. Something was stirring, something terrible. The air had become quiet. The night noises had ceased. The sea itself no longer heaved. Something terrible was about to happen! Something was arising. Yes! No! Yes...s!

Something arose! A slow ripple spread out from a distant centre. Glide trembled. A huge amorphous image popped into his mind. A word came with it, a whole bundle of words. And all of them were awful. The kraken, he thought, the kraken awakes. His logic told him that no such creature existed. But it stirred in the depths. His depths! In fearful confirmation, a huge mottled tentacle broke the surface. Slowly, the water heaved upwards.

Chapter 39

"It's the kraken!" Glide mentally screamed. "The kraken awakes!" In terror, he paddled one way with one arm while the other went the other way. Legs turned to jelly. Emergency! Emergency! The whistle was strapped around his neck. He tried to get it to his lips but his fingers shook too much. Fumbling, bumbling, trembling, he tried again. Impossible. A second tentacle broke the surface. Then a third, a fourth, and a fifth. Then a pair of glasses.

Glasses?

Glasses! Pince-nez? Spectacles? A pair of glasses. A pair of a pair. Then a quartet of a pair. What was going on here? Glide stared at the kraken. The kraken stared back. It had a huge mottled body with hundreds of writhing tentacles. It also had a hundred huge eyes and perched on top of a hundred huge beaky noses - the arithmetic might not be quite right here - were a hundred pairs of spectacles. It was quite a spectacle. It might even have been a spectentacle.

Glide went boondoggle. This awful creature was his worst nightmare. It was the cesspit creation of his youth. How many nights had he'd taken a torch under a blanket and read this story? How many nights had he awoken to this awful scene? How mightily had his youthful ability to visualise magnified the book's version of the terrible monster?

Nor was it just the fiction that terrified him. The story of the kraken was associated with so many problems of his youth. He'd hidden in fantasy to avoid the school bully, the girls who'd laughed at him, and the teacher who picked on him. Now, the creature lifted a dozen pocked-marked tentacles. Glide waited fearfully for them to come crashing down. When they didn't, he chanced a look upwards. The monster was pressing a dozen pairs of glasses more firmly to a dozen beaks. The kraken's tone was more resigned than threatening.

"Is there one of you or twenty?" It peered between water droplets on its glasses. "One, I think, pretending to be many. Harrumph!" The kraken loomed over Glide, slapping dozens of tentacles together. "Have I gotta lesson fer you," it/bully/girl/teacher said.

At these dread but familiar words, Glide reacted. He hadn't only hidden in the make-belief of fantasy. They'd been the other reactions, too. When the bullies had pushed him to far, he'd lifted his fists. When the girls had laughed at him for too long, he'd deliberately become the funny guy. If the teacher had picked on him too much, Glide had hissed. Push him too far and he would start to push back. Glide was no devil but even if he ever did manage to fly, he'd never be mistaken for an angel either. As the kraken spoke, Glide unfroze. The whistle virtually jumped into his mouth and a piercing shriek burst out of it.

In reaction, the kraken lifted a score of tentacles. Oh no, Glide thought. But it only poked the tips into its ears, causing waterfalls to cascade out. "Ah, that's better," it said. "Now, what did you scream?" The monster had a bit of a lisp so that *scream* came out as *shcream*.

Which did not, however, make him any less menacing. Indeed, Glide's teeth were chattering. He couldn't scream, couldn't even scream out what he'd screamed before. He was shivering with an icy fear. At the same time, he was hot and bothered. He had finally managed to blow the whistle. But nothing had happened. No Ne'vermaker! No Ne'wang!

Glide lifted his trembling hand ready to give one more blast.

"Olright, Olright," the air grumbled, "I heard you the first time."

"Well? I blew the whistle. This is an emergency, a serious emergency."

"I can't come right now." There was the vaguest hint of blue body against the grey sky. I'm tied up."

"What with?"

"Rope, of course."

"Rope! Bother!"

Glide swore. Actually, he swore something altogether different from *bother*. It might've been, "Damn and strawberries." It might've been something stronger. Certainly, the kraken heard something stronger. Its mottled skin sharply turned purple.

"Not to me, you won't!" it snapped and advanced threateningly.

"Help! Help!" Glide called.

The Ne'vermaker's voice sounded calmly in his right ear. "Give him a chocolate," it seemed to say.

"A what?" Glide echoed. "Give him, it, a what?"

"Another what? I reckon that makes a kilowhat, Glide. Just give him a chocolate."

Glide stared around wildly. He had no idea what the Ne'vermaker meant. All he could see were bits of seaweed, a misshapen body the size of a house and tentacles as thick as trees. Oh, yes, and moonlight glinting off numerous pairs of spectacles. Glide sniffed.

"Goodbye cruel world," he mourned. "Goodbye lovely Cascade. Goodbye strong, er, Strongarm. Goodbye dark chocolate. Goodbye... dark chocolate? Dark chocolate! Chocolate!" Big bars were streaming out of the sky. "Oh, good Ne'vermaker!" he cried. "Loverly beautiful Ne'vermaker!"

He grabbed a bar, ripped off the wrapping and threw the contents to the kraken. A tentacle caught it. A beak sniffed it. A mouth gobbled it. "Oh, yummy," the creature rumbled, "much better than a human." The sky continued to rain chocolate bars, allowing the kraken to catch its own. It stuffed them straight into its mouth.

"You could at least unwrap them," Glide shouted.

"Really? Didn't you know? The best vitaminsh are just below the skin."

A nutritional monster, Glide thought. *That's hard to believe.*

"The trouble is," a dark voice said inside his head, "is that you do believe. You really do. Try not believing instead."

"Huh?" Glide dodged to avoid falling bars. "Meaning what?"

"You know."

"I don't."

"You do."

This incipient argument was halted when the kraken suddenly burped. The sound was that of creaking timbers and its odour was that of undigested depths. "Flapping fishes," the kraken groaned. "I'm feeling sick. Too many saturated fatsh." It raised a dozen tentacles to its mouth. "Fish! I'm going to have to take something." It eyed Glide. "You for a start."

"Not me!" Glide yelled. "I've been eating pizza. I'm saturated with saturated fats!"

The foul-smelling, burp-making, person-swallowing monster advanced. Glide's craft heaved. So did Glide's stomache. His mind went into a fast spin. Fast enough to dry soggy clothes. This situation made real so many of his childhood nightmares. So many! How could that be? Who knew about them but him? A huge tentacle hovered above his head. *He was a sucker for a tentacle*, he thought. *Huh, punny. Who*, he thought again, *could know his fears but him?* Of course, him! His unconscious mind. That was the answer. That was what the Ne'vermaker had meant. The Witch had created the monster out of his unconscious mind. His imagination had then made it real.

Glide laughed. It was a slightly mad laugh and the kraken hesitated. Threatened by his own imagination! The kraken wavered. Glide shook his head in amazement. "I don't need to bother about you," he said.

"You don't?" The kraken suddenly looked sad and helpless.

It was no wonder chocolate had saved the day – this day, tonight. Choccies had always helped him when he was young. With that understanding, the falling tentacle shimmered. It smudged. It became a mist on the horizon. The whole creature teetered on the edge of transparency. Just like that. Too easy.

Glide paused. "No, wait."

He probed into the depths of his mind, tracking back to the origins of the kraken. Like a tongue on a broken tooth, he found a sunken sharpness. He made a shift in his mind, intending to dislodge the hook. But another thought, touched with the velvet edge of the Ne'vermaker, came to him. *Be clever, it said, don't let her know. Be clever. Be tricky.* With the stealth of a zen swordsman, he separated this thought from that and this image from another. The kraken solidified. In the grip of its many huge tentacles, it now held a human body, another Glide. Other tentacles held a canoe. With a piercing shriek, the kraken triumphantly held the body aloft. Then, with an awesome eddy, it sank beneath the waves.

In recreating the monster, Glide was on the verge of understanding how Strongarm was seen as an elephant and how Loopy had been possessed. He briefly contemplated going further in that direction. But no, he didn't want to be drawn in. Instead, he lifted his chin to the sky and called out, "Thanks, mate."

"No worries." And a final bar of chocolate dropped out of the empty sky.

"Thanks, again." He bit into it and smeared chocolate across his mouth.

Preoccupied, Glide glided across the face of the waters. Half of his mind was still concerned with maintaining the image of the kraken. Half of it mused on how chocolate provided the energy to maintain an image. The third half, Glide was good at halves, was concerned with letting the Witch see the image. His way.

***

In her castle, the Witch cackled. She caught waves of terror, anger and despair. She sensed the kraken's vast bulk.

"He-he-he," she burbled. "Ho-ho-ho. So much for your hero." She stirred the green brew. "Tomorrow, tomorrow, and none of your tomorrows." She dipped a strip of smooth leather into the pot. It came out as scaly as a dragon's tail. "Too strong, he-he-he. Don't want to kill you, do we? He-he." She snapped a finger and Cascade stirred. "I said we don't want to kill you, do we? He-he."

Cascade nodded. "Kill me," she said. "Kill me."

***

Still holding the kraken in mind, Glide approached the shore. Waves rose around him and crashed upon the rocks. His makeshift craft was picked up and pushed forward. He paddled occasionally. So far, it was no worse than Laguna Bay, Noosa Heads. But then, he entered a crosscurrent and it began to pull him towards the rocks. Paddling now didn't help. The waves picked him up, swirled him around and propelled him towards the sharp jagged edges. Glide reached for the whistle.

"Sorry," a voice said. "I do deserts. I don't do oceans. May I recommend a ship of the desert." A camel dropped into the sea. It immediately began to bellow. "Sorry, mate." The camel disappeared. "Try this." A rubber ring replaced it.

Glide snorted. He hadn't used one of those since he was three. Still, he supposed, it was better than nothing. He slipped it on. Then for luck, he crossed his fingers. And his toes. And his eyes. You could never have enough luck. Yet even cross-eyed, he could see that the rocks were coming closer. Glide uncrossed and stretched out along his board.

"Just have to go with the flow," he muttered.

And so he did. The waves carried him over the sharp points and the swirls pulled him between the jagged teeth. The air in the rubber ring gave him just enough buoyancy for lift. Finally, there was only the white wash as it surged over the pebbles. Well, more a grey wash than white but it still surged.

At the end, with the ring around his waist, Glide tried to stand on his board like a true surfer. But he was too weak. His legs were as rubbery as the ring. He sank down and let the waves deposit him. A weak wet bundle, he dragged himself onto the land and found a dry spot beneath an overhang. Taking off his clothes, he tried to wring them out. However, they remained sodden. With little hope, he addressed the air.

"You got any dry clothes?" he asked.

"Sure, mate." Ne'verman silver shorts appeared.

"I don't think so."

"No? How about this?"

Replacement fringed trousers and shirt drifted down. Gratefully, Glide grabbed them before they hit the sand. More clothes followed. Warm again, Glide sank down against a rock. He was exhausted. After all, he must've been paddling for hours. He just had to rest. It couldn't hurt if he just closed his eyes. Closed... his eyes. Could it? If he just... closed... his... eyes. He immediately fell asleep.

A clip around the ear awoke him and Glide reflexively leapt into a fighting crouch. A cautionary hand floated in mid-air then disappeared. "Heard you snoring across the gateways. Worse than Strongarm with a cold."

Awake, Glide looked and listened. Moments later, he heard noises. In the grey-green of pre-dawn, he saw that men were searching for him. Obviously, the Witch was taking no chances. He watched them carefully. Though they were not thorough, there was no way that they could miss him. And, although they might not want to report him, fear would force them to.

"Okay," he muttered, " how do I get out of this?"

"If I knew how to get out of this, I'd be happy to help," came the reply. "As regards the Witch, my hands are tied." There was a pause. "My legs, too."

Glide groaned. He peered over his rock. The men were getting closer and the light was getting brighter. He had to do something. And now! But what?

Chapter 40

Would they give him away? Glide tried to figure the odds. Undoubtedly, if they were free, they'd support the Ne'vermaker. But they weren't free. They were controlled by fear and hate, hate and fear. Hate? Glide certainly knew the feeling. Or rather, he had done. To his surprise, he found that the hate had gone. He did not hate the Witch. Fear her? Yes. Hate her? No. He had hated working in an office. Eight hours a day, five days a week in a sick building. It had been slowly killing him. Yes, he'd hated that. In comparison, the Witch had given him life. A short one, perhaps, but she'd certainly added a colour to it – bilious green.

The shouting of the men was clearer now. Words were carried on the breeze. He only had a few minutes. Hate? Fear? Hate? He understood what motivating forces they could be. It only needed their embodiment to energise his imagination. But who? He racked his brains? Who? Who? Who? His racked brains sent back the answer. The perfect who. He sent a mental message to the Ne'vermaker.

"Will do," came the reply.

In the distance, a cavorting Haggort was hurling detailed insults at the decoy that was Strongarm and his companions. "Yer father was a puff ov smoke," he shouted. "And yer movver was a giant snail."

Strongarm trumpeted on the far side of Slowtime. He didn't want to cross it. That might drive Haggort back to the castle. The Giant Dwarf froze, however, when a dark figure appeared in front of him and pointed a small black box.

"Smile," Ne'wang said.

In the dawn light, which ran from blue in Auslan to grey in Inklan, a light flashed. Haggort doubly froze. Usually when that happened to him, he was in Slowtime. Yet except for a few spots before his eyes, he now seemed all right. By then, though, through a bit of hocus-pocus through the gateways, Glide held a developed photo of Haggort.

With a concentration aided by the wind-carried voices, Glide focussed on the picture. Moments later, he startled when a hulking figure loomed over him. His heart pounded even though he knew it was just an image. The image he had just created! Cautiously, he peered out. The men were grumbling and were not too focussed on searching. Glide guided the image onto a rock.

"Aaargh, yous lot!" he bellowed. "Wotta yous lot doing?"

The men gawped. "I thought he was with the others," one gasped.

"Damned dwarves, he's everywhere."

"Wish the ground would swallow him up."

"Shush, he'll hear."

"He isn't here," Glide roared. "Yous go on that way. Go on, quick now. Yous want me to throw yers inta the sea."

The image made as if to come at them. The men slowly backed away. The pseudo-Haggort bent to pick up a stone. The men scattered. Glide moved the image behind a rock and out of their sight. He wiped the sweat off his face. Between him and the castle were only the image and the moat of Slowtime. He scampered forward, hiding as best he could behind tufts of grass. Every so often, he jumped the image to his side.

Maggot Thwacka sniffed the air, sensing the link with Glide. "Ho-ho-ho," she cackled, "something wicked this way comes." But the hook she'd sunk into Glide's mind was now two-way. He sensed her sensing him. But that only tickled her. "He-he-he," she wheezed. "The wicked? Who's more wicked than me? He-he-he." She stirred at her brew with satisfaction.

In that moment, Glide darted up to the castle. Now there was only the moat of Slowtime to cross. He checked that he still had Haggort's amulet around his neck. He checked that he still had the home-made ones in his pocket. He checked that he still had the whistle. He checked... Damn and strawberries! There was nothing more to check. Glide advanced slowly, unsure where the Slowtime actually began. In dawn's grey light, he was almost seeing through a castle window when a group of men rounded the corner.

There was a moment's hesitation then one called, "Hey, you!" He ran forward. But suddenly he stopped and clamped both hands over his mouth. The others careened into him and they all piled up. Glide didn't move as they faced him. "Er, you?" the leader mumbled. He looked at the man besides him as if he were the one that had actually spoken.

"Yes?" Glide said.

"Er, um, what're you doing?" The leader spoke without separating his lips.

"I'm going to rescue Cascade and biff the Witch. Want to help?"

"To, er, rescue Cascade? Biff the Witch, er?" The man looked at his companions. "Sorry, talking to meself." He slapped his head. "Must be hearing voices. I don't see anything. Do any of you?"

"The stranger?" one ventured.

"I said we don't see anything. Right?"

"But... Yeah, right. Too right."

"And if we did, we're not here. Right?"

"Right. Not here. Never been here."

"And if what we don't see does what can't be done, we're right behind him. Right?"

"Right."

"Otherwise, we're right on top of him. Right?"

"Right."

The leader rose, straightened his tunic and lifted his head high. The others copied him. They marched off, conspicuous by the brave terrified expressions etched into their faces. If Haggort could see them now, he'd immediately know they were hiding something. If they saw him, they'd probably have heart attacks on the spot.

"Bloody hell." Glide sighed. "How long d'you reckon we've got. Ten minutes? Twenty?"

"Don't look now," said a voice on the breeze, "but Greenvort is suspicious."

"Oh no! Where is he?"

"Tugging at Haggort."

"Can't you create a diversion?"

"Maybe, maybe. Nothing too drastic. Nothing to make her rash. Hmm?"

Haggort enjoyed hurling abuse at Strongarm. Actually, he enjoyed hurling abuse at anyone, but Strongarm was his particular favourite. Especially now. Strongarm was the only one that was retaliating. For once, the others were ignoring Haggort. They were probably too cast down by the particular fineness of his language. Instead, they continued at their tedious task, digging up blue wires and pressing them into clay. Just the sort of meaningless task that Haggort would have them do. It took a great deal of tugging on Greenvort's part before his stone-age mind began to turn in a different direction.

"Wot?" he demanded. "Wot? I've got 'em running, er, sitting scared."

"Where are the others...s?" Greenvort said. "They're not here. This is not where it's happening. We have to find the others...s."

"Olright, olright. Hey, yous," he bellowed to his silent army, "yous keep an eye out here. An' do it right otherwise I'll keep yers eye out fer yous. An' no defec... def... d..., runnin' away. We knows yer families, he-he-he." He tried to cackle. It sounded like a bear with a bad cough.

Haggort turned to run. His feet, however, only lifted very slowly. The message took a few steps to reach his brain. He looked down and saw that long grey strips connected his soles to the ground.

"Always wanted an excuse to eat the sugar off," a voice from nowhere said to no one, "and spit the chewy bit out. Good chewing gum, otherwise. Especially when mixed with superglue."

"Yark! Gerr! Gerroff!" Haggort bellowed. He clomped around in circles.

"Take ten," the Ne'vermaker said to Glide. "Be my guest."

"Right. Here goes," Glide muttered. "Got the tools?"

"Gottem!"

"If I'm wrong, it's curtains for us."

"It's not just curtains, mate. It's Venetian blinds, as well."

"If those others tell...?"

"I'll make 'em speak in Scotlish. Dinna chance o' bein unnerstood."

"If Haggort gets here...?"

"I'm chewing gum as fast as I can."

"Oh, well. Right."

Glide prayed. Even though he didn't know he had a prayer inside of him. Sounds bubbled up to his lips, took shape as words for a few moments, then floated up to the sky. He took a step forward. The stickiness of Slowtime gripped him. He paused. His body shook. This was the moment. He could still run away. But no, he couldn't. That would mean to creep away. He had to go through with it, shakes and all.

Against all hope, the amulets worked. Just about. One was designed for Haggort. One was home-made. Perhaps they partially cancelled each other out. Who knew? Glide advanced. It felt as if he were pushing through elastic bands. They first stretched, broke and then reformed behind him. Time slowed. What should have been a few seconds felt like a day inside school when outside there was a glorious sun.

The last step felt as if he'd burst out of tar and onto grass. He didn't know if the air had changed but if seemed fresher and purer.

There wasn't far to go from here. But Glide's nerves had him panting for breath. He stumbled towards the nearest window. Then a sound made him startle. The pounding of Haggort's feet? Thud-thud-thud, thud-thud-thud. But no, it was only the pounding of his heart. From around the corner, he saw his reluctant opponents. They were as pale as he must be. What was worse, much worse, was that Glide sensed that the weird homunculi in their strange armour were coming for him.

Cautiously, Glide peered through the window. What he saw froze him with shock. In one corner, the Witch held a goblin-shaped root. It was a thick-bodied thing, knobbly and wizened. Decorated with scraps of materials and jewels, it formed the travesty of a woman. A lock of silver hair plastered to its scalp made it quite clear which woman. The corner crackled with a magical charge.

Glide shifted to the left side of the window. He could see the other corner. It showed a sight hard to believe. A house left for a century in a mildewed waste dump would look like that. Webs formed a broken lattice from top to bottom. Dust was heaped on the floor. Twelve-legged spiders, three-headed beetles, and giant slugs were trapped there. Rotten fish, decayed meat and wormy flour littered the surfaces.

With tears blurring his vision, Glide could just make out Cascade. She was a dim figure behind a curtain of filth. Even the silver sheen of her hair was dulled. It was a miracle, he thought, that she had survived. In her situation, he would've gone to pieces centuries ago.

Time, Glide thought, to do something. Time to act. He didn't need a photo for what he was going to do next. The image that he wanted was etched in a deep well running from his head to his heart.

Chapter 41

Greenvort concentrated, spreading his hands. Grey-green energy oozed out of his fingers and the goo that connected his feet to the ground slowly melted. He directed the rays towards Haggort as well. Freed, the Giant Dwarf's straining knees immediately shot up and whacked him on the chin. He collapsed backwards, falling on top of Greenvort. The Ne'vermaker relaxed. That wasn't bad for delaying tactics. What next? Greenvort didn't have much magic but, then, it didn't take too much to deal with chewing gum. What else could slow them? Ice? Ball bearings? Both? Now that would be a nice challenge.

With his head still spinning, Haggort staggered to his feet. Greenvort immediately sprang onto his back, digging his heels in as if they were spurs.

"Go!" he urged. "Go, go!"

"Yarr!" Haggort bellowed and began to run. In the wrong direction. The imp beat on his head but to no effect. Instead, he pulled on the right ear. Pain impulses slowly moved along sluggish nerves. The foggy brain preferred, however, to ignore the messages. Reactively, Haggort tried to flick Greenvort off as if it were a mosquito biting on his ear. The imp ducked and shouted. The noise combined with the pain did the trick. Haggort veered to the right. That was when the Ne'vermaker did his next trick.

First the ground frosted over. Then a trickle of ball bearings appeared. Haggort put down a big foot. He slipped. He staggered. His upper body swung backwards and forwards. The pendulum motion shot Greenvort forwards, still in a riding position. There was a THUMP followed by a thump. Both rose and fell, rose and fell as they continued to move in the general direction of the castle.

With the echoes of pounding feet in his head, Glide concentrated harder. Positive that his scheme would work, he was pretty sure that the Witch was near to her end. Some intuition, though, informed him that this end would not be a happy-ever-after for him. Even so, he had to go on. This battle was bigger than him, bigger than the both of him.

Both of him? Yes, though one of him was now a her. The result of his concentration was twofold. One fold was a protective barrier. He hoped he'd set up a mental force field, a barrier to shield his presence. The other fold was Cascade. He had projected an image of her by the window. Glide wanted the Witch to see this image. The Witch, unfortunately, was still busy stirring her brew. To get her attention, Glide coughed in what he hoped was Cascade's baritone, er contralto, er pitch?

"What's that?" the Witch looked up. "Oh, you." She returned to her work. Then she jerked upright. "You! You? What are you doing there?" Blinded by hate, she screeched, "Back to your hole! Back to where you belong! Immediately!" Not daring to speak, Glide had the image shake its head. "You disobey?" the Witch fumed. "Get back this instant!" A blue discharge crackled over her body. Pointing a bony finger, her hair stuck out and a jagged bolt shot across the room.

It flared over the image. Since there was a psychic connection to its source, some of the energy flowed onto Glide so that Glide fried. As he concentrated to maintain the apparition, his whole nervous system lit up. He shook and flickered like a badly engineered neon sign.

"Don't resist," a voice murmured. "Glow with the flow."

"You mean go with the flow."

"Glow in this case."

Glide was angry. He'd not come this far to be beaten. No! He was furious. She was absolutely determined. She? He! No, she! No, he! Insight flashed through Glide, along with the electric bombard. His concentration had been so hard that he'd made a connection to Cascade through the Witch! Her frozen determination burnt within him. He opened up to her. The electric charge went right through him, reached down to the bottom of his psychic well and, like an elastic spring, bounced right up again. In imitation of Maggot Thwacka, the image of Cascade raised an arm and pointed its fingers. Blue light zigzagged around the Witch.

Maggot Thwacka screamed. Her blue hair jerked as if it would pull her off the ground. With the high-pitched squeal going on and on, she lifted her hands into the air. A monstrous blackness manifested in the cup of her hands. She hurled it. Its path swallowed space and engulfed the image. Glide felt the sharp pain of emptiness. He resisted and the hurt of loneliness multiplied a thousand times.

"Let go, let go," a river murmured in his ear.

He sought to let go. Instantly the image of Cascade dissolved and the pain went with it. Yet he immediately created another image so that it seemed as if the form had never been blasted. The Witch stared dumbfounded. Nothing should have resisted her attack. Nothing did. Not even the shadow of a nothing. She hurled another black hole of energy. And another image was swallowed. And a third and a fourth. By the fifth image, the Witch was slumped over a chair.

"How can you?" she wheezed. "How can you?"

Though he, too, was tired, Glide managed one more apparition.

Seeing it, the Witch's blue-wire hair curled into question marks and her head sank into her shoulders like an old crow. A black cloud hovered over her head. *Revenge, revenge*, her mind cried. *Revenge.* With an effort, she cracked her knuckles. The pain jolted her and brought back her control.

"You haven't escaped yet, my lovely!" The Witch reached for the brew. She drew back her arm and hurled it. Dripping green ooze, it flew through the air. It hit the image of Cascade and then... and then nothing. The Witch had thrown an image at an image. Blinded by rage, she hadn't noticed the absence of weight.

Uttering incoherent screams and enveloped in black clouds, she snatched a spear from the wall. In her rage, it hit the bottles. They spilt, creating a mess of ooze, slime and preserved innards. The Witch kicked them away as she dashed across the room. This was it. The Cascade image darted through the window and off to the left. The Witch leant out the window, drew back her arm and threw the spear. With the effort, her body was hanging way out. She was looking to the left. Glide had waited on the right, waited with a sandbag. Thump! Thump! And, just for luck, thump! Eyes crossed, the Witch slowly turned. She raised a hand. A trickle of concussed magic filtered out. Glide visualised a burst of compassionate white light. No one could say that he was merely out for revenge. Then he hit her again. The Witch keeled over.

Haggort skidded to a halt. Something had happened. Something good? Or something bad? He felt that a weight had been taken off his back. Greenvort getting off? Or something else? Greenvort also paused. Magic was in the air. But whose? Ne'wang's? The stranger's? Whose?

"The Witch," Goresh the raven cried. "The Witch!"

So that was it. She had done something. Or, was it possible, something had been done to her? What was it? They stared at each other. Could there be something more evil than her? Could they cope with that? Oh, oh! What to do? Which way to go?

Their ragged army felt it, too. The cringing fear began to change. They looked across the distance and saw Strongarm the elephant. They straightened their backs. They looked at Haggort and Greenvort then grasped their weapons in a quite different sort of way.

Greenvort, quick to catch the change, said in his most casual way, "Er, nice weather."

"Yeah," Haggort agreed in a remarkably quick apprehension for him, "nice day fer it." They all watched as Strongarm began a careful descent of the escarpment. Men, women and imps followed him. Haggort revved up his feet. "To der Witch," he bellowed. "She's our only hope. To der Witch!"

This was it, Glide thought. Then he reached for the body of the Witch as others might reach for a particularly nasty type of toad. "Scalpel," he said to the air.

"Scalpel," a voice echoed.

Gleaming steel appeared in his hand. "Scissors."

"Scissors."

Glide took a handful of the Witch's hair, put the blades around them and snipped. Or tried to. The hair just slipped out. He tried again. It was just too tough.

"Wire cutters," Glide requested.

"Wire cutters."

The Witch stirred. Glide acted quickly. He put a lock of hair between the wire cutters and grasped the shaft in both hands. He pressed down. Click they cut. Click-click went the shears. Click! Another cut. The Witch sighed. Her mouth sighed. Her nose sighed. Even her ears sighed. The air filled with fading blue-black smoke.

Cascade's corner shimmered. There was a hint of motion. The web of illusion flickered. Hernandes, for a brief moment, again thought he glimpsed the body of a man within the hide of an elephant.

Click, click went the shears. Click, click. In moments, the Witch was shorn. Glide grasped at a bundle of locks. Wire filaments! That was her hair!

In the corner, Cascade stirred. In bewilderment, she looked around her. At the same time, Strongarm stumbled. Bronzed shields! Why was he running on all fours? There was a great cheer. Even Haggort paused at that. He turned, saw, and paled. Strongarm the man was doing somersaults. A few scratches from ice and marbles no longer mattered, Haggort put on speed. In the reverse of Strongarm, he put his long arms down to make it easier.

The Ne'vermaker strained to move a ton weight through dimensions. Failing that, he made do with a large sack instead. Haggort went straight into it. The Ne'vermaker quickly tied a knot. With a wild Giant Dwarf inside it, the sack behaved like an enormous amoeba.

At that very same moment, Glide gazed in awe at the beautiful Cascade. Her silver hair caught the sun and enhanced it. She saw the stranger and approached. Though he looked friendly, she approached carefully. In other words, she picked up a sword.

"Who are you?" she asked. As her voice washed over him, Glide knew that he was drowning not waving. At the long admiring pause, Cascade risked putting down the sword. "Who are you?" she repeated more softly.

They gazed at each other across the sill. Then a black finger poked Glide in the ribs.

"He's your hero," the Ne'vermaker said. "He rescued you."

"Dad!" Cascade cried. "You! Him! Oh, thank you!"

She hopped over the sill. Arms outstretched and dress pressing against her body, she rushed towards Glide. This was it! This was it! At that moment, the Witch raised her head and Haggort, having bitten through the sack, burst into the throne room.

Chapter 42

This was it. This was the perfect moment. Or should've been. But confronted by the Witch, both Glide and Cascade froze. The Ne'vermaker, of course, had gone again. The Witch held out a hand, halting Haggort.

"Stay back," she screeched. "Don't interfere. They are mine."

Cascade tried to grab the Witch's outstretched hand but she snatched it away. Haggort bounded through the doorway and advanced threateningly.

"Run!" Cascade cried. She pushed at Glide. "It's your only chance. Run!"

Glide panicked. Despite his recent exercise in depilation, he felt caught. One half of him said *You're done. Trapped by the Witch, as effectively as a rabbit before a snake*. Another half said, *Nah you're beyond done. It's already all over*. The first half replied, *Don't believe everything you think!* He gulped. His sandbag was just a dead weight in his hand.

The Witch rose to her full height and reached her arms up to the sky. With a scream, she invoked dark forces. With a scream, she... With a scream... she... nothing. Just nothing. The cup of her hands remained empty. No evil pit of nothingness manifested. There was just a nothing.

Her face twisted. "Not obey me?" she cackled. "Won't? Well! Well, I'll see to them later. Now, you!"

She pointed a finger. The arthritic knuckles quivered. A fingernail glowed with a feeble gangrenous green. An olive drip fell to the floor. It hissed, did a bit of paint stripping and fell onto its back. The face of the Witch acquired a rictus. The right eye blinked open while the left one flicked closed. Her upper and lower lips twisted as if they would change places. Aghast, the Witch stared at her hands. Slowly, slowly, with the slowness of dread, she reached up. Her hands touched the stubble on her head. Her mouth opened wide. Without making a noise, like a painting by Bacon, she screamed and screamed and screamed.

A frozen tableau watched. Finally, exhausted, she collapsed onto the windowsill. A black shape appeared. A dark hand rested gently on her shoulder. At the presence of the Ne'vermaker, Haggort backed away. Then with a giant bound, he scooped Glide up under one arm and Cascade under the other.

"Don't," said a voice with quiet authority.

Haggort didn't. Glide looked around. He was used to voices coming out of the air but they were always from the Ne'vermaker. Yet Ne'wang was by the window while this voice had come from up high. Glide arched his neck and... boggled. On the roof was the most magnificent man that he'd ever seen. He was tall and golden-skinned and rippled with muscles. His face shone. Who could this be? Who? It could only be Strongarm. Who else?

"I, er, won't bother you," Haggort muttered. "I was, er, just going."

A dozen of his own army surrounded him, waving pitchforks.

"I think," Strongarm said, "that there's a score to settle."

He descended. With a pas de deux, a double frappé, and a flambé a gauche, Strongarm somersaulted from roof to ground. A pitchfork jabbed in the direction of the Giant Dwarf.

"Take your choice," it said. "Him or us?"

Haggort sneered. "Reckon I can fight any elephant," he jeered. "Wiv or wivout a trunk."

So saying, he kicked out with a massive foot. It flew right between Strongarm's legs. Glide doubled up in sympathy. But with an amazing lightness, Strongarm extended both palms, pushed with his calves and rode the kick straight up into the air. At the pinnacle of a parabola, he twisted. Haggort squawked at the painful twist put upon his leg and the Giant Dwarf was forced to flip onto his side.

Strongarm landed on his feet as Haggort rolled backwards onto his.

"Argh!" he roared. "Fancy steps. Well, I kin also pa der jetty."

He rushed forward and launched both feet into the air. Strongarm dropped onto one knee and grabbed Haggort's jerkin as it flew over his head. A bottom, of bottomless proportions, hit the ground in a shortened arc. Boots ploughed up the earth and the ground shook.

In the confusion, Greenvort tried to slip away. At the edge of the crowd, however, he ran into two people of his own size.

"The quality of mercy," Rosenstern began as he took the evil imp's right arm.

"Is about to be strained," Guildencrantz concluded, taking the left arm.

"I, er, was...sn't going nowhere." Greenvort pulled unsuccessfully against their grips. "Nowhere at all."

"That's for sure," Guildencrantz agreed.

Greenvort wriggled his fingers in an attempt to magic the other two.

"Oh, so you want to fight." Rosenstern raised his own hands.

"No, you don't." Guildencrantz pushed his friend's hands down. "I saw him first."

"No, you didn't."

"Yes, I did."

"Didn't!"

"Did"

"I'll biff you first."

"I'll biff you!"

In a flurry of dust, the two locked in mortal combat. Released, Greenvort holstered his hands and crept away. He didn't get very far. Hernandes was in his saddle and looking down at him.

"Goings places?" he asked.

"Er, no, no. Just walking."

"Then walks the other ways."

Greenvort again raised his hands. But quick as a flash, Hernandes whipped off his akubra and hurled it. It hit Greenvort in the face and blocked his vision. The corks twirled into his ears and around his arms.

"Hogtied!" Hernandes cried triumphantly.

He took Greenvort by the scruff of his neck and drew him back to the centre of activity. He arrived just in time to see Strongarm leap high into the air and land smack on Haggort's shoulders. Then he hammered so hard on the latter's head that it disappeared into his neck. Jumping down, Strongarm pulled Haggort's feet out so that he landed flat on his nose with a muffled gurgle. Strongarm sat on him and out of habit attempted a last thump with a trunk that was no longer there.

There was a silence. It was broken by Maggot Thwacka the Witch. "You'll never best me," she cried. "Not while there's breath left in my body."

With a terrible sadness, the Ne'vermaker indicated the wire cutters and clippers. "That will best you," he said. "There's science in your magic and Glide has shown us how to deal with it."

"So that's his name," Cascade breathed. Her gaze danced over him. "My hero," she said.

She came forward, arms open, her glance still dancing over him. Glide's heart pounded. At the last moment, however, he realised that her glance did indeed dance over him. Right over to Strongarm. Her arms encircled the warrior and the two hugged fiercely. The Ne'vermaker looked at Glide with regretful sympathy.

"You've done well." Ne'wang's expression showed that he understood Glide's desire. "But this place is not your home."

"No." Sad symphonies played in Glide's mind. "I suppose not. Then what now?"

The Ne'verman touched Glide on the chest. "Your heart knows what it must do."

Glide nodded. Despite his dreams of Cascade, he was pretty sure what would really happen. Strongarm and Cascade would guide a reunited Inklan to a state of happy anarchy. The Ne'vermaker would monthly give Maggot Thwacka a cut above so that she remained a cut below. This part of the world would be happy.

As for him... As for Glide...

Chapter 43

Glide didn't even have time to plan, even to think. There was a sudden sensation of spinning. It was followed by a falling, falling... falling upwards. It lasted for an infinite moment. It stopped with a soggy bounce. Heart pounding, Glide opened his eyes. He looked around. This was his bedroom. He was in his own bedroom, lying on his own bed. He stared uncertainly at the ceiling.

"Oh," he said. He looked at the familiar walls and window. "Was it all a dream, just a dream?" The answer, however, came immediately. "No. I feel too different. I am different!"

His whole core was different.

He rose. His arms were brown and his body was fit. Not gym fit but working-outdoors fit. Exhilarated, Glide went to the window. It was grey outside. The trees were bare. Bare? Well, not really bare. That didn't happen on the Sunny Coast. They just became a little less exuberant. It was autumn here. But last seen, it was summer! Had been summer? Glide scratched his head. Auslan must be nearer to the equator than here. It had certainly been warmer. He went to the mirror. Yes, his face was brown, too. But that was minor. Look at his clothes! He wore baggy trousers, fringed shirt and moccasins. Those months had not been a fancy. But they had been fantastical.

But forget season. Forget clothes. He had changed. He had been a pygmy. Now he was a giant.

Bemused, Glide turned on his computer. It took time for the valves to warm up after so long. But there in the corner was the date. It was May. May! March had just been a blink away. Well, well, well. Well, well, well. That was about as coherent as he could get. He went onto the balcony. It was cool. And he'd been away. He'd crossed some magic gateway. Well, well, well. Well, well, well.

Across from him, a magpie hopped onto a branch. It angled its head and turned a suspicious red eye on Glide. Red? Was that right?

Maybe it had been drinking? A rosella, bright with colour, flew by. A moment later, its mate joined it. The two birds bit into over-ripe fruit. Drunk on fermented juices, they shrieked joyously. He felt sure that they were giving him a message. What message? If only he could understand it. Well, well, well. Maybe he did.

A yellow-crested cockatoo wrote an invisible calligraphy across the sky. Glide read it. Magic was still about. He closed his eyes. In his mind, Hernandes slid off a big red roo. Rosenstern tumbled over Guildencrantz. That was a life. But he couldn't go back. No, he'd not go back. He couldn't. The Ne'vermaker had shown him how to live. Now, he'd have to go forward. A slow smile spread over his face. Still, Glide scratched his head, how to account for the missing months? He touched the whistle around his neck. He grinned. Had the Ne'vermaker forgotten about it? No, he wouldn't have forgotten. Well, Ne'wang owed him one – at least one. He put the whistle to his lips and made one tuneful blast. The air swirled. A vortex appeared like a plug being pulled in a bath. The vortex condensed.

"Keep playing, mate," the Ne'vermaker said. "I'm only in the middle of an Auslan Cabinet meeting."

"I need about ten minutes," Glide said.

"You got it." The Ne'vermaker disappeared for a moment. "Did I say the Cabinet meeting was at Plonkers? Take all the time you want."

"Okay, first of all what do I tell people?"

The Ne'vermaker snorted. "That's easy. Tell 'em the truth."

"But no one will believe me!"

"Exactly. Tell 'em you bumped your head and went ga-ga for a while. Add that you've had a breakdown. They'll believe that. You say you don't wanna go back to the office. They say, that's right, we don't wan't you back in the office, having another breakdown."

Glide chuckled. "You're a cunning old devil."

"It also means you keep your story straight. Start telling lies and they unravel like me old grannies woollie."

"Okay, okay." Glide began to pace. "But if I don't go back to the office, then what?"

"Then what? Mate, you're bloody young. The world's your oyster."

"I've become a vegetarian."

"Then the world's your brocolli."

"Yeah, but really, I still don't know what to do."

A look of sympathy crossed the smiling face of the Ne'vermaker. "You know, Glide, you're a rare bloke, but I've seen a few like you. A few and they've been quite happy."

"They have?" Glide couldn't believe it. "Where?"

"Up north Quinsland and over in Western Ausphalia."

Glide frowned with suspicious. "What have they been doing?"

"Technicians and engineers working on the coal mines, keeping the steam engines going."

Glide laughed. "Mate, I want to help the environment not rip it up."

The Ne'vermaker spoke urgently. "Glide, the main thing is to sort yourself out. There are wild blokes up there and semi-wild. You're one of the semi-wild. You could get an apprenticeship in electrical stuff or hydraulics."

"Even with a breakdown."

"Mate, they understand your kind of breakdown. You could work on the machines up there, get your hands really dirty. You'd be as happy as a kid in a mudpie."

"You think?" Glide could imagine it, a wrench in one hand, a wench in the other. "But what about my principles?"

"Once you're working, you can start bringing in solar power, wind power, and all that sorta stuff. You save 'em money, they'll be more'n happy to use it."

Glide laughed outright. "Solar energy on a coal mine?"

The Ne'vermaker was beginning to fade. "Undermine them from within." He also laughed. "Undermine the mine. That's a good one."

Like the Cheshire Cat his smile was the last thing to go. It hung in the air and filled Glide with a bubbly feeling. Glide went on to his balcony. The houses of Brissie filled his view in either direction.

No, he wasn't going back to the office. But work in a mine? What a way to go!

With a determined expression, Glide cranked up his phone to make some calls. Someone could rent his flat and cover the mortgage. A mining company would cover his costs at TAFE. *North Quinsland*, he thought, *here I come. I'm off to find some magic.*

A blue hand appeared.

A flower drifted down.

A chocolate voice said, "Go, Glide, go!" A moment later, a well-worn coin spun through the air. "Oops! Sorry, mate, I forgot. I meant ta give this dollar back to your mum."

Glide eyed the coin in wonder. It was made in the same year as he was born. He rubbed the metal between his fingers and received a warm tingle. Damn and strawberries, but he'd better ask his mum about it!

Grinning with wonder, Glide turned his gaze to the north. Up there were more Ne'vermen. More Ne'vermen and more gateways. Glide whistled. He'd met the blue man and he'd never ever be blue again.

About the Author

I was born in London but moved to Canberra, Australia, after completing a Ph.D in visual information processing. After a few more years of research, I became involved with tai chi and meditation. I left research and spent 12 years in teaching tai chi and yoga relaxation classes. Meditation manifested a mountain of poems, then plays, short stories and novels.

In 1987, I married Judith, a visual artist. In 1992, I started to do her picture framing. That led to woodturning and making wooden automata.

Since 1997, Judith and I have lived on the Sunshine Coast, Queensland.

Milton Keynes UK
Ingram Content Group UK Ltd.
UKHW010228020424
440421UK00017B/108

9 798223 990772